Bound

BY

Honor

ALSO BY COLETTE GALE

Unmasqued
Master

Bound
BY
Honor

An Erotic Novel of Maid Marian

Colette Gale

A SIGNET ECLIPSE BOOK

SIGNET ECLIPSE
Published by New American Library, a division of
Penguin Group (USA) Inc., 375 Hudson Street,
New York, New York 10014, USA
Penguin Group (Canada), 90 Eglinton Avenue East, Suite 700, Toronto,
Ontario M4P 2Y3, Canada (a division of Pearson Penguin Canada Inc.)
Penguin Books Ltd., 80 Strand, London WC2R 0RL, England
Penguin Ireland, 25 St. Stephen's Green, Dublin 2,
Ireland (a division of Penguin Books Ltd.)
Penguin Group (Australia), 250 Camberwell Road, Camberwell, Victoria 3124,
Australia (a division of Pearson Australia Group Pty. Ltd.)
Penguin Books India Pvt. Ltd., 11 Community Centre, Panchsheel Park,
New Delhi - 110 017, India
Penguin Group (NZ), 67 Apollo Drive, Rosedale, North Shore 0632,
New Zealand (a division of Pearson New Zealand Ltd.)
Penguin Books (South Africa) (Pty.) Ltd., 24 Sturdee Avenue,
Rosebank, Johannesburg 2196, South Africa

Penguin Books Ltd., Registered Offices:
80 Strand, London WC2R 0RL, England

First published by Signet Eclipse, an imprint of New American Library,
a division of Penguin Group (USA) Inc.

For all the women who prefer
Alan Rickman and Richard Armitage

PROLOGUE

"*A*re you not the Sheriff of Nottinghamshire?" Prince John said in that lazy way of his.

It was not a question; he knew full well to whom he was speaking. His eyes were darker than ever in the dimness of his private chamber, but they were hooded with heavy satisfaction. "Methinks there's none who knows the king's Forest of Sherwood as well as you." He stretched his broad shoulders, and gave a little, almost effeminate shudder.

"Indeed, my lord, I am quite familiar with the forest," replied Sir William de Wendeval, keeping his voice even and his attention from the generous breasts of the serving wench who was . . . serving . . . the prince at the moment, and had no doubt caused his shiver of pleasure.

Her lips were red and swollen, her jaw stretched wide as she accommodated her liege's well-used cock. Large breasts hung and swayed with each movement, her nipples threatening to brush the floor. She was breathing hard from exertion, her face red and glistening with sweat.

Prince John, who was lording his royal self about his brother Richard's country while the king was off fighting Saladin in the Holy Lands, had taken over the ladies' solar in Ludlow Keep for his own private chamber. His Court of Pleasure, as he called it.

Will was grateful for his choice of the room, for it was large and had two massive fireplaces and several narrow slits that allowed fresh air to come in—a welcome treat on nights like this, when the chamber was thick with the smell of sex and sweat and heat.

"Then . . ." John gasped, stilled, then grabbed the head of the doxy going down on him and jammed his cock deep into the back of her throat. Pleasure narrowed his eyes and thinned his generous lips as the girl coughed and choked and struggled beneath his hands.

John released her suddenly and she fell back onto the floor. Her tangled hair caught under her hands as she collapsed, gasping for breath. From where he stood, Will eyed her critically. She'd live.

Unlike the girl last week, who'd been a casualty of one of John's experiments that included bondage and a heavy hood.

Will transferred his attention back to the prince, keeping his face devoid of emotion. He enjoyed fucking as much as any man, and in many ways, and the more the merrier—but some of John's proclivities weren't to his taste. And, at the least, unlike this pitiful wench, he had some choice in the matter.

So far.

". . . 'tis inconceivable that you have not yet caught Robin of the Hood!" John continued his sentence as though he'd not stopped to spew his seed, wipe his cock, and then shove it back into his braies—all the while leaving Will, whom he'd summoned from his bed well past midnight, standing there. "He and his band of outlaws have poached from the king, stolen from the tax collector, and they continue to run rampant through the shire."

Will's face tightened. He bowed to his liege. " 'Tis a matter of great annoyance to me as well, my lord. Robin Hood has been able to remain a bare step ahead of my men thus far . . . but 'twill not be long before we capture him. His luck cannot last forever."

John shifted on his seat, which happened to be a massive wooden chair piled high with cushions and furs. He'd removed his jewel-encrusted tunic some time ago, and now wore only an undertunic, braies, and soft calf slippers. A goblet of wine sat next to him on a small table, and he lifted it to drink furiously as though he—not the serving wench—had labored for his pleasure.

Will cast a glance around the room. The window slits were uncovered by heavy tapestries this summer night, and a beam of moonlight shone in through the westward side.

The side that faced Sherwood Forest, where the outlaw Robin of the Hood had famously eluded the fearsome Sheriff of Nottinghamshire for nearly a year.

A miracle that the prince hadn't come to investigate before now, since his pocket had become quite a bit lighter since Robin had taken to stealing from traveling lords and ladies.

John, of course, collected taxes from the English people in the name of his brother, Richard, called the Lionheart, who had left him as regent while on Crusade. Well, to be more precise . . . he'd first left William Longchamp, that humpbacked dwarf, as England's justiciar and chancellor—completely in charge of the treasury and in control of the country. That was until John, with the support of the powerful nobility, had removed the power-hungry man and sent him scuttling out of England.

Now, flush with the surge of power obtained by the overturning of Longchamp, John plotted to seize even more control. But in a much stealthier manner. Thus, while he acted in the name of the king, a goodly portion of the king's tax money meant to fund Richard's war had been lining John's pockets, and anything that the outlaw Robin Hood made away with was a direct cut to the prince's coffers.

"Robin Hood's luck had best change sooner rather than the later," John grumbled. He cast his attention around the luxurious chamber and his eyes fell on another of the wenches he had collected for this night's entertainment.

Her eyes goggled and Will saw her breasts—barely covered by a thin shift—rise and fall as though she were running. But she dared not move from where she sat on her haunches, either to hide or attempt escape.

John, who was considered a rather handsome man, with his dark hair and well-trimmed beard and mustache, smacked his full lips and gulped again from his goblet, but did not call the girl to him. Perhaps he was sated for the time. Will hoped that was the case, for he had little interest in watching his liege, especially when his jaw was as lief to crack with a wide yawn. A long day it had been, patrolling the Forest of Sherwood, on the hunt for outlaws like Robin Hood.

"Bitches," John said, slamming the heavy goblet down. He glowered at the frightened girl. "They stink and scuttle in fear the moment someone looks at them. 'Tis a blessing that Isabella will leave for Westminster in two days. Then we shall have a much more interesting variety to sample."

Isobel of Gloucester was John's wife, and it was well-known among the prince's confidants that she demanded at least the pretense of fidelity while she was in residence with him. That simply meant that her husband refrained from tupping any of her ladies-in-waiting, or the wives and daughters of his vassals, while Isobel was about.

But upon her removal from the prince's residence, the ladies became the same fair game as the does John hunted during the day . . . whether they wished to be or not. And when John's two other bosom companions, Sir Louis Krench and Lord Ralf Stannoch, were also in attendance . . . well, Will thought 'twas rarely a pretty sight.

"Indeed, my lord." Will bowed, then attempted to divert the king back to the reason he'd rousted him from bed so late at night. "Did you have some news for me, my lord?"

"Ah, yes. But of course." John plucked a piece of cheese from his mother's homeland of Aquitaine and slipped it into his mouth, brushing tiny crumbs of bread from his neat beard. "I received word earlier today that Lady Marian of Morlaix shall arrive here at Ludlow Keep sometime in the next sennight. As she's returning from her dead husband's lands as a ward of the king, it is expected that her baggage will be extensive. A perfect opportunity for Robin Hood to make an attempt to ambush her carriage. And of course, the Sheriff of Nottinghamshire shall be waiting to thwart such an attempt, and to save the fair maiden."

"Indeed," Will replied a trifle later than he should have. His brain had turned sluggish as soon as her name passed the prince's lips.

Marian was returning.

Lady Marian, she was now. No longer the maiden he and

Robin of Locksley had known during their childhood when they'd been fostered with Marian's father. How wealthy she had become, and how far Robin had fallen—from the young landed lord to an anonymous outlaw resigned to hiding out in the forest. Yet, Will had recognized him the first time they'd come face-to-face during an aborted robbery.

Marian's father, Lord Leaford, was a baron well-known for his skill in training young boys to be knights, and until his death, he had been popular among the lower ranks of nobles who could not afford to send their boys to a more powerful lord for fostering.

Yet, it was the baron's daughter Will remembered best. The tart-tongued, quick-witted, coppery-haired girl who'd ridden circles around both him and Robin, teasing and pestering and laughing at them with her sparkling green eyes. Now she was no longer a girl of twelve, but a woman grown and widowed, a rich heiress . . . and returning to Nottinghamshire.

A woman who had haunted him ever since their youth.

A ripe target for Robin Hood, indeed.

And, Will realized, with a glance at the handsome, lascivious prince . . . a ripe target for John Lackland, who would be fascinated by any new woman at court. But especially one as fiery and bold as Marian.

By all that was holy, what was he to do?

Chapter 1

Lady Marian of Morlaix peered through the shuttered windows of her traveling wagon, but to her annoyance could see little of interest. The tall, close trees of Sherwood Forest allowed only dappled sunlight through on a bright day, but when there were clouds and rain threatening as now, the woods were as dark as night. The smell of loam and damp bark was thick in the air.

'Twas ripe for an ambush from a band of thieves, and she was glad of the six sturdy men-at-arms who accompanied her small caravan. They would have reached Ludlow Keep by vespers, but a broken wheel on her wagon had delayed them. If it had been one of the other wagons, with her clothing and belongings, she would have gone on ahead and allowed them to follow. But, alas, hers was the only wagon fit for a lady to ride in—although she would just as easily have ridden asaddle. Her longbow and arrows had been packed deep inside a trunk of clothing, but she had a dagger handy.

If the tales were true about the band of thieves led by a man called Robin of the Hood, she might very well need that blade. Even in Normandy, Marian had heard stories of the outlaw who stole boldly from rich travelers and then distributed the wealth among the villeins and townspeople—likely after keeping a good portion for himself.

And the Sheriff of Nottinghamshire, who was rumored to be just as blackhearted and brutal as Prince John, his bosom companion, had been unable to lay his hands on the band of outlaws or its leader. A rich caravan with the niceties of the widow of the rich Lord Harold of Morlaix would likely prove too much of a temptation for them. But there was no help for it, for the road to Ludlow ran through the king's Sherwood Forest.

It was hard for Marian to believe how much her homeland had changed since her father died—King Henry was now gone, and the new king, Richard, had hardly taken the crown when he left on Crusade. His mother, Queen Eleanor, had been traveling with him to the Holy Land, but was now making her way back to neglected England.

Upon her father's death, Marian and her mother had been sent from the small barony of Leaford to live in Normandy, where her mother had remarried. After the old king died, Eleanor had been released from prison and reassembled her own court. As the daughter of a man who'd been faithful to his liege, Marian had been sent to the dowager queen's court, where she'd become a trusted favorite of the queen. There she remained until she was wed to the much-older Harold three years ago.

With her husband's death only six months past, she acquired a portion of his estates. Thus, at the age of twenty, Marian had become a wealthy woman whose marriage could be used for political alliance. Five months ago, the king had ordered her to the queen's holdings in Aquitaine to await the queen's imminent return from the Holy Land . . . and a decision about a future husband.

Now that Eleanor had been back in Aquitaine for some months and renewed her friendship with Marian, she'd had her own purposes for sending Marian on to her younger son's court: to spy on her son in advance of the queen's own arrival.

Marian had heard rumors of what John Lackland's court was like, and they had left her wondering whether she had more to fear in the forest or at her destination.

No sooner had she those thoughts than the wagon lurched to a halt.

"What ho!" came a shout from Bruse, her master-at-arms.

Marian sat up, ignoring the stifled shriek of her maid, who'd done nothing but hold her prayer beads and move her lips soundlessly during the entire journey. Her heart pounding, she looked out the window again just as a loud thump came on the roof above her, followed by a second and third. Ethelberga, the maid, gave a full-blooded shriek and dived to the floor, screeching in English about how they would all be dead in mere moments.

Marian forbore to point out that it was unlikely anyone would be killed, even as she pulled the dagger from her sheath. The thieves would merely want to relieve her of her valuables, and, in the very worst-case scenario, take Marian off for ransom. She hadn't heard of this Robin Hood killing anyone, and in any case a thief wouldn't be foolish enough to harm a gentle-born woman. Although, she thought, looking wryly at Ethelberga, mayhap they might be induced to put the lady's maid out of her misery if she didn't stop wailing.

The thump on the roof turned to low, rhythmic thuds as the person—or persons—moved about up there.

"Stand off!" came another shout, followed by a sharp whiz that she recognized as an arrow's flight. A soft twang followed as it embedded itself in a target close enough for her to hear it.

Marian couldn't see what was happening, but she suspected she knew. The thieves had surrounded the two carts and now held the men-at-arms from moving. Most likely, they were holding them off with arrows nocked into their bows, ready to fly at any moment. The one she'd heard had probably been an accurately charged warning shot.

At least two of the thieves had landed on her roof, likely jumping down from a tree. But surely six chain-mailed men would be enough of a deterrent for a ragtag band of thieves, unless they were particularly good archers. The shouts had settled into silence, and despite her certainty that she wouldn't be harmed, Marian's heart pounded in her chest.

Before she could move to the other side of the cart, making her way over the prone Ethelberga, the vehicle began to rock violently. Ethelberga screamed anew, clutching at the hem of Marian's undertunic, tangling herself among the floor-length skirt and her legs.

With the rocking of the cart, and her maid's histrionics, Marian lost her balance in the small space and had to catch herself against the closed door. But at that moment, the door opened, and she tumbled out, the dagger slipping from her grip. Strong arms caught her awkward fall, and the knife landed on the ground between two dusty boots.

"Well, now," said a surprised voice. "This must be the famous Lady Marian come to greet Robin of the Hood and his merry men." His arms tightened around her. "You are well come to our Sherwood, my lady," he added.

In the midst of the furor, Marian heard the rumble of laughter from the surrounding men, and she turned to look at who had the effrontery to hold her in his arms as though she belonged there. Her angry words died in her throat as she met familiar blue eyes, sparkling with mischief and jest. Despite the beard and mustache that covered half of his face, she recognized him.

"Robin—!" she began, but before she could speak his complete name, he covered her mouth with an impudent kiss.

After not seeing him for so many years, she couldn't have been more surprised by the kiss. Although she'd always been attracted to him, his charming personality and handsome appearance in the past, he'd done little more than tease her into a fury. He certainly had never tried to kiss her.

By the time Marian had caught her breath and freed herself from the man she'd known as Robin of Locksley—not Robin of the Hood—he had swept her up and run into the woods with her. A moment later, he thrust her up onto the saddle of a horse, and Robin vaulted up behind her before she could untangle her legs from her skirts and slip back to the ground.

The outraged roars from Bruse and the responding threats from the band of thieves faded as Robin kicked his horse into a gallop, crashing through the brush with his captive. Branches slashed across her face and caught at her veil, pulling it half off, as they dashed through the forest.

"Robin! What are you doing? Are you mad? It is you, isn't it?" Marian hardly knew what to think. The last she had heard from the young man who'd fostered at her childhood home, Mead's

Vale, was that he'd gone on Crusade with the newly coronated King Richard.

"Aye, indeed, Lady Marian," he said, stressing her title a bit. "I thought it would be a fitting welcome to you as you journeyed to that blackhearted cocklicker's court."

"Robin," she gasped, all the air jolted from her lungs as they galloped through the woods. "What are you talking about?"

Suddenly, he wheeled the horse into a small clearing and slid down from the saddle. Looking up at her, he gave her the slow, easy grin she remembered from their youth, and rested his hands at her hips as though to help her down. But he didn't; instead, he curled his fingers firmly into her flesh and then slid all along the sides, from thigh to knee. Little bumps rose on her skin, tingling at his intimate touch.

"And little Marian is all grown up now, into a beautiful, rich lady. I am honored that you should remember me after all these years." His eyes sparkled with naughtiness, and the next thing she knew, he pulled her down from the saddle, sliding her body all along his. *All along* his, so that she felt every bump and crease of the mail hauberk he wore. And something that most certainly felt like the beginning lift of a cock. "You've grown quite beautiful."

"Robin," she said, truly happy to see him. She'd always favored him, always found him irresistible. With his easy personality, bright eyes, and handsome face, it would have been difficult to feel otherwise. "What are you about?" she asked again, aware of his thighs pressed against hers, her slippers captured between his heavy boots. And, most definitely, the growing bulge of his cock. Her hand didn't have anywhere to go but flat against his chest. "Are you truly an outlaw?"

"An outlaw of great repute," he said, his lips curling. "Have you not heard of Robin Hood and his band of men who make merry with the king's coin? I thought for certain tales of our waywardness had reached the court's ears by now. Alas, mayhap I shall try harder, take more risks . . . be more daring!"

His face swooped toward hers, covering her mouth with his for the second time in a matter of minutes. Before she could react, his tongue slid into her mouth, licking in and around and tangling with her own.

Marian allowed the sleek kiss this time, even kissed him back for a moment, surprised at how much she enjoyed it. As much as she might have admired him as a young boy, she never imagined that actually kissing him would be this exciting. Kisses and coupling with her husband had been little more than duty, and, thankfully, of short duration—not only in each time he'd come to her bed, but also in the number of years in which they'd occurred. She'd been married for only three summers before Harold died of a fall during a boar hunt.

Robin's arms tightened around her waist and his tongue thrust deep as she came flush against his body. His lips were soft, but there were other areas of his body that were hard and insistent, drawing another unfamiliar response from Marian. She felt a heightened awareness, and a low, twisting sort of tickle deep in her belly.

After a moment, he pulled back a bit, kissing her and smiling into her mouth as she opened her eyes. "Not so bad, was it, now, Lady Marian?" he said lightly. "Your veil is slipping too, sweetling," he added, giving it a good tug off the back of her head.

"Robin," she said, pulling the veil back up to cover her braided hair and trying to act as though she kissed men in the forest all the time, "tell me what has come of you. Why are you here, in the woods, instead of at Locksley Keep?"

Now the humor slid from his face to be replaced by an irritable expression. " 'Twas all a mistake, and now here I am, running for my life. I never made it to the Holy Lands with the king," he confessed. "We were set upon by bandits when we put ashore in Greece, and I took an arrow to the thigh. Fever set in and I could not travel, though I was not deadly. The king wanted to make haste, and continued on. And I had no choice but to return to England. And to Locksley . . . I thought."

"You thought?"

He shrugged, stepping back, and she saw that though he stood only a hand or so taller than she, his shoulders had broadened quite a bit from the last time she'd seen him. He'd been fourteen, and she had been only twelve. His hair had darkened with maturity to brown-streaked honey, and he wore it cut short across his forehead and long over his ears. "When I returned, it was to find Locksley having been entailed to the king—through the prince, of course—on the claim of treason."

"Treason!"

"It's a lie, of course, Marian. Just another way for John Lackland to seize as much control as he can whilst his brother is fighting the infidels in Jerusalem. He has raised taxes and raised them more, and he skims more than his share off the top."

Marian had heard about Prince John's propensity for sly coin . . . among other things. After the overthrow of the unpopular William Longchamp, King Richard had allowed his brother, John, to act as regent of England while he was out of the country.

Eleanor had also left England to go on Crusade with Richard, but word had reached her that John was conspiring with King Philip Augustus of France. John had been old King Henry's favorite son, but that hadn't stopped him from plotting against his father. Eleanor did not doubt for a minute that he was now conspiring against his older brother, Richard. Even at the cost of the family lands in Normandy—what Philip would certainly require as payment for his complicity—it would be worth it to John to get permanent control of England. Yet, the queen must first attend to business in her native Aquitaine. The delay would enable Marian to act as her own secret eyes and ears, and to report back to her about any possibility that John was communicating with Philip.

"But it is the king who raises the taxes, to pay for his war," she reminded Robin, trying to keep the bitterness from her voice. She had no liking for the Crusade. It had taken many of the young men away from England, including her own brother, Walter. He hadn't returned from the Holy Land, for he'd been buried there.

"And then John raises them that much higher, so as to line his own pockets."

"But how did you come to be an outlaw? How could they take Locksley from you while you were away fighting at the king's side?"

Robin looked distinctly uncomfortable. "As I said, 'twas a mistake. I returned to find Locksley closed to me, and then I went hunting in the woods—*my* woods—for a meal. Then I was arrested for poaching from the king's forest."

Poaching from the king was indeed a serious offense—punishable by hanging, gouging of the eyes, or cutting off of the hands. "But surely once the mistake was found, you were released. Even the cruel Sheriff of Nottinghamshire could not keep an innocent man of the king's in prison."

Robin laughed. "Released? Nay, Marian, I made my own escape from the sheriff."

At that moment, a deep voice interrupted their conversation. "Did you indeed?"

Marian whirled to see a powerful black horse standing at the edge of the clearing. Atop it sat an equally powerful-looking man, dressed in equally dark clothing, holding a sword at his side. She stepped back automatically, but he inclined his head regally to her.

"Lady Marian." He urged his horse into the grassy clearing.

Robin released her, fairly shoving her away so that she stumbled with the force as he moved quickly away from her, gathering up his reins. "Ah, so to speak of the devil himself," he said, launching into his saddle. "Sheriff." He nodded. "I trust you'll see my lady to the keep."

These last words floated back behind him as he bolted off into the wood, leaving Marian standing in the center of the grass, suddenly alone, and feeling more than a bit disheveled.

Marian turned to look up at the man who remained astride his mount, edging his horse toward her, but not, thankfully, chasing after Robin. She was grateful for his restraint, for he would have had to fairly run over her to go after the bandit.

The sheriff sheathed his sword, but still held the reins in one gloved hand. The hooves on the majestic animal were larger than the trencher plates at a court dinner, and he was pure coal black from hoof to mane to wild, flaring nose.

The man himself had dark hair that fell in thick curls onto his forehead and brushed the sides of his neck, and he was clean-shaven but for the shadow that comes late in the day after a morning's shave. His mouth might have been considered sensual if it weren't settled and thin—and the same could be said for his face, dark with tan as well as obvious annoyance. As she gazed upon the Sheriff of Nottinghamshire, Marian was overcome by the sense of expectancy, and indeed, when she looked up into those shaded eyes, she felt set off-balance again, as if she were mistaken about something.

"I trust you are unharmed, Lady Marian," he said at last. "I apologize for the delay in coming to your aid, but we had heard your caravan was held up and thought to provide an escort at Revelstown."

"Delayed for a broken wheel, aye, but 'twas fixed readily," she replied, realizing with a start that he would indeed think she'd been in need of rescue. And, truth be told, if it had been anyone but Robin of Locksley, he would have had the right of it. But Marian had no fear of her childhood friend Robin, outlaw or no. In fact, she'd already decided that she must find a way to enlist the queen to help rid him of the charge of treason.

"Have I changed so much, then?" the sheriff said, sliding abruptly from the saddle. He landed on two steady feet next to her, and the destrier shimmied and snorted at the loss of his master's weight. "Marian."

She looked up at him again, closely this time, and recognition washed over her. "Will?" Perhaps it was the way he'd said her name, or that he now stood on the ground next to her—still much taller, but at least not towering so from the saddle.

Aye, indeed it was William de Wendeval before her now. The boy who'd grown up with her and Robin of Locksley on her father's estate.

But a boy Will was no longer. Just as Robin had grown broader and taller than she remembered from the summer she'd seen them last, nearly ten years ago, so had Will.

Taller, aye, and broad of shoulder . . . but he had not lost the sharp edges of his cheeks and jaw, and the reserved chill of his gaze. A handsome man he might be if the tension and reserve left his face and stance. But that had always been his way. While Robin had the lighter hair and dancing sapphire eyes, and personality to match, Will had been the quieter, more thoughtful, and, at times, gloomier of the pair.

And as their personalities tended to clash like oil and water, so had the two young men. Competitive and intense, they'd been rivals serving the same master, with their differences buried beneath civility and honor.

Will bowed again, peremptorily but correctly. "It is I."

"The Sheriff of Nottinghamshire?" Marian supposed she could be forgiven for the note of surprise in her voice. The last she'd known of Will, he'd been knighted and under service to old King Henry's confidant William Marshal, but no other news had reached her ears in Morlaix, across the Channel. Will had been a landless youth, the son of one of Marshal's seneschals. For him to have risen as high as sheriff of a shire was surprising, as was his ability to pay the fees that were required to buy such a post. She wondered what he'd done to deserve such an honor, and whereby he'd acquired the funds.

"And Robin of the Hood's sworn enemy," he said briskly. "Shall we be on our way?" Before she could reply, he grasped her by the waist and lifted her into the saddle. The destrier, unused to such insubstantial weight on its back, shuddered and pranced. But before his ire could rise dangerously, Will launched into the saddle behind Marian.

The horse quieted and Marian looked down, horrified to see how far she was from the trampled grass below. Her own palfrey was much smaller and milder than this beast, and Marian was not fond of being very high off the ground.

Her discomfort could have nothing to do with the strong arm curling around her waist from behind as they started off with a great leap. Will's solid chest and legs provided a comfortable and safe chair as they blazed through the woods. But he was so very warm. And large.

When he ducked to avoid a low-hanging branch, Marian was

forced to do so as well, leaning closer to the destrier's flowing mane. She couldn't remember the last time she'd been required to ride pillion, and certainly never in this pell-mell fashion through the woods.

She closed her eyes and clung to the saddle's pommel.

Moments later, they reached the road, where Marian's travel wagons and escort remained. The horse had barely stopped when Will dismounted and reached up to lift her down, setting her, weak-kneed, near her wagon. It took only a moment to ascertain that the outlaws had taken nothing from her caravan.

"Though I don't expect them to return, please accept our escort to Ludlow, my lady," Will said formally. He opened the door of her wagon.

"Thank you, Sheriff," she said, climbing in.

As she settled in her seat and the wagons rumbled off, now flanked by the sheriff's men as well as her own men-at-arms, Marian had much to contemplate. Least of which was whether Robin had known it was her party traveling through Sherwood, and had never intended on stealing anything from her in the first place.

Or had it merely been happenstance that Robin had recognized her, and had thus called off his men?

Or had the sheriff arrived in time to prevent the outlaws from making off with her belongings?

The next time she saw Robin—for she would certainly see him again, she'd make certain of it—she would have words with him. And try to find a way to help him while she spied on Prince John.

And mayhap . . . she might allow him to kiss her again.

Chapter 2

"By the rood," Prince John said to Will that evening. They sat at a large table on the dais in the great hall of Ludlow, enjoying pheasant and grouse from Sherwood Forest. "The hall has for certain grown quieter without my lovely wife's presence."

"But all that much darker and unattractive for it," Will replied automatically. Other than flattery about his person, John liked nothing better than to hear about the beauty and desirability of his wife. And if he ever procreated a legitimate child, he'd most likely require compliments in that regard as well.

No sooner had the words come out than Will cast a swift glance at his companion to be certain he hadn't noticed the disinterest in his voice. His mind had been elsewhere since his return to Ludlow as Marian's escort. And though he appreciated the opportunity to be seated at the high table, where he could look out over the other diners if he wished to locate one in particular, he was wholly uninterested in attending John tonight.

Ludlow was one of Prince John's smaller, less-significant holdings. He'd come into it simply by chance, when the daughter of one of his vassals married the baron of the tiny fief. The daughter and the baron died without issue, and John expediently assumed ownership of the holding as its overlord.

As it turned out, Ludlow Keep was fairly comfortable despite its smaller size, and it happened to abut the king's Sherwood Forest, which was known for generous hunting. Thus, John found the insignificant fief more pleasurable than one would expect, particularly since his wife, Isobel, preferred Westminster for a variety of reasons and wouldn't be present to hamper his other activities.

This time, John had been at Ludlow for six months, not just because he enjoyed it, but because he was trying to lie low, as far from his mother's notice as possible. When John was in residence, he required Will to attend him, which forced the sheriff to leave the small manor house he held along with his office. It also meant that he was relegated to a chamber with the other unmarried men of rank, since Ludlow wasn't really large enough to accommodate a royal court.

John's wife, Isobel, visited briefly, then returned to larger and busier residences, leaving her husband to amuse himself with hunting and other activities. Despite the princess's absence, however, many of her ladies-in-waiting remained at Ludlow, as they were wards of the prince, or because their husbands, fathers, or other responsible male family members attended him.

"And so you've allowed Robin Hood to escape yet again," John said as he sloshed a piece of bread in the juices of the trencher they shared. Since there were no ladies attending them at the trestle table, the single hollowed-out loaf of bread filled with fowl and potatoes served them both.

Despite the critical words, John's voice was easy and casual, indicating that he wasn't particularly angry or disappointed with Will's most recent failure to clap Robin in chains and toss him in the dungeon. There were times when Will suspected that John, for all his fury and blustering at the band of thieves, might also find their continued freedom useful in some respect.

After all, if coin disappeared, it could always be blamed on them, even if it happened to end up lining John's own coffers instead of in the hands of the bandits.

Yet, more important, John did not like to look the fool—and Robin Hood's continued elusion of the sheriff and his men accomplished just that. Will did not like to look the fool any more than the prince did, but he had little choice in the matter.

"The man and his band become more bold as the days go by, my lord," Will replied. He glanced out over the rows of tables that lined the hall. The gentry sat nearest the high table, where the most choice and freshest of foods were served. As one moved to the rear of the hall, the diners became more simple and mean, ending with the lowliest of serfs and villeins in the very back.

"He is too clever to capture in the forest. Methinks a trap ought to be set for the man. Something that will lure him from the safety of the trees."

Will calmly broke a corner of bread from the trencher and chewed on it, trying to keep his mind on John's words rather than his eyes searching the hall.

"An archery contest, and mayhap a day of jousting, would be in order," continued the prince. " 'Twill draw him out, for Robin Hood is known for his skill with the bow."

"He is a most skilled archer," Will agreed. "He did, after all, skewer the cloak of Lord d'Arlande, pinning him betwixt hand and waist against a tree trunk."

"Drawing nary a drop of blood in the process, the lickspittle. An' from some perch in a tree," John added, with a combination of disgust and wonder. "Did he not also pin your man—what was his name?—to a wagon he was robbing?"

Will picked up his goblet of wine. "Aye, three arrows and—"

"God's blood," said John suddenly. "And wherever did that vision appear from?"

The note of deep interest . . . almost reverence . . . in John's voice caught Will's full attention and he put his cup down and looked at the prince. His mouth parted and lips shiny with grease from the pheasant, John appeared quite taken.

Will's fingers tightened, though he kept his face blank. He knew without looking what—or, rather, who—had caught the Angevin's attention. It was inevitable.

And now he had to tread very carefully. "Ah, so you have seen Marian of Morlaix," Will said casually. He reached for his wine again, the metal of his goblet cool and textured beneath his grip. "She is quite the comely bitch. I had the misfortune of coming upon her in the wood today after Robin Hood had taken her off during the robbery."

"Is that so?" John said, but his eyes remained fixed on Marian. "Misfortune?"

Will didn't have to look directly out into the hall to know where she sat now, for he'd seen a glimpse of that brilliant coppery hair shining in the torchlight. He kept his attention on John instead of the woman. "He left her in the wood and that was the cause of his escape this day. I dare not leave a gentlewoman alone in the forest to chase after him, as he well knew. So I was forced to bring her back to her escort. By that time, Robin's men had taken what they desired and had all disappeared."

"So he took her off into the wood, did he?"

" 'Twas merely a diversionary tactic, my lord," he said. "I'm certain he meant to draw me and my men into the wood after him to rescue Lady Marian."

"Lady Marian," mused John, his voice hollow as he lifted his goblet to drink. "I've never seen such hair. The color of flame, 'tis. And a face to go with it. Alabaster skin, full lips just right for sucking cock—"

"And the temperament as well," Will added, disregarding the fact that he'd interrupted his liege. "I'd like nothing better than to take that in hand."

"Indeed." For the first time, John seemed to hear what Will had said. "Do you know the lady?"

"I fostered with her father at Mead's Vale. She tormented us most handily, and hid behind her father's hauberk when we would have had our revenge. Even then she showed the sign of becoming a most annoying, mouthy woman." He closed his own mouth at that point, acutely aware that his companion's mother had long been criticized for the very same faults—and more.

"Damme, and she is a widow too," John said, rich speculation in his voice. " 'Tis almost too convenient."

Even the prince would be hard-pressed to excuse the deflowering of one of his wards, but a widow was the easiest fruit to pluck. No male family members to cry dishonor, and no maidenhead to broach.

"A sharp-tongued one. I trow, the woman should be taught to keep her mouth closed . . . unless she has it otherwise engaged,"

Will said with a meaningful laugh. He'd somehow picked up his eating knife and realized his fingers had curled tightly around it. Keeping his voice even, he continued. "I should like to take that task on myself, my lord. I've a desire to otherwise engage that impudent tongue."

John turned to look at him again, his eyes so dark they appeared black. "And how does it happen that I have long urged you to find a field in which to rut, but now that you have set your eye on one, 'tis that of my own desire." His voice, low and easy, nevertheless carried a warning note.

"My lord, I knew that woman when she was but a young girl, a tease and a tormentor. And it's long been my desire to teach the lessons that I was never able to at that time. And aside of that, 'tis indeed a ripe field to plow. But," Will continued boldly when he saw that the prince was about to speak, "mayhap I have a way that you might find pleasing as well. She is a fire-haired bitch, and 'twill be a task to tame her. If you set that task to me, I'll take it gladly, my lord. Thus, none of her complaints can be directed at you, but at me instead. Then, I shall promise you a tame and willing woman to warm your bed when all the spite is gone from her. A well-trained and willing one in the stead of a surly, mouthy bitch."

John had closed his mouth to chew on a particularly tough piece of fowl, if the way his jaw worked was any indication. A spark of interest had flared in his eyes and he reached for his goblet to drink, still chewing.

Will used his eating knife to spear the last bit of pheasant and bring it to his own mouth, keeping his attention firmly on the prince. He uncurled his fingers and let the small knife rest next to the trencher. And waited. Waited as if to learn whether he would be sent into battle on a cold gray morning.

"Aye," said John at last. "Aye, 'tis a good plan, Will. There is only one stipulation I must insist upon."

"What is that, my lord?"

"That whilst you are going about the taming of that luscious little cunt, you'll provide me some entertainment." John wiped his face with a small cloth. "I desire to watch."

Marian found the great hall at Ludlow cramped, close, and smoky. All great halls were, to some extent, but it was worse here than usual. A royal court—even if 'twas only that of John Lackland—required numerous serfs to keep things running smoothly, countless pages and men-at-arms, and all the ladies and lords who curried favors. In a keep as small as Ludlow, the swell of people pushed at the very limits of the space.

She'd managed to find a seat in the second row, not far from the wall, where a torch burned down a pleasant circle of light. Though it was late September, fires blazed in two different fireplaces: a smaller one behind the high table, and a large one on the opposite wall. Dogs slunk underfoot, looking for their daily fare, while serfs dashed to and fro with their platters of food.

Marian glanced at the high table, where she caught her first glimpse of Prince John. He was a handsome man, with a neatly trimmed beard and fine clothing. His dark eyes seemed too small for his face, but they gleamed with interest and cunning as he conversed with the man next to him.

His companion had turned away momentarily as John gave an openmouthed guffaw, and was speaking to a page behind him, so Marian couldn't see his face. She cast a quick look about the hall. Nottinghamshire's sheriff was nowhere to be seen, for which she was unaccountably disappointed. Yet there were so

many people crowded around the tables, she would not be surprised if he was there, but not visible to her. No doubt a man of
his rank would sit closer to the prince, Marian thought.

"My lady, I heard you were set upon by that outlaw Robin
of the Hood!"

The breathless question came from Alys of Wentworth, one
of Queen Eleanor's wards whom Marian knew from her days in
the queen's court. Though she was only eighteen, Alys had been
sent as chaperone to deliver one of Richard's very young wards
to John's court while the king and his mother were traveling to
the Holy Lands.

Tonight, Alys was with two women who were only passing
acquaintances of Marian's from previous court visits. Finding
Alys here, who not only had been a good friend but also had a
reputation as an excellent healer, was a welcome diversion for
Marian.

"Aye, he attempted a robbery of my wagons," Marian replied.

"What was Robin Hood like? Was he as handsome as they
say?" asked another of the ladies, who introduced herself as
Catherine.

"He was friendly for a bandit," Marian replied, noticing that
some of the other nearby gentry had turned to listen. "No one
was hurt, and he was quite gallant." What else could she say?
She wasn't about to admit that he'd swept her up on his horse
and stolen a kiss.

"And handsome?" Catherine pressed, her eyes dancing as
though she knew something Marian didn't.

"Quite handsome," Marian replied, smiling back. She happened to look toward the front of the hall at that moment, and
her whole body froze. It chilled, then suddenly exploded into
unpleasant heat in her cheeks.

Prince John was looking at her. Not merely looking at her, but pinning her with hooded dark eyes as though he wished to be doing so with his hands . . . or something else. Marian pulled her gaze away from his and felt her heart pounding rampantly. Her stomach suddenly felt unpleasantly heavy and disrupted.

"Is it true that the sheriff rescued you and his men chased off the bandits?" ventured another of the ladies.

Marian swallowed back the churning in her stomach that threatened to bubble up her throat. "The sheriff did arrive quite fortuitously," she said, and was unable to keep from glancing back at the high table.

John was still watching her, slipping a chunk of food into his mouth and masticating as though he meant to be feeding on her rather than the food. The expression was unmistakable. Marian tore her eyes away again and they skittered over the prince's companion, who, this time, was facing the front of the hall. Her throat dried again.

She hadn't recognized him before, or perhaps she hadn't looked closely enough. But 'twas most definitely Will there, sharing the most prominent seat in the hall with the prince as though he was his closest crony.

He, at the least, wasn't looking at her. Instead, he leaned closer to John and spoke intimately to him while lifting a chunk of meat to his mouth on a small eating knife. Even from here, she saw the tension and harshness in a face tanned the color of deer hide, and made even more shadowy by the dark hair that brushed against it. And then the sudden gleam of a humorless smile.

"Why does he sit with the prince?" she asked. "In such a place of honor?"

"Oh," said the lady who'd asked about him in the first place, and whose name Marian had forgotten, "he and the prince are inseparable companions."

"Indeed," Marian said, feeling her brows draw together in a frown. "Does the sheriff seek favor from the prince, then?"

"Nay, 'tis not so much that he seeks boons from the prince, but that the prince finds him amusing," replied Sir Roderick, who had barely taken his eyes from Marian since she sat across from him. "The prince must include de Wendeval in all his amusements and activities or he is displeased by his absence."

Will and Prince John? She looked again at the acquaintance of her youth and his royal companion. The depravity and lust shone unabashedly in John's eyes, and though Will's face was half-turned away, she recognized anew the hardness there. Unrelieved and stoic. Emotionless.

'Twas most definitely not the young man she'd known. If he and John had become constant companions, he must no longer be merely quiet and brooding, but as brutal and cruel as the unloved prince.

"The sheriff has not been able to capture Robin Hood," Marian said, wondering about those two men. As children, they'd been rivals of a sort. Had that rivalry grown into something more ominous? Will was charged with catching, sentencing, and, if necessary, executing bandits such as Robin. "I trow the prince cannot be happy with that lack."

"Nay, but the prince himself has been witness to Robin Hood's cleverness. John and Nottingham have plotted many traps for the bandit, each one more dangerous than the last. And Robin Hood seems always to slip through the smallest crack and to make his escape. The sheriff was to execute a boy for treason. Hang him on the dais in the Ludlow bailey, in front of all who wished to watch. He intended to make an example of the poor boy."

"Treason? 'Tis a serious offense." And must be punished if law and order were to be kept. But a boy?

"Aye. The boy claimed he took only a deer that was already dead from the forest, in order to feed his family."

Marian felt a little pang in her middle. It was treason to steal from the king, indeed, but . . . "Surely the beast was examined. It would be no hardship to determine if it had been freshly slaughtered."

Sir Roderick shrugged. "Aye, and there were those who claimed the deer had not been recently killed. But the sheriff meant to hang him anyway, the boy. Merely fourteen winters he was, and if it weren't for Robin Hood, the boy would have been swaying in the breeze."

"Robin Hood?"

"Aye. He rescued him right off the scaffolding, whilst the sheriff could do naught but look on furiously."

Fourteen. That was the same age Will and Robin had been that last summer spent at Mead's Vale. Hardly boys, but not quite men.

Again she wondered about their rivalry. Even that short moment in the clearing, before she'd recognized Will, the antipathy between the men had been palpable.

Was it possible that they hadn't recognized each other?

Nay, of course not. She had recognized Robin immediately; surely Will had done so. But Robin could not claim innocence. He was an outlaw.

And it was Will's duty to punish outlaws.

Duty.

Marian felt her mouth tighten. Oh, she knew well of duty, for 'twas duty that brought her here, into the court of the cruel and lustful John Angevin. Duty to her king, by way of his mother.

She loved Eleanor as much as one could love a strong-willed liege—particularly one of the lesser gender, but who moved among men as if one of them—but Marian was not ignorant of the queen's faults. It would be no surprise to her if Eleanor hadn't picked her for this task purposely, knowing that Marian would catch John's eye. For, in Eleanor's mind, one must make sacrifices, and one must use whatever skills and advantages one had in order to complete the task. She herself had done so, and expected those whom she trusted to do the same.

Marian was one whom Eleanor trusted, and as she felt the heavy salaciousness of John's gaze on her, she shivered deep inside. Perhaps it was no boon to be a favorite of Eleanor's after all.

Yet, what choice did she have? Duty. She would do her duty, regardless of what she must endure.

Though she feared it was too late to escape the prince's attention, Marian spent the remainder of the meal with her back angled away from the high table and as close to the wall as possible. Perhaps some other fresh face would attract him in her stead. Alys, who was much more beautiful with her spun-gold hair and big blue eyes, was safe from the prince, as she was the heiress to Clervillieres, one of Eleanor's strongest vassals in Aquitaine. She was still a virgin, due to the fact that her betrothed, a lord eight years younger than she, had recently died before they were wed. Even John dare not sully her maidenhead.

When the interminable meal ended after six courses, plus a round of jongleurs' entertainment, Marian thought to make her escape to the small chamber that had been put aside for her and Ethelberga. That she had a private chamber was in itself a sign of the queen's influence.

Making her excuses and slipping past the eager smile of Sir

Roderick, Marian edged along the stone wall. She took care not to brush against it, for it was covered with smoke and other grime. One of the pleasures—few as there had been—of being sent to Ludlow was that she'd been able to prepare a new wardrobe. In retrospect, Marian wondered if mayhap she wouldn't have attracted the prince's attention if she'd been wearing less-fine clothing. Tonight, her floor-length undergown, fitted from throat to hip and with sleeves laced from wrist to shoulder, was the color of butter. The burnished-gold overtunic—a sleeveless shift—had been embroidered with gold-shot thread and tiny amber beads along the hems and neckline.

Marian knew that the combination of yellow, gold, and amber made her fiery hair appear brighter, her green eyes sharper, and her skin color warm and peachlike . . . and at that moment she bewailed her choice. Vanity. Would it be her undoing?

Just then, she felt a presence behind her, too close. She felt the hair at the back of her neck prickle, and she whirled around.

"Leaving so soon, Lady Marian?" William de Wendeval loomed over her.

The torchlight danced over his face, darkening shadows further, and giving his expression a wicked glow. His eyes were flat and cool, and his lips settled in a half smile that held no humor.

"I'm weary," she replied easily, though her heart, for some reason, pounded madly. She could not pull her gaze away from those dark eyes, and his large hand closed over her arm.

"Ah, weary. Of course. You must have found it trying to fight off the advances of that rogue in the woods," he said. His fingers held her firmly, but not painfully, though now he stood so that she was between him and the wall, hidden to the rest of the hall by his great height and broad shoulders.

"Release me, Will," she said, again keeping her voice calm. She chose to use his name in an effort to remind him of their past. "I wish to go to my chamber."

Having spoken, Marian turned away, and in doing so looked beyond Will's arm . . . toward the high table. John sat there, his eyes fastened on her and Will as he raised a goblet to drink. The cup hid the expression on his face, but the avidity in his eyes told her that he watched with interest. She realized that Will had maneuvered it so that while he blocked her from most of the hall, his angle left a clear view for the prince.

"But you cannot," the sheriff said, and she felt his foot brush against hers. The next thing she knew, the wall bumped up behind her and she was crowded between a large body and the stone. "Your presence is required elsewhere."

Marian's throat closed and the pounding of her heart became stronger. "By whom?" she demanded.

"By me."

The next thing she knew, the world changed: his hands closed over her shoulders and his mouth descended. The wall pushed into her from behind, and his powerful body pressed against hers from the front, one knee shifting to push between her legs. Will's lips covered hers before she could react or twist away, and his fingers moved to grasp her chin, curving over the front of her throat. Not hard enough to choke her, praise God, but enough that she dared not move.

She realized her eyes had closed, and her hands had gone convulsively toward his chest, her fingers closing over his embroidered tunic, grasping at the heavy stitching as she tried to push him away. He was as immovable as his mouth was skillful, and Marian tasted the heavy wine on his lips and tongue as she gave in to the kiss.

It caught her by surprise, the intensity of his mouth pressed to hers, lips and tongue slipping and sliding in an angry dance. Her breath caught and she became aware of the pounding of his heart beneath her hands, and the matching stampede of her own pulse.

But when she realized what was happening, she pulled her lips, her face, away angrily. His fingers fell from her chin, and before he could fully release her, she whipped her palm back. Will's hand shot up and caught her wrist before she could slap his face.

"How dare you?" she whispered, fighting to pull free.

His half smile was back, arrogant and powerful and humorless, as he held her wrist with angry fingers.

"Oh, I dare. Do you not know to whom you speak? The fearsome Sheriff of Nottinghamshire." His lips twisted in a parody of a smile.

"I know who you are," Marian responded, her heart pounding. "Now take your hands from me, Will."

"I cannot in conscience do that, my lady. For it's to be me," he said, leaning down into her face, crowding his hip against her belly, "or the prince." He slipped his other hand back up to cup her chin again, forcing her to look at him, up into those hard eyes, flat and dark. "And I won't draw blood. Or leave bruises."

CHAPTER 3

Robin eased back into the shadows.

From his vantage point high up in Ludlow's great hall, he had a clear view of the diners below. After his men had distracted one of the men-at-arms standing watch, Robin had nimbly climbed the bailey's wall. A corner window slit had allowed him to slip into the hall unnoticed. Now he stood on one of the narrow balconies, hidden behind a tapestry.

The air up here was hot and dull, and his eyes stung from the rising smoke. But not so much that he missed the way the Sheriff of Nottinghamshire had made his way to Lady Marian of Leaford, backed her up against the wall, and fairly rutted with her right in the midst of the hall. 'Twas hard to mistake Nottingham's height and unrelieved dark tunic pressed up near Marian's blazing hair, set even more afire by the rich golden clothing she wore.

A lovely lady Marian had become. So much that it had taken him by surprise when he accosted her wagon earlier today. Of course, he'd known it was hers, but he hadn't expected to find such a pleasant surprise within. A gangly girl with pale skin and an overload of freckles, Marian had always had the beacon-bright hair, as well as the stubborn chin . . . but now all that had melded into a very lovely woman.

By all rights, Robin should have been down below, on the rush-covered floor, with all the other vassals of King Richard, sitting at the trestle tables and slamming fair maidens up against the wall for a kiss—or more.

When he was Lord Robin of Locksley, he had been a favorite with the ladies for his charm, wit, and skill on the lute. He had been counted one of the favorites of the ladies of the royal court, who'd enjoyed the tradition begun in Queen Eleanor's Court of Love, wherein the knights and lords worshipped them from afar (and sometimes from very intimate proximity). In the old days, Robin had little difficulty moving from that pose of distant worship to a closer hold beneath the laces of those tight-fitting undertunics . . . to the mutual pleasure of all parties.

And then the old king had died, and his son decided to go on Crusade, and everything had changed.

Now Robin of Locksley had become Robin of the Hood, an outlaw who ranged throughout Sherwood Forest, terrorizing those who passed through. And who must remain on the periphery of the court, no longer lord of his own fief. There were benefits to his situation, but at this moment, Robin found them little compensation.

He watched as William de Wendeval seized Marian's hand when she raised it to strike him, and held it steady as he leaned down into her face. The man appeared unruffled as he spoke with obvious intensity.

Robin gritted his teeth as he watched. His father had thought years ago of betrothing his son to Marian, and had even gone so far as to speak to her father about it. At the time, Robin had little interest in the pale, skinny girl who always wanted to follow him around and who beat him at archery contests more often than he liked to admit. But now he realized he didn't like watching Nottingham pushing himself upon her, not one whit. And he wasn't going to allow it to happen.

'Twould be a simple task to put an end to it, for one of the benefits of being an outrageously charming and handsome outlaw, he'd discovered, was that the women found him dangerously fascinating. Marian had been no exception today in the woods.

And there were plenty of other beautiful women, lush and ripe for the plucking, if that was what Nottingham had a mind to do. Many of whom Robin himself had already had the pleasure of meeting. And plucking.

As the sheriff led Marian out of the hall, Robin scanned the remaining ladies for a potential replacement for the sheriff's interest.

Pauletta of Yarnley was comely enough, but she kissed like a fish. Of course, one could get beyond that easily if one had a mind to. Lady Elizabeth de Guildern had fairly melted in his arms when he slipped up behind her in one of the keep's torchlit hallways last sennight. She was an eager partner, and in fact, her hands had been quite busy during their brief interlude behind a tapestry. Robin grinned at the memory and felt his cock lift in its own salutation. Lady Elizabeth would most certainly be worth another visit.

He shifted slightly, adjusting the crotch of his braies as he considered the other candidates. Joanna of Wardhamshire . . . Catherine de Meauville . . . Hie! Who was the wench?

Robin eased the slightest bit forward, risking a bit more illumination, as he peered down. He'd never seen her before. Petite with blond hair . . . mayhap it was Henriette de Hulvasen. . . .

She turned her head slightly, looking up at Roderick of Treyvern, who was much taller than she, and Robin saw her young, heart-shaped face. That was most definitely not Henriette of the knife-blade nose and abundant bosom.

A new female addition to John's court meant more than a chance to steal kisses in dark corners. It meant yet another source of information, another opportunity to learn who was traveling to and from Ludlow and what they might be bringing that Robin might find worth relieving them of.

Of course, Robin already had a variety of sources, including one that was very close to the prince.

And Nottingham and Marian had disappeared from the hall.

Together.

His lips pursed thoughtfully, Robin made his decision, and pulling the hood of his dark green cloak up and over his head, he eased from the shadows.

Nottingham had disrupted Robin's playtime this afternoon. Now 'twas time for his own entertainment to be aborted.

"Where are you taking me?" Marian demanded, trying to drag her arm away from Will's grip.

His face appeared even more dark and forbidding than before. They'd come to a narrow flight of steps and he stopped at its base. "Your presence is requested by His Highness," he said in a low, tight voice. "In his private solar."

Marian's belly fell to her knees. Oh God, already? "The prince?" Then she drew in a deep breath and straightened. It would do no good to show fear. Especially to one as formidable as the man before her.

Who was taking her to the prince.

"Nay, Will." Her voice came out in a gust of breath. "Not tonight. Please." She reached for him, her fingers tight.

Will looked down at her, standing so that his head blocked the merry flames of the sconce behind him. The details of his face were thus obscured by shadow, but she saw his jaw move, and his lips tighten into a line so thin it was probably white. "You must make your choice, Marian, for he will not be put off." His voice was not so harsh as it had been in the hall.

"Choice?" she responded, tamping back the wail that threatened to erupt. By the holy cross, she was Lady Marian of Morlaix, and she would swallow her weakness. Even though she'd fairly begged a moment earlier.

By her own example, Eleanor of Aquitaine had instilled in Marian the responsibility of duty and honor. And if one did not have honor, one had nothing.

"I have *no* choice, according to you," she said. "The prince wishes my presence and you are to deliver me to him." Now it was her turn to clamp her lips tightly, for fear that he might see them tremble.

In truth, what was the worst that could happen? Prince John might wish to tup her, and, well, she was no virginal maid. She'd endured Harold's attentions as his wife. 'T could be no worse under . . . dear God, *under* . . . the prince.

"Your choice is to submit either to the prince . . . or to me."

Marian looked up at him, feeling her jaw sag slightly. *It's either him or me . . . and I won't draw blood.*

Now his rushed words made sense to her, words that she'd barely heard in the blast of anger and mortification that he should have used her the way he did in the hall.

Or leave bruises.

She felt the waves of tension rolling off him as if they were heat from a fireplace.

"I've already made my claim," he said. The words came out sharp and hard. "But if you prefer the prince—"

"No," she said. "No, Will." She drew in a deep breath. She didn't really know this man any more than she knew the prince, and if the rumors were correct, he was as brutal as the Angevin. But his stark promise seemed sincere. *I won't draw blood. Or leave bruises.* "I do not prefer the prince." She snatched in her breath and looked around, afraid that her words might have been overheard.

"Then you have made your choice," he said after a moment frozen in silence.

"Make no mistake," she said, stepping back from him. "I prefer to make no choice at all."

"You haven't that freedom, Marian," he said. "Make no mistake: if you aren't with me, you will be with John. He accepts nay from no one. Nor is he swayed from his desires. You will attend him tonight, as my guest."

Marian looked up at him, trying to read his face. Shadowed, closed, he looked as frightening as John sounded. She swallowed back a little shiver and said, "So you will protect me from John?"

"Protect you?" He gave a short, edgy laugh. "That is a loose word for what will pass between us, but if you wish, you may consider it that." Once again, his fingers curled around her arm. "Now, come, before I lose what little patience I have."

"Drink this," Will said, shoving a skin of wine at Marian as they stopped just outside the door to John's solar. "And if the prince offers you anything to drink, take it." It would make things easier.

She looked up at him, fury mingled with fear in her green eyes, and for a moment, he thought she meant to refuse. Then she snatched the skin from him and drank. She might loathe him—and if she didn't now, she would soon—but Marian was no fool. She knew the wine would soften whatever would happen beyond the door.

Will turned away, feeling as though his entire body were a jousting staff. Stiff and stark. Immovable. Unfeeling.

But that was nothing new.

She didn't hand him the wineskin; she slapped it at his gut.

"Aye, that's it," Will told her. "Show your fury. Fight me. 'Twill keep him entertained." The skin was empty, leaving none for him—which was just as well. He couldn't afford any indulgence.

Folding the skin and tucking it into the belt of his tunic, Will gave a sharp nod to the two guards, then opened the door and shoved her in, making sure she stumbled.

She didn't just stumble; she fell in a heap of golden skirts and a bounce of glorious, intricately braided hair.

"Ah . . . already she is on her knees, I see, de Wendeval." The prince chuckled deeply. "How efficient you are."

One of the guards closed the door behind him and Will stepped farther into the chambers, trying not to breathe too deeply. The space smelled of indulgence: wine, food, sweat . . . and sex.

"As you requested, my lord," Will said, bowing briefly.

"Rise, Lady Marian," John said. "Allow me to welcome you to my private chambers. I do hope that you will visit oft, here, in my Court of Pleasure."

The prince sat on a massive wooden chair too heavy for even Will to move alone. The well-cushioned seat was situated to the left of the door, near one end of the large, rectangular chamber. Tapestries stirred on the wall from the shift of the heavy door closing, and thick rugs covered the stone floor instead of herbs and rushes. A long low table lined the wall directly across from the door. It was covered with wine flagons, platters, and bowls of food, drink, oils, lotions, and other indulgences.

The prince's chambers lacked for nothing in the realm of sensuality. He'd taken over this large, well-lit space that had been the ladies' solar at Ludlow and made it into a den of hedonism. Candles flickered on the table, from wall sconces, and throughout the chamber. Along with the fires crackling at each end, the candlelight gave the space a warm, golden glow.

Will made no move to assist Marian as she rose to her feet and smoothed her tunic, though he stood nearby. He realized his fingers had closed tightly into his palms, and knew there was little he could do if John took it into his head to forget their agreement.

He didn't need to look around to know that there were other women in the room—but not gentlewomen, not tonight. He could hear the faint whistle of breath, a little catch of a sob from a corner. A servingwoman or two, most likely, at the other end of the chamber.

"My lord," Marian said as she rose to her feet, giving him a brief nod. Will caught the trace of insolence in her voice and wanted to strangle her. "I am honored by your gracious invitation, but as I've told Nottingham, I much prefer to seek my own chamber this night. 'Tis been a difficult day of travel and I am quite exhausted." She said it in the same tone Queen Eleanor might have done: as if she expected him to care.

"Then I am *most* honored that you've attended me," John replied in his smooth voice. His dark eyes missed little, scanning her with interest.

Marian bowed again, and her hair, which had loosened sometime since they'd left the hall—likely when Will had shoved his fingers into it during the kiss—sagged over one shoulder. "Then you will permit me to take my leave, my lord?"

"Most certainly," John replied. Will felt Marian gather herself up to thank him. Before she could speak, the prince continued. "But you must stay for a bit. I should not want you to leave my private chambers"—he emphasized those words delicately—"without having been suitably entertained."

The prince's gesture directed Marian's attention to the other side of the solar. She'd been facing John since entering the room, so Will knew it was the first time she'd looked there. Her breath caught audibly and she took a step back.

He didn't have to look to know what she was seeing, and he caught at her arm from behind. His fingers closed around it tightly in warning, but that was all he dared do.

"Come, let us join them," John said, rising from his chair.

Will tugged Marian back from the prince's path as he moved to the other side of the chamber. She bumped into Will, and half turned. The expression on her pale face was no more than he'd expected: a combination of loathing and horror.

"Be glad you are my guest and not his," he hissed into her ear, then directed her forward.

"Mayhap you would like to join me for a game of chess, my lady?" asked John, sweeping his hand to the side. "Or would you prefer to simply watch the entertainment?"

Will had become fairly inured to the sight of activities conducted in this chamber, but when he propelled Marian toward the cushions and chairs at the other side, he saw them from her point of view. Certainly she knew what passed between a man and a woman—she'd been married for three years, and Harold had not been an elderly man—but God help her if she didn't.

Yet, John's proclivities ranged far beyond what normally occurred in a bedchamber, and the sights that Marian would experience were unblemished examples of that. Although, surprisingly, this night the whips were out of sight, and the manacles and other restraints hung empty on the far wall.

The largest bed Will knew of stood before them, not obscured by its bed hangings or curtains—they were pulled wide, the better to view the activities within. The soft mattress currently boasted three naked women. One of them had red-tinged eyes and nose from crying, and was likely the cause of the snuffling Will had heard earlier. He recognized none of them, which confirmed the fact that they were serf women, a small blessing that meant that Marian wouldn't—at least yet—be recognized by her peers.

"Chess, my lady?" John asked again when Marian remained silent. "Or mayhap you'd prefer to watch Nottingham and me play. He is quite good."

She stood rigid and unmoving next to Will. He swore he could feel the sharp, hard pounding of her heart all the way through her body. When she looked over at the chess game, he felt her shock rise anew. The heavy wooden board rested on the back of a naked woman positioned on her hands and knees.

Will knew how that particular game was played, and he was in no mood to participate. "Mayhap Lady Marian would simply prefer to watch anight," he said, giving her a little push toward a pile of cushioned seats far from the chess game and the bed.

"She does seem a bit shy," John said easily, his eyes scoring over her yet again in a way that put Will on his guard. "I do hope you'll relieve her of that propensity sooner rather than later."

Shy, but not the tigress Will had described her as, which worried him anew. John might decide that it wouldn't be much of an effort to tame her and renege on their agreement.

"You can be certain of it, my lord," Will replied, settling onto a low, wide chair made specially for more than one. Because John expected it of him, he drew Marian onto his lap, more roughly than necessary, and made sure his hands moved crudely over her breasts before settling at her waist.

She stiffened but, other than trying to move his hands away, said nothing. Will persisted, sliding his palms up and over the sides of her torso and around to cup her breasts again. He felt her shuddering breaths, but she remained silent and still.

Wanting, needing, to get a rise out of her in order to support his excuses to John, Will moved roughly, sliding his fingers up into her hair and tipping her head to the side. He buried his face in the side of her warm neck, giving her a little bite just below the ear. It was a bite that turned into more of a nuzzling kiss. Her skin tasted like warm salt, smelled like violets, and was smooth. Unbelievably soft. Closing his eyes, he lifted his lips, keeping his hands strong and tight at her waist. When he opened them, he was relieved to see that John had found another distraction.

The prince had settled himself in the chair closest to the

bed. One of the women—the sniffling one—knelt at his feet. She had removed one of his boots, and was unrolling the hose from that leg.

On the bed, the other two women had commenced with one version of the entertainment John enjoyed. Will couldn't stop himself from watching as the two kissed full on the mouth, naked bodies aligned, breast to breast. They rolled to the side, hands shifting and legs sliding with soft scrapes. One bent to the other, her mouth wide, mauling an offered breast as her fingers slid down to cover the slick pink quim revealed by her splayed legs.

Marian was hardly breathing, and Will could tell that her shocked attention was fixed on the tableau in front of them. The soft whimpers and gasps from the two naked women filtered through the air, bringing their pleasure—real or feigned, Will was never quite certain—to surround their audience.

It was impossible not to watch—and even more impossible to close one's ears to the sounds: the soft, wet suction of mouth to mouth and mouth to nipple, of fingers slipping in and around slick red nether lips, making their own wet, erotic sounds. The movement of flesh against flesh and fabric, the moans and gasps, and even the scrape of nail over the bed beneath . . . pleasure and sensuality permeated the room through sight, sound, and scent.

Will glanced over to see that the prince no longer seemed to care that he and Marian were present, and instead had focused his attention wholly on the large bed. His attendant had removed the other boot and hose, and had lifted his tunic to expose a purple-headed erection. Her activity produced more sounds: wet lips and tongue laced with the grunts of her own exertion as she knelt between John's legs. The prince's face was a mask of dark pleasure, his eyes fixed on the bed while his hand clamped over the top of the woman's head, holding her there. Even from the distance, Will saw the whites of his knuckles as he pressed his fingers into the sides of her skull as if wordlessly directing her, driving her . . . as one signaled a bridled horse.

Closing his eyes, Will drew in a long, slow, silent breath, keeping his own fingers rigid and still at Marian's waist. Impossible to look away, to ignore the sounds . . . and to keep one's own body from responding.

The scent of violets, the silk of skin and lush red lips were his for the taking. She'd made her choice, chosen him. Her breathing had changed, become quick and shallow, and she moved slightly against him in short little jerks that matched its rhythm.

When he changed the angle of his head and watched Marian from the side and behind, he saw that her lips had parted and her eyes were still fastened on the women in front of them. He couldn't read the expression on her face—was it horror or fascination?—but he no longer cared.

His hands moved of their own accord, no longer able to remain still at her hips. They slid up the sides of her torso, filled their palms with the weight of her breasts through the tunic and undertunic, and felt the hard points of nipples through the thin fabric. She made a soft noise, an erotic little gasp, and he rubbed his thumbs hard over the fabric, teasing over her jutting nipples, and felt her breath turn to little shudders as she squirmed.

Suddenly, her skin was beneath his mouth again, there at the side of her neck, where her pulse raced and jumped, and he tasted and nibbled. She moved on his lap, brushing against the raging swell of his cock, and he had to stop for a moment and close his eyes. Breathing in that violet scent helped not at all, nor did holding her breasts in his hands, though they were protected by layers of cloth. He could feel the soft little pants of her breath and the roundness of her bottom against him. . . .

The two women on the bed continued their play, and the sounds became more urgent. One lay back on the cushions, her knees bent upright and her feet planted on the bed. Her companion bent between her legs, and Will could see the strong swipe of tongue over the glistening folds of her quim.

Marian breathed harder, fairly in tandem with the girl on the bed, leaning back against him as if he wasn't forcing her to watch. His fingers slipped through the sides of the sleeveless overtunic, finding her nipples and the weight of her breasts through the thin layer of silk.

John gave a loud groan, followed by the unmistakable gagging and choking sounds of the woman in front of him.

The noise drew Will back to the moment, and had the effect of a splash of cool water. Not ice-cold water, and not a complete submersion . . . but enough that the urgency waned.

He removed his hands from Marian, forcing them to his sides, and watched the prince from the corner of his eye while avoiding looking at the bed. Either John would be sated, and fall into slumber, or he would merely have his appetite whetted and would expect more forms of entertainment.

Will had done his best to keep the prince's goblet filled with wine during dinner, and he was hoping for the former. For the moment, he focused on the stone wall beyond the bed, keeping his eyes from the tapestry—which portrayed a scene more lascivious than the one in front of him—and counted the stones. He couldn't block out the sounds, and now the scent of woman's musk filtered through the air, teasing his attention back toward the bed.

And then, he heard the sound of a snore. The faintest little tease of a rumble.

Relief washing over him, Will turned to look.

John was asleep.

The first night of torture had ended.

CHAPTER 4

Where had they gone?

Robin had been slinking through the shadows of the keep for more than an hour, dodging behind tapestries and into dark alcoves—alone, unfortunately—but he'd seen not a sign of the sheriff and Marian.

'Twas possible Nottingham had escorted her to her chamber and Robin had missed seeing them pass by as they made their way to the stairs on the opposite site of the keep. He had, after all, been considering which of the other lovely women would be an appropriate distraction.

But just as he considered giving up his search, he heard the unmistakable sound of a skirt swishing through the rushes. Robin eased once more into the shadows.

He always found it surprisingly easy to move about within the keep, in the midst of the very people who sought him. Of course, the rough and mean clothing he wore was fit more for a serf than a lord turned outlaw, and he took care to keep his face averted. He'd been gone from court long enough that the people who gathered here—most of them John's cohorts anyway—wouldn't necessarily recognize him, particularly with his beard. Other than Nottingham, of course.

Despite his disreputable clothing, Robin wore his own good boots, carried his own dagger, and always kept a swatch of forest green ribbon on his person to leave with a lady who accommodated him with a kiss . . . or more.

Ahh. Robin's mouth twitched in a very pleased smile as he peered around the corner. The swish of silk skirts announced the approach of Lady Joanna Wardhamshire, with the huge blue eyes and small, rosebud mouth. Her nose might be a bit large, but one could forgive that. And best of all, she was a young widow.

"And a good evening to you, Lord Burle," she was saying. "Thank you for the turn about the bailey. Shall I see you at the hunt on the morrow?"

Hmmm. A hunt? An activity that would draw the richly dressed gentry and jewel-clad women out into the wood? Robin nodded to himself in delight.

"I shall indeed hunt, my lady," replied the man. Robin had noticed Burle before and knew him to be a serious-minded sort of person with a tedious sort of earnestness. Never would an exaggeration nor a falsehood pass his lips, nor even, Robin wagered, the slip of a tongue during a passionate kiss.

Even better. Lady Joanna must be bored to tears after walking with such a monotonous person. Hadn't the man a better sense of romance than to propose a walk around the stinking, crowded bailey, among the pigs and hounds and stables? Why not on the high parapets, overlooking the yard and out beyond the walls of Ludlow, where the dark forest and rich fields lay?

Robin shook his head, smiling to himself. One man's missed opportunity was another's delight. He listened and heard a gentle, moist smack that sounded decidedly like a kiss on the back of a hand. Definitely not lip to lip.

And then the swish of skirts came closer, and the faint sound of Burle's metal belt clinking faded into silence. Along with the swish came a gentle scent of rose and then Lady Joanna paced on past Robin's hiding place.

He waited until she'd gone a few steps farther, then stepped out into the empty corridor. "My lady, have you dropped something?"

Joanna turned. "Oh," she said when she saw him standing there. Her voice held a hint of wariness.

"Does this belong to you?" Robin asked, taking one step—only one, and no more until he determined how skittish she was—and offering the scrap of green ribbon.

"Why"—she stepped closer to him, her eyes roving over his belted burlap tunic and tight but holey hose—"I don't know." Then she looked at his feet, clad in well-tooled leather boots, and raised her gaze.

" 'Tis a green ribbon," Robin said, letting his eyes glint warmly, knowingly at her. "Do you know of anyone who might miss a green ribbon?"

"Oh." Joanna's voice held a different note now . . . one of curiosity and fascination. "A green ribbon?" Ah. At last a multi-syllabic word from her lips, albeit an echo of his own speech.

"Would you like to have it?" he asked meaningfully.

"Are you . . . ?" Her voice trailed off, but she looked neither frightened nor skittish. Rather, delight seemed to have sparked to life in her eyes. And taken control of her tongue.

Robin was certain he could remedy that.

He moved toward her, the ribbon dangling from his fingers, and eased her back into a little notch in the brick wall. Her breathing came faster, and her hands clasped his shoulders.

"You're . . . ," she began, but he covered her mouth with his.

Ah. Nothing like the feel of warm, slick lips, and the press of womanly curves. Robin molded himself to her as she kissed him back—her tongue was working perfectly now—and allowed his hands to curve over the swell of her hips. She tasted a bit like smoke from the great hall, and rose, and woman, and he nibbled on her ear. The soft mewling noises she made had his eyes closing and his hands moving more boldly.

Not to mention his cock lifting in salute.

He pressed closer, feeling for the juncture of her thighs through the layers of undergown and tunic. His palms held her breasts, found the thrusting nipples, and rubbed over them as she moved against him in pleasurable little circles. 'Twould be no problem to lift her skirts and slide right home, here against the damp stone wall. She was more than willing.

He'd just begun to gather up the woolen fabric between them when he stopped, pulling away to listen intently.

'Sblood, that was Marian's voice.

Joanna opened her mouth to protest his retreat, and he covered her lips with two fingers. "We cannot be seen," he murmured, fainter than a whisper, and brushed his fingertips over her soft mouth to seal it closed. "I vow, I'll come to you again. Take you this," he added, pressing the green ribbon into her hand, curling her fingers over it. He gently but firmly pulled her out of the corner. "Go, quickly, before you are seen."

"But . . ." She looked at him with full lips and shining eyes, and Robin smiled back.

"You'll keep my secret, will you not?"

"Aye," she breathed, clutching the ribbon that dangled from her fist.

"Now go," he said, half-listening behind him. He heard nothing. Had he been wrong? Still, he'd nearly forgotten his resolve to find Marian in the heat of this moment of pleasure.

If it had been so delightful to pull Joanna of Wardhamshire into the shadows, it would be that much more so to have his hands full of the lovely Marian. All that fiery red hair and those snapping green eyes and lush curves.

"I'm well able to find my own chamber," she was saying. And she sounded displeased.

There. It *was* Marian, and her voice was closer.

"I will escort you," came Nottingham's deep voice, equally flat and hard.

"Have you not escorted me enough this night?"

"I will see you to your chamber," the sheriff said again, and they were nearly upon Robin's hiding place.

Peste. He flattened himself against the wall, wishing for a deeper alcove. If the sheriff found him lurking about, 'twould be the end of his pleasant evening. Not that his childhood rival's attendance on the lovely Marian wasn't enough to ruin the night anyway.

Yet, through the risk, it appeared he would have the unexpected pleasure of learning which chamber Marian had been assigned to. Robin had been known to slip into a room filled with sleeping ladies and locate the one he sought . . . even if she was double or triple bunked. All without making a sound. The liberties he'd enjoyed as an outlaw were, at times, greater than those he'd enjoyed as the lord of a manor.

Marian and de Wendeval walked past him and Robin observed from his corner. The lady walked erect and stiffly, apart from her companion, and the sheriff made no move to take her arm or otherwise touch her.

Robin smoothed his hand over the beard and mustache he'd taken to wearing and smiled. The language of their bodies told him all he needed to know. Nottingham was no closer to wooing Lady Marian than Robin was to walking freely into Ludlow Keep and supping with the prince.

Not that he would wish to, but he sorely missed the opportunity to play his lute for the ladies. They became all moonyeyed and fell into his hands like ripe plums. Or apples. Or, in some cases, small pumpkins. With nipples that begged to be sucked and licked, and quims that ached for his fingers.

Robin followed the pair from a distance as they walked silently along the corridor on this second level of the keep. The unmarried men were housed in chambers belowstairs, crowded and lined up pallet by pallet, while the women shared space on the second floor in two different rooms and actually had beds. A few fortunate married couples shared smaller chambers on the opposite side of the great hall, and the rest either rented houses in town or slept apart with their appropriate gender. Prince John had made the third-floor solar his own private area, and that was one place even Robin hadn't dared venture in his exploration of the keep. But he well knew the two chambers apportioned to the ladies.

Yet, Marian and Nottingham walked past the two doors that Robin knew led to those chambers, and continued past the garderobe and to a door at the very end of the hallway. Most curious. Did Lady Marian have a chamber to herself? Why would that be?

Robin grimaced. Mayhap Nottingham had arranged it himself. But even if he had, it appeared he would not be taking advantage of it tonight if the lady's stance was any indication. Again, Robin's lips moved in a pleased smile.

"Good night," Marian was saying as she stopped in front of the door, clearly dismissing her companion.

Nottingham ignored her and opened the door to the chamber, walking in without invitation.

Marian glared at him for a moment, then followed.

Then, to Robin's utter vexation, the door closed.

Marian looked at Will, who'd closed the door and followed her through the small antechamber into the larger room, instead of leaving. Her heart, which had not yet returned to its regular rhythm since the episode in John's chambers, took another great leap and began to pound anew.

You must submit to him . . . or to me.

"What do you want?" she said, trying not to think about how tall and dark he was, how he seemed to fill the room, make it closer and smaller. How his hands had been all over her. And how she'd squirmed and twisted and wanted them there.

Her breasts still ached with a heavy, unfamiliar weight. And she felt prickly all over, prickly and unsettled.

"I wish for a moment of privacy," he replied. To his credit, he'd not moved away from the door and there was a comfortable space between them.

It would be comfortable if she didn't feel so *aware* of the man before her. Where was Ethelberga? She should be here, waiting for her mistress, snoring on her pallet in the cozy antechamber, and not leaving her alone with a man who'd taken her some-where so depraved. Who'd made her watch what she'd watched.

Marian's throat was dry, but she kept her composure. Lifting her chin, she said, "So is it to be now? Shall I undress? As you can see, my maid is not here to assist."

Will's face grew darker, and her breath caught. Lord, he was fearsome. *I won't leave bruises or draw blood.* Please God, he would keep his vow.

"If that is what you wish," he replied through a tight jaw. "I'm no saint, Marian, and I won't deny 'twould please me greatly."

She looked up at him, where he stood against the door, as if fixed to it. His hands hung at his sides, large, powerful, scarred hands that had held her breasts, stroked them, and made them heavy and achy.

"I don't wish it," she burst out. "I don't wish any of this— you or the prince or even to be here at Ludlow. Are you mad? *I wish for none of this.*"

Yet, she had no other option. Duty and honor demanded her compliance with the queen's orders. And Will thought she had no choice as a ward of the king.

Will gave a sharp nod and moved away from the door. Her heart leapt into her throat and Marian held her breath, but he walked not toward her but to the wall opposite where a heavy tapestry hung. To her surprise, he lifted it, coiling up its sub-stantial weight as though it were a scrap of silk. Will smoothed his hands over the stone wall beneath it, then reappeared with an unreadable expression on his face.

"Look you here," he said, crooking his finger imperiously at her.

Marian hesitated, then walked over to the wall. Taking care not to brush against him, she leaned where he directed and looked up under the bundle of cloth. "A hole?" she said, seeing the gap in the mortar between two of the bricks. She knew the garderobe was on the other side of the wall.

"A peephole," he told her grimly, then let the tapestry flow back into place. "See you here?"

He smoothed his hand over the cloth, but she'd already found it. "The horse's eye," she said, poking her finger through the hole that had looked like merely a black spot. Until now. A skitter of discomfort swept over her. "I'll cover it up."

"Nay," he said, stepping away as she turned toward him. "If you do that, he'll simply make another one."

Marian stared at him, her belly churning. She had been right about the chamber being chosen specially for her. But was it John who'd made the decision, or Will himself?

"The prince enjoys his entertainment," Will said, standing at the door again. " 'Tis best not to fight it, else you may find yourself hurt, or otherwise . . . upset . . . in the attempt."

Marian was beginning to understand. Her stomach pitched, and all the arousal that had peaked through her body ebbed away, leaving her cold and empty. "And so it will continue. Nights like tonight."

"Like tonight . . . and more," he said. "You can be certain of it."

And he left.

The door to Marian's chamber opened after no more than a few moments. Robin was surprised by that, but he assumed either Nottingham's performance lacked finesse and was quicker than

a noosed man dropping from the scaffold . . . or he hadn't per-
formed at all.

By the look of the sheriff, Robin suspected the latter.

Nottingham shut the door behind him and turned to leave,
giving Robin a clear view of his black expression.

Though there was a weariness about him, the sheriff certainly did not look like a man who'd just tupped the lovely Lady
Marian.

Robin couldn't resist a smile in the dark of a deep alcove as Nottingham walked past. But then the smile froze and disappeared.

"If I were an outlaw," came the sheriff's voice wafting down
the corridor behind him, like an afterthought, "I should make
certain that I wasn't so foolish as to be discovered in the very
place I should not be . . . for I might find myself shortly dressed
in a noose."

Nottingham's solid strides never hitched or paused, and he
continued on, leaving Robin to glare after him.

Though her day had been exhausting, Marian slept little that
night. And when she did sleep, her dreams swirled with dark,
erotic images. She woke near dawn with aching breasts and a dull
throb between her legs, her body moist, warm, and unsettled.

Her long hair had become loose in its thick braid and was
clinging to her damp skin and wrapping around her arms and
torso. When she rolled beneath the linens, her sensitive nipples
brushed against the fabric and hardened even more. Her legs
pressed together, and the pulsing there between them seemed to
grow stronger.

The memories of last evening in John's chambers surged back
into her mind, though she tried to block them out. She'd never

imagined the sensuality of such sights, of red tongues and slick lips and white breasts, of swollen, glistening quims . . . the wet sounds of lust and pleasure, the soft moans and little gasps . . . the smell of body and musky heat and sex . . . the feel of solid male muscle behind her, beneath her, and hands on her own breasts, demanding . . . yet enticing.

Marian's breathing rose again and her fingers slid around to cover her breasts in an echo of Will's large palms last night. They felt heavy and soft, and her skin tingled, tightening under her touch. She circled one fingertip experimentally over the top of a nipple. A responding streak of pleasure zipped down inside her, and she did it again . . . and again, and then on the other side as well. Her nipples tightened so hard they hurt, and the pounding in her quim ached and her flesh drew up tightly, expectantly. She let her legs fall apart and moved one hand down to touch herself.

Her fingers slipped through heat and wet and found the hard little pearl, the source of the throbbing. Marian closed her eyes and used the pads of her fingers to tease and dance and flicker in and around her swollen quim and the engorged nib, the pleasure and heat collecting and rising in her belly and between her legs as she shifted and bent her knees, working faster and more furiously . . . and then at last, an explosion was shooting through her body.

Warmth rushed over her as she shuddered and sighed and felt her whole person quake and shiver . . . and then lull into quiet and satiation.

Her hands slid away. She'd never felt like that after the rushed beddings with Harold. He joined her in bed, parted her legs, squeezed her breasts a bit, and then pounded himself inside her five or six times, cried out, and rolled away . . . and that was all.

After the first few occasions, Marian had learned to ease the way by slipping her own fingers up inside her quim before-hand, using her own moisture—or butter from the kitchen—to lubricate her body before he came to her . . . but she'd rarely given herself pleasure like she had this morning. And when she had, the results had never been so intense . . . so desperate. So necessary.

She had a sudden flash of Will's face last night as he stood by the door.

I'm no saint, Marian.

She doubted that not a whit.

Yet he hadn't forced her. He hadn't even attempted it.

Even though in John's chamber Will had had his hands all over her—despite the fact that she'd felt his own heart slamming in his chest, his breathing harsh in her ear . . . and the unmistak-able bulge of his cock beneath her—he'd left her untouched in the chamber.

He'd left her still burning with a need she hadn't, until now, really understood how to resolve.

Marian looked through the gap of ill-fitting bed-curtains and glanced at the tapestry on the wall, where the telltale horse's eye peered over at her, black and empty. He'd warned her about the peephole.

And he'd just as likely gone back to join the prince in the rest of his salacious activities. Ones that she would be forced to witness again. Perhaps even join.

A pang tingled in her belly as she thought of Will rearing up and over her, his large body covering her, piercing her. His mouth and hands on her bare skin. Her eyes closed and she swallowed, her stomach swirling like a swarm of butterflies.

She could endure it. It would be no different from submitting to Harold; he had been her duty because he was her wedded husband, and a coupling with Will would also be in the name of duty. Duty to her queen, and ultimately to her sovereign.

Marian could think of worse ways to be dutiful. Like being imprisoned. Or feeling a noose around her neck. Or going off to war, where her life was at stake, and it was kill or be killed. Nay, this fate was not of her choice, but it would be proof of her loyalty. And mayhap she might even be able to help Robin if she got close to the sheriff and the prince.

It occurred to her then that she'd been kissed by two different men yesterday—two enemies, two men on opposite sides of the law, two who had very different perspectives.

Dashing Robin, laden with arrogance and charm . . . with the dancing eyes and sensual, smiling mouth. And Will, with a darker, different sort of fierceness about him. As though he was almost . . . unwilling. Even angry.

And yet, both kisses had left her breathless and weak.

A knock at the chamber's inner door drew Marian from her disturbing musings, and she bade Ethelberga to enter.

The maid had returned to Marian's chamber shortly after Will left, apologizing that she'd gotten lost in the unfamiliar building. After assisting her mistress for bed, she'd closed the door that separated the antechamber from the rest of the room, and settled on her pallet to snore the night away.

Now she was here, wide-eyed and well rested, ready to help Marian dress for the hunt that John had arranged for the day.

Marian would attend Mass and break her fast with the other ladies. She then planned to participate in the hunt in hopes that she might see Robin again, though she realized he should be prudent enough to stay far from the lords and ladies who would roam the woods. Yet, for some reason, she didn't think he would.

In fact, knowing Robin . . . she suspected he'd be in the thick of it, simply for the thrill of doing so.

CHAPTER 5

The ferocious black horse belonging to the Sheriff of Nottinghamshire caused the villeins and serfs of Ludlow Village to scuttle from its path. Eyes peered from behind shutters as Will navigated the beast through the narrow streets of the town, his expression as black as his mount's.

As Cauchemar clip-clopped along, Will's sharp eyes missed nothing: the sagging roof of the smithy, an abysmally small pile of wooden bands outside the cooper's, the scrawny chickens that scattered into the road ahead of him.

A small boy dressed in thin clothing dashed out after the chickens to chase them from beneath the destrier's hooves, nearly getting himself trampled in the process. A scream from his mother, restrained from rushing out after her son by an older boy, broke the silence, swallowing Will's own curse as he hauled back on the reins. His beast reared high, wheeled to the side by his rider's demands, then slammed back to the ground in a loud, forceful jolt that shook the shutters of the nearby leatherworker.

The boy escaped unscathed, but Will dared not stop to ascertain whether any of the chickens had had their brains smashed by a hoof. The Sheriff of Nottinghamshire's presence was not appreciated in this town, nor in any of the other twenty-some villages of the county for which he was responsible.

His reputation was as black as the clothing he favored, the warhorse he rode, the expression on his face. When he approached, the villagers stayed away from him, cowering behind their shuttered doors in fear of being dragged away for some criminal offense—real or invented.

Will knew this and did nothing to lessen those fears. He was an agent of the king and, through him, of the prince. The king had a holy war to finance, and it was the sheriff's charge to oversee the collection of taxes—regardless of whether the people claimed they could afford them—and the imposition of justice where necessary. If some of his peers thought it odd that a landless knight had been named sheriff of this lush green shire that was home to one of the king's most fertile hunting forests, few dared to comment on it.

Those did were told the truth: the king had chosen to reward William de Wendeval for his father's, and his own, years of unwavering service—the specifics of which remained unspoken.

But today, on this bright and sunny morning in late September, William de Wendeval was particularly aware of the fear and dislike emanating from behind doors and stable walls, for he saw it through the eyes of those who rode with him.

Most of the ladies of the court were intimidated and avoided him. Some of the men respected his father and had known Will himself before he became sheriff, but since his association with John they'd become cool and reserved. Will felt their defection more acutely than the coolness of the women, for some of the noblemen that had withdrawn their friendship were men that he'd particularly liked. And as for women . . . well, there were plenty of maidservants willing to part their legs for a bauble or coin, and they were far less likely to have possessive husbands or a need to be wooed.

The hunting party had ridden from the keep's stables through the bailey area, which was enclosed by massive, high walls topped by crenellations, and then over its surrounding moat. That had brought them to the narrow streets of the little town that sprawled beyond, protected by its own walls.

Now, as they neared the raised portcullis of the village's gate, the sound of hunting horns filled the air. The horses pricked up their ears and increased their gait as the dogs began to bay in enthusiasm.

Although he'd arranged the activity, John had declined to join them this morning. He'd been lethargic of late (as evidenced by the early end to his night last evening), and sent them off without him with the instruction to bring back a boar and some harts for dinner.

For a moment Will had expected to be asked to stay behind as well, but John was distracted by a traveling metalsmith who claimed to have word from the king's army in Jerusalem. Will suspected the man merely wished to show the prince his wares, but he took the opportunity to slip from the morning meal before John could speak to him.

Now that they were leaving the town, Will let Cauchemar

loose, ready to feel the wind on his face. They were the first to cross the bridge out of town. For a man trained to battle—and one who preferred riding, jousting, and hunting to indoor activities—the role of sheriff during a time of relative peace could be stifling. Today, he meant to unleash the energy and frustration that had been building inside of him, particularly for the last sennight.

He hoped Robin Hood wouldn't be so foolish as to make an appearance today, for it would truly try his patience.

Cool shadows and the pleasant smell of damp soil and leaves enveloped him as he entered the woods, and not for the first time he envied Robin Hood his freedom to roam the forest. Mayhap "freedom" was a poor choice of word, for the man was a wanted outlaw . . . yet despite that, he did have liberties denied Will, who must fulfill his duties and retain his honor.

Will yearned to go deeper into the trees, to let go and ride on forever, away from duty and honor and green-eyed ladies . . . but of course he could not, so he turned Cauchemar in a wide circle and cantered back to join the others.

As he approached, a gay laugh caught his ear and pulled his eyes to Marian, who rode in the middle of the group. This day she wore a green gown lushly embroidered with gold and white along its wide sleeves and a wide hem that fluttered along the side of her mount. Beneath this gown the tight arms of her bliaud were light blue, as was the veil pinned to her brilliant hair. Only a narrow swatch of the copper tresses showed at the top of her forehead, for the rest were bundled demurely up and behind, rounding generously beneath the veil.

A lot of hair, she had. He could almost feel the weight of it in his hands.

He looked forward to seeing it unbound, swirling around

her hips, in all its fiery glory. 'Twas only a matter of time until he did.

Marian hadn't hunted for more than a year, and she was eager to be in the woods. The hounds had scented something already, and with answering shouts of excitement, the party started off. She rode next to Sir Roderick, who'd looked at her in surprise when he saw the longbow and quiver she wore over her shoulder. She'd had to assure him she had no intention of using them for a boar.

"Of course I shouldn't use this flimsy weapon for a great beast like that," she said, laughing with the delight of the day. " 'Tis only for a hare or mayhap a deer if should I be so fortunate as to spy one."

"But you will stay far from the boar in any case," Roderick cautioned.

"I shall indeed, for I value my own neck!" She laughed again.

At that moment, the dark figure of William de Wendeval emerged from the shadows of the forest, cantering in their direction after having galloped off ahead of the group moments ago.

Already a tall, imposing man, he appeared even more forbidding on the massive horse, with his wide shoulders, hawk nose, and unrelieved dark clothing. Though the standard of Nottingham was embroidered along the edges of his tunic, those colors were muted: dark blue and green on black, with only a smattering of burgundy in the design.

He looked directly at her as she laughed, and Marian felt her gaiety quelled. Would he come over to her, publicly claiming her as he'd done last night?

Will's actions last evening in the great hall had not been commented on by any of her companions, and although it was likely a futile wish, she hoped that none of them had been able to see who it was that the sheriff had backed up against the wall. Many of them had been facing the high table or the center of the hall, where the jongleurs were still playing, and his large body may well have blocked sight of her own . . . from everyone except the prince.

Marian turned away from Will's gaze, which had lingered heavily. She pushed aside the awareness of what they'd shared last evening, and slammed her heels into the sides of her horse, ready to leave the thoughts—and him—behind.

She took off after the hunters who barreled through the woods, fast and furious, following the hounds as they ran down their prey. When the boar was sighted, shouts and cries rose from the men, who'd followed more closely than the ladies—for 'twas only a fool who came too close to the murderous red-eyed beasts without a spear to thrust home. Ladies did not have the strength to drive one through the tough brindle of the fast and furious boar.

As the men charged off, the women rode along together at a less frantic, yet still exhilarating, pace that allowed them the opportunity to gossip and chat. The tiny Alys rode next to Marian, who on her other side found Lady Joanna, who seemed to be particularly smug this day.

"And he wrapped this around my wrist and tugged me into a dark corner," Joanna said, waving what appeared to be a scrap of green ribbon.

"Were you not frightened?" asked Lady Pauletta, who'd pulled her mare up closer to the group to admire the ribbon.

"Nay, indeed, for he was so witty and charming. And of

course I knew that I could call for help if I must, for Lord Burle had just left my side. But I had no need for that." Joanna looked across Alys's horse at Marian. "Did you find Robin Hood frightening when he accosted your wagons, Lady Marian?"

"A bit disconcerting," she replied, "but not terribly frightening." Robin had been in Ludlow Keep last night? What on earth had possessed him to be so bold?

"He was in the keep?" Alys said, echoing Marian's thoughts. "How foolish of the man to be wandering about the very place his enemies sleep."

"I did not realize how brave he is," Joanna said, fairly crooning at her ribbon. "Brave and kind."

"Brave and kind?" Alys scoffed. "Foolish is a better word, aye, Marian?"

"But he did not kiss you, and leave you with his favor, did he?" Joanna said, fluttering said favor in the breeze. "He is a beautiful kisser. I vow you would change your mind if he did so."

"You say the man is kind?" Marian asked. "By kissing you in the corner?"

"Nay, of course not," Lady Pauletta said. "You must have heard the tales of how he helps the villagers—poor sots that they are. They consider him some sort of hero for delivering chickens and goats, and once even spreading a bit of coin among them."

"The goods he purchases with the money he steals from the king," Alys said drily. "An outlaw indeed."

"But he does not keep it for himself," protested Joanna. "He uses it for the good of the poor. And he is wickedly handsome, is he not, Marian? Or did he wear his famous hood when he met you?"

The others looked at Marian. Oh, indeed, Robin of the Hood was wickedly handsome, and charming . . . and a delightful kisser. And bold and brave and foolish all at once. To risk himself by sneaking into the keep when the sheriff could catch sight of him at any moment . . .

Marian realized her companions expected a response. "He is not hard on the eyes," she conceded.

"Ware!" came a sudden shout, followed by frenzied crashing in the bushes.

The women looked up to see swaying and shuddering deep in the brush, and in an instant saw that they were in the path of the hunt.

Marian gathered up her reins, wheeling her horse to the side and away, kicking it into a gallop. The other women scattered as the cries of the hounds became louder and more frantic, and the bellows of the men echoed through the forest as they bore down on the very place they'd been riding.

Smiling with delight, Marian bent low over her mount's neck as they tore through the wood, safely away from the path of the boar and deeper into the shadows. She ducked and dodged as the branches raced past and over her, and buried her face into the soft coat of her horse when they came too close. By the time she turned to see if the others had followed, the sounds of the pursuit had waned into the distance. She was breathing heavily from exertion and excitement, her heart pounding. She straightened in the saddle and realized the veil had been torn from her head during the pell-mell ride, and that half the arrows had fallen from her quiver.

The sound of a triumphant horn in the distance signaled that the boar had been brought down. Marian turned her horse, starting back toward the others. She hadn't gone far when suddenly a figure dropped from the tree, landing on the ground in front of her.

Half-expecting to see Robin, at first Marian wasn't alarmed. But when she saw the size of the burly man, and the threatening stance he took in front of her, she reared back in her saddle, pulling on the reins again. Then another soft thud sounded behind her, and then another on either side.

Twisting in her seat, she turned to look, hoping to see Robin . . . but none of the men were familiar to her. Nor did they seem at all friendly or good-natured. In unkempt clothing and with grimy faces, they didn't even appear to be members of Robin's band—for yesterday the bandits who'd accompanied him had been as well clothed and clean as he.

"Co'mere, fine leuedy," said the first man in deep, guttural English. "Wha' ha' ye fer our greed' hands?" He lunged for her horse's bridle, and Marian screamed, yanking frantically at the reins. The horse reared up and it was all she could do to clutch at her mane and pray that the saddle straps did not give way, and she did not lose her seat.

Hands pawed at her as the men moved closer to the dancing, skittish horse. The largest of them tossed a cloth over her mare's head, covering her eyes, and immediately the horse began to settle.

Marian screamed again, belatedly remembering her bow. Struggling to hold on with only one hand and her leg curled around the pommel of her saddle, she managed to reach around and pull one of her few remaining arrows from the quiver. Stabbing at the hands reaching for her, she hauled on the reins.

Suddenly a whistle sounded through the air, and she head the faint whiz of an arrow shooting past her. One of the men near her froze, then dropped to the ground as another arrow, and then another, found their marks.

With cries of anguish, Marian's attackers fell or ran away as Robin Hood leapt down from the branches above.

"Marian, are you hurt?" he asked as several other men emerged from the shadows. At first, she tensed, wondering whether they were his companions or other attackers. But when Robin did not turn from his concern for her, she knew they were his companions.

"I am not hurt, only startled and a bit frightened," she replied, realizing she was shaking—yet still clutching the arrow she'd been using as a weapon. It had been a very near thing, and the revelation that those men could easily have taken her off into the deep woods, and . . . well, it did not bear thinking about.

"What were you doing so far from the hunting party?" Robin chided, looking up at her from the ground. He'd taken the reins of her horse and looped them into his hand. His eyes danced brightly and his sensual mouth curved in a mischievous smile.

Marian had her breathing under control now, and saw that Robin's men had melted back into the forest, taking the wounded bandits with them. "The boar was coming, and we ran to get out of its way. I didn't realize how far I'd gone."

That was a bald lie, for Marian was honest enough with herself to admit that she'd allowed her horse to run far and long, away from the hunters, in hopes of this very thing happening: that Robin would find her. And from the expression on his face, he suspected the same.

Of course, she did not expect that she would have been set upon by a different group of outlaws in the same forest, as odd as that might be. If there hadn't been some very real arrows shot, and some definite cries of pain and the smell of blood, Marian might even have suspected that Robin had arranged the episode so that he would have the chance to appear to rescue her.

But she didn't care. She'd wanted to see him, wanted not only to talk with him about how she might be able to help him evade the sheriff . . . but also to kiss him again.

"You could have been hurt, or worse," Robin said. This time, there was a note of seriousness in his voice. Before she could respond, he pulled her down from the saddle. "There are outlaws that roam these woods," he added, his voice low in her ear as she half fell against him.

"How was I to know that there was *another* group of bandits besides your own merry men?" she replied tartly, pulling away to stand on her own. He stood very close and was looking down at her with a particular light in his eyes.

"My merry men, as you call them, are not so desperate as those men who accosted you this day," he said, again being serious. "These were men who have nothing to lose, and may even go so far as to harm a noblewoman in the stead of ransoming her. They have lost their homes and the lands they've farmed for Ludlow for generations. They hate the prince and his agent, the sheriff . . . and all the gentry equally."

Now he closed his fingers around her hand and tugged her away from the small clearing created by the altercation. The horse followed docilely behind Robin, who still held on to the reins.

"They've lost their homes? Because of the king's taxes, and the sheriff?" Marian knew that Robin spoke the truth and he was not exaggerating the role he'd played in saving her. There had been an empty, feral light in the eyes of the man who had first grabbed her, as if he, indeed, did not have anything to lose.

"The sheriff has collected the taxes, aye, of course, and that has left many of the people of this shire homeless and without position. Some of them are more desperate than others, for they also have resorted to stealing or murder for gain."

"You and your men," she asked, looking up at him, "do you murder?"

"Nay, Marian, what do you take me for?" Robin asked. "I may be an outlaw, a landless lord, but I still have my honor. That I shall never lose. And when Richard returns, all will be set to right." He paused, but did not release her hand as he looped the horse's reins tightly around a sapling. "And that which I st— *borrow* from the wealthy. What I take is no more than what John takes off the top of the king's coffers for his own trunks—none of which is accounted for to Richard. I keep only that which I need to live upon—and in the wood, 'tis very little—and the rest is shared among the villagers, Marian. I am an outlaw, but I steal to live."

She believed him, believed that while he enjoyed the adventure and the daring, he also meant his gains to help others.

"Where are we going?" she asked as he began pushing through the brush and she realized just how far they'd gone into the wood.

He looked back down at her, his good humor showing once more. "The sheriff will soon be on your trail—for your scream echoed through the wood and likely woke the bats and owls from their sound sleep. 'Twas only good fortune that my men and I were near enough to arrive first."

"Good fortune, or sly planning?" Marian asked, ducking under a low-hanging branch. She did not care that sticks and leaves clung to her sagging braids, or that the train of her riding gown—which was extra long in order to create a fashionable image while spread over the rump of her horse—dragged through the dirt. She was with Robin. Her heart pounded in anticipation and her lips curved in a teasing smile as she glanced up at him.

"Most definitely sly planning," he confessed with a grin. "Did you not know I wished to see you again?"

"I could not have guessed it, knowing that you have spread your favors among the other ladies. Joanna could not have been prouder if the green ribbon you gave her had come from the king himself." She realized she was still carrying her arrow, which was tipped with blood from the hands of her attacker, and she paused to wipe it clean on a mossy tree.

Robin snorted in a derisive fashion. "The king would no sooner gift a lady with his favor than I would grant mine to the Sheriff of Nottinghamshire."

Marian had heard tales of King Richard's disinterest in women—an anomaly, considering the lusty blood from both father and mother that flowed in his veins. Whether he suffered from a different affliction, and preferred men—as some believed—or whether he was merely too busy making war to care about the fair sex, no one was certain. At any rate, he had recently espoused Princess Berengaria of Navarre in a hasty wedding, and by all accounts had consummated the marriage.

Slipping the clean arrow back into her quiver, Marian chided, "But you were sneaking through the halls of Ludlow Keep! Robin, how foolish of you."

At that moment, he stopped and spun her sharply about. The quiver slipped to the edge of her shoulder. Marian felt the solid trunk of a tree behind her, and the rough bark under her hands, pressing into the back of her head as he crowded close to her.

"I wanted to see you, Marian," he said. "I was well aware of my risk." He gripped her arm as his other hand moved toward her head, and she felt her sagging hair loosen even further. "I hoped to see you last eve, to ensure that you returned to the keep safely."

"You know I was safe with the sheriff. With Will." There . . . she'd said it—reminded him that they both knew the sheriff from their childhoods.

Yet he avoided acknowledgment of that fact. "Being with the sheriff does not mean that you are safe," Robin said, leaning closer to her as he moved his hand from her hair. His leg slid between hers, his knee bowing into the heavy folds of her gown as his hands slid up and along her shoulders. "He is greatly feared, and with good reason. Tell me, now: what is between you two? I saw him leaving your chamber last night."

Marian would have drawn herself up in indignation and surprise upon learning that he had spied on her, but he was pressing her so close against the tree, lining his body up against hers, that she had nowhere to go.

She found it difficult to keep her mind clear and her thoughts focused when he did so, for, in truth, Marian was feeling more than a mild response to his hard body. If only 'twere Robin who had claimed her in the hall last night.

But she captured her wild thoughts and said, "You saw the sheriff leave my chamber?"

"I cannot stand to imagine you with him, Marian. He is so cold, so angry and cruel. Tell me he hasn't hurt you."

"He has caused me no injury," she replied, though the memories of the carnality in John's chambers brought a warm flush to her cheeks, and a renewed awareness to the pit of her belly. "He seeks to protect me from John's attentions, 'tis all."

Robin's face darkened and his sensual lips twisted. "Is that the tale he has told you? He must speak a lie for a woman to spread her legs for him?" His breath was warm, but not unpleasantly so, on her face.

"I have not spread my legs for him," she said, anger replacing the languor he'd begun to coax from her. She'd expected a kiss, not an insult, and she struggled to push him away.

But Robin had strong hands, and the pressure of his body kept her imprisoned against the tree. He captured her arms, pulling her hands away from where they pushed against his chest. "Forgive me, Marian," he said. "I should not have said such a thing. 'Tis true that I am jealous, knowing that you can be with him—or anyone, even that blockhead Burle—while I must lurk in the wood like a criminal."

She looked up at him. "And if you are jealous of Will, who simply left my chamber after ensuring there was no one hiding within," she said tartly, wondering why she chose to defend the sheriff rather than ask Robin for help, "all the while you confess your affections for me . . . how should I feel, knowing that you spend your time drawing other ladies into the shadows to kiss them?"

He smiled down at her, his disgruntled expression disappearing. "Marian, is it possible that you are jealous? My heart be still, I can only hope that it is so."

"Not jealous so much as befuddled by your foolishness in moving about the keep. What if you were caught? The sheriff—Will—could come upon you at any time."

"Have no fear. I shall not be caught." His lips came closer as his fingers curled around her upper arms. "I cannot resist being near you," he murmured as his mouth fitted over hers.

Marian closed her eyes, lifting her face to meet him. His

lips opened wide to devour hers, and his tongue was sleek and strong in her mouth, delving deeply as his hands slid to cover her breasts. Her nipples reacted to his touch, tightening beneath the pressure of his palms, and Marian realized that whatever she'd done to relieve her tension this morning had not fully tamped away her body's need. Or else . . . it had merely whetted her appetite for something more. It was as if she had awakened to pleasure.

"Why do you not stay with me?" Robin asked, pulling away enough to take in a breath and speak. "You will be safe here in Sherwood, and I vow," he said, pressing the bulge of his cock into her belly, "you will not regret it."

"Stay with an outlaw?" she asked, angling her mouth away even as the rest of her body moved closer. "But, Robin, I cannot."

"But there are so many delightful things about being with an outlaw," he murmured, drawing her hands away from his chest to above her head, pressing the backs of them against the rough bark of the tree. "The woods are filled with surprises." Leaning against her, hip to hip, leg merged with leg, he was smiling as he bent to kiss her again.

"But, Robin, that is what I wished to speak with you about," she began as she became engulfed in the kiss.

He transferred one hand to his other grip, leaving one set of his fingers free to slip down over the curve of her throat and to cup her breast while her wrists were captured above her head. Then his hand left her breast and reached down to lift the weight of her gown, crumpling it in an awkward wad between them. She felt the fresh air through her light woolen hose and the brush of his strong leg between hers.

He pressed his thigh up into her quim and she felt something near her wrist, twisting around it. . . .

"Robin, what are you about?" she asked, pulling her face away.

"The sheriff is coming," he murmured, slipping his fingers up beneath her gown and chemise, up until he cupped the warmth between her legs. "And I must go, but I shall leave you with something that Joanna of Wardhamshire cannot claim."

"Robin," she hissed, and then she heard it—the thrashing through the brush in the distance. Coming closer . . . and yet Robin's palm pressed down onto her mons as if he had all the time he needed.

"Nay, sweeting," he said, laughing into her mouth as his fingers slid inside her. "Ah, you are ready for me, aren't you?" he said, pushing his fingers up inside her slick opening.

Marian gasped, catching her breath as his thumb found the hard little nub that pulsed anew, teasing it back and forth, slowly. . . . The now-familiar tingle gathered there in the recess of her belly, and her nipples knotted, thrusting against the soft linen of her chemise. He rubbed and flickered against her, his fingers moving deep inside, up and hard, as if he were fucking her, as he breathed softly into her neck.

"Ah, yes," he whispered, "come along, sweeting, come along."

Caught by the pleasure, lulled by his voice, she ground her head back against the tree, her hair catching on the rough bark, her hands looped above helplessly to the tree by some trick of Robin's.

Robin leaned into her, kissing her neck, the pads of his fingers spreading up into the folds of her quim, jolting her hard little pearl. The crashing in the bushes became louder as her pleasure built, and Marian bit her lip as the needy ache tightened and she felt her body gather up as it did, ready to slip over.

"Hurry, my sweet, hurry," Robin coaxed, moving his fingers faster and deeper, using the pad of his finger to tickle her as he drove inside.

The bark pushed into her skull and her uneasy hips, her eyes closed and mouth parted as she gasped in the air, wanting . . . knowing . . . she heard the crash in the bush . . . the sound of her name . . . felt the frantic jiggling of Robin's fingers, and suddenly it all exploded into a burst of pleasure and noise and great, deep, gasping breaths.

She may have cried out; she definitely heard Will shout, "Locksley!" and was aware of the sudden *wuft* of her layers of clothing falling back into place. There were vague sounds that melded with her world of pleasure: a solid thud, the rustling of brush, a faint shaking of the tree as if someone climbed or danced past it. The erotic tremors still shuddered through her, and when she opened her eyes, it was not Robin's dancing blue ones in front of her but the hard, dark ones that had haunted her since yestereve.

Gasping in shock at their intensity, Marian pulled her gaze away, fully aware that she stood tied to a tree, flush with pleasure, sated. She dared not look at Will, hoping that he wouldn't recognize what had just occurred.

He stood in front of her, and suddenly he was pulling at the ivy Robin had used to affix her wrists to the tree. His face was inscrutable, his cheeks hollow as if he was drawing them in tightly. But he was empty-handed. And Robin was gone.

He'd escaped once again.

Will said nothing as he pulled sharply at the bonds that kept her to the tree, and Marian did not know what to say. As the fog of pleasure slipped away, she began to realize what Robin had done, and how his actions had enabled him to flee yet again.

Leaving her in dishabille and tied to a tree had allowed him to escape at the last moment—just as Will approached—for the sheriff would not pursue him and leave Marian in such a state.

"I would ask if you were hurt," Will said as the vines fell away, "but 'tis quite clear that is not the case."

Marian swallowed and felt heat rise in her cheeks. His dark eyes glittered as his large hand rested on the tree next to her head. She could see it from the corner of her eye and realized how close he was standing to her. Her breath felt heavy and she found that she couldn't find a safe place to look.

"Will," was all she could say, and she knew it sounded woefully weak and breathy.

He turned away, pulling a horn from his belt. Putting it to his lips, he blew a long, low sound . . . once, then twice . . . then replaced the horn.

"To signal that I've found you, and that all is well." His gaze raked over her again, dark and scornful. "If I'd known 'twas merely a lovers' quarrel, I would not have pushed Cauchemar into a lather to get here."

"I was set upon by bandits," Marian told him coolly. "They would have torn me off my horse and taken me away if Robin had not come upon us."

"Locksley's men are indeed fearsome," Will replied, his voice dry.

"Nay, they were no friends of Robin," she said. "They were desperate and violent. Robin intervened, along with some of his real men, and they had a battle in which many were injured."

" 'Twould not surprise me if Locksley arranged for such an ambush in order to show his outlaw heart in a new and sympathetic light."

Marian opened her mouth to retort, but found that she needed to close it. For had she not also suspected the same? "So you do recognize him," she said instead.

"Aye, how could I not? Locksley has not changed a whit from the rash boy I knew at Mead's Vale. A skilled longbowman, aye, and a pillow-hearted fool. But also a man with a very large opinion of himself who believes he needn't pay for his actions."

"But he is a hero in the eyes of the simple people," she said, taking a pleading step toward Will. "The villagers are bled dry by this war, and the greed of—" She stopped herself, aware of the accusation she was about to make to a confidant of the accused. "They lose their houses and lands—they haven't the resources to pay the taxes demanded of them. I saw them today, how they duck and hide. . . ." Her voice trailed off again.

"When I approach," Will finished flatly. "Aye, 'tis true. But you forget, Lady Marian, that I am bound by duty to King Richard to collect those funds, and to see that justice is served in this shire. If that includes fitting a rope necklet about your lover's throat, then so be it." He stepped closer to her. "But may I suggest that you have a care for yourself? For if the prince learns that you are . . . close . . . to Robin Hood, I cannot guarantee your safety."

Marian stepped back and felt the tree behind her again. "You cannot guarantee my safety anyway," she returned, conscious that her heart was pounding crazily. He was so large, and dark and tall, and his expression was so forbidding. Yet, she felt herself gather up inside, taut and keenly aware of the man before her. The man who claimed *I am no saint.* "And if tales are carried to the prince of my friendship with Robin," she continued, though her mouth had dried, "I will know from whom they've come."

When she stepped back, he did not follow but stood unmoving, looking down at her. "John is watching you . . . and us . . . very closely, Marian. You seem to be unable to comprehend his determination to have whatever he wishes. And he is very interested in having you."

Her stomach pitched at his stark words, and she could find nothing to say. There was naught in Will's face or demeanor that suggested softness, or worry.

"Now," he said, turning away, "I will return you to the hunt. Then I'll lead a party into the wood to flush out this band of desperate outlaws who attacked you." He glanced back at her as he approached his monster of a horse. "If indeed they do exist."

CHAPTER 6

Robin smelled Marian's musky scent when he raised his fingers to his mouth to make a grackle's call, announcing his arrival to the man on watch. He made the bird's cry, then sniffed his fingers again and smiled. A lusty woman, and one who would not soon forget him.

The responding call of a slightly higher-pitched grackle indicated that it was safe for Robin to approach the treetop hideaway he and his men had built. Deep in Sherwood, aloft in a cluster of sky-brushing pine and oak trees, they'd constructed a generous building higher than any man would tend to look. And even if he did so, he'd see little but shadows, branches, and thick pine needles.

A rope ladder dropped down and he clambered up quickly. Someone was nearly always left on guard in the tree house, but in the event that everyone had been called away, the rope ladder was left up inside the hideaway and the first arrival climbed up using the less direct route of branch to branch, tree to tree.

"What ho," Robin said as his head rose above the floor of the building. "Any news?" He glanced briefly around and saw that three of his men sat or crouched about the room . . . and then he saw *her*.

"Aye, now." Robin smiled and climbed the rest of the way into the room, pulling up the ladder automatically behind him. "And who might this be?"

At first he didn't recognize her, for she'd been sitting in the shadows . . . but at his greeting, she stood and moved into the dappled light that filtered through the leafy trees above and around them. "Release me at once," she demanded.

It was the woman he'd noticed last eve, in the great hall. The girlish one with the pretty heart-shaped face whose name he didn't know. She was also the one who'd been riding alongside Marian and Joanna today during the hunt. He'd heard just that part of their conversation as he watched their approach from high in the trees, hoping to catch Marian alone.

As he recalled, this woman had called him foolish, with great disdain dripping from her voice. She'd been jealous, for she was the only one of the ladies who hadn't had the pleasure of a visit from the outlaw.

Robin could easily rectify that.

"My lady," he said with a flourishing bow. "You are welcome to our little hideaway in the trees. May I introduce myself?"

"I am well aware of your identity," the woman replied. She was standing straight and as tall as her petite figure would allow—which was not so very tall at all. Mayhap she would reach to his shoulder. If she stood on her toes.

"Then you must have the advantage of me," Robin said, still smiling.

He glanced at his boon companion John Little, who for all his great size and burliness appeared to be more than a bit cowed by this slip of femininity. Despite her diminutive figure, she was most definitely a woman. A woman with breasts the size of the very large oranges Robin had eaten in Greece, a tiny begirdled waist, and rounded hips. And lush pink lips that, if they deigned to pout, would look like crinkled velvet petals . . . but at this moment were flattened into a line oozing with disgust.

"I demand that you release me, Robin Hood," she said. "Your men had no right to bring me here." She crossed her arms under those lovely breasts and, for a moment, Robin found himself distracted as they lifted, adjusted, and jiggled gently.

Then he realized that silence had fallen and all were waiting for him to respond. "But how did you come to be here?" he asked, allowing a sympathetic sparkle to come into his eyes.

"My horse threw a shoe," she said. Of necessity, her mouth relaxed a bit. Her upper lip was more full and luscious than her lower lip, and right then, Robin knew where he wanted that lovely mouth to be. His cock, which had been raging since he left Marian tied to the tree, lifted yet again, boldly reminding him that it had been much too long since it had been somewhere dark and moist and tight.

Mayhap she would be friendlier if they were alone.

Robin looked at the three men who'd edged away from the woman as soon as their leader arrived: John Little, Allan-a-Dale, and a most uncomfortable-looking Friar Tuck, dressed in his robes. "Is there aught you can attend to below while my lady and I converse?"

They didn't need to be asked twice, for John leapt out of his seat as quickly as his bulk allowed and tossed the rope ladder down without hesitation. "Aye," he said, giving no excuse as he disappeared down the ladder, the ropes straining and creaking against the wooden floor.

"A brace of hares would make a nice stew this night," Allan said, moving just as eagerly toward the opening. "Tuck, would you like to come along with me and carry my extra arrows?"

Moments later, Robin and the blond woman were left alone. She'd done nothing but stand there, arms crossed under her breasts, foot tapping on the floor beneath the overlong hem of her riding gown.

"I do hope you don't intend to rape me now," she said. Annoyance—not fear or even apprehension—blazed through every pore of her fine body.

Robin blinked and closed his mouth. Then opened it. "My lady, I should never resort to such an assault." He smiled comfortingly at her.

"Clearly 'tis because you believe you would never have to. I vow, the size of your head is like to burst the walls of this house."

He watched her, unable to take his eyes away from her rich honey-colored hair, and the lift of her dainty chin. Let alone able to formulate a response to such a statement. No wonder John Little and the others had fled. He wondered how long they'd been cooped up in here with her.

She turned away and paced across the room, the only sound that of her fine wool bliaud catching on the rough floor and a faint whistle through the trees. He watched the smooth curve of her bottom as it swayed enticingly with each step. Robin felt the urge to clear his throat, for it had suddenly become very dry.

"If you believe that I am one of those foolish ladies who cannot resist the lure of an outlaw, you are dangerously mistaken. I will not be swooning at the prospect of your kisses. I demand to be returned to Ludlow immediately."

"I will return you, my lady. I vow it. But, if you please, will you not give me your name?"

"Lady Alys of Wentworth," she said with a great sigh. "Now that your curiosity is assuaged, shall we go?"

"Alys," he said, savoring the taste of it on his tongue. "A lovely name."

The fascinating woman he itched to touch, to see if she was as soft and smelled as good as he suspected, gave an indelicate snort. "And the next I know, like every other man, you'll be waxing rhapsodic over my sea blue eyes, and the velvet of my crushed-petal lips, and my long flowing tresses of golden hair."

Robin closed his mouth again. Damn.

She made a sharp gesture of dismissal at him. "Do you think I have not heard it all before, O Robin Hood? Do you think I do not know how tongue-tied and cow-eyed men turn when they are near me? 'Tis a curse," she said, pacing the room in earnest now. " 'Tisn't enough that I must deal with the frog-eyed barons or high-reaching knights greedy not only for my lands but for my person—but now I must be whisked away to a treetop hideaway and suffer the courtship of an outlaw."

"I do not *court* you," Robin burst out in disdain.

"Indeed?" She stopped and turned to look at him. "You do not court me. You do not intend to rape me. . . . Why, then, Robin Hood, are we still here? Ah. It must be that you intend to hold me for ransom. It certainly cannot be that you've been giving me mooning dog eyes and preening about like a cock so that I will kiss you."

"So that is what you want," Robin said, his eyes narrowing

in delight. A smile tickled his mouth. He was in front of her in a moment, his hands closing around her upper arms, his feet planted on the hem of her gown. "A kiss. Why did you not say so, Lady Alys?"

Her blue eyes flashed sparks and her luscious mouth opened, but Robin found a most efficient way to close it. And to block out the pretend outrage in her eyes.

He dragged her up against him, his mouth on hers, at last touching those lush, top-heavy lips. She stiffened against him, pushing. He was gentle . . . but firm. Alys tasted as sweet as he'd expected, her tongue small and slick and naive, tangling with his stronger one.

He closed his mouth over that full top lip that so enticed him, gently sucking and licking it, unable to get enough of the taste, of the softness. Her breasts crushed into his chest, and the thick locks of her hair tangled in his fingers as he smoothed his hands up her slender back, pulling her close . . . melding her against him.

At last she wrenched her face away and the next thing Robin knew, his right ear was ringing from the slap.

He could not recall the last time he'd been slapped by a woman.

In fact, he couldn't remember any time that he'd been so rebuffed.

"I shall have the sheriff after you," she spit, her blue eyes furious. "How dare you!"

Robin didn't have the energy to laugh at her threat. He was out of breath, the room still spun, and 'sblood, her lips were even more lush now. Her cheeks burned pink; her hair—its fashioning having long fallen out—swirled about her hips, where her hands were now planted like those of an angry fishwife.

"I do believe the sheriff is already after me," Robin said when he'd caught his breath.

"I shall tell him where your hideout is," she retorted.

Robin couldn't help but laugh, though he wasn't quite certain why. He'd just been slapped by this little fairy of a woman, his cheek still throbbed from it, and he couldn't wait to get her back into his arms again. "You are fortunate that I am not of the ilk of some other bandits that lurk about in these woods. Such men would be more likely to slay you on the spot than allow you to carry tales."

For the first time, her bravado faltered. But then the sparkle was back in her eyes. "But you shall demand a ransom for me, and will move me, well hooded, I trow, to another safe place so that I cannot carry tales."

"My, how much you know of the tricks of an outlaw, Lady Alys."

"Nay, 'tis naught but common sense that I speak."

"But now you speak of ransom . . . so you've decided to stay with us, then, Lady Alys? Not in so much of a hurry to leave?" Robin asked. "And I would have returned you to Ludlow this very moment. But instead, I must cipher a ransom note." He *tsk*ed, shaking his head. "But how much are you worth, my lady?"

Alys tossed her head. "Send a ransom note, then," she scoffed. "The sheriff will use it as an opportunity to capture you."

"Nottingham could not capture me if I came and stood in his chamber at Ludlow," Robin felt compelled to say. He didn't care for the way she spoke about Nottingham, the certainty and admiration in her voice for the black devil.

"I trow *he* would not force his kiss upon a lady," she added, with a surprisingly sharp bolt to his heart. One of her blond eyebrows rose in a perfect arch.

"So 'tis Nottingham you desire," Robin said. "I find that difficult to believe, for the ladies I know turn tail and run when he approaches. They fear him as the villagers do."

"I do not think he is as cruel as he appears," Alys replied with startling perception. "He is angry, but he does not take it out on the innocent."

"The tales that come to my ears speak otherwise."

She lifted her chin again. "And they are tales, and nay more. I've not seen it. And he certainly doesn't force kisses upon the women."

"And so we are back to the kisses once more," Robin said, finding himself moving closer to her again. "Mayhap I shall demand a ransom of sorts from you, rather than money from your father . . . or husband."

"Is that your inept way of trying to learn who shall be after your head once I am freed?" Alys retorted. But she did not step back this time, instead standing her ground as he placed himself directly in front of her. A lock of her hip-length hair curled boldly out, nearly brushing against his tunic just above the belt.

"Inept?" Robin said, feeling his mouth twitch into a smile again. "I do not think many consider me inept . . . in any fashion." He stepped forward and felt the titillating whisk of another curl against his hand, which remained at his side. Looking down at her, he could see each of her thick lashes. "The only ransom I wish to collect from you, Lady Alys, is one kiss. Given willingly." His voice was rich and low even to his ears.

"And then you will take me back to Ludlow?" she asked. She sounded a little out of breath. Not quite as strident as before.

"And then I will take you back to Ludlow. If you still wish to go."

She raised her face, lifting those gorgeous lips, and Robin

bent to meet them. Softly, he pressed against her mouth, so softly. He barely touched her lips, brushing them with his, opening his mouth to close around her upper lip, licking its underside slowly . . . gently. He felt his breath gathering again, his eyes closing, his knees weakening.

And then it was over. She stepped away.

He opened his eyes.

She was looking up at him, speechless.

And then the mood broke when she said, "There. Now you shall return me. And I hope that the sheriff catches you when you do."

There it was . . . the sheriff again. Robin frowned, then tamped back his annoyance. "I'm certain you shall tell him everything you know," he said, matching her cool tone.

"I should warn you," Alys said, crossing her arms again, and this time, he didn't allow himself to be distracted, "I will keep no secrets from the sheriff. If you should approach me again— especially in the halls of the keep as you've foolishly done to Lady Joanna—I shall raise such a hue and cry that you will never see these trees again."

"Then I shall make certain if I do approach you that I shall keep that lovely mouth of yours otherwise engaged."

And with that, he dropped down the rope ladder.

"After you, Lady Alys."

Marian did not venture into the great hall for the midday meal. Instead, she sent Ethelberga to procure some cheese and bread for her repast while she sat in her chamber. Positioning a small table directly beneath the peephole, where she could not be seen by anyone looking through the hole, she took a piece of parchment from deep within her trunk. A bottle of ink and three quills followed, and she settled at the table to write to the queen. The foolscap had been scraped clean many times, but with care, so there was only a single hole near the bottom. As she wrote, Marian avoided the few thin spots on the parchment so that the ink wouldn't bleed.

Although Ethelberga was aware that her mistress could read and write—an unusual feat for a woman, and, indeed, for most men who weren't priests—Marian didn't wish for her to know that she was doing so at this time. A simple mention of her mistress writing a letter could lead to questions or curiosity from others.

It was one thing for a woman to send and receive letters that, in most cases, would need to be dictated to, or read to her by, a priest or other learned man, but Eleanor preferred that her ladies be able to do such tasks on their own. Fewer eyes and ears to notice them. She'd come to trust Marian after noting that the younger woman could hold her tongue after assisting the queen in scribing personal messages. At first they'd been simple, unimportant ones, but as her confidence in Marian grew, Eleanor had used her for more-sensitive communications.

Marian had little to report to the queen other than her safe arrival at Ludlow, so her missive took little time to finish. She'd sprinkled sand over it to dry the ink, then folded and sealed it long before Ethelberga returned.

After eating her cheese and bread, Marian left her chamber in search of one of the messengers Eleanor had told her to use when communicating. Just as she preferred her ladies to compose their own missives, she also trained them well on the trustworthiness of messengers, teaching them which ones to use. And which ones to avoid.

Down in the hall, which had emptied of most diners after the meal, Marian managed to catch the attention of one of the messengers she sought. She'd murmured for him to meet her privately in the bailey when she felt something stir in the room behind her. Without looking, she knew Will had entered the hall, and tension crept over her shoulders, along with an uncomfortable tingling in her belly.

She avoided looking at him and walked purposely out of the hall through one of the side entrances, planning to take a circuitous route to her meeting place with Twilly, the messenger.

Out in the warm sunshine, Marian moved quickly to the apple tree at the edge of the herb garden. It had long since bloomed, and now boasted a myriad of small green apples.

Twilly was already waiting, fortunately, and she quickly gave him the missive, along with her quiet, terse instruction to deliver it into the queen's hands only. There wasn't much of substance to report yet, but Marian wouldn't risk the security of future missives through carelessness. Satisfied that he understood the importance of discretion, she pressed a coin into his palm and turned to start back into the keep.

Her heart leapt into her throat when she saw Will standing there.

Praise God, he wasn't close enough to have heard anything she'd said, and he wasn't even looking in her direction . . . until now. As if her sighting him had been an invisible string that pulled at him, he turned and their eyes met.

Marian kept her face blank as she continued on her path and hoped that Twilly had gone on his way in a different direction before Will noticed that they'd been in the same vicinity. He would likely recognize one of the queen's messengers, and was smart enough to wonder at her conversing with him.

She nodded to Will and would have walked past if he had not moved into her path.

"Marian," he said. He looked at her, then glanced in the direction of the apple tree . . . where Twilly had been standing.

"Yes?" She couldn't look directly up at him, for he was too tall and the sun too bright.

"Have you seen Alys of Wentworth since we returned this morning?" As he spoke, he moved slightly toward her into the shadow of the small herbary.

This allowed her to step out of the sun and look up at him, her fingers brushing against the rough wooden wall. "Nay," she answered, recognizing something like concern in his face. "I've not seen her since we were separated during the hunt."

"Her mount has returned, limping, and without a shoe," Will told her grimly. "It appears she herself has not been seen by anyone since the hunt. I'm off to search the wood."

He turned away, but Marian grabbed at his sleeve. Will's muscles tensed beneath her fingers, and he turned back. "What is it?"

"Did you find those other bandits?" Marian asked, alarmed to hear that Alys might have been taken by the very men who'd nearly attacked her.

"Some. They're belowstairs in the dungeon until I can deal with them. The hands of one of them were a bloody mess."

Marian's eyes widened in understanding. "Oh, aye . . . my arrow. I stabbed at him when he dared try and lift me off my saddle."

"So he said. I do not think they'll heal, and 'tis almost punishment enough for him, I trow. His fingers will be crippled forever, if they do not need to be cut off."

Marian felt a momentary stab of conscience, but then pushed it away. The man had meant to do far worse to her.

"I've left three of my men to watch their camp for when the others return," Will replied. "But if you will release me, I'll be off to begin the search anew." He looked down at her hand on his arm as if it were a particularly ugly spider.

Just as she released him, a shout from the bailey entrance drew her attention. Will pulled away, heading toward the sound of the turmoil. Marian followed, watching his tall figure navigate quickly through the crush of hounds, rushing men-at-arms, busy serfs, and playing children.

By the time she reached the cluster of people, she understood that Alys had returned, presumably uninjured, and on foot. When she caught sight of Marian, her friend pushed away from Will and the other men-at-arms who'd met her at the gate.

"I am unhurt," she said in a tone that implied it wasn't the first time she'd made such a statement and that she was weary of doing so. "My horse threw a shoe and I was a bit lost in the wood until I found my way back. Now, there is Lady Marian. I am certain she will see that I'm taken safely to the chamber where I can change my clothing."

Marian needed no further suggestion. She moved forward and linked arms with Alys, drawing her away toward the keep.

After ensuring that her friend was indeed unscathed from her experience wandering about in the forest, Marian left Alys to the other ladies. She walked back out into the bailey, glad to find herself out of the smoky, dark keep.

The herb garden was large enough to offer wandering paths that would keep her occupied for a time. She brushed past the silvery sage and lavender leaves, the brilliant orange calendula growing in low clusters, the dark blue green woad, basil, thyme, and others. As her feet wandered, so did her mind, and Marian couldn't help but feel apprehensive about the night ahead.

Would John invite her and Will to his chambers again? What would happen this night?

Though the sun burned warm, Marian shivered, remembering the knowing lift of Will's hands at her breasts, the feel of his mouth on the tender skin of her neck. That tingling, unsettled feeling returned to her stomach and she drew in deep breaths scented with rosemary and lily.

She knew, understood, that it was only a matter of time before Will coupled with her. And though 'twas Robin who'd made her tremble and sigh earlier today, Robin whose smile she saw when she closed her eyes, Robin who risked his life to do what was right for the people of Nottinghamshire . . . she also felt a deep tug in her belly when she thought of Will touching her, kissing her, settling his big body over hers.

Her mouth was dry; her heart pounded steadily. Her cheeks felt warm.

But she must remember she was here with a duty to the queen. Mayhap tonight she would find the chance to look about John's chambers and discover evidence of treason he planned against his brother. The last thing the prince would expect was a woman who not only could read but also would be looking for something.

If indeed John was plotting with the French king, Philip Augustus, to overthrow Richard, there must be some planning, and some negotiation. Philip wouldn't assist John without some compensation. Eleanor claimed he would require the return of all of Normandy, leaving John only England to rule. But now that Richard had wed and could produce an heir, the chances of John ascending to the throne without a bit of help were less than before.

Thrusting those thoughts aside—there would be time enough to deal with any suspicious evidence later—Marian left the herb garden and made her way back into the keep. She would be expected at the evening meal, and much as she would prefer to remain closed up in her chamber, hiding would get her no closer to learning whether John was indeed planning a threat to his brother's throne. She must be out and about, listening and speaking to the barons and lords—the ones John trusted and the ones who hated him and loved his brother. And if that included visiting his private chambers and overhearing pertinent conversations with Will, or anyone else, then that was what she must do. Even if it meant submitting as she'd done to Harold.

Once back to her chamber, Marian ordered Ethelberga to arrange for her bath. As she watched the serfs carry in bucket after bucket of steaming water, slopping their contents into the generous tub that had been rolled in on its side, she glanced briefly at the horse-eye peephole. The garderobe door had been open when she returned to her chamber, but someone could be in there now.

Or not.

'Twas unlikely that the prince would be spying on her during the midafternoon. Not that he would be praying at Nones— John didn't strike her as a particularly devout man—but he was likely holding court.

Thus appeased, Marian dismissed the serfs, who left several buckets of clean water for rinsing, and allowed Ethelberga to disrobe her. Sinking into the steaming water, on which floated crushed violets, gillyflowers, and lavender, Marian rested her head back against the edge and allowed herself to relax. And to think about how she might direct a conversation to get her the information she wanted.

Ethelberga might be skittish when it came to being stopped by highwaymen, and have a poor sense of direction when in a new building, but she had magic fingers. The tight, heavy braids uncoiled from Marian's hair left her scalp loose and relieved, and Ethelberga's strong fingers massaged and scrubbed until her mistress groaned with pleasure.

The length and weight of Marian's unusually colored hair was such that the maid had kept a smaller tub nearby, also filled with warm violet water, so that she could more easily wash the long tresses in their own water.

By the time Ethelberga had finished soaping her hair and rinsing it with the extra buckets, Marian had decided that Lord Burle would be a worthy candidate to pretend to flirt with. She might loosen his tongue and learn whether he was still loyal to the king or lining up behind John.

Just as Marian had settled this plan in her mind, there was a loud knock on the door of her chamber. Ethelberga squeaked in surprise and Marian sat upright in the tub.

"See you who is there, but close the inner door so that I cannot be seen," she ordered. "Tell whoever it is I will attend them in a moment."

Ethelberga did as she was told, hurrying from the room and closing the door behind her. Marian sat in the rapidly cooling water, straining to hear what was happening beyond. She didn't have long to wait.

The inner door opened suddenly and Will was there. "Leave us," he commanded over his shoulder to Ethelberga, who lurked behind him. Her eyes were wide and frightened in a pale face.

Marian smothered a gasp and sank to her collarbones under the water, which thankfully was murky with the herbal additives as well as the soap she'd used. "Will, I beg you give me a moment to finish my bath," she managed to say in a steady voice.

As if men burst in upon her bedchamber while she bathed every day. "And then I will—"

"Leave," he ordered, turning back to look at Ethelberga, who appeared as if she might collapse. "I'll not say it again."

The maid's mouth was a large round O, and she looked apologetically at her mistress, fright casting a shadow over her face, before she whirled and dashed out the door. Marian didn't blame the girl; if she had been confronted with the wild, black-haired, dark-visaged man who now stood in her chamber, she would have run too.

Apparently, that was not a luxury she would be afforded.

"Will," she said, keeping her voice steady with an effort. "What has befallen—"

"Be silent," he said in a strained voice. He was looking toward her, but he wasn't looking *at* her.

He came fully into the chamber and closed the door behind him. Bolted it. And when he turned to face her, Marian felt as though her insides had been turned inside out, and back and inside out again. A face that had always been harsh and cold now wore an expression of . . . nothing. As if it were made of stone or wood. Unmoving and set.

"Get out," he said, and when she didn't move, a hand whipped out and his fingers closed over her arm, pulling her upright from the water.

It fell from her in a cascade, splattering his clothing and the floor. Her wet hair was plastered over her like a copper cloak, clinging to breasts, hips, thighs, buttocks, and arms.

By now, Marian could not speak. Her heart was racing out of control, and she was well and truly frightened. There was a horrible pause as he stood there, his eyes scoring her nudity as he gripped her arm.

Then he shoved her toward the bed. "You'll deny me no longer."

Marian gasped, stumbled when she slipped on the wet floor, and fell onto the mattress, narrowly missing the bedpost.

"Will," she whispered, shivering from fright and chill. Her teeth chattered and she breathed as if she'd just run into the chamber. She snatched up the blanket hanging over the chair between the fire and the bed, covering herself with it as much as she could. Her hair was still dripping and cold, still clinging to her body everywhere. "What—"

"Silence," he snarled as he kicked off his soft boots. "By God, woman, do not make me say it again." His voice was cold, without inflection. And he did not look at her.

Something was wrong. So wrong. Marian felt the unaccountable urge to reach for him, to touch him and try to read what had happened . . . but suddenly, he was on the bed next to her, his large, warm hands covering her shoulders and pulling her against him. She felt the rough scrape of the embroidered hem of his tunic, the weight of his powerful hose-clad thigh sliding over hers, the slickness of her damp skin.

"Nay," she gasped, trying to twist away from him. She knew it would happen; she knew she couldn't prevent it. But not now. Not this way.

She wasn't ready.

His fingers curled into her shoulders, tangling in hair caught between them, and held her from pulling away. She closed her eyes, felt tears begin to leak from her lids.

Not yet.

Not here.

Not like this.

But his hands held her still and his great weight covered her.

One knee pushed between her legs, and she squeezed her eyes tighter, twisting and bucking beneath him, trying to keep her breathing from running away with her. Trying to keep from crying and pleading.

He muttered something in her ear, hard and so quiet it was unintelligible. She looked up at him through watery eyes, saw that his face was turned away, his lips pressed together so tightly that his mouth was white. Through a fog of fear and disbelief, she noticed details, as though the world had slowed to a crawl: beads of sweat dampened the skin along his dark hairline, and one trickled down his cheek. He smelled like horse and smoke, and something else unidentifiable. An occasional dark hair that stubbled his face glinted gray. A scar, white and thick, marred one smooth temple.

Will grasped her hands and pulled them above her head, curling strong fingers around her wrists so tightly, grinding them together, causing her to cry out.

"That's it," he muttered from between clenched teeth. She understood his words this time. "Fight."

She didn't need to be encouraged. Unable to help herself, she kicked and arched beneath him. "Nay, Will," she breathed, catching the sob in the back of her throat.

His other hand slipped between them, moving along her damp belly, and Marian felt it down between her legs. She closed her eyes, trying to breathe easier, struggling to make herself lie still.

It hurt less if she didn't fight it. If she lay still and relaxed. She knew this. But this man, so large and dark, his face feral and wild . . . he was different from Harold. Demanding, violent. Angry. So angry.

He propped himself up with the elbow of the hand that held her wrists, and she felt the unmistakable shifting between their bodies as, with the other, he lifted his tunic, loosened the tie of his braies, quickly, sharply, and then before she could plead once more, he made a sharp move.

She braced herself, willing herself not to whimper, but there was nothing but a jolt of the bed. She cried out in surprise and shock.

"Aye," he said in her ear, his voice hoarse and tight. Will jerked against her again, then again, faster and harder . . . but his hand had settled between them. Covering her. Not penetrating.

Protecting her?

She looked up at him, at the tense, averted face, the perspiration that gathered at his temples and near his closed eyes. His brows knit together in an angry furrow and he gave one last thrust and sagged forward over her with a low, heartfelt groan that tugged deep at her belly.

His fingers loosened over her wrists and she pulled them away, aware that they were both out of breath.

"Will," she began in a rough, bewildered voice.

"Stop it." His voice sounded like a whip cracking. "I'll not listen to your sobs." He rolled away, tossing the blanket back over to cover her.

Marian gathered it over her hips and breasts and watched as he snatched up his boots and one of the empty buckets. "Do you not attempt to hide away in here tonight," he said, half-turning back toward her. "You will be seen at dinner."

From the distance, she saw that his eyes remained dark and flat. They swept over her briefly, but did not linger. And then he pivoted and slammed the door's bolt from its moorings, leaving the chamber before she could speak again.

Marian heard the outer door close behind him, and she was

alone on a bed damp from her own body . . . but not from Will, or his seed.

She lay there for a moment, bringing her trembling body under control, scarcely able to comprehend what had just occurred. Yet, she did—she realized what Will had done.

Or, more accurately . . . what he had not done.

One thing was certain: John had most definitely not been holding court this midday.

Will passed Marian's sniffling maid, who'd loyally waited in the hall despite his orders to leave. She cowered back as he stalked by, but did not flee.

"See to your mistress," he snarled, still carrying the bucket, folding his boots under his arm.

He made it down three steps of the shadowy side stairwell before he lost control and had to stop. Leaning against the wall, he emptied his stomach violently into the bucket, heaving until his belly ached.

Swiping the back of a hand over his mouth, he looked up to find Alys of Wentworth standing at the top of the stairs.

"Are you ill?" she asked, her blue eyes wide.

" 'Tis no concern of yours," he snapped, standing upright with effort. Without a backward glance, he turned and made his way down the stairs, his fingers still trembling.

CHAPTER 7

John the Angevin, Lord of Ireland, Earl of Gloucester, Count of Mortain, and current regent of England, was displeased.

He sat at the high table next to one of his most trusted cohorts, one who shared his ambition and confidences, as well
as participated in his most private and vulgar of activities. A
man so clever and determined John might have feared him if he
hadn't known that he was as determined as John to rid the country of its rapacious king. Richard's foolish war had left England,
lush, green, beautiful England, stripped to bare and bone. John
could not abide by his brother's vainglorious ways, his ignorance
of the land he had the blessing to rule while he traipsed about
far away in the Holy Lands.

He cast a sly, corner-of-the-eye glance at William de Wendeval. His performance this afternoon, though brief and—from

the prince's perspective—not nearly violent enough, had awakened John's desire for the luscious Lady Marian.

Nay, "awakened" was too mild a word. "Emblazoned" was more appropriate. Emblazoned upon his heart—and his cock—the need to have her.

The sight of that glorious hair alone, strands of mingling gold and bronze and copper, streaming down the sides of the tub as her maid gathered it into a huge bundle to wash and rinse it, had sent frissons of lust through his body. He imagined it twining around him, thick, shiny, and heavy. But when Marian had been yanked from her bath, breasts jouncing and smooth hips shining with the cascade of water, that long glossy hair had plastered itself to her from shoulder to thigh like a well-fitting glove and set his cock to throbbing.

And Nottingham, knowing that his liege watched, had paused for a moment, holding her in clear view, so that John could admire the display of her long legs and creamy skin. From that moment, John knew he'd not be satisfied until he had Marian thusly garbed in his own chamber, at his own hands, beneath his own body.

He licked his lips, sliding his glance out over the occupants of the hall . . . then back to the dark, silent man sitting next to him.

Therein lay the problem, and the root of his displeasure.

The man had claimed the woman for himself, and John had foolishly agreed to allow him to have her. For a time.

But he no longer wished to wait. The soft cry she'd made when Nottingham slammed himself into her could easily be imagined as one of pained passion—one of John's specialties. Her wild struggles against the large, fully clothed man who strained over her John found arousing and delightful. Who did not want a woman who knew better than to lie there like a dead fish? He had a wife who did that. She could have been a statue made from ice-white porcelain for all she responded to his caresses. The most beautiful of women, true, with long, perfect golden ringlets of her own . . . but Isobell was stone in comparison with Marian's lush heat.

And yet Marian was, at the moment, unavailable to him.

John didn't like to admit it, even to himself, but he knew better than to breach his agreement, such as it were, with Nottingham. The man knew too much about him, too many secrets, too much of his cunning plans to ally with Philip Augustus of France and to split Richard's kingdom between them. Aye, 'twas true that Nottingham was nearly as deep into the plot as John himself, collecting funds and making allies here at Ludlow, even strategizing with him in between bouts of pleasure taking.

But most important, John knew that without William de Wendeval his plans to displace Richard would never be realized. For no traveler through the forest, from any direction to Ludlow, could reach the keep without the Sheriff of Nottinghamshire knowing who he was and from whence he came.

Thus John received no surprises, no messages that he did not wish to receive—for those messengers, oddly enough, often did not make it to the keep. Or if they did, it was after a delay . . . and mayhap even to their physical detriment.

The outlaws were blamed, of course, but it was Nottingham and his control over the area that allowed for that selection. Aye, Robin of the Hood thought that he had full reign over the forest, but some of that freedom was at the pleasure of the sheriff. For if there were no outlaws, they could not be blamed for the ransoming or capturing of the messengers John wished to avoid or otherwise prepare for.

John's real complaint over Robin Hood was that he stole his money, and those funds collected for taxes, not that he roamed the wood and frightened the travelers. The vassals would pay their fines whether they were robbed or not. John cared little for their hardship.

Thus he did not intend to offend the loyalty of Nottingham, who played such a vital role in this plot. For now, John had no choice but to make his way with care.

And Nottingham had never made any request of him before this. He had a personal grudge against the woman, and John could understand his need to put her in her place.

Nor was he the sort of man to look away, or to accept John's reasons—whatever ones he might manufacture—for the breach of the agreement. De Wendeval was that rare breed of man who could be convinced to change his loyalty, yet maintain a strong sense of honor to that misplaced loyalty. And he expected it in return.

Thus, 'twas most unfortunate, but John could not afford to insult Nottingham, especially over a woman.

Even a woman such as Marian.

Yet . . . John could not concentrate on the conversation he meant to have with Lord Tenselton, who sat to his left, when he was aware that the man to his right had had the delights he himself so lusted after. And had not even partaken of them as deeply or devoutly as John would.

Thus, during the meal, while Nottingham ate sparingly and spoke even less, the Angevin's mind wormed about, seeking a way to have what he wanted . . . but without offending the valuable, and dangerous, man next to him.

Aye, the man's loyalty was worth more than the riding of a woman, but John intended to find a way to have both.

"She does not seem the worse for her experience this Nones," John commented to Will idly. His eyes fastened on the lady in question, who seemed to be finding that brickhead Lord Burle quite fascinating.

Nottingham drank from his goblet, then settled it precisely on the trestle in front of them. "To the contrary," he replied. "The lady wishes nothing more than to retire to her chamber after the meal. She claims, to anyone who will listen, of an ache in the head." He gave a knowing rumble of laughter and drank again.

John chuckled along with him, suddenly full of good humor. His tactic had become clear, and he cast a sharp eye on the amount of wine the man next to him was drinking, with the intent of increasing it generously. "An ache in the *head*? I should have expected one elsewhere."

Nottingham settled his goblet once again. "Aye, and mayhap elsewhere as well. I thought to give her a chance to contemplate her . . . options . . . this night. Mayhap after taking her ease, she will be more interested in the lessoning I mean to give her."

Unfortunately for her, John had no intent of leaving that lovely piece to wallow in her chamber alone this evening. Smiling, he gulped largely from his own wine. His mother might be a bullheaded manipulator who loved her elder son best, but she was immeasurably generous with the excellent wines from her lands. And in addition to that, she'd bestowed upon her youngest son her own crafty mind. Which he had put to good use in planning strategies for overthrowing his brother . . . and for luring gentlewomen into his bed.

"Indeed. Then I must presume your visit to the Court of Pleasure this evening will be solitary."

John smiled to himself, as he did every time he uttered the

phrase of his own making. Court of Pleasure. A more earthy, hedonistic version of his mother's famed Court of Love.

"Aye, that it will," Nottingham replied.

John frowned behind his goblet. He'd expected the other man to seize an excuse to decline the invitation. It hadn't escaped his notice that Nottingham had seemed less than enamored of the pleasure taking as of late. Oh, he participated . . . or, more accurately, most often watched and occasionally partook from a willing maidservant . . . but more likely than not, he merely provided the audience for John's activities.

Then John's eyes narrowed in speculation. Mayhap this would work out best after all. If Nottingham arrived before Marian and was otherwise occupied—or incapacitated—when the lady arrived . . . it would be incumbent upon the host to make her feel welcome.

He gestured for the page behind them to refill their goblets.

John was, if naught else, a most accommodating host.

"Come in, come in, my lady."

Marian hesitated on the threshold. She did not wish to take that step over, into the chamber, into the den of iniquity. John's voice sounded jovial, but there was an underlying command beneath it.

Her palms damp but her head held high, she stepped into the room and the door closed behind her.

Already this was very different from last night's experience.

Will had escorted her back to her chamber after the evening meal and bidden her good evening. She'd gone eagerly inside, fully aware that he'd said nary a word to her but "Let us go" when he approached her in the great hall, and "Good evening" when he left as soon as she was inside the chamber.

Nor had he looked at her, other than a quick impersonal glance, during the few moments they were together. He simply walked with long strides next to her, his solid arm angled out for her fingertips to curl around, his thigh brushing occasionally against her gown. This all made her exceedingly aware of his presence, his size, his strength . . . and what had occurred in her chamber earlier this day.

When they reached her accommodations, Ethelberga had been there, and she'd helped her mistress disrobe and prepare for bed—a circumstance Marian had readily welcomed. Despite the fact that she had left the hall before the evening's entertainment ended, and the sun still sat above the horizon, she was glad to be in the solitude—and relative safety—of her chamber.

But no more than two candle marks later, when the sun had barely set and the bailey below had not yet begun to quiet for the night, a solid pounding came at her door. Marian's heart leapt into her throat and she considered ignoring the knocking. Ethelberga had been dismissed and had gone belowstairs to visit with some of the other maidservants—and mayhap a handsome groom or two—and there was no one but Marian to answer the determined knock.

It could be Will. Likely it was. Her stomach gave another flutter and she resisted the urge to look toward the horse-eye peephole.

The knocking did not cease, and she had no choice but to respond. But when she opened the door, she found it was not Will, as she'd expected. And, in truth, half anticipated.

Nor was it Robin.

Thus, even before he spoke, when Marian saw the page

standing outside the door, she knew he would say, "The prince requires your presence, milady." Knowing she could not deny a royal summons, despite the sharp pinching of her insides and the parched sensation in her mouth, she quickly dressed and pulled on a enveloping cloak, drawing the deep hood up and over to shadow her face and hair. At the least she could attempt to avoid being recognized by anyone who might wonder why she was about alone . . . and going to the prince's chambers.

The page walked quickly, and was followed by a stoic man-at-arms who joined the party as they made their way to the third level of the keep. Apparently, John was taking no chances that Marian might get lost or otherwise delayed.

And here she was now, the door bumping closed in her wake, most definitely not lost or delayed.

As before, the room, which stretched well to her right and not quite so far to her left, was lit by candles and sconces throughout. The number of candles, along with two fires that blazed at either end of the chamber, gave off a sensual golden glow that cast yellow and bronze and brown across the room's furnishings and occupants.

She smelled the heavy rich scent of good wine and something else . . . a lingering, musky, close smell that hung in the air. It mingled with the ever-present wisps of smoke and settled a sort of lethargy over her.

"My lady." John's mellow voice came again, and she looked to the right, seeing him for the first time.

He sat on the side of the room where the bed was, where the two women had rolled and kissed and touched the night before. Marian caught a glimpse through the half-open bed-curtains of a woman's bare leg, the rise of a hip, and other human-shaped shadows within. Mayhap the girls had already completed this night's performance and now took their ease.

Her suspicion of this was reinforced when she noticed that, instead of having a woman kneeling in front of him with her face buried between his legs, the prince sat in a low chair. On a table within easy reach was a flagon of wine and several goblets. In front of him was the human chessboard—a nude woman on her hands and knees with an arrangement of low, squat chess pieces on her back.

Marian didn't know if it was the same woman who'd been there last night. She wouldn't have recognized her even if it was, for the woman's rear end faced her, knees apart, the hair of her quim readily visible between her spread legs.

"My lord," Marian replied, her voice low. Her mouth was dry and her palms were slick. She was torn between looking around the room to see what other surprises might lurk in the shadowy corners—and whether mayhap Will was there—and keeping her attention on the prince, to shield herself in ignorance.

"Would you care to play chess?" John asked, gesturing to the table. Then, as if noticing her cloak for the first time, he said, "Divest yourself of that. I prefer to admire the womanly form in my Court of Pleasure."

Marian allowed the cloak to slip from her shoulders and reluctantly draped it over a cushioned chair that had only a back but no arms or sides. She dared not consider what sort of activity it might be used for. As she did so, she glanced around the room, hoping to see Will lounging in a chair in the corner. He was not.

Her heart began to pound harder.

When she turned back, John was looking up at her, the weight of his dark eyes heavy. He was a handsome man—not a surprise, being the son of two comely parents. His coloring was nearly as dark as Will's tanned skin, likely a gift from his French mother. He had walnut-colored hair, thick and straight, and he wore it long over his ears as was the style, but short across his forehead. A neatly trimmed beard and mustache encircled a small but sensual mouth that glistened red and plump as if he'd been chewing his lip . . . or nibbling on something else. His shoulders were broad, and he was a solid man, but he was not as tall as his golden-haired brother, nor even his regal mother. Marian suspected he would be only a bit taller than herself, for his legs were rather short for his torso.

Instead of wearing a jeweled or gold-threaded tunic and belt, he wore a hip-length tunic with a deep vee in the unlaced neckline that showed a large amount of dark hair, and braies that clearly displayed a healthy bulge.

"Now, shall we play chess? You do know how to play, my lady?" he asked, his rings glinting as he beckoned to a chair on the other side of the woman's narrow back. He reached for one of the goblets next to him and poured bloodred wine into it, then licked the rim with a thick red tongue and offered the cup to her.

Trying to hide her reluctance, Marian took the goblet and sat. Then she realized that there was no chessboard. Someone had . . . drawn . . . the lines of the squares on the woman's back. The irregular crisscrossing lines looked like . . . Marian swallowed, and involuntarily looked up at John, horrified.

His dark eyes were fastened on her, glittering with delight. "Aye, you are correct. The sting of the whip created our game." He gave what she supposed he meant to be a heartbroken smile. "Hilde was not behaving as I required and needed to be punished. And I needed a chessboard, and 'twas only after I'd begun her punishment that I realized how she could accommodate me. That is why some of the squares are a bit . . . uneven."

Marian swallowed. She looked at the woman, who was clearly not one of her class but likely a serf or maidservant—but a woman nevertheless. Her shiny black hair, knotted loosely at the nape of her neck, sagged to one side and her head was bowed. She hadn't moved, nor made a sound, since Marian had come into the room. God help them both.

"I do know how to play," Marian replied, her mind working quickly.

She'd not been one of Eleanor's favorite ladies because of her dull wits and spinelessness, despite the fact that she wasn't the most accomplished chess player.

"Good," John said. "But you must understand . . . the rules are a bit different for this game." He smiled again, and this time the stretch of his red lips carried a hint of slyness. "If you lose a piece to me, you must remove an article of clothing. And of course, I will do the same."

Marian had expected naught less and was prepared. "But you have so few items to remove, my lord. I should hate for you to be sitting in the chill whilst I am still fully clothed." She offered a small smile that she hoped appeared confident, and not tense. "I propose a slight alteration in your rules: if you lose a piece to me, I replace an article of my clothing. I shall begin with my cloak when I take the first piece."

John laughed then, loudly and delightedly. "And so it shall be, Lady Marian, if for no other reason than your boldness."

"And the winner?" she asked, wondering if there was enough wine in the room to send him under his cups before the game was over.

"Can you not guess?" John replied, folding short, wide

hands over his lean belly. A ruby the size of a chestnut glinted on one.

"If I win," she replied, conscious that he'd appreciated her boldness a moment ago, "I will require a boon of you." She swallowed, because she knew what would happen if she lost. Those stubby, beringed fingers would be all over her bare flesh, touching, pinching, poking.

"A boon?"

A pardon for Robin Hood. Those words nearly passed her lips—she wanted them to do so—but she stopped them. Not now, not yet. Too soon, too great of a request . . . and too close to her heart. If he knew of a desire like that, he could use it against her. Instead, she said, "Aye, a boon of my asking. Yet to be decided."

"If your request is within my power, you shall have it . . . if, of course, your king remains standing alone at the end."

She dared not ask what would happen in the case of a draw.

John sat up in his chair. "Now, then. Shall we begin our battle with a kiss of peace?"

Before she could respond, he stood and leaned over the human chessboard, grasping the back of Marian's head with a very strong hand. His fingers curled into her skull, sliding into her hair as he tipped her face up by the force of his kiss. His lips were as soft and full and wet as they appeared, and Marian felt the scrape of teeth at the edges of her mouth as he forced his tongue through. He thrust brutally into her mouth, crushing her lips, sucking on her tongue, sweeping so strong and hard that she nearly gagged. He tasted of wine and thick, unpleasant heat, and he took . . . and took . . . holding her so hard that her head began to pound.

At last he released her, pulling a long strand of hair free

from her braid, and she sat back shakily. The back of her head pounded from his grip, her mouth felt raw and swollen, and her heart slammed rapidly in her chest. He must have fully loosened her braid, for a long, two-finger-thick coil of her hair fell down over her shoulder and curled in her lap.

"That was lovely," John said, reaching for one of his pawns—black of course. "I look forward to the spoils of my win." He moved and then lifted his goblet to drink, watching her over its rim.

Marian blinked, trying to clear her mind. She was a passable chess player, and this was the most important game she'd ever played. She'd need every bit of concentration she could muster.

They'd each made two moves when, without a word, John stood. Marian caught her breath as he unlaced his braies and began to move toward her. A wild protest caught in her throat, but before she could utter it, he stopped at the rear end of the chess table.

Grasping the woman's hips, he knelt behind her and exposed a long, turgid cock. As she watched, he spit down onto its length and used his hand to rub the spittle over his erection. It glistened with the simple lubricant, and before Marian could look away, he slid it inside the waiting quim from behind. The woman barely moved, and made only a squeak.

John gave a quiet, satisfied groan and reached toward the woman's neck, and at first Marian thought he was about to strangle her. But instead, he coiled a thick mass of hair around his fist, using it to raise the woman's head as if she were a horse and he held the reins.

Marian watched as John pumped her steadily, easily, from behind, and noticed that the woman's arms strained with the effort of keeping herself still so that the chess pieces did not fall.

What would happen to her if they did?

But they were short and wide pieces, obviously made for this purpose, and John was not rough. The pieces slipped only a bit.

The woman's breasts swayed from side to side, and John moved one hand to close over and pinch the nipple of one while the other maintained its hold on her hair. Marian was surprised to see through the heavy hair that obscured much of her face that the woman's eyes were closed and her mouth parted slightly, her breath rising audibly. She even gave a quiet groan of her own that almost sounded like an expression of pleasure. Was it possible she was enjoying this? How could that be?

For a moment, Marian was caught by the rhythm, the sounds, even the rising scent of woman. Her lips felt dry and she wanted to lick them, and she was aware of a quiet tingling beginning between her own legs, deep inside her.

Ashamed that a woman's degradation should cause even the slightest excitement in her, Marian looked away and found herself captured by John's dark gaze. It glittered with lust and depravation, and a clear message that she did not want to see. She tore her eyes away and heard his low gasp of laughter.

Where was Will?

Why wasn't he here to protect her?

At that moment, John gave a heartfelt groan and eased inside his chess table one last time. Hilde released her own breath in a low sigh. Marian saw her lick her lips and then as John released the hank of hair, she lowered her head so that it hung down once again.

Not one chess piece had fallen.

John picked up a cloth, wiped his cock, and settled back in his seat. "Now, then," he said, refilling his goblet and renewing

Marian's hopes he would drink himself into a stupor. "Whose move?"

Marian applied herself to the game, and only pretended to drink when John urged her. She did get her cloak back, but only for a few moments. And then she lost it, as well as her braided leather girdle and then, to her rising concern, her long overgown. This left her clothed in only the tightly laced bliaud, and while that garment covered her from neck to floor, it left her feeling quite exposed with its close sleeves and formfitting fashion. She moved a rook, trying to concentrate on the game.

John's eyes gleamed as he moved to take her knight, and he raised his face to look at her. "This time, you must remove your braid and allow your hair to fall loosely."

Relieved that she had a reprieve before removing her undergown, which would leave her clothed in naught but her hair, Marian took her time unbraiding the rest of her hair. John watched in fascination as she pulled it over her shoulders, partly on each side, and allowed it to fall so that it nearly brushed the floor. When she leaned forward to make her next move, some of the shorter strands in front slipped against the bare skin of the chess table's torso and the woman shuddered.

Marian saw the little rise of bumps on Hilde's skin, and felt her own flesh pebble beneath her clothes. There was something about seeing her hair touching another's skin so intimately. . . .

She looked up and found John watching her, again that knowing look in his eyes. She swallowed and just as she reached for a piece on the chessboard—any piece, anything to break away from that look—she heard a shifting and a groan behind her.

A male groan, from the sound of it. It seemed like rustling and shifting, movement . . . from the bed behind her.

John looked up over her shoulder, and she thought she caught a glimpse of annoyance flash over his face. But then the *shush* of movement stopped and there was silence again.

" 'Tis your turn, my lady," the prince said.

Marian replaced the piece she'd lifted, realizing if she made a bad move and lost another piece, she would be as exposed as Hilde. Her hand moved above the pieces and she tried to pull her scattered thoughts together.

She hovered over her bishop and there was a low cough from behind her, drawing John's attention once more. Marian looked again at the board and this time saw the trap she'd been led into—a trap that a movement of the bishop could foil; it would save her from not only losing her undergown but also checkmate.

She made the placement and looked up to find John once again watching her. Yet he said naught of her spoiling his plan and, after a brief consultation of the pieces, moved again.

Marian stared at the game, realizing her breathing had become rushed again and knowing that she had no way to win this battle. He was obviously a much better player than she was on a good day, but with all the other distractions she had to contend with, Marian knew she was playing miserably.

She looked desperately at the board, curling her hands in her lap and around and through the hair that amassed there. It took a moment before she realized that John was not watching the game, but was eyeing the way her fingers slid in and around, playing with her hair as she tried to keep her desperation at bay. His breathing had changed, and when she closed her fingers around a piece of end curl and began to idly stroke it, the prince appeared fixated.

Marian drew in a deep breath and leaned forward, allowing a

wide swath of hair to brush over Hilde's round hip like a coppery curtain. As she hovered over her queen, two things happened. John gave a quiet moan and his lips parted, and she heard another movement behind her, another faint groan, almost like a heavy breath, that . . . stopped as she moved toward the rook.

She moved her hand back over the queen and there came a renewed shifting from the bed, and then when she picked up the knight, it stopped.

As she fingered her hair more seductively, Marian looked at the queen again and realized her move . . . and with a burst of relief, she understood. He was helping her. From the bed.

Whether 'twas Will she didn't know, but it didn't matter.

She made her move with the queen and looked up at John, taking care to hide the triumph in her eyes. "Check," she said.

He pulled his eyes from her fingers, which were busily making a little braid in her lap, and looked down at the game. Then he looked up at her again. "A fascinating move, my lady," he said. "But not good enough."

And he reached swiftly forward and captured her queen.

Holy Mary, Will silently groaned.

She'd moved the right piece . . . but to the wrong place. If she hadn't placed the prince in check, she would have been safe. Saf*er.*

Pah. She wasn't safe at all. Even when he was here with her.

Will understood the prince's game. He'd realized it at the evening meal, when John had become overly solicitous about keeping Will's wine goblet filled, and urging him to enjoy the fine vintage from Aquitaine.

Fortunately Will's squire, Tristan, stood with the prince's

pages and helped to serve. A quick whisper to Tristan resulted in the squire's keeping his master's goblet filled, but with much more water than wine.

When John had invited him, as he always did, to his chamber, Will had been careful to stumble and slur as he made his way to the solar along with the prince, taking care to litter his words with profanities about Marian.

John had promised him pleasure to take his mind off the problem, as well as even more wine. As planned, Will was easily able to pretend to slip off into oblivion once he climbed into the half-curtained bed with two of John's naked consorts—and none too soon, for they'd divested him of all but his braies by the time they realized he was no longer with them.

Will's diligence was rewarded when he heard John order one of the pages to go and fetch Marian to the solar. So he waited as the girls fell asleep next to him, likely just as eager for a bit of rest as he was.

And now, as he lay sprawled in the bed, he could see Marian facing John across the prince's own special chessboard. She stood slowly and lifted her heavy hair, brushing it back over her shoulders. Reluctance showed in every movement and Will knew he could wait no longer.

With a loud groan, he shifted and pulled the bed-curtains to the side.

John looked up at him, and Will was shocked to see the unbridled venom in the prince's expression . . . and then it was gone. Marian dropped the hem of her gown, which she'd begun to raise, and turned toward the bed.

Will looked away and gave one of the naked rumps next to him a sound slap. Its owner shrieked and bolted awake, and so did the other, and the moment of tension was broken.

"I beg your pardon, my lord," Will said, making a show of rubbing his eyes. He gave a nearby breast a fond little jiggle as he made his way off the bed. "I must have dozed off. Too much wine anight."

He didn't look at Marian, but he was fully aware that her attention was focused steadily on him.

"You've interrupted our chess game," John said in a velvety voice.

"Indeed?" Will said, standing beside the bed now. "It appears by the state of your clothing . . . and my lady's . . . that my lord is on the verge of claiming victory."

"I would have done," John continued in that soft voice, "if you had not interrupted us."

"Ah, then do go on with it." Will made a careless gesture and walked over to the other part of the chamber, where he pretended to pour another goblet of wine.

When he turned back moments later, it was all he could do to keep his breath even. She had removed her gown and sat clothed only in her rippling hair. Now that it was dry, it didn't cling to every curve like a second skin. A pink nipple peeked out from the golden red curtain, but other than two slender white arms, she was nearly as well covered as if she were wearing a cloak. Marian's face had paled and settled into a tight mask and now she looked at him with loathing.

Of course she'd thought he'd save her from this eventuality . . . and so had the prince. Which was precisely why Will had not done so.

Yet, that sword was double-edged, for now he must also be confronted with what he'd touched and crushed and manipulated earlier this day. At that time, he'd allowed himself naught but blurred impressions and impersonal touch—although the feel of her soft skin, the smell of her body, ripe from the floral bath, the silk of her hair . . . all had been impressed on his memory.

Will drank from his wine and sauntered back over to the chess game. The flash of hatred in John's eyes had indicated just how keen the man's disappointment had been . . . and how deep his lust had burrowed.

'Twas time to tread most carefully and cleverly. A balance between reminding John of his agreement and not letting him feel his loss too deeply.

He came to stand behind Marian. She tensed perceptibly and her breathing changed, but she did not look at him nor acknowledge him. Good. John must believe, at the least for now, that she loathed Will.

And of course she did. After what he'd subjected her to earlier this day, and now, as she sat here naked, what was likely to come . . . how could a noblewoman like Marian not despise him?

And yet, though he knew it would only feed the fire of her resentment, he was unable to resist touching her . . . this time without haste or furtiveness.

He reached forward, brushing his fingers over the top of her warm head, noticing details that he'd been unwilling to allow himself to see before. The palm of his hand cupped the top of her skull, then slid down over thick waves made of infinite shades of gold, bronze, copper, auburn . . . even ruby and garnet. Truly, she had the most magnificent hair, miraculous in its fire. 'Twas no wonder John lusted for her.

And, in truth, John was not the only one.

Marian lifted her hand to make another poor move, and Will tightened his fingers slightly. She paused and Will felt John's interested gaze lift briefly. Damn.

But before he could say or do anything to alleviate the prince's suspicions, someone knocked on the door.

John looked over and bade entrance, while Marian gasped and reached for something with which to cover herself. Will looked away as she snatched up her cloak, the curve of a smooth hip and the roundness of a breast jolting teasingly from beneath her hair.

The prince greeted the newcomers, and Will felt his momentary relief at the interruption fade. 'Sblood. The arrival of these two men—Sir Louis Krench and Lord Ralf Stannoch—only made the situation worse, for they were two of John's long-time confidants and companions. Will had appreciated their absence, for while they were gone, John was left to his own devices—which were not quite as extreme as what the three of them dreamed up together.

At the least, no one had died while Krench and Stannoch were gone.

"So you have at last returned," said John. "I'd begun to fear you'd joined my brother's camp." He laughed heartily at what he obviously intended as a jest.

He invited his friends into the chamber, and Will was slightly mollified to see that they weren't alone: three tittering women accompanied them. Whores, serfs, or freewomen, Will didn't know, and he didn't care who they were except for the fact that they were additional quims and breasts.

He moved now and pulled Marian firmly onto his lap as he settled into an armless chair in a shadowy corner. She settled there stiffly, warm and lush. As far as he was concerned, the chess game was over. To ensure this eventuality, as John was inspecting the new female arrivals, who were already being coaxed out of their clothing, Will swept his hand over the chess table and knocked the remaining pieces askew. Then he curled his arm around Marian's belly to keep her in place, folding his fingers into a fist.

Marian stiffened even more in his lap, and hissed, "Now he shall blame Hilde for that and punish her further." Her mouth was near enough for him to smell the wine on her breath, but she was not close enough to kiss.

Foolish woman. Will looked away from the soft, sweet-smelling body and tightened his fist as he struggled to keep from uncurling those fingers and touching her. "John will know 'twas I. 'Tis yourself for whom you ought worry," he murmured into her ear. "Krench and Stannoch are no weak weasels. But at the least they've brought their own playthings."

"Then let us leave." She turned and her hair spilled differently over his arm, tickling him and raising fine bumps there.

Aye. They must leave.

But Will did not move. His body was frozen, and he feared if he allowed it to thaw, all would be lost.

"Nottingham." The sound of John's voice cut through Will's haze of indecision, and Will looked over to find John looking at him. "You must join us."

It was not a request.

CHAPTER 8

*M*arian had nowhere to look, so she closed her eyes.

But the sounds pervaded, the sounds and scents of coupling. Of cries and gasps and desperate begging, the sharp slap of braided leather on skin, the groan of satiation, the smells of spent seed and sweat and spilled wine.

She didn't want to think about the fact that she was naked, bare but for the cloak she'd grabbed up at the knock at the door.

Will stood slightly behind her, leaning against the tall bedpost, arms crossed over his bare chest. He'd said naught to her, nothing to ease her fears or worries except the warning that she should have a care for herself. Even when John ordered them to join his other companions, Will had done nothing but acquiesce.

Now, acutely aware of the tableau before her, her nipples were drawn tight and the little hooded knot in her quim had begun to come alive, and she knew that she'd leave the chamber much less innocent this night than she had been before. She dared not open her eyes and look at Will for fear of what he might see in her eyes, and she was relieved to no longer be sitting bare-bottomed on his lap, held in place by a steely arm.

During the chess game, when he'd crawled out of the bed leaving two women in the shadows behind him, Marian's tentative relief had been washed away by the sight of his half-clothed self. Though that strong body had trapped her against a wall, and been poised over her earlier today, she'd never seen the powerful slabs of muscle and the square angles of his shoulders. Harold's pale, hair-covered torso and belly had looked nothing like the tanned, rippling one that emerged from the bed-curtains.

At first, as he'd crawled forth, he had reminded Marian of a lean cat, dark and sleek with rich black hair rumpled from whatever he'd been doing behind the curtains. Shadows gathered in the hollows of his collarbones and along the sweep of his muscled shoulders. His face was dusky and dark with stubble, his eyes heavy-lidded, his mouth set. Black hair grew in a wide patch over the upper part of his chest, but as he came into view, she saw that it narrowed into a slender line that ran down the center of his flat, ridged belly . . . and then disappeared into the shadow of his loose braies. Braies that hung low on lean hips, exposing their bones and a thick dark thatch of hair . . . and looked as though they might slip down with the slightest tug.

All this had been impressed upon Marian in an instant . . . and now she could not erase the image from her mind. She'd had no idea . . . no idea a man could look like that. Beautiful . . . and yet frightening, dark and smooth and lean . . . the beauty marred by white battle scars.

"Why so shy, my lady?" came a velvety voice in her ear. "Open your eyes."

She didn't. She kept them closed and though they did not touch, she felt the tension from Will, who stood like a powerful, impersonal tree trunk next to her chair.

The prince spoke again. "You'll watch, my lady, or you'll join them."

Marian's eyes flew open and John's mellow chuckle fell heavily into her ears. "Very good. Now tell me which of these . . . arrangements . . . suits you the most."

He settled in an armless seat next to hers, close enough to brush against her. She drew her cloak closer about her shoulders, but he noticed . . . and with a flick of his wrist whisked it away, sending it crumpling to the floor. "Do you not recall that you lost your cloak by fair play, my lady?"

Marian could do naught but huddle beneath her hair, grateful that it was so thick and heavy.

"My lady," that mellow voice purred again, "which is it? Which scene has captured your attention?" John had leaned very close to her and she felt the warmth of his skin brush against her. He'd removed his tunic and now, like Will, wore only braies tied at the waist.

And yet the proximity of his bare chest and arms, darkly haired torso and belly, prompted a very different response from Marian. One closer to distaste than desire.

"Is it the woman there?" John persisted. "See how she takes them both at once?"

Marian could not help but see the woman, arranged on her hands and knees, naked, of course. One of John's friends, the shorter one with sharp, weasel features, had loosened and dropped his hose so that it bunched around his ankles. He slammed into the woman from behind, his fingers grasping her hips so hard the skin was white where he gripped.

And in front of her stood the other late arrival, a man with pale skin and pale hair, and colorless gray eyes that had scanned Marian with bald lust. Dressed in only a tunic, he'd dispensed with his hose completely and his pale, spindly legs bowed slightly as he worked his erection in and out of the woman's mouth.

"Would you enjoy that, my lady?" John murmured in her ear. "Two sleek cocks sliding in and out, one at each end?"

As before, once she began to look, she found herself unable to turn away . . . to block out the sounds and images. The long, shiny lengths pumping the woman from either side . . . her cheeks hollow and her eyes wide as one man held her face steady, lifting her chin to make her throat a long, easy curve, her breasts hanging free, jolting with every movement . . . and at the rear, the slip and slide of another red cock, in and out in a smooth, sticky rhythm, faster and faster . . .

Marian swallowed, her breath rising faster as the pounding became harder and the two men lost their synchronized rhythm, slamming into the woman haphazardly so that she could barely keep her balance, breasts bouncing and swaying. Marian felt it as if it were inside her, the rise, the tension, the urgency. . . . The hot tingling in her stomach swirled lower, almost painful in its intensity, tightening at the center of her quim.

She didn't realize she'd given a soft gasp until she felt John's mouth near her ear.

"Ahh, so you do like that," he said. "Drink, my lady." He lifted a cup to her mouth.

Drink if he offers, Will had said. She opened her mouth and gulped the heavy, sweet wine and felt it flush warmly through her.

She drank more, and John's tongue thrust through the curtain of her hair, into the depth of her ear in a parody of the activity before them. She shuddered at the invasion, even as her body began to warm, loosen. He leaned closer, and his hand slid up over her belly, her skin trembling and lurching from his touch as she tried to pull her eyes away from the scene ahead, knowing vaguely that she wanted to get away from him.

But he was the prince . . . and even though her mind was dull and murky, she knew she could not offend him.

Will, protect me.

"Nay, don't close your eyes," he said. "Watch as they come, watch them spew their seed and see how she takes it . . . how . . . *oh.*" He stopped with his own sudden low groan as the pale man whipped his cock from the woman's mouth, and gave it two hard jerks, spurting his seed over the woman's head.

The man behind lunged forward hard, and the woman bent her arms, resting her head on the floor as he pummeled her from behind. Her bottom rose higher now than her shoulders, her sighs and grunts filling the air with erotic sounds. Marian saw the glistening red of her quim as the cock slid in and out . . . and knew that her own was as swollen and wet, that her breathing was caught up in the same rising rhythm.

John had turned, straddling the edge of the chair, pressing against her. His fingers filtered through her hair, his breath rasping hard, low, and harsh in her ear. She could not mistake the bulge of his cock against her hip.

"More," he ordered, lifting the goblet to her mouth again . . . and she gulped down more, the sweet wine sinking more easily into her this time.

After she swallowed half the libation, he found her hand, drawing it from where she'd clasped it against her belly, and forced it down over him . . . into the depth of his braies, where it was hot and damp and a pulsing erection raged like a smithy's iron.

"There," he sighed, a half command, half groan. He forced her fingers around its width, closing his hand tightly over hers, pushing his body up closer. "Now . . . mmph . . ." His command lurched to a halt as the weasel-faced man arched his back with a last violent thrust, calling out the pleasure of his orgasm with a loud moan.

Marian could not look away. The man appeared to be in agony, his face stretched and dark and pained . . . but something primal gouged her; watching him find his pleasure made something tug deep inside, leaving her skittish and out of breath . . . her heart slamming as if it had been she on the floor . . . she accepting the slick length of a cock.

John's fingers closed tighter, and he showed her the stroke, the rhythm, and then he murmured, "And what of her?" He directed her attention to another side of the room. Though his breathing was heavy and raspy, the cadence of his voice remained smooth. "Should I bind you like so?" He lifted the wine to her lips again.

She turned to see what John was looking at and then didn't know which was worse . . . the feel of his hot, hard erection, its skin sliding beneath her fingers . . . or the sight of the dark-haired woman splayed against the wall. Head tipped back, nude, her hands held high so that they raised her breasts, and her feet spread wide and bound in place. Another woman with short dark hair stood nearby with a whip that had clearly already left marks on her companion's belly.

Marian swallowed, tried to catch her breath. . . . She felt the chamber walls pushing closer, warmer, redder on her until there was naught to see but the woman against the wall.

The pale man moved to take the whip, pausing to fondle the breast of the woman he'd taken it from.

"Mavis, go to her," he ordered, and the short-haired woman moved to the wall.

"Ahh," John sighed in Marian's ear, forcing her hand to move faster. "Glynna is delicious, is she not? The one on the wall?"

Even if she'd had an opinion, Marian couldn't have voiced it. She concentrated on breathing, on moving her arm in a non-stop rhythm . . . her body taut and quivering, pounding, swollen, wet . . . tight.

Her arm moved faster and faster, and she could not ignore the scene in front of her. . . . Mavis knelt in front of the bound woman, spreading wide her bare knees so that the deep red of Glynna's quim was exposed to the room.

Marian's breath caught as that dark head bent to the woman in front of her, and the sounds of lapping, of sloppy damp laving, filled the air over the rising harsh breaths of the prince, and the roaring in her own ears.

Almost . . . she almost felt the strokes on her, over her, her quim full and ready. . . . Her mouth was dry as she watched Glynna, bound and helpless, writhing against the wall as the kneeling woman bent to her . . . and then pulled away, running her fingers all along the insides of her thighs as the bound woman struggled and arched . . . and then the tormentor bent again as Glynna begged *Please, please.* . . . Marian felt the teasing, the stop-starting, the pounding and wet of her own little pearl . . . the damp growing between her legs.

"Faster," John ordered, releasing her hand to grope for her

breast, his breathing heavy and hot in her ear. Her arm ached from the motion, and yet she dared not stop. . . . She could do naught but focus on the women in front of her, and watched as the pale man pulled Mavis away, sending her tumbling across the room.

The man shoved himself inside Glynna, and Marian saw her eyes fly wide, watched as he pumped inside her, his hands clawing at her breasts. . . . Marian's arm screamed with pain, and yet she continued on, faster, matching the rhythm of the man fucking the woman against the wall . . . her breath, her heartbeat, her eyes, all focused, centered, *there.* . . .

John cried out, and she felt the surge from his cock, the wet over her hand, the shuddering in his body. She pulled her hand away, turning from him, wiping his seed on the first cloth she groped, the woman's pleading cries still filling her ears, the sounds of body slamming into body, the gasps and groans.

She couldn't catch her breath, and the room felt close and small around her. The cries and the heavy sweet wine made her soft and loose . . . yet tight and desperate. . . . She couldn't get away, couldn't look anywhere but at the woman's mouth, open in pleasure or pain, her head rolling against the stones behind her, the taut, spare muscle of the man slamming into her, his buttocks moving, his slender, ropy arms tense as they groped at her.

Suddenly, Marian felt strong hands on her . . . strong, solid hands, warm . . . and she was pulled away, turned from the sight of them fucking, her hair catching painfully. . . . Dizzy, lightheaded, she stumbled and fell. . . . Those strong hands caught her and she tumbled against him, his solid, bare skin . . . an exchange of deep rumbling voices, a sharp response, and *aye* . . . Will.

Will.

Her dull mind recognized him, his touch, the way he moved, the rumble in his chest as he spoke something she couldn't understand. He was around her, holding her, his hands smoothing over her body, up along her back, through the masses of hair, pulling her close to his chest with a powerful arm, and then shifting her away.

She rolled free in a swirl of hair, falling onto something soft . . . the bed. . . . It dipped when he joined her, the yellow light from the chamber about them disappearing as he yanked the bed-curtains around closed, leaving only a narrow strip of light on either side.

And then . . . nothing.

She lay there, heart still pounding, breathing heavily, unsettled, irritated. . . . The images still haunted her, teased her. Beyond their curtained space, Marian heard the unmistakable sounds of coupling, of wet, slick strokes, the slap of skin against skin . . . the pleasured moans, the pained cries. . . . She needed something . . . to move, to be touched. . . . She needed relief, to be rid of this tightness, this incessant throbbing and pounding that made her feel like crawling out of her skin.

"Will," she whispered. . . . It came out like a soft moan, like a little plea. She reached out, felt for him, found the warm tension of his arm next to her. She became aware of his breathing, rough and heavy, and the absolute stillness of his body. As if he were frozen, bracing for something.

"I . . . please . . ." She didn't know, didn't know what to say, how to ask. . . . The unsettling, squirming feeling roiling inside her was strong, desperate.

He made a soft noise, like a sigh deep in his chest, and suddenly his hands were on her. The next thing she knew, he'd dragged her on top of him, half over his wide, solid chest, and he brought her face down for a hungry kiss.

His hands moved over her, catching up her breasts where they tipped above him, finding the nipples that had tightened. He released her mouth and grasped her waist to move her up, above him, settling her full, wet quim over his belly. Unable to help it, she moved, pressing her throbbing little pip into his skin, seeking relief, grinding madly into him.

He made a noise—mayhap it was her name—planting his hands on her hips as he lifted his head. Will found one of her nipples, closing his warm mouth around it.

Marian gasped. Her face lifted, her head tipping back at the sharp pleasure—at last!—shooting down, from breast to belly to the little throbbing piece between her legs. As he sucked and licked over the top of her sensitive nipple, she cried and squirmed against him, feeling his breathing roughen beneath her, conscious of the little pulses between her legs. More . . . more . . .

At last, he released her breast, tumbling her off and to the side next to him. Will moved with her too, somehow managing not to catch her hair under an elbow or a hip or leg as he levered his torso half over hers, one hand propping himself near her hips, the other near her shoulder.

Yes, aye, oh . . . please, she was ready. She wanted . . . She made a little noise, another desperate gasp, and hitched her hips impatiently. He buried his face in her neck, hot and damp, kissing her shoulder, using his strong tongue to glide along the tender part there as she twitched and writhed and thought about begging.

Urgent, desperate, she reached, her hand glancing over his belly, still damp from her moisture moments ago. She felt the rough hair growing there, then the waist of his braies. . . . She slipped her hand down into the heat.

"Nay," he said suddenly, the word a clipped order. Lifting his face from her neck, he shifted out of reach and her hand fell away. And then she forgot all, for his fingers moved between her legs.

Marian cried out, arching up into his hand as he found her swollen pip. Oh, aye . . . he slid a finger deep inside, and then another one, filling her . . . moving in and out, sliding through the pool of dampness. He used his thumb to massage in and around, caressing her swollen labia, gently flicking over her tight little pip, slow and easy . . . and then, as she began to breathe more urgently, feeling the pleasure gather there, he teased and rubbed harder, faster, his own breath hot on her neck, his skin sticky against hers.

Marian's eyes were closed, and she knew naught but the rise and tightening of pleasure . . . the climb toward relief, as it coiled—almost painfully—there beneath his hand strokes . . . and all at once she slipped over with a cry, bursting into delicious warmth and gasping with the rolling waves of relief as she shuddered against him.

Oh, aye . . . aye . . .

Her face was wet, her body still twitching, the little pearl between her legs heavy and pulsing, the gentle weight of his hand against it, as she sifted back to reality. Then he moved away, eased his fingers free, and she blinked her eyes open, finding the lit seam of the bed-curtains and a haze over her vision. Despite all that had happened, Marian could not keep a satisfied smile from curving her lips. . . . She had needed that so, needed the blast of release, the touch of a strong body, sure fingers, skillful mouth.

But Will . . . he'd moved away, and before she could speak,

or reach for him—she wanted to touch him—he sat up, flung the curtains open.

"Come," he said sharply, quietly, looking not at her but into the chamber beyond.

Only then did Marian become aware that the sounds of pleasure beyond their curtained sanctuary had not eased. But Will had opened the opposite side of the bed, out of sight of the others. When he beckoned, she moved sluggishly toward him, still languid and dazed from the wine and pleasure.

Will grabbed her arm and pulled her along, unspeaking, away from the bed. He snatched up a wrap of some sort and flung it over her: a dusty cloak with a hood that would hide her distinctive hair, and the rest of her body.

From the other end of the chamber, beyond the bed they'd just vacated, came the sounds of pleasure and pain, of flesh slaps and guttural cries, galvanizing Marian to move more readily. She wanted to escape before John noticed them, and she understood that silence and speed were imperative.

To that end, she couldn't be concerned with the pile of her discarded clothing, yet Will snatched it up, bundling it under his arm and towing her along with his other hand.

Moments later, they were safely outside the chamber, and she noticed that he'd left his own clothing behind. He still wore only the low-hanging braies, which defied the law of nature and remained at his hips.

"Come," he hissed again, without a look at her. One of the guards made a move as if to question him, but Will turned and gave him a cold order. "Yield."

Thus, dressed only in a cloak, Marian hurried behind him—bare of foot, cloak flapping, propelled along by his grip to keep pace with his long strides.

She was breathless by the time they reached her bedchamber, and Marian pulled from Will's grip. He'd said naught during their quick negotiation of hallways and staircases, rushing her along as if he couldn't wait to be rid of her. She'd caught a glimpse of his set face, but he made no move to speak or to otherwise acknowledge her presence.

Ethelberga did not answer the door, and the antechamber, where the maid should have been sleeping at this late hour, was empty. A fire burned therein, along with a well-placed wall sconce, giving the chamber good light. Turning to close the door, Marian found Will standing there, his eyes sharp. His presence gave her a start, for he'd seemed so eager to get her back to the chamber and be on his way.

"Your maid is not here?" he said.

"Nay, and what a tongue-lashing she'll get from me," Marian said. "Though," she added with a self-conscious laugh, "I trow I am in no need of her assistance to disrobe this night."

He didn't respond to her attempt at humor, and instead stepped over the threshold into the antechamber. She looked up at him, very conscious of the fact that they were alone, and that much had happened this day.

In this chamber, where he'd burst in earlier today and . . .

Pretended to rape her. And then tonight, in the prince's quarters, when she'd tried to touch him, he'd rejected her overture. Why?

I am no saint, Marian. I do not deny 'twould please me greatly.

Yet . . . he did not touch her when he had the chance.

Nay . . . he *had* touched her . . . but not for his own pleasure. She swallowed harder as something fluttered in her belly, and she glanced up and found him watching her. Behind him the door gaped open.

Feeling exposed, she pushed it closed, sensing that he was about to speak. Yet he did not appear friendly or the least approachable; his mouth had settled into a flat line and he looked at her as if he didn't know her. Distant, impersonal.

But she found it difficult to look away from the breadth of his shoulders and the faint sheen on his tanned, dark-haired chest. Marian could see a band of white skin above his low-hanging braies, testament to the fact that he must train or practice in the sunlight without a tunic or shirt.

She'd been gathered against that solid torso, shuddering and trembling, only moments ago. Her mouth became dry and she licked her lips, aware of her nakedness beneath the cloak. His mouth on her breast, his hands between her legs. She swallowed. Heat flushed over her.

"Marian," he said, his voice rough, impatient. "Are you . . . ?"

She looked up at him, and her insides flipped. He was reaching toward her, his hand moving toward her face. Marian's heart started pounding and then he touched her, brushing a strand of hair from where it had caught at the corner of her mouth.

A musky scent reached her nose, and she grabbed his wrist, barely able to fit her fingers around it. Though her grip wasn't strong, he didn't pull away as she brought his fingers closer. 'Twas her own scent there, still strong on his skin from when he'd stroked her.

Their eyes met over their joined fists, and she gently moved them up and toward his nose. His eyes darkened to black, a tiny glow of the fire reflected there, and his nostrils flared as he drew in the scent. Marian felt weak in the knees at the expression in the black depths. Hunger . . . remorse . . . fear.

"Will," she whispered. "Thank you."

Her words seemed to break the spell. His face sharpened;

he extricated his hand and stepped back. "You have naught for which to thank me."

Then he seemed to look around as if seeing the chamber again for the first time, cocking his head. "Step away," he said, his voice sharp. "I'll look inside." He gestured to the door behind her, and she realized with a start that he meant to go into her chamber.

He brushed past, obvious in his attempt to avoid touching her as she stood in front of the door. Shoving it open, he went inside.

"I suspected as much," she heard him say in a cold voice.

"Nottingham," came an even response. "I cannot say the same."

"Robin?" Marian exclaimed, rushing into the room, cloak flapping at her heels.

Indeed. None other but Robin Hood sat comfortably on the stool in the corner of her room, beneath the horse-eye peephole. A fire burned happily, lending a soft glow to the room. He seemed more annoyed than apprehensive about the arrival of the man sworn to hang him.

"Marian! What has befallen you?" Robin shot to his feet when he saw her. Then he spun toward Will, a menacing look on his face. Before Marian could react, he had a knife in his hand. "What has happened?"

"The prince," Will replied flatly. Ignoring the knife, he advanced. "And you are more a fool than I believed possible." He looked as if he was about to lunge toward the other man.

But Marian intervened. "Robin, what are you doing here?" she asked, frightened. Will's face had gone from blank and cold to deadly furious. Why had Robin been so foolish as to come back to the keep?

She moved closer to him, as if to block him from Will . . . an odd thing, she realized belatedly, for 'twas Robin who had the blade and not the sheriff.

"The prince? It looks as though he had some assistance," Robin said cuttingly. "Am I to believe he acted alone, without the help of his black cohort the sheriff?" He was looking, not at her, but at the half-dressed Will, and he still held the knife as if prepared to use it.

Will muttered something foul under his breath and Marian felt the loathing rolling off him. "Take care at whom you throw accusations, Locksley."

"Robin—" Marian started to plead, but she was cut off.

"What has happened?" he asked again, still looking at Will.

"Naught as of yet, but 'tis not for lack of trying." Now Will glanced at her, eyes glittering black. "Mayhap you wish to cover yourself, Lady Marian."

Marian looked down and saw that with her sudden movement toward Robin, the cloak had slipped and caught on the edge of a trunk. The fabric gaped wide open, clearly displaying her state of undress. She gathered the edges together, wondering, *What did it matter?* Will had seen all there was to see, and Robin had felt most of it.

"Naught has happened, you say?" Robin said, lifting his chin belligerently at Will. "Then how came she—"

"*Robin,*" Marian began again, more frantically. She grabbed his arm, pulling him back, ignoring the further slip of her cloak. The expression on Will's face frightened her, and Robin's bravado was not assisting matters. He must get out of here before the sheriff arrested him.

How could he have been such a *fool*?

"Cover yourself, Marian," Will ordered, then grabbed her by

the arm and yanked her from his path. She stumbled but caught herself against the wall, pulling the cloak tighter.

"Will," she tried. "Please don—"

He turned on her, lips so tight they were white at the edges. "Do not be a fool, Marian. I am not about to slay your lover in these chambers."

"Slay me?" Robin snorted. "How? You have no weapon." He looked pointedly at Will's simple attire.

"If I chose to put you in your grave, I would need no weapon. So I suggest you leave before your presence here is found out."

"Mayhap Lady Marian shall accompany me back to Sherwood," Robin said, moving now too. The next thing she knew, he had his arm around her belly, and the knife blade at her throat. "I trow I can keep her from the hands of John better than his cohort the Sheriff of Nottinghamshire."

Marian wasn't the least bit frightened of the dagger at her throat; it was Will and his black look she feared. For a moment, he looked as though he might lunge forward, knife or nay . . . and then the feral light died from his eyes to be replaced by a malicious gleam.

"Aye," he said. "If the lady is kidnapped and taken by the outlaw Robin Hood, not only will she be safe from the lecherous eyes of the prince . . . but I shall also be obliged to gather up every able-bodied man to flush the outlaw and his band from the forest. I am certain you would wish for that."

Robin's fingers had slipped between the edges of the cloak, and she felt his warm hand on her belly . . . and then up to brush over her breast. She snatched in a little intake of breath and resisted the urge to stomp his foot. Instead of trying to escape when cornered, he did naught but taunt his enemy and play games.

"But you know they will never find us," Robin said, inching her a bit toward the door. "You may send all of the king's men into the forest and never flush us out." Behind the neatly trimmed beard and mustache beamed a sly smile, clearly taunting his opponent. His fingers brushed the underside of her breast, and a thumb slipped up over her nipple. She remained rigid, despite the fact that he caused a little tingle to rise.

By the saints, she knew how to put an end to this standoff.

"You are the veriest of fools, Locksley," Will said in a biting voice. "You would risk the safety of your lady and her reputation by openly making her your consort, your accomplice. And would you then be willing to allow her to hang from the scaffold next to you?"

Judging the moment right, Marian pulled free from Robin—after all, his hold was more for show than for anything else—and whirled toward Will. 'Twas unfortunate . . . or mayhap not so unfortunate . . . that her captor had been holding the cloak more tightly than he'd gripped her person. The covering slipped from her body as she moved, leaving her once again clothed only in a swirl of hair.

"God's teeth, Marian," Will snarled as Robin simply stood there, holding the sagging cloak.

"Robin, you fool," she cried, "go!" She flung herself at Will, knowing that while she had little chance of stopping him by force, she might befuddle him enough that Robin could escape. She slammed against him, causing nary a jolt to his stance, but knocking the breath from her lungs and acquiring the sharp dig of a wayward elbow. His hands automatically closed around her arms, steadying her.

"Blast," Robin said lightly, indeed slipping past her toward the door, " 'tis a hardship to leave that sight. But I am not the fool you think I am, Nottingham. Until the morrow, sweeting," he said to Marian—and he was gone.

Will fairly shoved Marian away from him, but to her vast relief, he did not rush out the door after the outlaw. She would have launched herself at him if he had, little good though that would do.

"I should have sent you with him," he said, looking down at her with a very different expression. "Marian, for the rood's sake, cover yourself." This time the command sounded more like a plea than an order.

Realizing she was not only breathing heavily but very naked, Marian backed away from Will and reached for a fur from the bed to gather it up in front of her. The fox felt silky and luxurious against her bare skin.

"Mayhap he is right. Though he is an outlaw, you would be out of the prince's reach if you hid with them in the forest," Will said in the softest voice she'd heard him use.

And then, without another word, he turned and strode out. "Lay the bolt," he ordered, pausing in the antechamber, then exited into the passage.

Marian moved to comply, peeking out after him to ensure that Robin had gone, and that Will was not giving chase. The hall was empty but for the figure of a half-clothed Nottingham, striding smoothly away without a backward look.

She bolted the door, once again annoyed by the absence of her maid, and retired to the inner chamber.

Will's words gave her pause. She could go with Robin. Stay with him, be with him. They would likely become lovers . . . and she would leave behind the threat of the prince.

But Will would come after them, even more fiercely than before. He had the right of it: the gentry would be incensed by the abduction of a noblewoman by the bandits. And if she admitted her desire to be with Robin, not only would she then be regarded as an outlaw and thus subject to the reach of the law . . . but she would no longer be in Ludlow, able to spy on John for the queen, and on Will, for Robin himself.

Not that, Marian admitted, she'd yet found anything of import to tell the queen. Or to help Robin. When in John's presence, she'd spent more time in a state of unease or discomfiting arousal than anything else.

Nay, much as she might wish to be with Robin, she could not go. She must stay in the keep, within reach of the grasp of the prince.

And Will.

CHAPTER 9

*A*lys of Wentworth pulled the cloak's hood up and over her head, hurrying through the hall. Empty of diners and drinkers, the vast room offered shelter to the half dozen hounds twitching and groaning by the fireplaces near the dozing serf boys charged with keeping the blazes going. A man-at-arms well beyond his cups slumped in one corner, and another, propped up on the trestle table by naught but his nose, snored loudly.

Long past vespers, hours since the evening meal had finished, the night was fading toward dawn. It had been a tiring day, and Alys was quite ready for her bed.

It had begun with the wild hunt, and all the gossip of Robin Hood . . . and then for her to have been so unfortunate as to fall into the clutches of his men! Of all the things to have happened when Sandy threw a shoe. And then for the blackhearted rogue to steal a kiss from her . . . but most of all, to believe she might actually welcome it!

She pursed her lips as her fury at Robin Hood and his silly games rose anew. A bandit with a love for himself so great that it threatened to explode his head! So foolish of him to have crept into the keep last night. Why would he travel into the nest of the very hawk that wished to devour him?

'Twas simple. . . . He believed he would not be caught! Well, he would have a fine surprise if he ever accosted her in the keep. Joanna of Wardhamshire might giggle and blush at his kisses, but Alys had no misconceptions. The man was an outlaw, and he must be made to face the laws of the land.

As had happened throughout the day since her escape from Robin Hood, Alys felt the anger boiling inside her. A slick, cowardly bandit slipping through the night, stealing from good people—why, her friend Lady Marian had nearly lost her belongings to the outlaws! And then to make light of it by—

A faint noise from the shadows startled her. She paused, heart thumping, and looked . . . but saw nothing. Raising her chin at her foolishness, Alys continued on along the rear passageway of the keep toward the staircase that led to the second floor.

She had just turned the corner and seen the steps at the far end of the passage when she noticed a tall figure walking toward her.

The yellow light of a wall sconce cast illumination over his face and—saints! bare torso!—and Alys recognized him immediately. Nottingham.

He didn't appear to see her moving swiftly through the shadows, for his head was bowed, as it had been earlier today when she'd found him near the same place. At that time, he'd seemed ill and out of sorts, very troubled . . . and to see such a handsome, powerful man so vulnerable had tugged at her healer's heart. Not to mention her womanly desires.

Now he merely paused at one of the window slits and looked out into the night.

She drew near, her heart thumping and curiosity dampening her palms. He was so very large and dark, with an aura of annoyance that most often put people off . . . yet there was something about him that caught deeply at her. And she had seen the expression on his face earlier today; he'd looked disgusted, ill, and yet resigned. Now he stood, staring into the dark, an image of tension and frustration.

As she approached, Alys tried to think of what she might say to him, to ease whatever it was that ailed the man . . . but before she could, he looked up and saw her.

"Lady Alys," he said, turning from the window. "What do you about this time of night?" His voice cut sharply, coldly into the silence, and if she had not had a grandfather with much the same temperament, she might have been frightened by his discourtesy. As it was, she felt a shiver at his unfeeling expression. He was a man one did not wish to anger.

"Good morrow, my lord," she said, moving closer. "I seek my bed at last, though the sun is nigh ready to rise."

" 'Tis not safe for a lady to be out alone in the night, even in the castle." He stepped toward her, and for a moment her lungs seemed not to work. He was so large, and dark, and forbidding . . . and even more so with naught to cover his chest and belly. He was broad and haired and scarred . . . very daunting. He made no move to cover himself, nor did he seem to care that she saw him in such a state.

She swallowed and pulled her eyes away from his imposing chest . . . and found her gaze snagged by cold eyes. "I had my maid with me, but I allowed her to stay behind. Her sister lives here in Ludlow—a freewoman, married to Frederick the fishmonger—and she had taken ill. Rose—my maid—knows of my skill with healing, and she begged that I might assist her." She moistened her lips, aware that her voice trembled a bit.

"And so you came from your soft warm bed to help your maid's sister." His words came out more quietly, but only a bit. Frustration and impatience colored their tone much more strongly than empathy.

Alys shrugged. "I have oft been called from my bed at Wentworth for the same purpose. 'Tis nothing new." She looked boldly up at him. "I am a healer, my lord. Will you not tell me what ails you?"

At this proximity, despite the wavering torchlight, she could see the lines etched on his face, the weariness in his eyes. A brittleness too, which she feared might crack.

"There is naught that ails me, Lady Alys," he replied flatly.

She reached for him, touching his warm arm. "I would that you trusted me enough. If you are ill, you know where to find me. I . . ." She felt a rising flush warm her face, but she continued. "I would have a care for you if you wish." She drew in a deep breath. "I should very much . . . like to."

"A care for me?" Incredulity laced his voice. "Do not be a fool, Lady Alys. There are others for whom you should cast your heart in the stead of my black one. I am fit for no lady."

She'd expected nothing less from such a man, and would have spoken again, but he drew aside, turning his face away. "Take yourself to bed, Lady Alys."

Then, as if gaining control of some runaway emotion, a breath later he added, "If you have need of going to the village again at night, send for me and I will find a man to accompany you. 'Tis foolish of you to take such a chance. This is not Wentworth, and you are not the lady of this manor. And now . . . I will escort you to your chamber to ensure your safety."

She shook her head. "Nay. There is no need. I can see the steps from here, and there is no one about . . . for you have just come from above, is that not so?"

Why that simple question should turn his expression even blacker, she did not know. But she did step back at the look in his eyes, heart thumping.

He said nothing, however, and turned away. "I will escort you to your chamber, Lady Alys." And with that, their discussion seemed to be at an end.

But just as he gestured for her to accompany him—and she hesitated at touching his bare arm, so close to such a naked chest—there was a loud shout from the direction of the hall. Nottingham stiffened and listened, and when there was a similarly violent response, he cursed under his breath.

"I must investigate," he said. "Yet I am loath to leave you to make your way alone."

"I am in no danger of losing my way here, Sir William. As I have said, I can see the steps from here, and you forget—I have also made my way from the village across the bailey and through the hall . . . all without incident. I am certain I shall find my way without mishap."

A nasty crash from the hall pulled his attention from her, causing his lips to flatten even farther. "Very well, then. But make haste." And with that, he turned and hurried off toward the hall.

Alys could not help but watch, noticing how gracefully and smoothly he moved, despite the bulk of his body. A man that large and powerful should not have the grace of a cat . . . yet he did.

She turned and began to make her way toward the stairwell, the noise of whatever altercation had begun in the hall echoing behind her. A mere three steps away from her climb, Alys felt something behind her.

She spun, heart pounding, just in time to see a figure emerge from the shadows.

"Lady Alys," said Robin Hood, moving toward her. "What a delightful surprise." His smile was charming and a bit self-deprecating, as if he was encouraging her to join him in a bit of humor—but uncertain if she would. And mayhap . . . mayhap that grin was a bit forced. "I hope I do not interrupt your tête-à-tête."

He was comely to look at; that she could not deny. Though the light was dim, she remembered his sparkling blue eyes from earlier, and she could even see a hint of that gleam now. Though half his face was obscured by his beard and mustache, she could make out the strong lines of his jaw and sculpted cheekbones, and his elegant brows arched beneath the thick fringe of his dark blond hair.

"What are you doing here?" She stepped back, yet only a bit. Fascination and exasperation at the man's foolish boldness kept her steady. She had no fear of him, of course. Naught but abhorrence for his imprudent ways. "And unless you caused the disturbance in the hall, the interruption was none of your doing."

To her surprise, Robin smiled ruefully. "Alas, I am discovered. I have disrupted my lady about her business of wooing the cold, flat-eyed Sheriff of Nottingham."

It took her a moment to comprehend, but then she did. "I did hear you earlier, then. I thought I felt as if someone followed me. You sneaked back and caused some fight in the hall in order to draw him away, did you not? You are indeed a sneaky fiend!"

She would have pushed past him, but he stepped forward and blocked her way.

"My lady, I could not resist. 'Twas fairly painful for me to witness your attempt to seduce the man."

Alys felt a flush begin to creep over her throat. Horrid of him to have seen Nottingham's flat-out rejection. "You are beyond foolish to come inside his stronghold yet again when he hunts you so fiercely."

He shifted toward her, crowding her toward a shadowy alcove. He smelled fresh and woodsy, like crushed pine needles. "I had business to attend herein."

"Someone to rob?" She became aware of the shift of darkness over her face, enveloping her person as he edged closer. The stone wall brushed her hand and she realized that her heart had begun to pump a bit faster.

"Nay," Robin replied. "But I would find it no hardship to steal a kiss from a lovely lady."

"Ah . . . so if your business was not to rob a slumbering rich lord, it must have been to visit some woman who sighs at the mere mention of your name . . . and who sleeps with your green ribbon favor."

"I don't believe they sleep with my green ribbon favor," he said, the corners of his eyes crinkling and his dimples showing beneath the beard, "but mayhap I ought to make such a suggestion. Alas, I cannot be everywhere at once."

"And so your head grows the larger! Soon even the forest will not be vast enough to accommodate it," she said, rolling her eyes in disgust. "I cannot fathom that the ladies swoon and gasp when they see you."

"Do I sense a bit of envy that you've not received a pretty green ribbon, Lady Alys? Do not be ashamed to admit it." He leaned closer. "For you are speaking to the one who can correct that situation."

'Twas all she could do not to laugh in his face . . . but the light in his eyes, a lingering intensity there, kept her from more than a scoff. "I have plenty of ribbons, Robin Hood, and several of them are green. I am in no need of yet another frill."

"Come now, Lady Alys. A green ribbon would look very lovely twined in your honey gold hair," he murmured. His eyelids had become heavy and he was looking at her in such a way as to make the insides of her belly flutter.

'Twas a feeling she did not welcome in the least.

"Robin Hood, I do not wish to have anything from you . . . least of which a green ribbon, which was most likely stolen from some other lady," she said, the wall very close behind her now, and the warmth of his person seeping into her awareness. "Did I not tell you most clearly today that should I be accosted by you, I should not hesitate to raise the alarm?"

"Aye, that you did." And still he did not release his gaze . . . which had somehow become fastened upon her lips.

"And yet you string my patience taut."

He gave a low little chuckle. "My lady Alys, I am most accustomed to a woman speaking what she *believes* is on her mind . . . but more oft than not, I find that what she speaks is not what she truly means."

"And so now, sirrah, you accuse me of not knowing my own mind?" she replied, raising her hands to push at his chest.

Not as tall as the forbidding sheriff, nor as powerfully built, he was nevertheless muscular and graceful. Lean and strong, and more wickedly handsome than she would willingly admit. And he did not make the slightest shift when she shoved at him.

"But 'tis quite obvious, Lady Alys . . . for if you'd truly intended to cry ware, you would have done so long before now." His grin was wide and knowing and he leaned in.

Infuriated—for he was partially correct, curse the man—Alys drew in her breath to shriek to high heaven.

The scream was forever caught in her mouth, for he timed his assault perfectly and covered her lips at that moment.

This kiss was violently different from the one they'd shared in his treetop hideaway; his lips were much more demanding, much less tentative and coaxing. He ate at her, his tongue thrusting into her mouth as if he'd die if he did not kiss her . . . and she found herself closing her eyes, opening her mouth to take him in farther.

His hands, fingers trembling, shoved into her hair, pulling it free from the braids that had long since loosened, and his hips pressed her against the cold, damp wall. Alys found that her fingers had curled into his plain-cloth tunic; instead of pushing him away, as she'd attempted a moment ago, she drew him closer. She didn't know why. She didn't care.

She loved the long, strong lines of his body, the warmth of him pressing her against the wall as her hands moved over the planes of his chest, feeling the swell of muscle there, as she tasted the heat of his mouth. Her knees began to loosen, and she felt herself falling. . . .

When she fully realized what she was doing, that she'd become weak-kneed and mind-boggled, she yanked her face away from his. Breathing heavily, she opened her mouth and screamed.

Robin reeled away from her, his eyes wide and shocked as she continued to cry warning at the top of her lungs.

"Foolish woman!" he said, every trace of good humor gone. His eyes flashed sparks instead of charm. "Do you want me killed?"

"Foolish man," she gasped, still out of breath. "Did you not listen when I warned you thus? I am no simple and easy woman, Robin Hood. I will not be wooed by falsities and a flattering tongue."

"Viper!" he accused, and as they heard the pounding of footsteps coming toward them, he disappeared into the shadows.

"I do not care for your green ribbons!" she hissed after him, and leaned against the wall, pressing her hands against her lips. Trembling.

She knew that she would lie to the man now coming to her rescue. Just as the Sheriff of Nottingham had lied to her earlier.

The cloak fell away, leaving Marian chilled and warm at the same time . . . an odd sensation. Her hair, braided and coiled heavily around her head, left her fully exposed. Her nipples puckered tightly, her skin heated from the fire, yet pebbled where the warmth could not reach. Her body stood, stretched, pale and creamy, dusted with brushstrokes of rich, golden freckles. The dance of flames warmed every swell and hollow.

Robin covered her mouth with smiling lips, laughing with great humor as they curved over hers . . . his hands sliding over her, slender and elegant, drawing her close to his warm, lean body . . . and she was falling, falling. . . .

The bed caught her, the slick, smooth furs embraced her . . . and he landed next to her, his hands sliding between her legs, his fingers finding her hard little pearl, covering it, teasing . . . and when she rolled over, there was Will, dark and heavy, on the other side. His eyes, shadowed and flat, filled her vision as he came closer, bending to her. His mouth covered hers, masking her soft little moan as Robin knelt before her, his fingers warm on her hips.

Hands all over her ... too many, sliding, caressing, cupping ... large, dark ones on her white breasts, lifting, stroking ... a swarthy face bending to cover her lips again, blocking her view as someone drew her knees wide. The brush of his silky hair over her legs, on the sides of her thighs as he bent there ... teasing, taunting, as she lifted and rocked her hips, desperately seeking completion, her mouth filled with a slick hot tongue, devoured by hungry lips.

Her quim opened, ready, hot, and wet ... then a dark head at her breast, sucking long, hard ... pulling away and then slipping a strong tongue around and over the tip of her nipple so that she gasped and arched and writhed.

But strong hands held her hips, her knees wide ... elegant hands, and she could see the top of a blond head bending between her legs ... the swipe of a tongue that sent her twisting and careening under the large dark hands that held her shoulders, pinning her to the bed. She couldn't see. . . . She could only feel the delicious assault on her body ... sleek, slick strokes at her mouth, at her quim. . . .

She cried out, restless; she lifted and twitched and begged ... and suddenly there was John, his dark face rapt and intent ... and she felt the stone wall behind her, scraping rough over her back and buttocks as she struggled to free herself from the manacles.

Her wrists and hands were fixed and John moved closer, kneeling at her feet, his fingers sliding in and around her swollen quim, his fingers pressing into the soft flesh of her thighs ... his lips thick and moist and red, moving forward to cover her mound, his tongue sliding strong and delving deep as she looked around and saw Robin, and Will ... watching.

... Watching with avid eyes, full lips, as John licked and

sucked on her, forcing her into the rough masonry, scraping her skin as she struggled to get free . . . to find release as the prince teased her, pushing her to the edge and then stepping away to leer and laugh at her as she writhed and moaned, pleading for more.

And then he fell on her again, driving his tongue deep into her until she cried out, begged . . . and then he stood to cup her breasts and torture them, with long dragging pulls, sucking her nipples hard and sending painful whorls of pleasure as his fingers slipped inside her.

And then they were gone . . . all of them. 'Twas only darkness and a cold room, and she hung helplessly from the wall, the manacles heavy and tight on her wrists, her ankles . . . her pip swollen and needy, her body humming and desperate, her breasts sore and tight and heavy. . . .

The insistent knocking on her chamber door drew Marian from the depths of her dream.

"My lady, can you be awake?"

Groggy. Heart pounding.

Marian forced her eyes open, banishing the images. She rolled to the side, aware that though the dream had gone, she still throbbed between her legs as if John and Robin and Will truly had been there, their lips and hands on her.

"Ethelberga!" she said crossly. "Enter."

The maid came in and Marian blinked, trying to dispel the remnants of the arousing, disturbing dream.

"Where did you go last night?" She sat up, becoming aware that the sun was high enough to indicate that she'd missed Mass. And she smelled a tinge of smoke in the air.

"I am very sorry, my lady," Ethelberga said, and at that moment, Marian saw through the doorway that Lady Joanna waited in the antechamber. "I received your message to await you in the hall, but you did not come, and it became very late and at last I returned to here. When I did, I found you already returned and well asleep."

Marian had opened her mouth to flay her maid for her irresponsibility, but now she closed it. Robin. It had to have been Robin who had sent Ethelberga away so that he could wait for her within. Clever, but he was still a fool . . . he who had not expected Nottingham to be with her upon her return.

What had he thought would transpire, meeting her privately in her chamber?

The insistent throbbing between her legs, the memory of his hand sliding expertly there as he pressed her against the tree . . . she had no reason to wonder what he had hoped.

When her mistress didn't speak, Ethelberga took that as permission to continue. "My lady, I only woke you because Lady Joanna be without."

"I can see that," Marian replied a bit tartly. Still shaky and trembling from a dream that had felt much too real, she knew nevertheless that now was the time to rise. Glancing out the window slit, she saw that something seemed to be burning beyond the keep's walls, which explained the strong smell of smoke. "Joanna, I shall be only a moment."

"Hurry, Marian," Joanna said, her voice urgent. "Do you make haste—we must go see. They say he is burning the village!"

"Who?" Marian gestured sharply to Ethelberga, who closed the door a bit and hurried into the room to dig through her trunks for a bliaud and an overgown—a task that should already have been done. Pressing her lips together in annoyance, Marian slid from the bed, acutely aware of the pressure of her legs over her swollen quim.

"The sheriff! They say he is burning the village. I cannot believe it!"

Marian stilled, absorbing her words. Will was burning the village? No. He couldn't. Why?

A blast of disappointment and then anger washed over her—and then she wondered why she should be so shocked and appalled. She knew what he was, whom he was loyal to. Why would she expect anything different?

Moments later the two women hurried out into the bailey, where a groom had their saddled horses waiting. A black billow of smoke curled from Ludlow Village beyond the bailey's gate, giving credence to the rumor that the blaze was no small incident.

Marian and Joanna rode quickly through the throngs of people, the villeins shuffling away from their path.

As they approached the crowd that had gathered along the main thoroughfare of the village, the first thing Marian saw was Will, tall and imposing in his saddle, towering over everyone about him. He watched the proceedings impassively, holding the reins easily in his lap as the black curls of smoke filtered around him.

He appeared powerful and implacable, just as he always did. But Marian was struck by the memory of how he'd looked last night . . . that moment of vulnerability or . . . something . . . when she'd lifted their joined hands. That moment of tangled gazes, the remorse and shame and anguish she saw there . . . it seemed at such great odds with this unfeeling, emotionless . . . *cruel* . . . man.

Villagers had gathered and watched with dumbstruck faces streaked with dirt and smoke. What had been three houses along the main road roared with flames, the heat so fierce that the thick crowd was forced to stand away from the hot, wavering air.

"And the cooper's house as well," Will ordered, lifting an imperious hand to point at a fourth structure, which had a sagging roof and wide cracks between the boards. A mean hovel, barely inhabitable. Marian had noticed it the day before, as they rode out for the hunt.

"But they are so poor," she cried to Joanna. All soft thoughts about Will had evaporated. Now she knew who he was. "And he takes away what little they have! A blackhearted man."

Her companion appeared fascinated, rather than revolted. "He is a frightening man, but methinks he does what must be done to keep the villagers under control. He has instilled fear in their hearts, and they dare not naysay him. 'Tis best that they are cowed and do not seek to rise above their stations. They do not wish to pay the taxes that are due, and 'tis incumbent upon the sheriff to support the tax collector."

"But see how poor they are! One cannot squeeze water from a dry rag no matter how hard one twists it!" As her father's only heir and a landowner herself, through her husband, Marian knew of the gentle balance between managing the land and those who worked it, culling what it could yield without destroying those who would reap the harvest.

Galvanized and infuriated, Marian urged her horse forward, passing through the crowd and then the cluster of men-at-arms who stood nearby to assist the sheriff.

"Will!" she cried, urging her horse up next to him. "What are you about?"

He turned at her voice, and from the great height of his destrier glowered down at her. "This is naught of your concern, Lady Marian. Begone with you."

"But, Will, how can you—"

His cold face turned even harsher. "Take yourself off or I shall have you taken off." He turned away, his unshaven jaw shifting. He must have risen early this morrow to have accomplished this task so quickly. Had he slept at all?

Marian did not move at first, so stunned was she by the destruction she was witnessing and the cruel expression on his face. The sheriff was bound to uphold justice, and to care for the people of his shire by enforcing the law and protecting them. Not by destroying their homes and livelihood when they could no longer pay their due.

She reached for him, determined to have his attention. But when she leaned across to accost him, he merely pulled his arm away as though she meant to give him the plague.

"Gavin, Hugh," Will shouted to his men-at-arms without looking away from the blaze in front of them, "see that Lady Marian is returned to the keep. Immediately."

She didn't wait for the two soldiers to move toward her. Marian wheeled her palfrey about and started away, sick at heart.

And then she realized what she must do.

CHAPTER 10

The forest grew thick and dark, allowing just a dappling of light over the bushes and leaves. Only a few patches of straggly grass and shade-loving bushes had the tenacity to rise from beneath the thick covering of pine needles and rotted leaves.

Far from Ludlow, whose tallest tower could be glimpsed through a thin segment of trees, the forest was quiet and empty. The occasional call of a thrush or grackle or the rustle of a four-footed creature stirred the silence. A faint hint of smoke from Will's fire wafted through the air, mixing with the rich, loamy scent of the forest.

Marian rode fearlessly through the wood, head high and shoulders straight . . . and eyes lifted to scour the high branches of the trees. Well behind, but near enough to come to her aid should the need arise, followed her master-at-arms, Bruse, and two of his men.

Despite Robin Hood's presence in the forest and the fact that Will had imprisoned some of the outlaws that attacked her, Marian knew better than to ride out alone. Bruse and the other two men had escorted her on her journey to Ludlow and indeed had been loyal to her since she was but a babe. She knew they would have their tongues cut out before they would wag them in news to others about her business.

Thus, secure that no harm would befall her, yet obviously available for a clandestine meeting . . . should that opportunity arise . . . Marian could enjoy the cool silence of the shadows. It wasn't often that she rode without purpose, and had the opportunity to admire the variety of nature. And though she had a reason for coming out today, she knew it could be some time before Robin found her.

For she was certain he would.

And she was not disappointed.

The filtering sun had not shifted more than a half candle's mark, rising to its highest point in the sky, when something streaked past her head. It slammed into the nearest tree trunk, the arrow's feathers quivering as it settled into place.

Marian smiled to herself, and rode toward the arrow, plucking it from the tree. A serviceable weapon, she thought, smoothing the fluff of goose feathers so that they lay flat. But a trifle crooked in the making, and enough so that the arrow would not fly true. Nevertheless, she slipped it into her quiver and continued to ride along.

Moments later, another arrow whizzed past her, lodging in a tree beyond and to the left, and she veered her palfrey in that direction. Retrieving the bolt, she continued along until the next one guided her path in a slightly different direction.

Each arrow she pulled from the tree and added to her own

quiver, knowing that soon she would see Robin. Her heart beat faster in anticipation, and her palms became a bit damp.

After a short time following Robin's path, she paused and peered back into the forest.

Bruse had ridden closer, and she could see him through the trees. She gestured for him to remain where he was. Aware that Robin was near, she knew she would be safe.

Indeed, it was only moments later that another arrow slammed into the tree near the knees of her horse, necessitating that Marian dismount in order to retrieve the weapon. Glancing up and about, she slid down, holding the reins, and pulled the bolt from its spot in the bark.

As she turned back, arrow in hand, a pair of feet landed silently next to her. The cushion of pine needles covered all but the slightest rustle from his legs as they passed by.

"I do believe you've dropped something," Marian said, offering the arrow to Robin.

His eyes danced, matching her own mischievous smile, and he reached . . . not for the arrow, but for her arm. "I don't *drop* arrows," he said, pulling her close. "An archer with my skill aims true at all times." His eyes glinted with an entirely different meaning.

Still holding the arrow, she wrapped her arms around his waist. "That may be the case," she replied, looking up at him, "but 'tis a shame your weapons are of such inferior quality."

"Inferior?" His brows knit together. Then he laughed, his humor echoing through the forest. "Do you still swear by the bolts made by the mad blind man at Mead's Vale?"

"He is not mad . . . any more than you, for being so foolish as to wander through the keep at night. And with his skill in casting the heads and trimming the feathers, Tesh creates arrows that fly faster and farther than any others."

"I would match my skill against the madman's arrows any day," Robin said. "And would come forth the winner."

"I should be pleased to accept your challenge," Marian said, shifting her shoulder so that her arrows shifted meaningfully in their quiver.

Robin's grin grew wider. "Ah, so you are still trifling with the longbow, my lady? I do hope you've acquired a greater skill than what you had at Mead's Vale. If I recall correctly, your target then was more like to be the ground or the high branches of a tree rather than the painted circle."

Marian felt a little rise of temper. "Trifling? I would not say my skill with the bow is a trifle, Robin, and I should be quite pleased to demonstrate how well it shows with Tesh's arrows. A combination I trow you shall not beat."

He seemed to realize he'd overstepped, and pulled her hips close to his, where she could feel the evidence that his mind was on other things. "But of course, Marian, it would be an honor to match longbows with you. Yet . . . I had rather hoped you'd come searching for me for a reason other than to decry my arrows and skill."

Without waiting for her response, he bent his face to hers. At first, she felt petulant, and nearly turned her face away. Trifling with a bow? He knew not whereof he spoke . . . and even when they were younger, she'd shown more than a passing skill.

Mayhap he merely teased . . . but she'd seen no humor in his eyes to indicate that was the case.

But then she thought no longer . . . for his lips had covered hers, and she did not turn away, instead accepting the kiss as a peace offering. And something more.

An edge of desperation colored his kiss, as though he'd been waiting for this and needed it. His mouth was harsh, devouring hers, covering her lips and scoring the sides of her mouth with his teeth. Tight arms crushed her against him, compressing her lungs so that she found it difficult to breathe, and she had to pull her face away to gasp for air.

Looking up, she realized he wasn't as tall and forbidding as the darker Will was, and that should have made her feel more comfortable. Softer. More willing to melt against him, to arch into the hand that had moved to cup her breast. Robin's mouth was supple and more finely drawn, elegant, where Will had not a bit of elegance about him . . . no elegance, but something else.

A rough, deep sensuality. Power. An underlying fury.

And ruthlessness. The scent of smoke wafted anew to her nose, reminding her of the scene she'd left behind in the village. She must not forget the ruthlessness.

She pushed all thoughts of Will from her mind and smoothed her hands up and over Robin's chest to cup his shoulders. His fingers had curved around her breasts, thumbs finding the tightening nipples beneath two layers of cloth, and he smiled down at her.

"My lovely Marian," he said, groping lower to raise her skirts. "You'd not lure me in with lovely kisses and then cry ware down upon me, would you?"

"Nay, of course not, Robin," she murmured, wondering why he should say such a thing. She'd not betrayed him. The cool forest breeze brushed her exposed legs as his hands busily moved her hems higher.

"I did not think you would be such a viper," he muttered, his mouth sliding along her jaw.

Fully aware that the last two times she and Robin had embraced in the woods, Will had come upon them, she pushed him back when he would have buried his face in her neck again. "I . . . Robin," she murmured, wishing they were somewhere she wouldn't feel so exposed. After all, Bruse and his men were nearby. "I do wish to speak with you."

He stepped back and looked down at her, a strangely intense gleam in his eyes. "Ah," he said, a full-blown grin spreading beneath his beard. "Of course you do. Out of earshot . . . and sight," he said, his eyes dancing again, "of your trusty men. I should be happy to oblige, my lady."

" 'Tis not my men who worry me," Marian said, stepping away from his grip. " 'Tis the sheriff." She glanced beyond his shoulder, half-expecting her words to cause the large dark horse and its rider to materialize. What would he think if he found her with her skirts up around her hips here in the forest, after moaning and gasping beneath his hands last evening?

But that was different. She hadn't *wanted* to be in John's chambers . . . and she had purposely sought Robin here in the forest.

Although she *had* wanted Will's hands on her.

Marian pushed that thought away. She'd not been thinking clearly.

"Ah, aye, the sheriff. That bastion of justice, a man of ice whose demeanor must be melted by the soft hand of a woman."

The steely glint in his eyes didn't match the light, airy words, and caused Marian to wonder if he was jealous of Will.

The idea pleased her more than a little—after all, she was a woman, and she found Robin Hood so charming and handsome—but she replied, "Nay, Robin, do you not fear that I am setting about to soften the heart of that blackguard! For that is the reason I came to look for you. Have you not heard what he's done in Ludlow Village?"

"Nay, I have not. What is it today? The hanging of a poacher? The stripping and whipping of a cooper who makes leaky barrels?"

"Robin, he is burning half the village! He stands and orders the buildings to be set afire as the villagers watch. They are the meanest of hovels, but all they have, and he has destroyed their homes."

"Ah, aye, the fire. Aye, 'tis a brutal thing for the sheriff to do," he added, glancing off toward the spiral of smoke. "But the villeins will soon rebuild, I trow."

Was this sort of destruction so common that he was hardened against it? "A man such as that," Marian said, all those odd liquid thoughts of Will disintegrating, "cannot be softened. And does not wish to be."

"Aye, and I am sure that the tale will be good gossip for you and your lady friends," Robin said. "Joanna and Pauletta and Catherine, along with the lovely Marian . . . and who is the child? The blond girl with the blue eyes? The very young one?"

"Alys," Marian replied, looking at him, struck by the brittleness in his voice.

How difficult it must be to be thought a villain when one was really a hero. Her heart swelled with pride and sympathy for him. Dear Robin . . . she must find a way to help him.

"Ah, aye . . . Alys. And so all of you ladies will wag your tongues and discuss how cruel and blackhearted the sheriff is, aye? For, of course, he is. And he will keep you busy with your gossip."

"Aye, mayhap," she said. "But, Robin, I came to ask you for help. For those people. Can you help them?"

"But of course I shall," Robin said airily. "That is what Robin of the Hood and his band of outlaws do, is it not? We are not the sly, greedy men some think us."

Marian realized that as they conversed, he'd begun to lead her gently after him, deeper into the dark part of the wood. "Are you taking me somewhere safe . . . where we can talk freely?"

He flashed a great smile at her. "Indeed. If that is what you wish to do. Talk. But I thought mayhap there are other ways we might find to occupy our time."

A little wave of surprise fluttered in her belly and she matched his smile. How wonderful it would be to have his elegant hands, his long slender fingers, on her bare skin—in the stead of heavy ones, groping and grabbing all the while she wished to be anywhere but there. And to have it without the furtiveness, the quick risk of discovery, while in the glades of the forest. To have the time for bodies to slide against each other, skin to skin. To taste and touch and stroke.

The memory of John forcing her fingers around his turgid cock, sliding them back and forth while he squeezed and pinched her breast, breathing heavily and roughly into her ear, caused an unpleasant rush to pass over her. Her stomach pitched with nausea.

She did not wish to return to the keep, to be forced back into that Court of Pleasure, waiting and wondering whether this would be the night that John had his way.

Or Will.

A flash of memory had her heart thumping hard and fast . . . that moment in her chamber when she'd raised their joined hands to his nose and seen the blatant desire burning in his eyes. When his nostrils had widened and his mouth tightened and for a moment she thought he might tear off the simple cloak she wore . . . and take her then and there.

Her throat had dried and she could not ignore the memory of his dark hands covering her white skin, there in the shadows of the bed-curtains . . . the way she curved and arched against him, trembling as she cried out her release. Her face felt warm, her quim full and slick, as she remembered. . . .

Then all those thoughts were driven from her mind when Robin pulled her beyond a flush of bushes into the depths of a dark cave. She realized they were at the base of a small hill, and the cave entrance was well hidden from even a sharp-eyed passerby.

"Is this one of your hideaways?" she asked, moving closer to him in the darkness. In the event that it was not, she didn't wish to be surprised by a flock of bats—or a wild cat—swarming out.

"It is indeed," he said, that smile back and more visible as he lit a torch. "And there is no one about, no one to disturb us here, my lady."

He gestured into the darkness of the cave, pulling her with him. She saw that it was indeed a hideaway, for deep within, concealed behind a cluster of rocks, several pallets were arranged on the ground. The boulders had been cunningly arranged to appear to be a wall, but instead they provided a generous hiding place.

And privacy.

Marian allowed Robin to draw her deeper into the cave, the small torch casting tiny, flickering shadows. He set fire to a small pile of kindling in the corner, and she saw that there must be a hole somewhere in the high ceiling, because the smoke rose and left the space without choking them.

Despite the fire, inside the hideaway was cool and dark, and dampness seeped into her skin immediately. But she was with

Robin . . . at last, Robin . . . and when he turned her to face him, and pressed her up against the rough, damp cavern wall, she allowed her quiver and bow to slide from her shoulder and gently down onto the floor.

He wasted no time, for he'd barely covered her mouth with his, in that insistent, reckless manner, when his hands tugged at her woven leather girdle, untying it with surprising ease. She pulled at his tunic, made of coarse material that would scratch her skin, yanking it up and over his torso.

His lips moved against her forehead, and she thought she heard him begging.

Please.

As the fire crackled to life, casting more warmth, more soft light, they undressed, leaving a pile of clothing near one of the pallets. Robin saved Marian's veil for the last, and he tore it from her head, then shoved his fingers roughly into her braids, loosening Ethelberga's handiwork only a bit before drawing her down onto the pallet with him.

The soft slide of furs beneath her bare skin awakened her, and Marian closed her eyes, lifting her arms for the warmth of his body. But it wasn't Robin who came to her then, whose face and broad shoulders filled her mind.

Marian's eyes flew open, her heart slamming in her chest. But it *was* Robin there, who bent toward her, whose hands smoothed along her torso as he lowered himself, settling partially over her. She kept her eyes open, even when he came so close that he filled her vision with a shadowy face.

His beard gently prickled her skin, not so smooth as the rabbit pelts beneath her, but more coarse, like the coat of a fox. Much better than when Harold had come to her, with short, rough whiskers.

Marian's feet were cold, for he'd drawn her hose down and away, leaving them bare. And the chill of the floor seeped through the thin pallet beneath her. Something hard was digging into the back of her shoulder, and she shifted to move away from the pointed rock.

Robin reached for her hand and brought it down between their bodies, lifting away from the breast he'd been sucking to press his lips to her fingers, then directing them down. She knew what he wanted, and eager to erase the memory of the prince's similar demands, she closed her fingers around a longer, more slender cock than the one they'd held last night. Yet it was just as warm and smooth, pulsing beneath her touch.

He released a long, pent-up sigh as she began to stroke, and lifted himself so that she could move more easily. Now she was even colder as his warm body shifted away, and Marian became aware of their legs twined together, his heavy, haired ones against her lighter, more slender ones.

"Marian," he sighed, "please."

He kissed and fondled her breast, lying next to her on his side as she reached between them, slowly lifting and lowering her hand over his cock. Strangely detached, she found herself watching his face as she varied her movements, slower . . . then more quickly . . . tightening and then loosening her grip. His mouth moved, making soundless pleas, and his eyes closed.

Fascinated by the concept of the power she literally held in her hand, Marian watched and listened, noticing his breathing, his eyes fluttering beneath half-closed lids. She felt him gather up next to her, the tension simmering beneath his skin . . . the burgeoning of his cock in her hand.

She felt a little drip at the tip and used her thumb to slide it around and over, using it to lubricate her way, and felt a little tingling rise inside herself. . . . He breathed faster, had released her breast, and now simply lay there, one hand resting on her hip, gripping with his fingers.

"Please," he said, sounding horribly desperate. "I need . . ."

Something shimmered up under his skin, beneath her fingers, and she moved faster, watching him, still strangely detached, her arm aching but her lips parted, matching him breath for breath, rising with him. . . . He stiffened, gave a low, sharp cry, and pulsed beneath her fingers, his seed spilling warm over her hand.

After a moment Marian released him, wiping his semen off herself on the edge of the fur pelts. As she did so, she realized that her own body was thrumming quietly.

Robin opened his eyes and, for an instant, she saw regret there. Then it evaporated, replaced by a hint of chagrin and a saucy smile. "Ah, Marian, you've no idea how badly I needed that," he said. "But, my lady, now that that little distraction's been taken care of, let me attend to other necessities."

His hand moved easily between her legs, finding the soft down of hair there and the sleekness of her full nether lips. She sighed, opening her legs a bit, allowing the slide of his fingers for a moment.

But then . . . she stopped him. She was too aware of her chilled body, and the fact that her men had been waiting a long time for her. "Nay, Robin," she said mildly, and pulled his hand away. "I have been away too long, and my men will come looking for me if I do not reappear soon. And aside of that," she said when he would have opened his mouth to protest, "I have taken a bit of a chill here in this damp cavern."

Easing away, she reached for her bliaud and began to search for the bottom to pull it on over her head. She was cold, and . . .

'twas God's truth, but she realized she did not desire those elegant hands on her after all.

"Marian," Robin said, his voice low. And hurt. "I am sorry. I did not mean for things to go . . . this way."

"Robin, 'tis of no account. I found it all quite . . . interesting." Marian spoke the unvarnished truth, for while her experiences of the previous nights had occurred in an environment of fear and shock, along with her own unbidden lust, this experience had been simply . . . enlightening. Fascinating. So fascinating and arousing, to watch a man taking his pleasure, so vulnerable and open during those moments. To see a strong, powerful man helpless and trembling because of the simple touch of a woman. Completely tantalizing.

Her mouth dried and she realized her breathing had risen. Marian swallowed hard and pushed away the thoughts teasing the edge of her consciousness—not of Robin, the man next to her, but images of Will's dark hair, shadowed eyes, and strong shoulders, corded with tension.

"And aside of that, Robin," she said, emerging from the other side of the bliaud's neckline, "I suggest that any future trysts you might arrange with a lady not take place in this damp, cold cave."

"Marian," Robin said, reaching for her hand and clasping it in his, "I do not have trysts with ladies. Truly. This is the first time I've brought one here—"

" 'Tis just as well, then, that I was the first, for I am not offended in the least. But heed my warning, Robin. A soft bed and a warm fire does much more to make a woman ready than wet stone and a bit of a fire."

"Marian!"

But she'd already pulled her hose on, and now stood with

her overtunic. "But you will promise me, will you not, that you will help those villagers?" A resurgence of horror over Will's actions eclipsed her remaining good humor. At least she was warm again, now that the overtunic settled in place.

"I have already vowed to do so," Robin said. He'd pulled on his own hose, moving slowly, as if reluctant to admit that the moment had passed. "Marian, truly, I—"

"Robin, please. I prefer your charming devil-may-care grin to this mealymouthed person you've become. You need feel no remorse over our tryst this afternoon. I feel none myself."

And she found to her surprise that it was true. Robin no longer held the fascination for her that he had when they were younger, and even as recently as yestereve. Instead of worrying about when she might be able to steal a kiss from the outlaw in the forest, she would focus on finding out what she could for the queen. And then she would leave Ludlow and go far away from Prince John. And the Sheriff of Nottinghamshire, whose image seemed to intrude on her thoughts much more often than such a cruel man's should.

"Stay with me, Marian," he said, suddenly grabbing her arm. "Don't go back there. Stay with me."

Temptation overcame her for a moment. To be away from John, from those lascivious fingers and burning eyes and the demands . . .

"I can't let you go back to him, Marian. I see the way he looks at you. Please."

She nodded, felt her belly sink as though it were stone. "But I must. I have a duty." She couldn't explain what the queen required of her even to Robin.

"Marian."

She was shaking her head, even as she reached for her girdle.

"Nay, Robin. I know what 'tis I must do. And know you this . . . I am under the protection of the queen. Her reach is far, and I will come to no real harm. But you must help the poor villagers, and I will do what I can inside Ludlow to keep you safe. How can I send a message if I hear of something that will help—or hurt—you?"

He didn't speak for a moment. Then with a great sigh, he pulled on his shirt and reached for his tunic. "There is a large oak, five paces from the great stone marker—do you know the one? At the fork between Revelstown and Carts Grange?"

"I'll find it," Marian told him.

He nodded. "Five paces north from that marker, there is a large oak. With a hollow on the south side, so high from the ground." He measured a hand at his waist. "Like this. You can place any messages for me there, but put them in deeply so they cannot easily be noticed." He frowned, then smiled. "I never thought that Friar Bellamy's sacrilegious teachings of a girl to scribe and cipher would come in so helpfully."

Marian nodded, but at that moment, her heart sank. Robin and Will had both known that she'd learned to read and write from an elderly monk.

Which meant that the sheriff could mention such a thing to the prince. And that she could not feign ignorance if she happened to see a message or paper that she should not.

Which meant that she must take even greater care than she'd thought.

"*Peste,*" Robin said as they emerged from the cave. He was looking up at the sun. "It's much later than I realized. I must go, Marian, and leave you to your men."

Marian raised her brows. "I need merely whistle for them. But, Robin, if you must rush off just now, 'tis fortunate then that we did not spend overmuch time inside." She gave him a meaningful smile, and was rewarded as a faint ruddiness flushed his cheeks.

"Aye, Marian, indeed. And I apologize once again for my . . . unchivalrous actions. I am sorely shamed that I took from you and did not give in return."

She shook her head, still smiling. Will had been correct: Robin was a rash, pillow-hearted man. Charming and amusing, but not as long on thinking ahead as she herself was. She raised her fingers and whistled for Bruse, and when she heard his response in the distance, she turned to Robin. "Go off with you. And if I have need of you or have news for you, I'll secret a message in the oak."

He bent forward and pressed a lingering kiss on her lips. "Until we can meet again, my lady."

She patted his cheek, her feelings for him having evolved from infatuation and fascination into more sisterly ones. All in the space of an afternoon. "Do not risk yourself to do so," she warned.

Moments after Robin disappeared into the trees above, Bruse and his men came trotting through the wood.

The smell of smoke had faded from the air during her time inside the cave, but as she rode back toward Ludlow, Marian could not help but think of Will. What had happened to him since their younger days that had turned him so cruel? He'd always been serious as a lad, but never mean-hearted. Was it simply being in the company of John? Or had something else occurred that had made a serious young man become unfeeling?

Certainly, most nobles didn't worry overmuch about the villeins who worked the land for them, as long as they paid their tithes and produced from the lord's land. But nor did a smart and cunning overlord seek to harm or ruin the human machine that generated his wealth. In fact, it was to the manor's benefit that the village be well maintained enough for the inhabitants to remain productive.

And they certainly couldn't be if their homes were razed to the ground, and they were overtaxed into poverty.

These thoughts occupied Marian's mind as they approached the bridge that led to Ludlow Village, the keep and its protective walls rising on a low hill behind it.

Though the acrid smoke had dissipated, Marian saw that the cluster of villagers had not. And as she drew nearer, she saw that they gathered in the center of the square. Immediately, she recognized Will sitting on a balcony that overlooked a platform, and that dais was the center of the crowd.

It took only that moment to understand what was happening: a young woman stood on the platform, her hands bound behind her back. Even from a distance, she could see that the young woman had been badly beaten. Her face was bruised, and dried blood on her matted hair bespoke of violent treatment. Her clothing was more than decent, indicating that she came from the family of a tradesman or shopkeeper. She was likely a freewoman, and not bound to the land here at Ludlow.

And she was about to be hung.

Marian looked up at Will, wondering what crime this woman had committed that justified her execution. As always, his face held an impassive expression. He sat back in his chair and watched as if unmoved by the event.

Hanging was a common enough activity, and regardless of where or who the criminal was, crowds turned out to watch. But there was a different feel to this crowd . . . an unsettled one . . . that made her want to stop and see more.

"Do you know about this?" Marian asked Bruse.

He nodded, his face grave. The man had reached past forty summers, yet his eyes still shone clear and gray. He was also one of the strongest men she knew, and amusing as well. But at this time there was no hint of humor in his expression. "See you that the woman has been beaten?"

"Well and truly, it appears," Marian said, wincing inwardly at the pain she must have endured. They'd stopped their horses near the edge of the crowd and were watching the proceedings.

"Aye, and 'twas from a man who wanted more than the cloth she weaves. He was her betrothed husband. He took her off behind the apple orchard and forced himself on her. Then he used his fists and a knife to mark her, and she managed to get his dagger. While trying to escape, she struck him in the neck."

"And so her crime is murder?" Marian asked.

"Aye. She'll hang for murder." Bruse looked at her, and she read the bleakness in his eyes. "If my daughter were set upon by such a man, I would cry delight if she sliced him open. This was not the first time he did this to her, and 'tis a fact that he planned to wed her and did not wish to wait for the priest's blessing. But the sheriff has no mercy and she's to be hung. He'll tolerate no breaking of the law in Nottinghamshire."

So in the stead of living a life of beatings and rapes, the woman defended herself and killed her assailant while doing so. The sheriff cried murder and would make her an example.

Marian felt ill when she realized the man who'd only last night made her quiver and cry with pleasure would raise his powerful hand and end the poor woman's life. If she'd thought he might have any mercy, her belief in that possibility was now gone.

Were these the sorts of things—destroying property, hanging

abused women—Will did every day? Was this how he went about his business?

Disgusted and horror-struck, she wheeled her horse and started back to the keep. She could not watch such a travesty, for she knew naught would veer William de Wendeval's black heart from its purpose.

The only thing that kept her from hating him more than Prince John at that moment was the fact that he conducted his foul affairs openly, rather than slyly behind closed doors. At the least he was honest about who he was.

CHAPTER 11

*W*ill watched Marian ride away, then turned back to the crowd.

The horde was angry, but of course it was a fury that simmered beneath the surface. Someday it might rise to the top and spill over into a force to be reckoned with. He didn't wish to be there when that time came, for 'twould be bloody and violent.

He already sensed a sort of independence growing among the barons, which had begun to churn mightily after Richard's appalling choice of Longchamp for justiciar and chancellor. John's love for England and lust for power had resulted in some good when he and the barons united to run the despicable man out of the country.

Having seen how easily the barons allied themselves when faced with such a vast problem, Will knew that the day they required their king and liege to give them more authority and equality was not so far off—mayhap even closer than Richard and his current heir, John, realized. 'Twas possible that one of them would need to negotiate with their vassals, and relinquish some of their absolute control, before the reign of the Plantagenets was over.

But here in Ludlow Village, the villeins and freemen had even less power and influence than their overlords, and had no choice but to accept the decisions inflicted upon them. Including this one, in which Will had chosen to obey the law down to the letters in which it was written.

Ella Weaver was a favorite in the village, and although their world was already one of simplicity and violence, the bruises on her face and the deep cuts on her body had horrified men and women alike. In truth, the sight of her battered face and what little he'd seen of her other wounds had moved him more than he would have liked to admit.

Yet, she had killed a man. And as per the law, a woman was beholden to any man who owned her—from her husband to her father, to her liege lord. This man had been her intended husband, and therefore had claim on her thus. She could be beaten, raped, or otherwise punished if necessary to keep her in line. Even if she was killed in the course of such discipline, the law hardly noticed.

And if she retaliated, she must be punished. It was the law.

And Will, above all, was beholden to the law.

He glanced up and noted how far across the sky the sun had moved, and gritted his teeth. He'd delayed as long as he could. If Robin Hood did not act soon, Ella Weaver would hang by her slender, bruised neck.

Taking his time, Will stood, clasping his hands behind his

back. He walked to the edge of the balcony and looked down over the crowd. Anger shone in the faces he saw there, overt in some, subtle in others. Once again, he had made an unpopular decision that blackened his character further in the eyes of the village and his peers.

And it mattered not. None of them had any choice in the matter. It was the way of the world. Duty. Honor. Fealty.

Just as he raised his hand to gesture for the hood to be placed over Ella's head, an arrow whizzed through the air. Just missing his fingers.

The crowd responded with gasps and undercurrents of joy, and Will turned to look, slowly lowering the hand that had nearly been skewered. By God's teeth, the outlaw was an insolent bastard. There were moments when he'd as lief toss Locksley in the gaol for his impertinence as much as for his crimes.

Or, better yet, strip down to naught but his braies and pummel the snot out of the man.

But now the buzz of the crowd had risen, and Will could do naught but watch as his men were held at arrow point as Robin Hood swooped in to save the day. Feeding the legend, Robin of Locksley pirouetted onstage, bowing to the delight of the crowd and then turning to do the same to the young woman. Then he swung the smiling Ella Weaver over his shoulder and leapt off the dais onto a waiting horse and galloped off down the street, kicking up dust and leaving the roar of approval in his wake.

Will just stood there, appearing ineffective and stymied by the outlaw.

"Mayhap a stroll along the parapet, my lady?" asked Sir Roderick. "The moon is full and fat this evening."

Marian glanced at the high table. The meal had ended some time ago, but the entertainment provided by a troupe of tumbling acrobats had kept the diners amused after the trenchers and platters had been taken away. But the high table was now empty, and John and his companions were nowhere in sight. Only a few remained at the lower tables, mingling with the hounds that skulked about for their meals and the serfs clearing away the last bit of remains.

A reprieve tonight, perhaps. Especially if she was to disappear for a time, walking in the moonlight with Sir Roderick, where no one would think to look for her.

"I should find a walk most enjoyable," she said, slipping her fingers around his arm. The sooner she disappeared from the hall, the better.

"Then let us go." He turned, but stopped just as suddenly, for their path between the tables was blocked.

Marian looked up into the expressionless eyes of the sheriff. Her heart sank and she squeezed her eyes closed for a moment. But when she opened them, he was still there. Implacable and clearly in poor humor.

"Lady Marian's presence is required elsewhere," Will said. Though his countenance was unemotional as usual, she recognized a deep weariness in his demeanor. He held himself stiffly, as though unwilling to trust himself to unbend for fear he'd show a trace of weakness. His cheeks were hollow, his mouth was tight and controlled, and the lines radiating from the corners of his eyes were deeper than she recalled.

Sir Roderick looked down at her, and Marian hesitated. He must have felt her fingers tense around his, and from the expression on his face, she knew he would intervene if she indicated unwillingness. But before she could speak, Will reached forward and took her arm, smoothly and quickly, and the next thing she knew, she stood next to Will instead of Roderick.

"Do not make trouble for the lady," he said to Roderick . . . but it was Marian on whom his glare settled. She read the meaning there: he was warning her not to put Roderick in a position that would cause problems for the knight.

"Nay, sir," she said lightly, looking at her would-be escort. "I am simply a bubblehead and had forgotten my other responsibilities." She couldn't help a bit of bitterness in that last word.

Before Roderick could speak or even excuse her from leaving, Will turned and maneuvered Marian along with him. She had no choice but to follow, for any scene she might make would simply end poorly for anyone who intervened.

And her fate would still be the same.

Yet, fury boiled up inside her as the sheriff directed her with sharp, rough movements through the hall. Could she not have one night of peace? Could she not have one night away from the pawing hands of the prince?

And her loathing of Will himself bubbled to the surface. She yanked her arm away from the fingers that gripped it and paused near the back of the hall. "What a glorious day you've had, sirrah. Burning the village, hanging a poor woman . . . and now on to the carnal pleasures that await you abovestairs. How amusing it must be for you to take such advantage of those weaker than yourself."

Then she pressed a finger to her chin in a pretense of sudden comprehension. "Ah, but not everything went as planned, did it? Robin Hood, hero of the poor, saved that unfortunate woman while you could do naught but grind your teeth. And now you intend to drag me abovestairs to take your fury out on an unwilling woman of your own."

His face grew even stonier. Blanker. Except for his eyes. They pierced her with silent rage, so dark they appeared completely black. She felt him shift, and knew he balled his fist, ready to silence her with the same violence he used against his underlings.

But she did not cease. Her emotions—exhaustion, loathing, fear—boiled over, spilling forth in words as sharp and cutting as his stare. She did not care if he struck her. Mayhap then she would be too damaged to attend the prince.

"And if I were to raise a hand to defend myself, you'd black hood me and raise me on the dais with a rope necklet about my throat as well, would you not? An evil, vile creature you've become, William de Wendeval. My father would suffer greatly if he knew how repugnant his ward had become."

His hand flashed out and she nearly recoiled, but the wall was behind her, and instead of raising a fist to her face, he merely snatched up her arm once again. She felt the vibration of his rage in the fingers that closed over her, but he said nothing, merely directed her forcefully from the hall.

Her heart beating harder, she tried to pull free, suddenly sure he would kill her. She struggled and kicked, trying to wrench her arm away.

"Cease," he spit, "or, by God, Marian, I'll wrap my hands around your neck and stop you myself."

She realized then that he was directing her not to the stairs leading to John's chambers but to the ones that led to her own. Now her palms grew damp and her heart raced, but for a different fear.

Up the stairs he propelled her none too gently, and every glimpse of his face sent a new frisson of fear down her spine. She'd pushed him too far. She'd seen how tense and taut he was in the hall. He had plenty of cause to retaliate, and no reason to hold back.

At her chamber, he shoved the door open, sending Ethelberga scuttling from the anteroom without a command from him. He released Marian with a little shove and stalked into the rear chamber, leaving her to look after him with shaking and weak knees. Moments later he reemerged and walked past her in an angry swish.

At the door to the hallway, he turned, his mouth pressed tightly and his eyes angry. "You won't be bothered any further this evening—at the least, not by me. The prince has declined your presence this evening. Rest well this night, my lady, for you will need your strength on the morrow."

He closed the door behind him and she heard his heavy footfalls fade into silence.

Moments later, she heard the door open again and Ethelberga walked in. "He has placed a watch outside the door, my lady," she said, her eyes wide.

And so he would ensure that she was bothered by no one this night.

He'd granted her a reprieve.

Marian slept poorly, but she did sleep.

She cared not to revisit the dreams that had haunted her slumber when at last she opened her eyes and found the sun streaming through the window slit. Instead, she tucked away the tendrils of images that had again left her body feeling skittish and yet expectant and called for Ethelberga.

After helping her mistress dress, the maid arranged her hair in two fat braids and twisted them into intricate coils over each ear while Marian chewed on a few mint leaves and some cloves.

When she entered the great hall to break her fast, she found the other ladies buzzing with news. A quick glance at the empty high table told Marian that John either had chosen to break his own fast elsewhere or had come and gone.

She was glad she did not have to face Will this morning. Yesterday had left her unsettled and discomfited, and he'd been a prominent part of last night's dreams.

"Have you been invited, Marian?" Lady Joanna asked, her eyes bright with glee. "I have, and Catherine and Pauletta too. Poor Alys has not, but mayhap 'tis because she is a ward of the queen and not the Crown. He dare not overstep his mother."

A prickle of unease trickled over her shoulders, though Marian didn't know why it should. Mayhap simply because the prince's name had been invoked. "Invited? I don't believe I've been invited to anything."

"To the prince's gathering anight," replied Lady Pauletta. Her eyes gleamed like those of a cat with its paw dipped in the cream. A mysterious smile tipped the corner of her mouth as she looked at Marian. " 'Tis too bad if you have not been asked. The prince is very generous to those who attend."

"But even if you do not attend that, at the least you will be pleased to hear about the archery contest. The prize for that is a gold arrow, and 'tis certain that Robin Hood himself will make an attempt to win," Joanna said in a placating tone. "We shall be able to see the great archer and how he handles his arrow."

Pauletta and Catherine tittered along with Joanna, looking at Marian over hands covering their mouths.

"My, such a great bit of news this morning," Marian replied. "What sort of gathering is the prince hosting?"

Pauletta's feline smile widened. " 'Tis a very special night. I have attended in the past, for my lord has given such parties before. He calls it his night of living statues. There is a contest, and he is most generous to the winners."

Now Marian understood the prickles at the back of her neck. Of certain, anything related to the prince would make her uneasy. But a night of living statues? Yet, mayhap her trepidation was misplaced. After all, Pauletta and Joanna seemed delighted at the prospect.

But then again . . . Pauletta's smile had a wicked twist to it that reminded her of John's depraved one.

Marian shrugged and took a piece of bread, examining it for weevils before breaking off a bite. "I do not know if I have been invited," she replied honestly.

Rest well, my lady, for you will need all your strength on the morrow.

Had that been a warning? Or her invitation? Or both?

" 'Twill serve that fool Robin Hood well if he comes to the archery contest," spoke up Alys suddenly. "He will be well and truly captured if he is so bold—and rightly so."

"You would not say such a thing if you had met the man," Joanna said, a dreamy look in her eyes.

"Indeed, you are mistaken, for I have met the arrogant ass."

The ladies all gaped at Alys, not only because her statement was so unexpected . . . but because her tone held such unusual bitterness.

"Did he not kiss you, then?" Joanna asked, a sly look coming into her eyes. "I trow if he had, you would not wish him ill. The man has a fine, sweet mouth."

Alys merely looked at the other lady and replied, "He would not dare to do so. I find him arrogant and misguided. And I hope that he is caught by the sheriff and imprisoned for his crimes."

Marian noted that Alys was not bloodthirsty enough to wish for Robin to be hung, and found that a bit interesting when coupled with the fact that Robin had obviously met her . . . but had not recalled her name. Or so he said.

She also noted the wash of pink over the fair-skinned girl's cheeks.

"You had best hope that the sheriff does not capture him," Pauletta said, her eyes slanted wickedly, "for he'll do more than imprison the man. He's as lief to tear him limb from limb with his bare hands as string him up with a black hood. I pray that he'll attend the gathering tonight, for he's one who fascinates me. So dark, so angry . . . I should love to be the woman who brings him to his knees."

Catherine sniffed. "Not I. Every time I look at him, I vow, my blood runs cold."

Pauletta merely smiled in a manner that Marian found both interesting and annoying. "Our dear Alys doesn't find the sheriff frightening at all. Have you managed to stoke the man's fires yet, my dear?" Her deprecating laugh indicated that she believed she already knew the answer.

Alys forbore to respond, but Marian noticed that the girl's fair skin tinged pink again.

But before the conversation could go any further, the man himself entered the hall. He strode quickly to the front where a duo of barons stood next to one of the great fireplaces. He barely glanced at the ladies.

Marian stood, stuffing a last bit of bread into her mouth and selecting an apple to munch on as well. Not only did she have news to report to Robin via the oak tree—a warning that the archery contest was likely a trap meant to draw him out—but she was also revolted by the way Pauletta's catlike eyes had narrowed, homing in on Will as he walked across the room.

How could she not find the man as repulsive as she?

Although Marian did her best to avoid Will for the rest of the day, hoping to evade any invitation the prince might wish to extend to her, she knew she was fighting a losing battle. If the prince required her to attend his revelry anight, hiding from Will would make no difference. And despite the fact that she didn't wish to be in Will's company, she also knew that if she had to attend, she would much rather do so with his escort than without it. It was simply a question of the lesser of two evils.

Thus, when she came down to dinner and saw that the high table was empty yet again, her relief was short-lived. The ladies buzzed with gossip that John had spent the day holed up in his chambers with his companions preparing for the night's festivities. And no sooner had she finished her meal and attempted to slip unnoticed back to her chamber than Will appeared as if from the shadows.

His face was as haggard as the previous night, but when he bowed and offered his arm, his countenance remained expressionless.

"What, no reprieve anight?" Marian asked, then, without thinking, added, "I trow, Will, you look as though you've not slept in days."

"Ah, the lady's tongue speaks ever the truth," he said.

"Why have you not slept?" she persisted. "Have you been up all the night plotting ways to destroy the village? Or how to squeeze more from the villeins? I should not sleep either if I had those sins on my conscience."

"I've those and more," he said, his words flat like the slap of a hand. "The wicked find no ease, do they?"

He turned and tugged her with him, but not before she caught a glimpse of his eyes. And she saw something there that did not match his harsh words. Something that looked like anguish.

Then it was gone. Or mayhap it was a trick of the shadows, for she'd never before seen anything soften his gaze. At least, not since she'd arrived at Ludlow. There'd been times when they were younger that a less rigid Will might smile or relax over a jest. As she recalled, once when they'd come upon a nest of newborn hares in the field, he'd been almost reverent as they examined the tiny creatures.

But she'd seen nothing like that of late.

Marian remained silent as they walked the now-familiar route to the Court of Pleasure. It was not lost on her that Will hadn't specifically indicated that they were attending something unusual this evening. Either he wished not to scare her, or he assumed that the ladies had gossiped about it enough that she knew.

But tonight, she thought, with what she expected would be more occupants in the chamber than usual, she might have the chance to search for letters or documents that would give credence to the rumors Queen Eleanor had sent her to investigate. And mayhap she'd find enough that the queen would release her from her task and allow her to return to her lands—at least until a husband was found for her.

By focusing on that purpose, Marian was able to quell the nervousness spiraling in her belly as they climbed the stairs to the third level.

After all, how terrible could the gathering be if the other ladies were invited as well?

But immediately upon their arrival, Marian learned the terrible answer to that question. The meaning of "living statues" became horribly clear to her the moment she entered the chamber.

Now, stripped of her clothing, she stood near a post of the massive bed as one of her arms was lifted, her fingers curled around the column above her head. The prince, his eyes gleaming wickedly, posed her himself, taking his time to arrange the angle of her arm just the way he wanted it. Surprisingly impersonal in his touch, he seemed to have aesthetics in mind as opposed to carnality . . . or mayhap the two were inextricably entwined.

No sooner was she arranged thus at the post than the prince beckoned the woman Marian recognized as Glynna over to them. Glynna, the woman with the whip marks on her belly, was just as naked as Marian. And so were all the other women in the chamber, including Catherine, Pauletta, and Joanna, as well as others Marian had not seen before.

To her mortification, Marian was commanded to remain frozen. The prince arranged Glynna in such a manner that the other woman's hand cupped Marian's quim, curving over her mound to slide fingers between Marian's parted legs. Then he brought Glynna forward so that her warm, wet mouth covered one of Marian's breasts, centered over her nipple. Marian could hardly breathe and she felt her whole body flush with warmth and awareness. Her nipple hardened beneath the moist lips, and her little pip began to swell at the very brush of pressure.

Then, still impersonal and concentrated, John took Marian's free hand and settled it in a similar position between Glynna's legs. Marian gasped and would have jerked her hand away, but he tightened his fingers around her wrist.

"Tsk, tsk, my lady," he said, leering close to her so that she could smell the vast amount of wine on his breath. "You mustn't move. You are a living statue."

And then he carefully arranged one finger so that it slipped between the warm, wet folds of the other woman's quim, and the others so that they spread over the springy hair of Glynna's mound. Satisfied, he stepped back to admire his handiwork.

But he wasn't finished. "Your hair," he muttered. And then he began to systematically, and none too gently, pull it loose from her braids so that it fell down her back in a long swath. Then he took one wrist-thick lock and arranged it over the breast that was not covered by Glynna's mouth, draping the bottom part of it over the maidservant's shoulder.

He stepped back and surveyed his work, then stroked his beard and nodded. "Lovely," he said, then turned to look about the chamber with satisfaction. "All of you are quite the most beautiful sight I've had the pleasure of seeing."

The other ladies and maidservants had already been arranged in similarly provocative positions throughout the room. They were indeed a garden of living statues.

"Be warned, the first one of you to move, to do other than to blink your eyes or change your breathing, will be punished." He gestured to an odd-looking item that looked like half a large barrel, rounded side up, in the center of the room. Empty manacles settled at the base of the curve. "But those of you who remain like the statues you are shall be generously rewarded."

He moved out of Marian's eyesight for a moment, and she became aware of a low murmur of male voices. She dared not turn her head to look to the other end of the chamber, but she knew that Will was there, along with John's other companions. Instead, she remained unable to think of little more than the pressure at her breast and the hand at her mound.

Moments later, the prince came back into view, and he was carrying something. When he spread his hands, standing in front of her, she saw that it was a heavy necklet of square gold links, such as a man might wear. In the center of the five largest links garnets the size of walnuts had been inset. He lifted the necklet and placed it around her shoulders, over her loose hair, and settled the garnets just below her throat. Heavy and cold, the jewels seemed to imprint themselves into her bare shoulders and chest.

"Such will be your reward if you are the last to move," he said, his hands lingering on her hair. "I considered topazes, but the garnets look magnificent with your hair." He leaned closer, brushing his lips over hers. "I vow, I cannot decide if I wish for you to win, or to lose, Lady Marian."

Then John turned away to adorn the other ladies in a similar manner, with different jewels in girdles, necklets, or bracelets. The maidservants received much smaller baubles in the form of slender silver chains.

"And now . . . let the contest begin," John said, spreading his hands wide and gesturing for his male companions to join him.

During this time, Marian had gone from flushed hot to bitterly cold and fairly trembling, from horrified to numb. She could hardly believe that she was to stand thus . . . to have such intimate liberties taken with her body. And that she could not move or find relief from the position! Already her limbs ached.

But as John shifted about the room, readying for the contest, the heat of Glynna's mouth burned into her breast, and the weight of her fingers, positioned over her quim, began to feel less like an invasion . . . and more titillating. Her shield of numbness faltered, and she became aware of the pressure of gentle finger pads against her quim lips . . . and the weight of a mouth, of lips parted wide over her nipple.

Yet Marian refused to allow herself to think about where her own fingers had been placed, and instead stared unseeingly across the room at a tapestry on the wall. If she ignored the sensation at her nipple, the pressure within her quim . . . the heat and dampness of the nether lips of this woman next to her . . . she could bear it.

The thought occurred to her that she might move, might pull away, and end her part in the contest, removing the other woman's hands from her body . . . but she feared John's punishment even more. This . . . was awkward, but not painful nor even as humiliating as the other nights.

The men had moved from the far end of the chamber and now came into view. Marian kept her gaze focused straight ahead, fully aware of the trickle of saliva that had begun to run down her breast and torso from Glynna's open mouth. It tickled, making her want to move and brush away the itch. She drew in a deep breath, staring into nothingness, willing the little discomfort to go away.

What were the men going to do? Try to make them move?

She was already having a hard enough time remaining still. . . . If they—

Suddenly, Glynna's tongue flickered over her nipple. Marian snatched in her breath sharply and barely kept herself from jolting.

John turned to look closely at her, and she stared straight ahead. "Do you surrender so soon?" he asked, moving so that he came into her line of vision. "I had thought you more stubborn than that, Lady Marian."

She didn't move, didn't allow her eyes to focus on him. Instead, she stared straight through him, his hair and handsome face nothing more than a dark blur.

Glynna's tongue darted around her nipple again, secret and sure behind her open mouth. Marian caught her breath and nearly moved again as little frissons of sensation blasted through her. *Nay* . . . oh, this was *not* . . .

John moved very close, and she could barely breathe, knowing that if she moved, he would notice even the slightest twitch.

Please, not again . . .

"You may of course move your eyes, Lady Marian," he said, adjusting her hair once more. "And look about the chamber at your competition."

She closed them, struggling to maintain her composure, measuring her breathing.

"You may move your eyes, but you must keep them open, my dear, or the others will cry foul," John said in a deep voice near her ear.

Marian had no choice but to raise her lids to see that he was watching her with satisfaction. Then a faint sound from behind him drew his attention, blessedly, away. Marian nearly relaxed, almost biting her lip—which would have ended the contest—when she saw that Sir Louis Krench was watching her closely.

He licked his thin lips and she recognized the glint in his eyes. "Come now, my lady. Would you not rather a randy cock betwixt your legs than a whore's fingers?" He would have moved up into her face, she believed, had a large dark figure not edged between them.

"I rather doubt she would find your cock all that randy,"

Will said in an obvious jest. His voice held a tone of good humor that Marian had never heard before. " 'Tis more than a bit overused."

"Step back, sirrah," Louis replied in the same bantering tone. "For I doubt you can even find your cock, considering the amount of times you've used it."

Will laughed, a short hard bark, as if he had to force it. " 'Tis not the measure of frequency but the manner in which it is wielded that concerns me. And the ladies."

Glynna's tongue flickered out again and Marian could barely contain a surprised gasp, and when the finger that had settled over her swollen labia began to move gently, yet purposely . . . she went rigid. Her mouth dried and she struggled to maintain control.

Breathe. Concentrate.

And then she could ignore it no longer. . . . The wave of sensation swarmed over her . . . heat, pleasure, the tightening of her nipple, suddenly jewel hard beneath the rhythmic tongue . . . the insistent, teasing pressure of a light finger over her hard little pearl. Oh, nay . . . she couldn't breathe, could barely keep herself from twitching, from spinning away from the silent torture.

And then she felt Glynna move . . . beneath her own fingers. She felt a little pulse against her, and noticed the slickness of the hot folds of flesh as if they burned down into her hand.

Marian closed her eyes, breathing deeply, holding herself stiff and unfeeling, even as the secret little tongue moved wickedly over her tight, sensitive skin. Trails of sensation coiled down, deep into her belly, and her breathing rose, became harsher, as she fought to keep from giving in to it.

A soft cry drew her attention and her eyes flew open in time to see Pauletta and her female partner separating, being pulled apart by John and Lord Ralf.

Marian could not recall exactly the position in which they'd been arranged, but she knew it had been just as provocative as her own. The maidservant was sent to the corner, where she crouched with a complacent look on her face and fondled her winnings: the silver chain.

Mercifully, her own private torture seemed to have stopped for the moment, giving Marian a chance to gather control and fight the increasing sensitivity in her own body. Vaguely, she also realized that now she was to see exactly what awaited her if she could no longer restrain herself.

Pauletta didn't seem dismayed as she was arranged over the huge half barrel, feet flat on the ground, back arched over the fixture, belly facing up. Her arms were drawn up over her head, and reached nearly to the floor behind her, where they were manacled in place. Her breasts lifted, her legs spread and chained, her dark hair spilled down the side of the barrel into a pool on the floor.

Her pale skin gleamed like soft pearl skin in the yellow light, her pink nipples and the dark bush of hair over her mound the only color in the living statue. Pauletta breathed hard, her breasts shimmering with each gasp, her hips twitching, and Marian could see the dark folds of her quim glistening.

She licked her lips, then realized she'd moved, and her eyes darted quickly around to see if anyone had noticed. They were all watching Pauletta, praise God, and no one had noticed her weakness.

Even Will, who stood nearby, his face like marble, had his eyes focused on the long, slender body on display before him.

I should love to be the woman who brings him to his knees.

Pauletta's arch words settled in Marian's mind and burrowed there deeply. *He fascinates me.*

Would he touch her? Marian couldn't take her eyes off the scene in front of her, her heart thumping madly. Her belly felt tight and expectant, but, mercifully, Glynna chose to remain still. Mayhap the woman realized that no one would be watching if she continued her torture.

Or mayhap she wanted to listen to the proceedings—for she could see nothing from her position.

But Marian could see it all.

John moved first, so quickly that Marian didn't realize what was happening. But then she heard the light *smack* of leather striking flesh, followed by a soft grunt of surprise. She saw Pauletta's body twitch as John raised his hand and rained blows over her belly and thighs.

They were light ones, for there were no corresponding blood lines drawn onto her skin. But each touch of the slender leather caused Pauletta to gasp and jerk and cry out in pained pleasure.

Marian could not look away, and the sight of her confined body, spread so, roused her own emotions. And when Glynna decided that the truce was over and began to slide her tongue around in circles . . . around and around and around her taut nipple . . . Marian felt the lust rise from deep inside her.

Yet she could not look away as John stepped back, thrusting the slender whip into the hands of one of his men. He breathed heavily, his mouth full and shiny beneath the beard, and he lifted his tunic, untied his braies.

Pauletta cried out as he shoved himself between her legs, his hands closing over her upthrust breasts as he stroked between her legs. He stroked and Marian kept her mind blank by counting the number of times he slammed into her . . . five . . . six . . .

seven. . . . She lost count as Pauletta began to roll and cry beneath John's onslaught.

And as the prince cried his release, stumbling back and away, Pauletta whimpered . . . begging for more. "Please," she sobbed, her hips moving desperately against the smooth wood beneath her. The red folds of her quim shone bright, and then Ralf shoved his way into place between her hips.

Pauletta cried out in relief, and as Ralf rode her, his fingers curling into her white hips, Louis walked over and straddled the barrel at the location of her neck, facing Ralf, who pumped away at her hips. Marian watched as he pulled out his slender white cock and began to jerk hard on it, faster and faster, and she watched the two men as their pleasure shone on their faces . . . growing tight and pained as they seemed to race to the end.

Glynna's fingers began to work again, and her tongue ceased its swirling and began to tickle over the top of her nipple, where it was the most sensitive. Marian watched, horrified, fascinated, titillated . . . unable to take her eyes away, as her own pleasure grew and swelled. Pauletta's low little cries filled her ears, along with her own breathing, and she heard the other woman gasp her relief . . . sobbing her pleasure in a long, keening moan.

Marian closed her eyes, struggling desperately to retain control of her own body. Her breathing rasped louder—her mouth had opened and she did not care. . . . She shuddered and trembled deep beneath her skin, fighting to remain outwardly frozen.

Her nipple grew tighter and more sensitive, the twitching fingers between her legs more insistent . . . and yet . . . not enough. Not enough to bring her over . . . to give relief.

She rose and fell, gathered up and then eased, beneath the

very skillful fingers . . . and suddenly she felt the surge of wet-ness around her own fingers.

Glynna gasped, pulsing around her, and Marian nearly cried out in surprise as she felt the quivering sensation from the woman next to her . . . the woman on her, around her, sucking and licking and teasing. Marian's breath came faster. Her hips threatened to move, to buck against the post behind her. . . . Her head wanted to roll from side to side as she waited for her peak. . . . She climbed, and grew closer . . . tighter, pulsing, trembling . . . felt her insides tighten . . . ready. . . .

And then she realized Will stood there, in front of her, his face tight and dark, and Marian felt herself trapped by his eyes. Even as the dancing finger wriggled insistently over her pip, another finger pressed secretly inside her, shoving deeply and working in and around, the torturing tongue flickering faster than John's whip. . . . She felt herself drowning . . . ready . . . so ready. . . .

And then the pressure eased . . . ceased. The tongue stopped, leaving her nipple hard and hot and wet beneath the open mouth . . . her little pearl pounding uselessly next to a finger that had frozen and merely teased itself between her thick, swollen lips.

Marian gasped, realized she was breathing as if she'd been running, and . . . she moved.

She moved; she couldn't resist any longer. Her hips thrashed, her body shuddered, and she heard the cry of victory from somewhere in the room.

Dimly, she was aware that Glynna moved away. . . . The pressure between her legs receded, leaving her quim throbbing and slick, needy . . . and her breast cold and wet, dripping with saliva, hard and painfully pointed at the nipple. The necklet still heavy over her shoulders, no longer cold, shifted, clunking against her, as she moved.

Hands were on her . . . pulling her arm down from the post.

Marian stumbled. She was next. . . . She knew it. . . . She felt strong hands, warm ones, moving her, sliding over her skin . . . the sharp deep voices . . . then the smooth wood of the barrel behind her, beneath her.

Her arms drawn long and tall, her back stretched so that her breasts shifted toward her shoulders. Her legs . . . opened, revealing the need throbbing there for all to see. She didn't care. . . . She wanted it, needed it there, touching her, filling her . . . *please*. . . .

She breathed, gave a little sob, thrashed her head against the cool wood, heard the delicate clank of the chains that bound her. Felt the ungainly slide of the necklet to one side.

Shadows filtered about, harsh voices, and then strong hands at her hips. The brush of warmth against her, rough cloth. She opened her eyes. Aye . . . Will loomed over her, just as she'd imagined . . . just as he'd done before. *Please* . . .

He blocked the light, his face turned away. She had the impression of closed eyes, cheeks sharp and hollow, jaw dark and scruffy. . . . He settled there, and she tried to lift her hips, tried to rise onto her toes and meet him. . . . She needed this . . . needed him . . . *needed* . . . *please* . . . Will. . . .

She felt him, hot and smooth against her, then the sudden filling of her center . . . the sweet relief of joining . . . and she cried out and her body surged around his hard cock, tightening as he moved in and out, fast and urgent and desperate . . . over and over . . . yes, aye, yes . . . and her body coiled, readied. . . .

She needed to move, to rock and thrust and touch. . . . Her

fingers curled helplessly against wood instead of flesh. She cried out in frustration, in rising desire . . . *needing*. . . . Then she felt it . . . closer . . . the promise, the fulfillment . . . coming, coming . . . and then the sensation of shattering, of breaking apart, as she slipped over into rolls of pleasure, waves of relief, shuddering violently against her chains, against him as she cried out.

A short, sharp moan, low, followed, and he arched into her one last time. She felt him tense, then sag, his own pulsing filling her core as his fingers tightened painfully into her sides, dark hair falling to obscure his averted face.

Her breathing settled into long, low gasps, and the warmth of satiation settled over her. And then she realized where she was: her position, her vulnerability. . . . Her eyes flew open as Will pulled away, leaving her cold and empty and suddenly frightened.

Nay. She could not. . . . He'd turned so that his back was to her; she could not see his face . . . but beyond him she saw John's glittering dark eyes and his full red lips. . . . He'd be at her in a moment. Looming over her, shoving himself inside her.

Nay, Will. *Please.*

Marian tried to move, to pull free. . . . She may have cried out . . . but she was well and truly caught, and the remnants of her pleasure disappeared. Vulnerable, open, helpless . . . she closed her eyes, holding back a sob.

Nay.

And then her arms were loosened, her ankles freed. . . . Someone dragged her off the barrel and she stumbled away, collapsing to her knees. . . . Then Will was gone. . . . He stood across the chamber, still fully clothed, with John and Ralf. . . .

Marian could not stand, and she crawled across the floor, over the rug, moving as quickly as she could, *away*.

She trembled with relief and chill and shock. Hearing the sounds behind her, she glanced over her shoulder and saw Catherine taking her place over the barrel, John and Ralf standing over her. Louis and Will and others . . .

Marian scuttled out of sight, beyond the large bed, toward the other side of the chamber, searching for something to cover herself with. The necklet had fallen off or been taken, and she wore naught but her long hair, catching under her palms and knees.

Dare she leave? She was near the chamber door now, and they seemed not to notice her absence, for Catherine was providing much distraction as she cried and pleaded in a high-pitched voice that could reach the hall below.

Marian curled into a shadowy corner for a moment to catch her breath and survey the chamber. Louis wielded the whip and was slicing it over Catherine's buttocks, which rose, white and plump, from over the half barrel, writhing and twisting and bucking. John stood watching, his own hand curled about his cock for once, and Will . . . leaned against the wall, watching. And Pauletta . . . she had her long, white body pressed up against his darkly clothed one. One strong arm wrapped around her waist, and her white hand lay flat against his tunic.

Turning away, Marian tasted something foul deep in the back of her throat. Her fingers still trembled, and she could not forget the feel of him moving against her, inside her . . . nor his flat, expressionless eyes. As if he despised what he was doing.

Yet, he took pleasure from it. She knew it. She'd felt it. . . . She'd matched his rising lust with her own.

She pushed the memories, the uneasiness, from her mind. She did not want John's hands on her again tonight . . . nor anyone else's. She must get away before they realized she'd not received her full punishment.

There were bound to be guards outside the door. Dare she try to slip out? Would they allow it? Would an aborted attempt to escape only draw their attention back to Marian?

The fog of lust and need had filtered away, leaving her mind clearer than it had been for some time, and she cast a quick glance around this end of the chamber. This was her opportunity to see if she could find any evidence of John's perfidy.

Keeping her attention half on the activities behind her, morbidly glad that Catherine made no attempt to keep her voice low, Marian crawled past the table of food and wine, toward the far end of the chamber. It was the only place that might hold messages or documents.

If she was caught, she could claim she was looking for the chamber pot.

Quickly, quickly, she hurried over, found a low table with a quill on it. Foolscap curled atop it, but Marian ignored those parchments. John wouldn't leave important messages lying out in his chamber, even if he didn't think his visitors could read.

Glancing behind her, noting that the others were still busy, she slipped beyond the table, staying low to the ground, and found a small chest. Mayhap . . . she tried to open it, but the chest was locked. And then she saw a packet of oiled leather behind it . . . one that might be used to protect important documents. Quickly, with trembling fingers, she untied it and began to unroll the packet.

She scanned the documents, quickly—difficult in the flickering candlelight—keeping one ear and eye trained on the activity at the other end of the chamber . . . and was rewarded by the sight of a royal seal. Not of England, but of France. Of Philip Augustus.

Drawing in a deep breath, she knew she'd found something . . . for John would have no reason to be in contact with Philip unless it was for some treacherous reason. But all she saw in the letter was the odd words, "The wild dog shall be contained. An emperor shall cage him."

Hearing a change in the mood behind her, Marian quickly stuffed the parchments back into their leather wrap, rolling and tying it back into place. She'd barely shoved it behind the chest, back into its hiding place, when a pair of boots came into her view.

She looked up to find Will staring down at her, an inscrutable expression on his face. Dimly noting that he hadn't even removed his footwear during the entire evening, Marian pulled to her feet—helped by his imperious hand.

"What are you doing?" he asked in a low, deathly voice. "Are you a fool?"

"I was searching for a chamber pot," she replied breathlessly, no longer even bothering to attempt to cover herself.

"Liar," he said, and thrust her away more sharply than necessary. "Do not let John find you sneaking about, or you'll discover that tonight was a delight compared to what he can do."

"Please," she said, glancing past him, "may I leave? Will?" She cared not that she begged. She needed to escape from this place.

His mouth settled into a hard line, he gave a sharp nod. "Aye, 'tis safe enough now, for the others are beyond caring. But let us be quick."

Once again, she bundled herself simply in a cloak, her clothing scrabbled up into her arms, and Will drew her firmly out the door. The guards did not try to stop them, but from the way they looked at them, Marian knew it would have been a mistake to try to leave on her own.

Will's heavy footsteps rang dully on the stone floor, down the stairs, and over to the other side of the keep as she trotted along beside him. Back up to the chambers on the second floor, and to her door. This route too had become horribly familiar.

And, once more, he spoke not at all, gave nothing away with his expression. If possible, she found his face even more implacable, more unreadable.

When they reached her chamber, he opened the door and preceded her inside. Feeling awkward yet expectant, Marian followed, closing the door.

Ethelberga snored on her pallet, and Will made no move to send her away or awaken her.

He stalked into the rear chamber, and Marian followed, as if drawn by a string. When he turned to leave, he fairly walked into her, standing there in the entrance between the two rooms.

He froze as if afraid to move closer, and she saw his hand curl into a fist at his side.

She was fully aware of her nakedness beneath the cloak, and how tight the chamber felt. Warm and dark and close . . . and how easily he'd slid inside her, how glorious it had felt.

Marian licked her lips, not certain why she stood there, why she'd moved thus . . . what she wanted. Her heart pounded and she looked up into his face, saw the glitter in his eyes and the tight press of his lips. Tension filled the space, pounding in her ears along with her heartbeat, and she swallowed hard.

"You are not hurt," he said suddenly, his voice low. The words came out like short little bites, as if dragged from deep within. He would not meet her eyes, but instead she felt his gaze score over her.

"Nay, Will. You . . ." Her voice gave way, her mouth dried, as the awareness became too much to bear. How could she want him to touch her with those hands . . . hands that had set fire to those houses, hands that would have gestured for the hanging. . . ? Yet she did.

"I warned you," he said in a harsh voice. "That you must submit. You made your choice."

"Aye," she breathed, surprised at the anger. Did he truly think she would have preferred John? She opened her mouth to tell him she'd wanted him—reached, even, to touch him—but he pulled her aside and brushed past, into the antechamber.

At the door to the passageway, a full room between them, he turned and looked at her. "I warn you again, Marian. . . . Do not allow John to find you reading his papers, or even I won't be able to protect you."

Then he was gone, leaving her alone. Suddenly bereft and empty.

And wondering if he would return to the Court of Pleasure . . . and the sinuous white body of Lady Pauletta.

Chapter 12

Whenever Will had cause to spend any length of time with his knees grinding into a chapel's stone floor, he was reminded of the night vigil before his knighting, more than a decade earlier. Long and silent, spent fully prone on his face, the hours had gone by in a drone of noiseless prayer and anticipation for the great accolade.

His life had changed that day, and until he'd become one of King Richard's most trusted men, he'd had little trouble keeping the oaths he'd made before the archbishop of Canterbury. The oaths of loyalty to his liege, to honor God and protect women, to despise and renounce traitors.

Now the cold stone beneath his knees served as reminder of his faults, his weaknesses and failures. And, for the first time, Will could no longer see the way to fulfill those God-sworn oaths. There was no way to obey his liege while retaining his honor and protecting the weaker gender . . . for to do one, he must renounce the other.

'Twas an appalling dilemma. One that had drawn him to the chapel, to his confessor, these last nights . . . he'd come from the debauchery of John's chambers to spend hours on his knees doing penance for the desire to forswear his vows. Seeking solace. Searching for an answer.

But at last, the balancing act had taken its toll, and he'd succumbed this night, stepping over the line and beyond reason. He gritted his teeth, squeezed his eyes closed at the realization of what he'd done.

How far he'd gone.

The vow he'd shattered.

Even now, as he knelt, holding himself fully upright, his legs trembling from exhaustion, from lack of sleep and from intense physical activity, he could not dismiss the sordid details of his transgression.

He told himself he'd had no choice. That it had finally come to the point from which there was no turning away.

His greed, his perfidy, ate at him, gnawing deep in his belly . . . yet, to his great shame, his body remembered. And could not deny the moment of bliss, of relief, of fulfillment . . . of triumph.

It was that last—the sense of victory, of attainment—that made the nausea roil sharply in his belly and brought the foul, metallic taste to the back of his throat.

The faint scuff of a slipper, the nearly soundless rustle of a hem over the floor, pulled Will's attention from his personal misery. He looked up, noting the dark gray cast of predawn sun filtering over the altar, and saw the slender figure standing there.

"Lady Alys," he managed to say. His voice was rough from disuse and gruff with annoyance.

"You are like to fall over," she said, moving toward him.

In the spare candlelight, he saw kindness in her pretty, heart-shaped face, genuine concern in her expression, and as before, it disgraced him. That this little slip of a girl could see something that simply wasn't there, or, at the least, wasn't there any longer . . .

Will pulled to his feet, aware that his knees ached and trembled in protest. When was the last time he'd slept more than two hours? He spent his nights in John's chambers, or taking Marian to hers; he was here . . . or tossing and turning on his own palliasse. Taunted by dreams of the unattainable.

Or he was burning houses in the village. Or condemning a woman to her death.

Did Alys simply not know of his wickedness?

Marian certainly did.

And now, God help her, she comprehended it firsthand.

The wave of anguish stunned him, and he felt his empty stomach rebel. His fingers shook, and he clasped them tightly together.

"My lord," she said, moving closer to him. Alys barely reached the center of his chest; she must know that he could crush her skull with two hands, or use the back of one to send her flying across the chamber.

After all, he was the Sheriff of Nottinghamshire. Brutal, cruel, without conscience.

Yet, she lifted her hand to touch his arm and he tensed, unwilling for her to feel his weakness.

"What do you here?" he demanded, pulling from her fingers. "And alone, at this hour?"

"Something woke me early and I came to pray," she replied. "But I see you, and methinks I've been drawn here for a different reason. You are ill. Or troubled. Will you not let me see to your needs?"

There was Pauletta, whose obvious interest might have been satisfied once upon a time . . . and might yet still be, if only to keep himself from going mad. There was Marian, on whom he could barely allow himself to think. And then there was this girl, Alys.

Why could it not be she?

Forcing strained kindness into his tone, Will nevertheless knew that his expression remained forbidding. "You have the right of it. I am troubled, but that is why I sought my confessor. All is well."

"Pardon me for saying so, but . . . it does not appear as if you have met with success. Please, my lord," Alys said, opening her hands in supplication. "Will you not at the least allow me to fix you a draught? It may help you to sleep a bit. I see the weariness in your eyes."

In his eyes? It fairly weighted his whole damned body . . . not to mention his conscience. Still. "Nay, my lady. I have much to attend to this morrow."

"But the sun has not even risen, and Mass is hours away. 'Tis clear you've seen no rest this night. A simple draught to help you sleep. And then you can be back to your tasks with a clearer mind."

"Aye, to the burning of villages and the heavy weight of the law's sentence in the form of a knotted rope," he said bitterly, then regretted the weakness of such an admission.

But Alys looked up at him not with condemnation but with understanding. " 'Tis no easy task you bear, I trow, my lord.

Whilst the rogue Robin Hood dances about, flaunting the law, you are left to do the work no one wishes. Yet without you, there would be no order."

She was looking at him as if he was . . . he did not want to acknowledge—or even to recognize—what was in her eyes.

"Please." She reached, boldly, closing her fingers around his wrist and tugging at him. "There is a pallet in the herbary where you might take your ease for a bit."

"Nay," he began to say, but then he stumbled and realized how clogged his mind was, how slow his reactions were . . . and it startled him.

Will was no stranger to physical duress—he'd fought in enough sieges and wars that he'd gone for days with little sleep, little food, and great demands on his body. But in those times, the goal had been clear . . . the intent unambiguous, and he had not been torn in two.

'Twas the mental anguish that was destroying him.

Returning to the chamber where his pallet lay, one among the rows of many men, would do little to ease him toward rest. The snores, the snorts, the snuffles . . . all served to assist his already active mind from succumbing to sleep.

In the end, he followed Alys.

Out in the bailey, with the sun still below the horizon, even the texture of the keep's stones was barely visible and the yard was as quiet as it ever got—which was to say that there were only a few serfs scurrying about. The night watchmen posted above paid no heed to them and Will was glad for it. Alys did not need to be seen in his company.

She made her preparations swiftly while he looked beyond the narrow window slit, uneasy and yet acquiescing. If he could push the thoughts, the shame, the memories, from his mind for a bit, mayhap rest would clear his mind. And help prepare him for what would come.

The draught Alys pressed upon him carried the taste of chamomile and something else he could not identify. He sat on the simple bed in the small, quiet structure and found that, in doing so, it brought his face just a bit lower than Alys's. When she turned toward him, he stilled and lowered the cup.

The look in her eyes was unmistakable and before he could rebuff her, she rested a light hand on his shoulder. And leaned forward.

The first brush of her lips was featherlight, little more than a tickle. And then she pressed harder, fitting her top-heavy mouth against his more closely. She slipped the tip of her tongue out, over the seam of his mouth. Will did not move, did not close his eyes. Did not shift closer for more.

Nor did he pull back. He would not offend her thus.

Alys stepped aside, her hand falling from his shoulder. "Would that I could ease you in other ways. But it appears that I cannot. Rest you well, my lord. I pray you'll find the ease you crave."

She turned to go, and he stopped her. "Alys." He groped for the words; he was unused to speaking gently, to taking care with his language. "I am most grateful."

"Rest you well," she said quietly again. And she left him.

He moved to lie supine, guilt-ridden, unsettled, weary.

And yet . . . by the grace of God . . . he slept.

Alys grimaced as she stepped out into the bailey, quietly closing the door of the herbary behind her. Her fingers trembled; her heart beat madly . . . but she did not regret it. With a quick swipe of fingers, she dashed away the trickle of tears.

Why?

Anger rather than shame coursed through her. Frustration, in the stead of humiliation.

Although if she thought much deeper on it, the humiliation might yet come.

Something moved in the shadows, and suddenly the outlaw was there. Again, as if conjured by her fury. Her heart thumping harder, mortification rose within her. Had he seen her crying?

Apparently still wary from their last meeting, Robin remained at a prudent distance, leaning against the wattle-and-daub bakehouse.

Cloaked in shadow that would soon ease, for the sun was ready to begin its climb, he watched as she walked toward him, heading for the keep.

"You had little success with the sheriff, I see," he said, scuffing the toe of his boot into the dirt, as she drew closer.

Alys continued on, and soon she would pass him. Her mouth was dry and she saw no reason to respond to his taunt. Yet, he was here. Spying on her? What a fool. Surely he would get caught if he continued such boldness.

Why, she could bring Nottingham down on him in a trice.

"Alys," he said, and the desperate tone of his voice caught her, putting a hitch in her step.

But she kept walking. "Did you not learn from our last meeting?" she said as she passed by.

"Aye . . . I learned . . . something," he replied in a low whisper. His voice filtered to her ears over the soft shift and clink of the watchman's chain mail as he strode by on the wall above.

She kept on, feeling his gaze on the back of her neck, ignoring the prickles on her palms, the flipping and shifting of her stomach. The side door to the keep was only a few paces away.

"Did you have no success with Nottingham?" His question followed her. Insistent.

"You already supposed that I did not. Why should I be the one to say you nay?" She flung the reply over her shoulder and slowed her pace . . . but did not stop. Then, behind her she felt him moving, shifting closer. The hair on her arms lifted; her stomach fluttered. "Robin, do you test me yet again?"

"I wish only to speak with you," he said. "Please, Alys. Only for a moment, may we have a truce?"

She hesitated, and that was her undoing. Before she could respond, he tugged her into the shadows. She could have raised a hue and cry, calling the watchman down on them. But she told herself that if she did, then Nottingham's rest would be disturbed.

And she had no fear of Robin Hood. He wanted from her only what the other ladies gave him so readily. She'd heard men speak of it—little nicks in their bootheels for each kiss they stole, each noble lady they bedded.

She had no intent of being another nick. Especially on the bootheel of an outlaw.

To his credit, he released her arm as soon as she was out of sight of the watchman, encompassed by shadow in the corner between the bakehouse and the alehouse. He released her arm, aye . . . but he stood so close to her, with the wall behind her, that she felt closed in. Trapped. She swallowed and pressed the pads of her fingers into the rough straw and mud wall behind her. In the near dark, she felt his gaze heavy on her, saw the faint gleam of his eyes.

"A truce?" she said, simply for something to say. Her mouth was altogether too dry, making it difficult to swallow. "Or did you wish to lure me into a dark corner for something else? Did you not learn the last time?"

"I learned how well your voice carries," he said, and she saw the flash of white behind his beard. The contrite Robin had gone, replaced by the charming outlaw. The one who wooed lady after lady in dark corners such as this one. Who flaunted the law, and dared to show his face where it did not belong.

A wave of disgust rose anew and Alys thought for a moment she would push past him and stalk away. But then . . . she looked up consideringly. Since he'd learned naught of her the last time, mayhap she must teach him a better lesson.

The night waned, yet it still floated gray about them . . . gray and subtle, enclosing them in a sort of private fog. Too early for anyone to be up, too late for revelers to be seeking their beds. The knowledge emboldened her, and the sense of being awake at such an odd time gave her the impression of acting in a dream.

She realized he was looking at her, and that the air felt charged with the same sort of tension as a thunderstorm, jagged with lightning.

She'd done it already once this night . . . why not a second time? At the least, she knew Robin would not stand like a statue. And mayhap she remembered it wrong. Mayhap on the heels of Nottingham, it would be no great incident.

"Alys," he began, but he never finished. For she reached up and pulled his head down to hers.

The first touch of lip to lip was not so different from moments ago when she brushed over Nottingham's set mouth . . . but only for that first breath. Then his mouth softened in welcome and she shifted closer, felt his lips gentle and part slightly, the brush of his beard and mustache like prickling silk. She felt the whoosh of breath from him, his hands resting tremulously on her shoulders as if unwilling to pull her closer, as if he was afraid to touch her, but unable to keep from doing so. Light and tentative.

Then she became lost in the kiss, their lips forming to each other and tongues slipping between them to curl and stroke. His mouth was sleek and warm, fitting to hers, making her close her eyes, forget who this was and where they were. Her hands came to rest on the front of his chest, feeling the solidness there, the warmth, and the pounding of his heart.

It matched hers.

Now his hands moved with more freedom, his hips pressing into hers, trapping her between him and the wall. His hands at her back, pulling her close, as if he wished to draw her into his body. A sensual mouth, sliding along her jaw to kiss an ear, then down to close his lips on the soft skin of her neck, over and over, his strong tongue stroking, pushing into her sensitive skin. She gasped and seized up, arching against him at the sensation . . . the tickling pleasure that swarmed her, settling low in her belly.

"Ah, Alys," he murmured, lifting his face away to look down at her. "I knew it. . . ."

She shoved him away, her mouth open in shock, the languid pleasure evaporating. Nay. Not him. The anger she'd felt earlier, leaving Nottingham's side, came back in a great wave.

"Alys," Robin said, reaching for her again, his mouth in a smile that she could suddenly discern. The sun had begun to spill its rays over the horizon, and now she could see more. . . . She saw the man who loomed over her now. His twinkling eyes, his disarming grin.

"Nay, Robin," she said, pushing against his chest when he would have gathered her up again.

The light ebbed from his eyes, and his mouth settled. He

resisted her attempts to shove him back, held steady against her effort. "Is it Nottingham?"

Nay. And that infuriated her the most. What she'd felt when she kissed the sheriff was nothing, *nothing*, compared with what this man did to her. This outlaw, who kissed every lady who was foolish enough to be wooed into a dark corner.

"Release me," she said, her voice rising mayhap higher than it ought.

"Hush," he said, looking with concern at the rising sun and the nearness of the watchman.

"Release me." She shoved hard at his chest, frightened by the way her knees trembled and her heart raced. She would not succumb to this, to him. "I have no desire for your green ribands and your stealthy kisses. Give them to your other ladies."

He took her at her word—or mayhap it was her strident voice that caused him to step back, eyes wide and hands outspread as though facing a spitting cat. "Alys, please—"

"Do not come near me again," she said, brushing past him. "If I had my wish, you'd rot in gaol."

"You must tell me," he said, his voice grinding after her. "Is it Nottingham?"

"I wish it were," she said, a horrible sob catching at her voice. "Leave me be or I will call him down on you. The next time I see you, I will." She managed to force out the threat as she picked up her skirts and ran.

Away.

Why could it not have been the sheriff?

Why did it have to be this man, this scoundrel . . . this *fool*, this shallow, deceitful *outlaw* . . . who owned her heart?

*   *   *

Marian woke the following morrow feeling restless.

She'd been unable to keep from reliving those moments in John's chamber, writhing and moaning over the back of the barrel . . . and the relief and pleasure Will had given her. A combination of mortification and discomfort accompanied memories of her wantonness, yet she still felt the fulfillment of coupling with him, such as it were. That lovely, full slide of him filling her . . .

She closed her eyes fiercely. She would not think of it.

Naught changed the fact that he was a blackhearted brute, but she could not deny that he'd given her what she needed. And that he'd taken what he obviously wanted.

Or had he?

She couldn't banish the memory of his face, his hard, tortured expression, as he moved inside her. And afterward, he'd been just as rigid, just as stoic as ever. Even . . . angry.

Marian rose and called for Ethelberga to assist her in dressing, then went belowstairs to the chapel. She was a bit surprised to find that Catherine, Joanna, and Pauletta attended Mass—although their faces and frequent yawns bespoke the lateness of their night. After all, Marian and Will had left before they did.

Although . . . it was more than possible that Will had returned after depositing her so unceremoniously in her chamber. Marian found herself eyeing Pauletta in a different light—all three of the ladies, in fact, but Pauletta most of all. Watching the woman, she noticed for the first time how sly her eyes were. And the way her mouth twitched in a feline smile.

Had Will returned to the chamber, and partaken of her offerings?

And why would it matter to Marian if he did?

It did not.

It *could* not.

She swept from the chapel after Mass, bestowing upon the trio of ladies what she hoped was a smile that matched theirs in smugness, and went through the great hall. She did not wish to sit at the trestle table and watch them break their fast, particularly if Will happened to be there.

She was not quite ready to face him yet.

At the back of the hall, she stopped a serf boy and bade him fetch her a piece of cheese and an apple with which to break her fast. When he returned moments later, she left the hall and went out into the bailey.

The September sun shone bright and warm this morning, and it took her a moment to adjust to the brightness. As she crunched into her apple, she saw Alys emerge from one of the smaller outbuildings.

"Good morrow," she greeted her friend.

"Marian," Alys said. "My goodness, the sun is high. I trow I've missed Mass again, haven't I?"

"Aye, but what were you doing in there?"

" 'Tis the herbary, and I had prepared a draught in the night and came to see if it had taken for its patient."

Marian fell into step next to her friend, noticing the dark circles under her eyes. "You look weary, Alys. Did your maid's sister call you out again in the night?"

She shook her head, smiling a bit sadly. "Nay. I could not sleep and went to the chapel. There I came upon the one in need of my assistance. But now he is gone."

At that moment, Marian realized what her friend had said, and a sudden thought . . . a wonderfully brilliant idea . . . settled into her mind. "A sleeping draught?"

"Aye."

"Could you make one for me? One that would put a man to sleep?"

Alys looked at her shrewdly and at first, Marian thought she might decline. But then her friend nodded and said, "I could do such a thing. But mayhap you will tell me about its purpose whilst I brew it?"

Marian nodded. "I will."

Inside the herbary, Marian found herself intrigued by the long wide table covered with neat stacks of wooden and clay bowls. Clay jars sat on shelf after shelf with markings on them, and a variety of utensils, buckets, platters, bowls, mortars, and pestles arrayed the table and another counter behind it. In a smaller room beyond, she caught sight of a narrow bed. A black cauldron hung over a happy blaze in the fireplace, steam coming from within.

"We are alone," Alys said. "The alewife comes in to build the fire in the morning, but she has gone back to her house to check on her brew. The leechman and midwife who use these stores are busy in the village. Now tell me who it is you wish to put to sleep . . . and why."

Marian considered for a moment whether to tell Alys the entire truth. After all, putting medicinals in the prince's drink could be considered treason, even if it wasn't meant to harm him.

"Mayhap I should tell you my great secret first," said Alys. "And then you will know you can trust me."

Marian looked at her with interest, but remained silent as her friend spoke again.

"There are few who know that I am the queen's half niece. As such, we have a rather close relationship, as she appreciates the fact that we are secretly bound by blood . . . and that she can trust me. She oft speaks—or writes, as the case may be—of you," Alys said, crushing dried leaves into a small pot of water drawn from the steaming cauldron. "You are well-thought-of in her mind."

And the queen was well aware of the propensities of her youngest son. Marian considered, but in the end decided to be safe. " 'Tis a suitor of mine who is more than a bit too . . . ardent," she explained. "I do not wish to offend him, but nor do I wish to spend the night in his bed. I thought mayhap to find a delicate way to deny him."

Alys placed the small pot over the fire, removing the larger cauldron, and glanced at Marian sidewise. "The prince?"

Marian let out a small huff of surprised laughter. "What do you mean?"

The little blond woman spewed out her own puff of air, blowing up the wisps of hair that had fallen into her eyes from her braid. Her sky blue eyes rolled. "I may appear young and naive, Marian, but I am not. 'Tis obvious by the way he looks at you that he lusts for you . . . and if I had not suspected, the conversation yester-morrow in regards to the prince's festivities would have told me so. The expression on your face made it known to me that you did not welcome his advances."

" 'Advance' is a weak word to describe the truth," Marian admitted. " 'Tis well near force."

"Then use this well," Alys told her, turning to strain the infusion into a small bottle. "There is little taste to it, so he will not notice if you add it to his wine. But it takes some time to work, so you must administer it early and be patient." She continued and gave Marian instructions for dosage. "It will cause him no harm, so you may use it without fear."

"I cannot thank you enough," Marian said, hoping she had not been wrong to trust the woman.

"You are loyal to the queen, and that is all the gratitude I need. She has been very kind to me and I owe her much more than simple fealty." Alys looked at her steadily. "I know why you are here, Marian. If there is aught I can do to assist, you have only to ask."

Did she know of her mission for Eleanor, then? Marian looked at her and their eyes met again. Aye. She knew of it. Or something.

"In fact, I have received word that she expects to arrive within the next sennight. Or sooner," Alys added, looking at her meaningfully. "I've journeyed with her often enough to know how quickly she travels."

"Indeed," Marian said. "I've heard that even her men cry for rest before she does."

"She will allow for little delay; of that you can be certain."

Marian nodded, feeling more optimistic. She thanked her again and sent for Bruse to have her palfrey saddled. While he did that, she took the tisane, secreting it in her chamber.

When she returned to the bailey, Bruse and another of her men were waiting, and they followed her as she rode out through the portcullis. In the distance, beyond the village, she saw the preparations being made for the next day's archery contest. Shaded stands were being erected in a large, grassy field for the nobles and ladies in front of an area that had been cleared for the competition.

She had no doubt that this contest was merely a way to entrap Robin Hood, for he simply would not be able to resist the prize of a golden arrow—nor, more importantly, the opportunity to be proclaimed the best archer in Nottinghamshire and beyond. And though she was certain he wouldn't heed her warning, Marian meant to put a message in the hollow oak advising him of this. But since she expected he would dismiss it, she had her own plans to keep him from being captured and tossed into the gaol.

She and her men rode briskly along the road to the fork where the large boulder sat, and when they were nearly there, she sent them to wait behind her where they would be close enough that she could call for assistance, but far enough away that they would not see what she did. Although she trusted them with her life, she was fully aware that aiding an outlaw was considered treasonous . . . and by keeping them in ignorance, she protected them as well.

Leaving her palfrey tied to a tree near the road, Marian approached the oak, moving quietly into the forest.

She found the place Robin had told her about with no difficulty, and tucked the small piece of foolscap deep inside. Just as she turned to walk back to her horse, she heard a soft rustle and the low murmur of voices deeper in the wood.

Curiosity niggled at her, and Marian could not resist. She moved silently through the forest, taking care to step only on the thick covering of pine needles, which muffled any sound, and to avoid sticks and bushes. The ability to move thus was a skill she'd learned long ago, when she sneaked after the fostering boys at Mead's Vale and spied upon them. When she heard the voices clearly enough to recognize that they belonged to two men who were speaking in low rumbles, she crouched and peered around a tree.

Will sat atop his massive black horse in the midst of a dark, thick section of the wood. The trees grew so close here that little sunlight reached the ground. Leaves and pine boughs created a canopy above Will's head, but he stood unfettered and fully in view in the middle of the shadowy forest.

At first, Marian thought he must be alone, and that his companion—or whomever he'd been talking to—had gone. But then she heard a murmured reply filtering from somewhere, and she looked up into the trees.

Robin?

Robin and Will were talking, there in the midst of the forest?

Or had Will chased the outlaw deep into the wood, and now Robin sat high in a tree, taunting the sheriff from his perch?

Marian strained to hear their conversation, but just then, Will gave a loud disgusted sound and wheeled his horse sharply about. He slammed his heels into the destrier's side, and with a great leap, they began to bound toward her. Heart in her throat, Marian stumbled back, out of the warhorse's path, and ducked behind a fallen tree. She tripped over the huge trunk, tumbling onto the other side and landing in a pile of gown and kirtle.

Worried that Will had heard her ungainly escape, she pulled herself up and peered over the top of the trunk, half-expecting him to come galloping over to yank her out from her hiding place. But he barreled on past, and she watched him go with another worry; he might not have found her, but if he kept on in that direction, he would see her horse and mayhap her men.

Marian scrambled up and began to run, not back on the route from which she'd come, but at a slightly different angle. Will would certainly come back into the forest, looking for her, and she wanted to be as far from this place where he'd been with Robin as possible.

She also wanted time to think about what she'd seen: Will and Robin, talking in the middle of the wood.

Had they met intentionally, and Robin taken the opportunity to taunt Will from his place in the tree? Or had it been happenstance, and the sheriff had once again allowed the outlaw to slip through his fingers? That hardly seemed to be the case, since Will had left first. But even so, she suspected that the sheriff would be less than pleased to know she'd witnessed their dealings.

She tripped and fell once because she wasn't watching the ground, so worried was she that Will might come bursting through the wood upon her. Pulling herself back up, Marian realized her veil had been torn from her hair somewhere along the way, and that branches had pulled tendrils from her thick braids. Her skirts were soiled and she was out of breath by the time she heard what she'd been expecting: the bellow of her name, and the dull thud of hooves on the forest floor.

Pausing to catch her breath, she smoothed her hair and her skirt and tried to appear as if she were merely examining a growth of moss on the side of one tree. She'd seen one of the healers use moss to pack a wound once—

"Marian!"

She forced herself to look mildly surprised to see him, but it was difficult when faced with the dangerous black figure before her. The warhorse pawed and pranced as Will drew him up and around, coming toward her.

"Madwoman!" he thundered. "What do you here alone? Was not one attack by outlaws enough for you? Do you *wish* to be taken off and assaulted?"

"Nay, of course I do not," she shouted back, startled into anger. However she had expected their next meeting to be after the events of the night before, this was not a scene she would have imagined. "My men are nearby, in fact. They will like be coming to my aid, for they're certain to hear how you have attacked me thus." Her voice had calmed and now bore a tinge of disdain.

"Or mayhap you simply troll through the wood in hopes of meeting Robin Hood," he continued furiously, as if she'd never spoken, his voice infused with venom. He took little care to keep the destrier from pawing and snorting, fairly atop her in his close proximity.

If she did not know how well he controlled his horse, she might be frightened enough to step back from the four-legged beast, but Marian was not about to show any further weakness. Instead, she stood her ground and glared up at him, hardly able to accept that only last night he'd been sliding in and out of her body, making her cry and writhe with pleasure.

"I presume this is yours?" His fist whipped out and she saw that he was holding a scrap of blue ribbon.

Marian looked at it, immediately recognizing the bit of fabric. She hadn't even noticed the narrow trim was missing, but quickly realized where she must have lost it: in the cave where she and Robin had . . . been . . . two days ago.

And Will had found it. And made . . . the right . . . conclusion. She grimaced.

"In the future," he continued as the sound of more dull hoofbeats came pounding, "I suggest you find a safer place than the middle of the forest to search for your lover. 'Tis foolish to wander where any might see or find you."

Before she had the chance to reply, Bruse and Fargus burst into view brandishing their swords as they galloped up.

"Hold!" she shouted, raising her hands to stop them. The last thing she needed was for them to attack the sheriff. Although 'twould likely be an overmatched battle, with the sheriff and his warhorse coming out the victors.

"Lady?" Bruse asked, slightly out of breath, eyeing the sheriff warily. He moved toward her, maneuvering his horse adeptly between his mistress and Will.

Marian thought she saw a glint of approval in the sheriff's eyes as his mount flared his nostrils furiously, but it disappeared.

Instead, he asked, "Is this yours?" Dangling the ribbon from a dark hand, he caught her with his dark eyes, his gaze piercing her coldly.

He wanted confirmation that she'd been in the cave with Robin, and by the saints, she'd give it to him. "Aye." She walked easily past Bruse and reached to pluck it from his fingers. "I had no idea I'd lost it. Many thanks for returning it."

"Mayhap next time, you'll take better care not to leave evidence of your presence languishing about. It could be dangerous to you."

"More dangerous than the Sheriff of Nottinghamshire?" she asked pertly. "That I cannot fathom."

He scowled at her well-placed barb, then wheeled his mount and started off toward the keep without another word. She watched him go, admiring his easy grace in the saddle . . . and the width of his shoulders, the thick dark hair that just brushed them, the powerful thighs that clamped around the warhorse.

And she wished that he were not the man she knew him to be.

CHAPTER 13

The day of the archery contest dawned gray and wet, and showed no inclination toward changing into more pleasant weather. Droplets glittered in the morning light and gray drizzle cooled the air as the sun rose behind smoky clouds. Nevertheless, the competition would commence just after the midday meal in the hall, for John would not be denied his pleasure—for the match, nor for springing his trap upon Robin Hood.

After coming upon Marian in the forest the day before, Will had returned to the keep and managed to keep the prince occupied, distracted with his plans to capture Robin Hood the next day. They'd plotted, drinking wine, throughout the evening and into the night before John sought his bed. This gave Will a needed reprieve and, he supposed, Marian a quiet night.

Unless Locksley had found his way into the keep and her chamber.

Better him than Will. At the least, she would welcome the outlaw.

His jaw tight, he dismissed those thoughts and turned his attention to the archery contest. Will knew that Locksley would be unable to resist the challenge to attend the competition, and that he would win the contest. There was no one in the county who had the same skill with a longbow; hence, John had made the prize too rich for the man to pass up. A gold arrow, which could be melted down to share among the poor Locksley made such a show of protecting, would be an irresistible lure.

Though he didn't sit at the high table during the midday meal, Will could not help but search for Marian, as if to ascertain whether she looked rested . . . or not . . . after her night away from the Court of Pleasure.

But he didn't see her. Instead, no sooner had he left the hall and strode outside than Marian's master-at-arms accosted him in the rain-dampened bailey.

His ruddy face appeared strained, and his eyes were lit with worry. The man gave a little bow, just enough to show respect but nothing more. "My lord sheriff," said the man. "I do no' wish to trouble you now, but I bear bad tidings."

"What is it?" Will asked, actually stopping in his tracks.

"My lady . . . she is gone. She ha' said she willn't stay in Ludlow any longer and she ha' gone. . . ." Here the man's voice dropped low and he glanced around, then back to Will. "She ha' gone to that Robin Hood. She claims she will be safer there, though I cannot trow how it could be safe . . . being wi' a bandit in the woods."

Will was enraged. *The woman was mad.* If John learned that she'd joined the outlaw . . .

And yet, Will could not deny her reasons for doing so. He'd even considered sending her off with the bandit. At the least with Locksley, she would be safe from John . . . and from himself.

Aye. From the both of them.

But he had a bigger concern at the moment. "She went off . . . alone?" Surely she wouldn't have been so foolish.

The man shrugged, his face worried, his skin glistening from the misty rain. "I do not know, my lord. I do nay think she would, but none of the men went with my lady."

Will drew in a slow breath. Marian was not that much of a fool. Either she had something planned with Locksley or she found some other way to ensure her safety. She would not have gone alone. He believed that.

And her plans aside, Will had sent men to patrolling the forest even more heavily since Marian's experience with the outlaws who had attacked her. None of his men had seen a sign from that group of bandits.

Mayhap Locksley had sneaked her from her chamber late in the night while Will attended to the prince.

"How do you know of her disappearance?"

"Her maidservant ha' told us just this morning."

Will allowed himself to relax a bit. 'Twas possible that his last guess was correct: Locksley had helped her slip from Ludlow late in the night while the maid snored on her pallet.

And then he wondered if having Marian with him would keep Locksley from attending the archery contest. John would be most annoyed if things did not go as planned and Robin Hood did not end up in the Ludlow dungeon.

He would soon find out. Will's attention was drawn beyond

the walls of the bailey to the faint sound of horns calling the competitors to appear.

"Send word to me if you learn anything further," Will said. "But I do not believe she is in any danger from Robin Hood—most likely he will hold her for ransom in order to fill his cup. He dare not harm a noblewoman."

Harming Marian was most definitely not what Locksley had in mind.

Striding through the bailey, Will took up Cauchemar's reins from his waiting squire and launched himself into the saddle. Beyond the walls, against the dreary gray sky, he saw the colorful pennants raised over the covered stands that had been erected in the last few days. They sagged flat and limp beneath the incessant damp. John's raised platform was in the center with a clear view of the targets that had been arranged along the tree line.

Placing the circular targets near the forest had been Will's suggestion, for he explained that it would make Robin Hood overly confident of his escape, should he think it necessary. John and Will had made other plans, however, to thwart such an attempt.

Yet Will didn't believe that Locksley would leave without his golden arrow, regardless of the danger he might find himself in. He would wait to claim his prize, and then make some bold escape.

And, as always, the Sheriff of Nottinghamshire would be unable to stop him, and appear to all as inept and slow.

As he drew closer, Will eyed the contestants that had begun to gather. Men of all ages and social classes, from noble to freeman to villein, held longbows and adjusted quivers over their shoulders. They milled about in small clusters, their boots and hose dark at the ankles from the damp grass.

He meant to ride down to the green where the match was to take place, but one of John's pages hurried up and caught his attention. Still high atop Cauchemar, Will found it necessary to look far down at the boy when he delivered the message that the prince required the sheriff's attendance.

Gritting his teeth, certain that John merely wished to review once again the plan to capture Robin Hood, Will turned and directed his mount off toward the tallest of the stands, at the center of the field. The prince had required chairs to be brought for himself and a few of his closest companions, and the oiled fabric roof tented high enough above the seats that he could walk fully erect beneath it—but not so high that the sting of rain angled through.

"Aye, my lord," Will called, bringing Cauchemar to the front of the stand, which stood as high as his head. "How may I serve you?"

"Where is Lady Marian of Morlaix?" John replied. He rose from his seat to come toward the edge of the stand. " 'Tis my wish and desire that she join me here. I have a seat prepared for her. Bring her to me before the match begins."

Will's face froze in the pleasant but emotionless expression with which he always faced the prince. "I have not seen Lady Marian, my lord. Is she not with the other ladies?"

"No one seems to know where she is," John said, looking down at Will. His unfriendly eyes fixed on him darkly. "Find her. I wish to have her company whilst I watch the proceedings."

"I have not seen her since supper yesterday," Will replied. "Mayhap she is ill in her chamber."

"Nay. I have sent for her, and I know for certain there is no one in her chamber." John's eyes gleamed maliciously. "You do not know where she is?"

"My lord, I truly have not seen her since last evening's meal. As you recall, you and I spent the remainder of the evening planning for today's events," Will said in an effort to redirect the prince's attention to the matter at hand: capturing Robin Hood. He did not care for John's sudden and overt interest in Marian's whereabouts.

John looked at him for a moment, then seemed to ease off on his intention. "Aye, then. You will find her after the match, and after we have the outlaw in our custody. Lady Marian will be honored when I invite her to sit next to me at the celebration meal anight."

Will gave a brief nod and turned his horse away before the prince formally dismissed him, but he did not care about the snub. His muscles jumped and his belly had tightened, for the sands seemed to be running out for Marian.

'Twas a good thing after all that she had left and gone to Locksley. Although how Will would handle it when John found out, he had yet to determine.

The first round of competitors was, of course, the longest and the least exciting. But by the end, twenty-three archers had been culled down to ten. The targets were moved farther away and the stands had begun to fill with the ladies and nobles, as well as men-at-arms and other spectators. The gray world was chilly, but they would not be wet beneath the covered stands.

Will watched as the ten lined up, readying themselves for this next challenge, and he examined each one to determine which was Locksley. He knew that even Robin Hood wasn't bold enough to appear without being in some disguise.

Though the gray mist softened some of the details of each person, Will found it easy to dismiss the two men-at-arms he recognized, and also two men who were too short. Another man was too fat, although Will didn't completely count him out, knowing that Locksley could easily pad his tunic. But in the first round, that man had not shot his arrows true enough to be Locksley.

There were three others who wore hats to keep the drizzle from their faces—a convenient way to obscure their features. But he discounted them simply because of the way they moved—not as smoothly nor as confidently as Locksley would. Will knew the man for whom he searched extremely well.

That left two candidates, and he watched them closely. One stood apart from the other competitors, and it was difficult to tell if he was tall enough to be Locksley. The curls showing from beneath his low cap were black, much darker than the outlaw's, and he was clean-shaven, unlike Locksley had been the last time Will had seen him. He seemed to hunch beneath his tunic and the loose cloak, but that was not surprising due to the dampness.

The other man was also hunched over a bit, and Will saw that his knees were slightly bent and he seemed to tip to the side, as if one shoulder was heavier than the other. When he shot his arrows, he seemed to pull himself more upright. Yet, he moved awkwardly, as if he was attempting to hide his age or true height. This man wore a voluminous cloak, and its deep hood obscured his face.

An obvious disguise, but because it was so obvious, it caught Will's attention. It might be Locksley himself beneath that cloak or it might be a decoy meant to draw the attention of the sheriff and king. The truth would be told during the competition, for Will knew no man who could match Locksley with the longbow.

And if there were, surely he would have heard of it.

The rain became thicker, yet the match continued. The second round eliminated all but three of the contestants, and Will's eyes narrowed in satisfaction as he looked them over again, moving closer to the archery row. He'd been right, of course. One of the two men who'd caught his attention must be Locksley: either the clean-shaven man with the dark curls showing from beneath his cap or the awkward man in the cloak. The third contestant was one of the men-at-arms that Will knew.

The targets were moved even farther away, and made smaller. The rain increased, making it even more difficult to see them. This was the final challenge. Each man would shoot three arrows, and the results of all three would be accounted. The one with the most arrows closest to the center of the target would win the golden arrow.

Yet even as he focused on the contest, Will could not easily dismiss his conversation with the prince. He was certain it had been John's way of telling him that their agreement was over. And now Marian was secreted away somewhere in the forest while her lover risked his life—and hers—by competing in this bloody contest.

Did Locksley not realize he put not only himself but Marian in danger as well? By showing up here, and winning? For if Robin Hood was captured, as John fully intended he should be, his band of men would no longer have their leader. They would easily be flushed out of the forest, and Marian with them, and her allegiance to the outlaw exposed. Or she would do something even more foolish and try to bargain for his release or pardon from the prince.

What would she offer—or what would John take—in return for his mercy?

Gritting his teeth, Will turned his attention from those

unpleasant thoughts and looked around the stands, and at his men-at-arms, who'd been stationed about. Some of them wore their hauberks of mail and carried swords, but others had been dressed in the garb of villeins or freemen. Their swords were hidden beneath long, rough tunics. Will had even bidden three of his men to hide up in the trees at the edge of the wood, near the row of archery targets. They would not only keep watch for members of Robin's band but also be there to stop the man if he tried to escape.

But the golden arrow would be awarded in the center of the open field, given by Prince John to the winner. And there would be nowhere for Robin to run or hide when he came forward to receive it.

Will moved down past the stands, ignoring the heavy gaze from Pauletta as well as the curious one of Alys of Wentworth. He should thank the little blond woman for the chamomile draught, for it had helped him to sleep well for several hours yester-morrow . . . but he had avoided doing so, for he didn't want a repeat of their last meeting. The hurt look in her eyes still haunted him, while her kiss did not.

The cloaked archer had stepped forward, still awkward . . . but when he nocked his arrow, he seemed to straighten fully. He was definitely tall enough to be Locksley, and the arrow flew true, slamming into the target just left of center.

Will nodded to himself and eased Cauchemar closer, the damp from the grass having long soaked the destrier's hocks. The man-at-arms shot next, and missed the center of his target by the width of his own broad thumb. Next was the dark-haired man, who'd remained apart from the other two archers. Will saw that he wore a tunic that was too large for him, and it made him look bulkier from a distance. The real man beneath, Will realized, was too slender to be Locksley at any rate, and mayhap too short.

Having confirmed the identity of his target as the cloaked longbowman, Will watched the remainder of the proceedings idly. He himself was fairly skilled with the bow, and John had at first suggested that he compete as the king's champion. If he won, then the prize would not have to be awarded, and John would have not only drawn Robin Hood from the forest but also kept his golden arrow. But Will had declined, explaining that he would prefer to be free to trap the outlaw, and so now he merely watched.

The dark-haired man's arrow flew, arching gracefully across the field, and found its mark, true. It was the only arrow to hit the center of the target.

Will straightened and looked at him again more sharply. Nay, it could not be Locksley. The man was too slender. And not tall enough.

And then he moved, sidling away as the cloaked man stepped up for his second shot. Will froze as he caught a better glimpse of the dark-haired man's profile.

By the saints, that was no man. That was Marian!

Will blinked and looked again. Was he mistaken?

Nay, indeed. He'd forgotten how enamored she'd been of the bow when he knew her at Mead's Vale—although he could never have imagined she'd become so skilled as to compete thus with Locksley. But now that he suspected the true identity of the dark-haired "man," he saw the confirmation in the way she moved, the way she raised her bow, and the fact that she was not tall enough. She stood on a bit of an incline that made her appear to be closer in height to her competitors. That explained why she'd stood at a distance for nearly the whole of the match.

He almost smiled at her cleverness, but caught himself in time. There was naught to smile about. She was here with Locksley—unless it had been a carefully planted lie that she'd gone to him in the wood—and it appeared one of them would win the golden arrow. If he'd thought Locksley was foolish before, now he was furious with him. How dare he bring her and flaunt their relationship in full view of the prince?

The prince, who had demanded to know where she was.

Tension rose within him, and Will realized his fingers had closed into tight fists. By the bloody cross, he did not need this to contend with. 'Twas bad enough trying to keep John from sniffing between Marian's legs. Now he would seek to punish her for consorting with England's most wanted outlaw. He could not even fathom what John would inflict upon her. And there would be naught he could do to stop him that would not involve treason.

The second round of arrows flew. Locksley's hit his target squarely in the center and then the man-at-arms's bolt lodged closer to the center than his last effort. Will watched as Marian stepped up to let her second arrow go, and he realized he was holding his breath.

He made himself release it, but watched the bolt whiz through the air. It lodged nearly atop the previous one, in the dead center of the target.

By the rood, not only was Marian in the final three; she was winning. Was that Locksley's plan? Or did he mean only for her to be a distraction?

Will glanced at the outlaw, who seemed to be standing straighter now, and no longer affected an awkward stance. One might imagine that he was annoyed with his lover's skill. That thought did make Will smile, although the humor faded almost immediately.

If Marian won, John would surely recognize her when he awarded her the golden arrow. Would she then escape, returning to the forest with Robin Hood? That would seal her fate in the eyes of the prince.

But surely she would not be foolish enough to reveal her relationship with Locksley. Will relaxed marginally. He must credit her for her intelligence. She wasn't that much of a fool.

Marian sensed the moment Will recognized her, for from the corner of her eye she saw him tense completely, drawing himself even taller in his saddle. It appeared he was not terribly pleased with her ruse.

She was surprised he'd seen through her disguise. The large, soft cap that sat on her head covered her bright, bundled hair, and she had affixed black horsehair to its edges to create the appearance of black locks. A bit of dirt on her face to darken her skin, men's clothing, and taking care not to lift her face too often or too far had helped keep her identity a secret.

Since he had recognized her, she hoped he wouldn't do anything about it. Or, if he did, he would not do so until she was awarded the arrow.

But Will's reaction was naught compared with that of Robin's. Marian had to bite the inside of her lip to keep it from twitching at the annoyance that blasted from his stance. She was fairly certain that he had not yet recognized her, for she had taken care to remain at a distance from him, with her face averted. But whether he had or had not, 'twas clear that he did not enjoy meeting up with a longbowman—or woman—as skilled as he was.

Or more so.

Marian realized with a start that it was her turn for the last shot. She had purposely not looked at the other targets during this round, so she was not aware of how well she was doing against her competitors . . . but Robin's demeanor suggested that someone, at least, was challenging him.

Stepping up to the archer's position, she pulled one of Tesh's arrows from her quiver. She'd warned Robin that the woodworker from Mead's Vale made the best, straightest, and fleetest of arrows in England, and she was about to prove yet again that she could hit her target with them.

The bolt felt familiar and steady, and she took her time, aiming through the misty air. The target sat at the tree line, with the dark forest looming behind it, its red painted circle already host to two of her bolts.

Will's gaze bored into her back, right between her shoulders, but she couldn't let that bother her. She pretended that the target was John's raging red cock, then closed her eyes and let the arrow fly.

When she opened them, it was over and the crowd was cheering. Marian looked at her target and saw that her third shot had landed precisely where she intended it—in the center of the target. Her three arrows created a small triangle in the dead middle of the small circle. She glanced over at the other targets for the first time, but found that she didn't need to—for Lord Beghely, the man who'd led the three judges, had turned toward her, congratulations in his expression.

Delight coursed through her. She'd won! As Lord Beghely approached, she looked over toward Robin and saw that he was staring at her with a shocked expression. Clearly he was only now recognizing her. Marian swallowed a giggle. She'd told him she wished to challenge him—and he'd belittled her chances.

Now she'd won the match in full view of all. Although no one else would ever know it was Marian of Morlaix who earned the golden arrow, Robin would. And that was enough for her.

Before Marian could bask any longer in the knowledge that she'd bested Robin Hood, Will's large black horse pranced into view. After a brief congratulations, Lord Beghely stepped back with the sheriff's approach. Marian looked up into Will's face and couldn't help the twitch of a proud smile as their eyes met.

As usual, he bore only a staid expression—one that could be called forbidding, in this case. Could he not see the humor in the situation just this once? He knew Robin of Locksley as well as she did; he must know that the man's pride would be bruised. Or perhaps that wasn't what annoyed him. Maybe Robin's humbling was nothing compared with what he saw as the outrage of a woman besting a man?

But how absurd! Marian thrust away her moment of glory and realized how foolish she was being. There had been one reason and one reason only for this archery contest—she was smart enough to realize it had been a trap for Robin Hood. And he had indeed attended, and now he was to be captured.

Unless her ruse would sufficiently distract and confuse people from being able to do so successfully.

Yet, before she could speak, the sheriff said, "So you have won the golden arrow. And what might we say is your name, when I *present you to His Majesty the prince*?" There was no mistaking the emphasis on those last words, and Marian felt a trickle of apprehension run down her spine. Will was telling her that she should continue with her charade and not reveal her true identity. Was there a chance that the prince wouldn't recognize her? Only a slim one, she was certain.

"I am called Tesh of Thane's Green," she replied in a voice deeper than her normal one.

A sudden shout drew her attention, and she spun to see Robin Hood streaking toward the forest. A slew of arrows followed him, and dark shadows emerged from among the trees, converging on him.

" 'Tis Robin Hood! Capture him!" cried the prince.

Marian caught herself before she showed any reaction. Revealing her true identity or her allegiance to an outlaw would do no good to anyone and most certainly bring great harm to herself and Robin.

Will's horse stamped and whuffed next to her as she watched the activity. She realized she had her fingernails curling sharply into her palms. The shadows at the forest's edge were not clear, and she couldn't see what was happening as Will and his mount leapt away, pounding toward the wood.

Robin. Please be safe!

Moments later, Will and three of his men rode triumphantly back into the field. Ahead of them, they pushed a figure that stumbled as the three men on horse and two on foot herded him forward. Ropes trailed from his body, causing him to trip and giving him little range of movement for his arms and legs.

The roar of the crowd seemed muted—or mayhap it was Marian who felt dull fear settle over her. They'd caught him at last. She moved closer to the stands, edging along so that she could be near enough to attract Robin's eye. Let him know that she would do all she could to help him.

As she watched, Will and his men brought the man forward roughly, moving rapidly toward the stand where Prince John awaited them. He looked down, smoothing his sleek beard and mustache eagerly as the prisoner stumbled and fell in front of him.

As he drew nearer, Marian saw that Robin was wrapped up in some sort of netlike covering. It appeared he'd become entangled in it, trapped like a wild animal. The crowd roared and hissed as Will's man pulled the prisoner to his feet. From where she stood in front of the spectator stands, she caught a glimpse of his face.

It wasn't Robin.

Marian knew that straightaway. The man looked like him. . . . He did indeed resemble Robin Hood with dark blond hair and a beard and mustache, but it was not Robin of Locksley who stood there before the prince.

She glanced up at Prince John, eyes wide, and saw that the triumph had not leaked from his face. The prince did not recognize that his man was not the outlaw!

"What a great day for Nottinghamshire!" John crowed. "We have taken into custody the bandit known as Robin Hood!"

Marian glanced at Will, ready for him to announce the mistake . . . but he sat stiffly on his horse, facing the prince, and gave no indication that they'd captured the wrong man. He said or did naught to disabuse John of his misunderstanding, and certainly made no move to look in her direction.

Did this have something to do with them speaking in the wood? But why? And how could it?

Before she could think on this turn of events any further, the horns sounded again and she heard the crowd roar with approval. Everyone was looking at her, and Lord Beghely beckoned for her to come forward. As the sheriff's men took the hapless prisoner—who was the poor man?—off toward the keep, where he would be thrown into gaol, Marian stepped reluctantly forward to receive her prize. As Lord Beghely presented her with the golden arrow, Prince John, in an obviously jovial mood now that his trap had been sprung, beckoned her to come even closer.

She tried to look down in a stance of humility, fully aware of Will's steady eyes on her. But because Prince John sat so high above her in the stands, their respective positions already put her in a position of obeisance, and when he spoke to her, she had no choice but to lift her face a bit in order to hear him. But she tried to appear shy, keeping her face trained at the festooned stand in front of her.

"Tesh of Thane's Green," John said in a booming voice. "Do you not look on the eyes of your benefactor, and thank him for his generous prize? Do you have no gratitude for your liege?"

Marian caught herself just before she fell into a curtsy and instead moved into a smooth bow. On the way up, she adjusted her cap so that it tipped forward onto her brow. She hoped it would obscure her face a bit more from the height at which John looked down at her.

But when she looked up at last, their eyes met. The prince stared at her for a moment, a long moment, and then the flash of recognition washed over his face. Marian braced herself and sensed Will moving closer behind her.

Why was it so important that he not recognize her, now that the contest was over and Robin was caught? Her only reason for wearing the disguise was to make the prince and the sheriff believe that she might be the outlaw, in order to allow him a chance to escape. Not only had he done so, but clearly it was with no help from her. All she had done was win the match. Despite Will's obvious concern, she could fathom no reason to conceal her true identity from the prince now that it was all over.

And perhaps she was right not to worry. Other than a glimmer of amusement in his dark eyes and the hint of a smile beneath his beard, John gave no indication that he knew who she was. "Very well, then, Tesh of Thane's Green," he boomed, looking around expansively at the audience. "You are now proclaimed the greatest longbowman in the county, and you have taken possession of the golden arrow! All proclaim *fiat*! *Fiat!*"

"*Fiat! Fiat!*" the crowd roared.

And then John leaned forward, speaking for Marian's ears only. "Congratulations, Lady Marian. That was well played. I wish to extend my personal felicitations to you this evening in my chamber." He glanced at Will, a smile playing beneath his well-trimmed beard. "Alone."

CHAPTER 14

"Alys," Marian hissed, pressing into the mudded walls of the alewife's house to conceal herself.

The delicate woman paused as she crossed the bailey, looking toward Marian where she hid in the shadows. "Aye? Who calls me?"

" 'Tis I, Marian." She kept her voice low, and tugged the cap from her head so that Alys could see her bright red hair in the drizzling rain. "I must speak to you."

Moments after the archery contest had ended, the misty sprinkles had become a full-fledged rainstorm. The spectators had all dispersed quickly, ready to change out of their damp, chilled clothing. Marian had hurried off as quickly as possible, anxious to be away from the prince's dark eyes as well as to make her own plans for the evening. Joining John in his chamber . . . alone . . . was not something she wished to do.

The very thought made her stomach pitch and flutter in an unpleasant manner. She thought she might vomit at the thought of being John's plaything.

And that was what had given her an idea that had prompted her to wait in the bailey in order to catch Alys's attention.

"What do you, going about dressed like . . . ?" Alys's voice trailed off as she caught sight of Marian's disguise. "That was you? The winner?"

"Aye." Marian could not smother a smile of pride. Will might not care that she'd won, and Robin seemed to be full of the sulks over it, but at the least Alys's expression was one of beaming admiration. She'd rather celebrate with Alys than the prince.

"You bested Robin Hood in the contest?"

"Aye!" Marian replied, aware that her pride was showing overmuch. She softened her grin to a mere smile and tried to remind herself of humility.

"I cannot believe he was very pleased with that at all," Alys added, linking her arm through Marian's. She'd obviously taken seriously her friend's request to speak, for she began to direct them once again to the herbary. "And now he is captured and sits in the prince's gaol. 'Tis a ripe meal to serve up to a fool such as he. He should have stayed in the wood."

Marian bit her tongue to keep from telling Alys the truth, but then she looked at the woman and saw that she was looking back at her . . . with a meaningful expression on her face. Did Alys know that the man who'd been captured was not Robin Hood? Did she know, or merely suspect? And since the woman bore no love for the outlaw, would she cry the truth to John? Or Will?

She would worry about that later. For now, she was in need of Alys's assistance. The door to the herbary opened easily and the two women slipped in. The small building was empty, and as Alys stoked the fire and lifted a switch to light candles from it, Marian moved to close the shutters of the single window. Though it was raining, and everyone hurried to the warmth inside, one could not be too careful of eavesdroppers.

Just as she reached the window, she caught sight of Will striding quickly and purposefully across the bailey. Mud flew from his boots, and his dark hair was plastered to his jaw and temples. The shadow of the day's growth of a beard darkened his face, giving him a more threatening appearance than usual. He was coming from the stables, no doubt on his way to check on the false Robin Hood in the dungeons.

"Nottingham," Alys breathed, having moved to peer over Marian's shoulder when she paused at the window. "He is a fine sight, if a fearsome one."

Unable to disagree, Marian quickly closed the wooden shutters before Will noticed them gawking at him.

Why *was* she gawking at the man? She despised what he'd done to his people—his rigidity with the law and cruelty to them. Regardless of what had passed between her and Will, whatever was really going on between him and Robin, she could not put his sins out of her mind. He was no better than John. Aside of that, he'd clearly not found her charade amusing today, and he must be quite furious that Robin Hood had escaped his trap yet again.

Yet again.

Marian frowned. Robin had escaped Will yet again. It seemed as though the outlaw had naught but good fortune, and the sheriff naught but bad. Yet, Will was the last man she'd call a fool, and Robin could ofttimes be one himself. After all, why would the outlaw continue to sneak into the keep? Or speak to the sheriff in the forest? She wondered again whether he'd been merely taunting him from the tree-tops, or whether they had been talking. But if they had been talking, why hadn't Will made a move to capture him? Was there some other reason?

She turned from the window and saw that Alys was looking toward the small pallet in the back of the herbary. When she realized Marian had noticed, Alys raised her gaze, her cheeks lightly flushed.

"Do you recall when I told you that I'd made a sleeping draught for a man?"

"Aye, of course." Marian nodded.

" 'Twas Nottingham." Alys hesitated, then continued. "I came upon him in the chapel, well in the early hours of the morrow."

"Nottingham?" Marian would have been no more surprised if she'd said she found John therein. "In the chapel?"

"Aye. I know that he is no favorite of yours, or of anyone's, but . . . I must talk plainly to you."

"You already know you can trust me, Alys. You say you found him in the chapel, in the early morn?"

" 'Twas more of night than morn," Alys said. "I woke early and thought to visit the chapel for prayer . . . yet I found him there on his knees. He was none too pleased to see me, and he looked like death."

Marian sat on a stool and waited for her friend to continue. Her stomach had begun to twist and flutter, and she wasn't certain why.

"I have seen him thus—dark, angry, in pain—on two other occasions, and I was certain he had some illness. But he insisted he did not. However, I could see his weariness and I pressed him to allow me to make him a sleeping draught. I swear, I feared he would shatter into ugly pieces if he did not have a care."

"He took the draught?" Marian could not imagine Will acquiescing to anything he did not wish to do—especially to urgings from this delicate sprite of a woman.

"Aye . . . I brought him here, and he agreed to rest." She looked past Marian into the smaller room, where the bed sat. "I kissed him."

Marian's mouth went dry and her stomach fell like a stone. She could not reply.

Alys turned to look at her, and Marian saw the remorse in her eyes.

"He did not hurt you," Marian exclaimed in disbelief.

"Nay! Of course he did not," Alys replied. "He would not. Marian, I know he is hard and mean, but I do not think ill of him. I have cared for many people, I have this skill with the medicinals . . . and I am used to understanding people. I knew he would not hurt me. I wanted merely to . . . relieve him. To ease whatever it is that has wormed inside him and causes him to be so angry and dark."

"You . . ." Marian found she could not speak.

Alys and Will?

"He did not touch me." Alys had begun to pace the small space, curling and uncurling her fingers. "And I left."

Absurdly relieved, Marian said, "You were very kind to him."

"I do not think many are."

Marian looked at her, wondering, faltering for a moment.

"He is the sheriff; he must keep order in the county," Alys said. "He has no choice but to uphold the law."

"Aye, but he does not have to burn the village," Marian

replied flatly. "And he could look the other way or find some manner of leniency when a woman is terrorized by her betrothed."

"And he could allow the outlaw Robin Hood to run free and rob from the nobles?" Alys said, her voice bitter. "Nay, Nottingham must capture that bandit. Oh, aye . . . he already has. Has he not?" The arch tone in her voice told Marian that Alys was indeed aware that Robin Hood was not the prisoner who'd been presented to the prince. She wondered briefly on the fact that Alys seemed to be the only other person besides herself—and Will—who'd noticed.

"But if he caught Robin, he would hang! And Robin Hood . . . he has tried to do only good," Marian argued.

Alys looked at her. "But he is a *thief*." Her voice held only rebuke.

"But a good-hearted one, Alys. Not for his personal gain. He shares with the poor—the villeins who lose their homes because of Nottingham. If not for him, they would starve. And if Robin had not intervened, that woman would have been hung."

"I did hear of that." Alys appeared to sober. "But what is Nottingham to do? He must uphold the law. He is consigned to do so. Even if he sees the strain on his people."

"And thus is the importance of Robin Hood's actions. He can act where Nottingham cannot."

Freezing, the two women looked at each other. Marian saw the comprehension flare in Alys's eyes at the same time she realized what she'd said. And what it could mean.

"Is it possible . . . ?" Alys trailed off. She shook her head. "Nay, of course not."

But Marian was thinking the same thing. And she was remembering the times Will had come upon her and Robin in the woods . . . and in her chamber. The sheriff had made no real move to capture the outlaw.

And Robin had said, with great confidence, that he would not be caught. On more than one occasion.

Of course, the two men had known each other long ago.

Had Will not wanted a witness to their meeting in the wood? Was that why he'd been so angry at Marian's presence—he'd feared she'd seen something she should not have?

Had it been more than happenstance that they'd come upon each other?

And, most damning of all . . . that Robin Hood had once again miraculously escaped from the sheriff and that a false prisoner had been presented to the prince as the outlaw himself. In truth, how could such a thing be accomplished *without* Will's help?

" 'Tis absurd," Marian said, though her voice was filled with wonder, and a smile tickled the corner of her mouth. The possibility was . . . fascinating. She looked at Alys. "If we listen and watch carefully, mayhap we'll know for certain." But . . . the prickling of her skin, the lifting of the hair over the backs of her arms, told her that they had to be right. "And the queen will soon arrive as well."

Alys nodded. "Aye. I received a message this morn confirming it. She is on the move, though the prince doesn't know to expect her."

A weight seemed to lift from Alys's shoulders, and her troubled blue eyes grew lighter. Then they darkened. "But, still, outlaw or no, sanctioned or nay, Robin Hood still cannot be trusted."

"I am not so certain of that," Marian said, her mind still working frantically. "Mayhap . . ." But she could not risk putting her suspicions into words quite yet.

And she did know that she now had more need of Alys's assistance for her plans this night. "I wanted to talk to you because I am in need of your help once again."

"The sleeping draught did not work?"

Marian's lips twitched. Suddenly . . . suddenly, she felt so much lighter. "I believe I will need something stronger than a sleeping potion for this night," she replied. "Something that will bring a man to his knees as he begs for mercy. And not in a pleasant manner."

Alys looked at her for a moment, and then understanding dawned. Her eyes narrowed in thought and then she nodded, her blue irises sparkling. "I know just the thing."

"Aye, indeed," John said, leaning ever closer to Marian.

His thick thigh and warm knee brushed against hers, and his elbow seemed to find the softness of her breast more often than not. She could feel the expectancy, the lust, rolling off him. It made her stomach tight and the backs of her knees damp.

"Your trick was well played this day, Lady Marian. My mother would have been proud of your gentle deceit."

Marian smiled demurely at the prince and looked down at the platter before them. She'd been given the dubious honor of sitting at the high table on his right side. For whatever reason, John had insisted that Will be seated on the other side of Marian. On the prince's left side sat Lady Joanna, proudly wearing the necklet she'd apparently won during the festivities the night before. On her left sat Lord Beghely.

Thus, she felt the oily, rich presence of John on one side, and the solid, stoic persona of the sheriff on her other. Mayhap this very seating arrangement was meant to be a reminder of her fate, trapped between the two men.

Regardless, Marian had no intention of submitting to John, at the least this night. That he was intent upon having her to himself had become quite clear in his words and actions, so much so that she could barely force down any of her meal.

John noticed. "Why do you not eat, my lady?" he murmured, his bristling black mustache much too close to her cheek, the heavy wine of his breath hot on her skin. "You will need your strength for this evening."

"The meat," she said, gesturing to a platter of boar that John had already begun to sample. "I do not care for the smell, nor does the taste seem right. Mayhap 'tis spoiled."

"Spoiled?" John leaned forward to sniff the piece he'd speared with his knife. "Nay, 'tis not spoiled." He shoved the bite into his mouth and began to chew rapidly. "But if you do not wish to eat, then I cannot help it. Mayhap you will drink, then?"

Marian had indeed been sipping the wine offered by the page behind her, but only in small quantities. Even so, her head felt a bit soft and her body felt loose. She was aware of every move Will made next to her, though he never touched her, nor spoke to her.

"The meat has a taint to it, my lord," she said firmly. "I have tasted such in the past and I've never been wrong. There was a time at Morlaix in which the whole of the house became ill."

John snorted and a bit of that very meat flew from between his lips onto the table. "Nottingham, do you hear this? Does the meat taste rank to you?"

Remembering the way Will had guided her during the chess game in John's chamber, Marian moved her foot very carefully, but swiftly, toward Will. She took great care not to cause the heavy cloth that covered the table to shift. She pressed her foot against his as hard as she dared while looking at the prince and his lean cheeks, bulging with victuals.

Fortunately, she saw out of the corner of her eye that Will had just lifted his goblet to drink, giving him a moment to pause before speaking. "I do not claim to be expert," he said as he lowered the cup. He did not move his foot away, to Marian's surprise. "But the meat does have a strange taste."

"Bah," said John. "I do not taste it." He leaned toward Lady Joanna and asked of her the same question. Her response was unintelligible, but since it was accompanied by giggles and overt flirtation, Marian did not think the other woman agreed with her.

Marian did not eat any of the meat in question, and she noted that Will did not touch the remainder of the slice on his trencher. But she dared not look at him and instead focused on keeping her conversation with the prince light and banal as she hid her apprehension.

The meal was only half-over—that is to say, the meats and breads had been served, but there were still potatoes, carrots, and beets to follow, as well as fruit tarts—when Marian became aware of movement under the table.

Something brushed against her legs, bumping near her feet, and she knew it wasn't one of the hounds. It felt too . . . human. Hands, most definitely . . . *moving along her thighs beneath the table.*

Marian froze, her breath catching in her throat. She carefully looked to her right, toward Will. The cloth hanging over the table had bunched and moved slightly, and she noted that he seemed to be holding himself as rigid as she was holding herself.

But now hands were lifting her skirts. Warm fingers eased up along her hose-encased legs gently, so gently they tickled her sensitive flesh, prickling the skin beneath the thin fabric . . . and then onto her bare skin at the tops of her thighs.

She knew her eyes had grown wide and that her lips had parted in shock. Clearly it was not Will who accosted her; he was too still beside her. Nor was it the prince. She dared not look at John, for from the activity happening beneath the table, bumping and nudging her leg on the left side, she knew that he was fully involved in his own pursuits. In fact, the bumping and nudging became a familiar rhythm next to her, and it took little imagination to confirm that someone had knelt before John and was working his cock in and out of her mouth. This knowledge, combined with the pressure of the hands on her legs, pulling them apart, sent a warmth flushing over Marian's face.

But whose hands were they?

Next to her, Will had remained completely still, yet she could feel the same sorts of movements happening on his side. The brush of his leg as it shifted against hers, and the flush of cool air over her now-bared thighs. The cloth of her undertunic and overgown had been bunched up in her lap beneath the table, and Marian stifled a little gasp as her legs were spread wide despite her attempt to keep them closed.

Her knees bumped into the rhythmic legs of the men on either side of her, and something warm and wet buried itself in the folds of her quim.

She could not move away; she could barely squirm in her seat as the tongue drove relentlessly into her warmth, tickling and teasing her little pip. Fingers spread her nether lips wide, and she felt the gentle scrape of teeth over her flesh, followed again by the strong thrust of a tongue . . . deep. Long, smooth strokes, licking around the inside of her as if it were a gentle knife spreading soft cheese.

Marian gripped the edge of the table and realized that John had turned to speak to her. His own eyes held a glassy look of pleasure, and the rhythm between his legs had become faster and faster.

"And how do you like my little . . . surprise, my lady?" he asked in a strained voice. His lips stretched in a pleased smile even as a tiny gasp burst from him. "Ohh . . . ," he said softly, his eyes fastened on her, still murky with pleasure. Yet there was a dark glint there that made Marian's belly twist.

"I prefer to confine . . . such activity . . . ," she said, working hard to focus on her words, and not the insistent sleek thrumming between her legs, ". . . to the bedchamber."

John smiled wide, showing yellow teeth and glistening gums. "That . . . can be . . . arranged."

Nauseated, yet flush with warmth and the need to twitch and move, Marian turned away. The pressure between her legs, the focused tip of a tongue vibrating against her, the gentle pull of lips . . . she could no longer ignore the delicious torture.

She wanted to free herself . . . but she couldn't. Or she needed to close her eyes . . . give in to the pleasure swarming like warm water over her . . . but she could not. Not here, not at the front of the hall, where everyone would see.

John might not take great care to hide his lust, but she could not—

A sudden shudder caught her by surprise, and her fingers tightened at the edge of the table. She needed to move . . . away . . . away from the demanding mouth and tongue that drove into her, sliding in her sleek warmth, teasing and luring her to a place she did not want to go.

As her attention skittered, trying to focus somewhere safe, she glanced at Will. His tanned face was flushed at the cheekbones, and his eyes seemed to be focused elsewhere—on a tapestry in the corner, mayhap, or even on a flickering torch. Marian watched him, drawn to the profile of his dark, emotionless face, to the strength of his firm chin dark with stubble, the full lips flattened in concentration . . . and as her own desire spiraled higher, she gave in.

She wanted it. She wanted *him*.

She no longer fought to ignore the slick heat between her legs, the throb of her tight little pearl . . . and she could not turn away from Will. She watched him as his own pleasure grew, and knew that she matched it, low and deep.

His cheeks sharpened as if he'd sucked in his breath, and she felt the faint trembling in the thigh pressed against her knee . . . and then, as she watched, his eyes fluttered for a moment, he drew in a short, sharp breath . . . and then, his cheeks flushing darker, he tensed . . . then silently eased.

The beauty of his harsh face, the controlled intensity, the way his eyelids swept down for a moment, then up again . . . the gentling of his mouth . . . *oh, God* . . . made her belly swirl deeply, then suddenly shoot lower, down, and she let herself go, arching a little beneath the table.

She may have gasped or closed her eyes, or even sighed. . . . Marian didn't know. . . . But when she came back to herself moments later, no one seemed to have noticed anything. She felt flushed and warm, and a trickle of sweat trailed down her spine. Her belly had softened and she still throbbed between her legs . . . but the insistent tongue had retreated. The demanding hands had moved away. Warmth pulsed gently through her.

And she looked over and saw Will watching her.

Their eyes met and then he tore his away. But not before she saw the truth in their darkness.

The truth that made her belly burn again with want.

At last, the meal . . . which had seemed to go on much too quickly at first, but then had slowed to an interminable crawl after John's little surprise underneath the table . . . rolled to an end.

Marian, whose knees had recovered, felt her belly begin to pitch with nervousness. Either her plan was going to work or she was going to find herself alone with John in that room with the massive bed, the restraints and whips . . . and the memories of nights past.

Or, worse, in that situation *and* accused of treason.

Her mouth felt parched, and when she clapped a hand to her belly, the nausea wasn't completely feigned. "I do not feel well, my lord," she said. It was not difficult to appear wan and weak. " 'Tis the meat, I am sure of it."

"Now, my lady, 'tis no sense in delaying the inevitable," John told her. Yet, he didn't look as robust as he had appeared earlier. Or mayhap, she only hoped he didn't. " 'Tis not the meat but your fears, methinks. Come, now, and I shall put your worries to rest."

He offered his arm, and Marian, her belly swirling, took it reluctantly. She felt the weight of Will's stare on her back, but of course she dared not look at him as she straightened her spine and allowed John to lead her away.

"I feel a bit ill," Lady Joanna said in a shrill voice. Marian paused, looking back at her in relief, and noted that the woman's face did appear to be a bit pale. *Aye, oh, aye!*

John turned toward the other lady and Marian took the opportunity to duck slightly and jam a finger down her throat. As the prince turned back, her belly revolted, and she upended its contents on the floor, splattering John's fine boots.

"Peste!" he exclaimed, stumbling away. His face glowed with annoyance, but Marian didn't care. She just hoped that Alys's special decoction would begin to work soon.

At the least it seemed as though Joanna had been affected already, and mayhap the others would soon follow.

"My pardon, my lord," Marian said, wiping her mouth with the back of her hand. She grasped the edge of the table, trying to appear weak. It wasn't difficult.

"Your false illness will not keep you from my bed this night," John hissed, grabbing at her arm with strong fingers. Yet, a fine sheen glistened over his forehead that Marian hoped meant he would have his own problems soon enough.

But then Lady Joanna coughed, and became sick in the rushes behind the great table. The pages leapt away, but the hounds lunged. And in the next moment, Lord Beghely, who had also eaten of the "tainted" meat, was bending over, retching from the depths of his belly.

"My lord," Marian said, "I am sorry. But I—mpph!"

She clapped a hand over her mouth as if she were to vomit again, making the appropriate gagging noises, and the prince sidestepped her with alacrity. Turning away, she faced Will, whose countenance had paled beneath his tan. Their eyes caught, and he looked at her with accusation and fury. She saw the illness in his face, lighting his eyes and making his skin appear clammy. Realization blazed in his eyes, and fear lurched through her. Would he accuse her here and now?

By now, there were others in the hall who'd become ill. The

excuse of the tainted meat seemed to have taken hold, for Marian heard others speaking of the odd taste of the boar's meat . . . despite the fact that she knew for certain that it was only a bit of boar's meat that had been tainted.

Only a particular hunk of that cut had been shared among the high table and a few rows below it. But the power of suggestion was strong, and the sight, smells, and sounds of illness tended to raise the same in other spectators.

Of the residents of the hall, only the hounds were in their glory.

" 'Tis the meat!" John said, as if it were his own realization. He appeared pale and weak, and when he gagged, Marian lurched away, bumping into the solid arm of Will.

The sheriff too appeared ill, but he did not bend to empty his belly as the others. Marian assumed it was because he had ceased eating the tainted meat after her gentle warning.

Thus it was with great relief that, moments later, Marian watched a weakened John, doubled over in pain, being escorted from the hall by two of his men. From what Alys had told her about the decoction made from the herb called broom, the illness would soon manifest itself from both the upper and nether regions of the prince . . . and others.

"What have you done?" Will asked fiercely, grabbing Marian's arm and yanking her away from the crowd, toward a corner of the hall. The sheen of sweat had grown on his forehead, and now dampened his cheeks. "You have committed treason!"

"Nay," she hissed back, pulling away. "No one will die. 'Tis only a brief illness, just enough . . ." Her voice caught. "Just enough to keep him at bay for a night. Will . . ." She looked up at him, even about to reach for him, when he pulled back. This response, after her confused and varied feelings today, sparked a bit of anger. "At the least, your Alys tells me it will not cause but a day's worth of illness."

"Alys?"

"Aye. Alys." Marian glared up at Will, fully aware of the damp wall behind her and his looming person in front of her. The bitterness of vomit lingered in the back of her mouth and she swallowed hard.

Just then, his face changed, and he spun away, heaving the contents of his belly into the corner. Braced against the wall by his splayed fingers, he lifted his face to shoot her a furious look as he swiped the back of a hand across his mouth. "Get you from me, madwoman," he whispered. "And pray that John does not learn of your perfidy."

Marian stepped aside, still watching him, and then turned and fled when he spun back to the corner, his body convulsed by the illness. For the first time, she wondered if Alys could be trusted. What if she hadn't known what she was doing?

What if she'd given her poison for the prince?

What if she'd poisoned Will?

Marian hurried from the hall and made her way up the stairs to her chamber. Ethelberga, for a wonder, was there . . . although she was not alone.

"Get up!" Marian ordered, rushing past the two figures writhing on the maid's pallet and into her chamber. She'd told them to wait for her here, not to attempt to add to the world's population. Ethelberga's companion was one of the steward's sons. He would also be able to lead Marian to the dungeon gaol.

By the time Ethelberga extricated herself from the young man, Marian had yanked off her vomit-splattered overgown and was unlacing the side of her tight-fitting bliaud.

The maid rushed to her side and quickly helped divest her

of the undergown and her sagging hose as her mistress drank watered wine to wash the bitter bile from her mouth. Moments later, Marian was dressed again, this time in a simple kirtle. She'd cleansed her face and hands with violet water. In the loose-fitting gown, tied only with a leather girdle and new hose beneath it, she felt more comfortable. And she thought the less-formal attire would make her less noticeable as well.

Ethelberga hid any impatience she might have had to return to her evening's engagement, and worked through Marian's braids to loosen the intricate coiffure. Once she had, she gathered Marian's locks at the nape of her neck, twisted the mass of hair, and tied it into a large loose knot, leaving the rest to hang down her mistress's back.

"I will take your wrap," Marian said, speaking of an old fox-lined cloak of dark blue that she'd given her maid some time ago. It had a deep hood and would serve to hide her face well. "If anyone should ask for me, I am ill and cannot rise from my bed. Do not allow anyone to enter."

Marian then piled a good amount of pillows and clothes under the blankets of her bed so that if anyone should defy her maid, or peer through the horse-eye peephole on his way to the garderobe, he would believe she slept there.

She made Ethelberga's lover peer out into the passageway first to ensure that no one was about. No one was, which was not surprising, as some of the women were likely still emptying their bellies in the hall, and the others were certainly hovering around them, offering assistance.

The garderobes would be busy this night.

Marian hurried silently through the passage behind her guide, and down the stairs that led to the hall. More than a few diners remained in the great chamber, and the serfs bustled about clearing away the remnants of the meal. Her guide took her past them to the back stairwell leading to the dungeon, and showed her the dark passage.

"Shall I go wi' ye, my lady?" he asked.

"Nay," Marian told him. "I will carry this torch. You must return to Ethelberga and entertain her." She gave him a silver coin, and when he hurried off, she turned to the darkness that yawned before her.

Down, down, down she'd go.

She must see this prisoner, this purported Robin Hood, and, if he was somehow an innocent pawn in a game of the prince and sheriff, find a way to help free him. She must act quickly, while the prince and the sheriff were ill, for she wanted no witnesses to her task.

Her torch cast flickering lights and eerie shadows that followed her down the long, curving stairwell. The walls gleamed damp with sweat and lichen, and the scent of rat droppings and stale air filled her nose. She'd pulled the hood so far up over her face that she had to turn her head to look to the side, and the wrap's hem draped silently down the steps behind her.

At the bottom, she was met with a gray stone wall and two choices of direction. The steward's son had told her he believed that the new prisoner was held in the last chamber to the right, so Marian turned that way. Her torch exposed a long, dark passage with barred doors along one side.

The sounds of little scrabbling paws, the drip-drop of water, and the stench of death and darkness consumed her. Marian continued on, gripping the torch, determined to get this over with as quickly as possible. She wasn't certain how she'd release the man once she found him, but she'd figure that out when the time was right.

At the end of the passage, she found the fourth and final chamber did indeed hold the man who'd been taken off the archery field today, the one who'd been snared in some sort of rope trap in the wood. The one who was supposed to be Robin Hood. She identified him in the low light as the new prisoner because he was the only one of the inmates who looked up and appeared to be aware of his surroundings, and because she recognized his clothing.

When she paused at his imprisoning bars, casting the light more fully between them, he pulled to his feet and limped toward her. At this close range, she immediately recognized him, and despite the iron studs between them, she stepped back in surprise. The prisoner was one of the desperate men who'd attacked her the day of the boar hunt, when Robin had come to her rescue.

Will told her he and his men had found some of the outlaws in that band. . . . Either this man was one of those who'd been captured before, or he had been caught today. Either way, he was no innocent man or unfortunate villein used as a scapegoat.

He growled at her, rattling the bars, but she turned away, heart skipping with relief and alarm. The clanging iron studs echoed like a fury in the silence, sending uncomfortable jitters up her spine. Could anyone abovestairs hear it? Would the noise call a guard or man-at-arms down to investigate?

And then, as if a signal to the other inmates, the ratcheting, rocking noise drew them from their stupors to rock their own gates of iron. Soon the dim, damp passage was filled with the horrible sounds, the desperate bids for release and freedom, exuding anger and despair.

Head ducked, hood falling forward, she rushed back toward the stairs, using the torch to light her way as her heart pounded.

Just as she reached the stairwell, she found her path blocked by a pair of large black boots standing in a shallow puddle at its base. Marian's heart thudded and at first she didn't look up, afraid that she would be recognized and John would learn that she was not ill at all this night. She would have slipped past him—or tried to do so—but his words stopped her.

"Have you thus assured yourself he belongs in captivity?" Will's voice lashed out, low but nevertheless rising above the clamoring that filled her ears.

Marian looked up, her torch held so that the light illuminated his visage from below. His eyes were in shadow, and his dark, whiskered jaw and mouth fully alight.

That mouth was pressed in the firm line, an expression that had become so familiar to her, that disparaging, annoyed, tightly controlled look. As the cacophony reverberated around them, he grabbed her arm and began to tow her up the stairs. She managed to grab her hems in one hand to keep from tripping, while the other still held the torch.

"Will," she said, speaking the first thing that popped into her mind. "You aren't ill?"

"Not any longer. I give no gratitude to you for that good fortune." He stopped on one of the wider triangular steps at a curve in the stairs, leaving the metallic clamoring below as nothing more than a distant echo. With a sharp movement, he shoved the hood from her head, leaving her without a place to hide. "You thought I'd imprisoned an innocent man."

Marian felt the rough stone against her, its chill seeping through the sleeve of her light kirtle. She still brandished the torch, lifting it higher now between them, casting his face in better light. "What else would I think?" she returned. "A man who would burn the homes of poor villagers would not hesitate to incarcerate a man simply because it pleased him to do so. Would he?"

"Nay, he would not." He stared down at her, eyes dark and fathomless, and Marian felt something shift . . . as if the world had fractured, and then righted itself, but in a slightly different way. Her chest felt tight and she found it difficult to swallow.

"Will," she began, but he cut her off.

"If John learns what you've done, your punishment won't be confined to his chambers and his bed. Do you not understand that?"

"What is it that I have done?" Marian asked calmly. Her heartbeat thudded harsh and strong through her body. Her palms dampened, and she felt . . . odd.

"You tainted the meat," Will said in a low, seething voice.

"There is no proof. And why would the finger point to me? Was I not the one who first complained that the meat was rank? Was I not the first to become ill? Did I not warn the prince?"

Though she'd not thought it possible, Will's lips tightened even further. Now the only part that showed was white with tension. "If anyone dies, Marian, you know what will happen. Particularly if something befalls the prince."

Marian resisted the urge to reply that she and much of England would find it no great loss if John were to slip into an early grave, but she did not. "Alys has assured me that no one will die," she replied. "After all, the draught she pressed upon you did not kill you." She looked up at him, watching for something in his face. But it remained harsh and unyielding, without that flash of vulnerability and softness she'd seen earlier at the table.

At the memory—the image of his eyes fluttering and the smooth control of his face as he sighed with release—a flush of warmth surprised her, blushing up from her throat. Her belly shifted, deep and low. She wanted to see that in his face again. And she wanted to be the cause of his release.

"Why did you do it?" he demanded, standing as far away from her as the step would allow.

"But you must know why," she burst out, one hand shifting to reach for him, then falling to her side. "Will."

He crossed his arms as if to ward her off, to keep the distance between them. "And what of the morrow? And the night after that? And after that? You cannot think to hold him off forever—or do you plan to make your escape into Sherwood? To go to Locksley?"

"Nay," Marian told him. "I'll not go to Locksley." She held his eyes for a beat, a long heartbeat, and then she looked away.

For a moment, she contemplated telling him what Alys had said—that the queen would arrive within the sennight—but she held back. She had suspicions, but she did not yet know for certain where his loyalties lay. "I know 'tis only time until I find myself with John, but if I can delay it for a night or so . . . I shall. I have no desire to submit to him."

He stepped away at that, down one step, as if she'd shoved him back. "Should I count myself fortunate that you didn't see fit to poison me as well?"

Marian simply looked at him. Though he stood a level below her now, more than an arm's length away, she still had to lift her face to see him. The torch's flames tangled up inside themselves, softening his marble features with wavering light. "Why did you burn those houses, Will? Why did you do it?"

"Why not? Is it no more than is expected of the Sheriff of Nottinghamshire? Senseless cruelty in order to prove my power over those weaker than me?"

"Why did you burn them?"

"They were old and falling down, hardly worth keeping," he said with a sneer. "I merely helped them get rid of the useless structures."

"And Robin Hood has already begun to assist them to rebuild."

"A paragon of virtue, Locksley."

Marian pursed her lips. She'd seen the cracks in his expression; she'd recognized the quickly obscured pain in his eyes. The backs of her shoulders prickled with awareness. She was close to the truth. "You met with Robin in the woods."

She didn't see him draw up and back, for it was the slightest change in his demeanor . . . but she felt it.

"What do you mean?"

"I saw you together. You made no move to capture him. What would John say if he knew this?"

"What are you suggesting, Marian?"

She'd never heard his voice so soft . . . barely a whisper. As if he could only force the words out on a breath.

"You've been protecting Robin. And thus he goes behind you, cleaning up the dung you create on the orders of the prince—in exchange for his freedom. Is that it, Will?"

"Marian, you speak treason." Again, quietly. With a whisper of disbelief. "I am beholden to my liege. Do you not impose such dishonor on me."

"Your liege, you say. But who is that, the king . . . or the prince?"

"Richard, of course. Always Richard. 'Tis an insult to say otherwise. But John acts in Richard's name, and I cannot avoid that."

Marian simply looked at him. His eyes held hers, and the argument, the tension, between them stretched and changed into something deeper.

"Marian . . ." Her name came out on a low whisper, laced with anguish . . . and anger.

Her stomach did a somersault as he reached for her. Not gently, not as his voice would have implied, but roughly. Strong fingers curled into her arms, not painfully, but not easily either. Then one hand moved, plucking the torch from hers. He tossed it down so that it rolled three steps below them, away from the hem of her skirt, resting harmlessly on the stone.

Its weakened flame danced tall shadows and a muted glow up around them as he dragged her against his chest. His fingers bit into the backs of her shoulders as he bowed toward her, his mouth covering hers as she lifted her face to meet it.

At first, she felt the desperation and drive in his kiss, the harshness. Was he trying to frighten her with brutality?

Yet after a moment, his lips softened, and he sagged against her, gathering her body up into his, loosening his grip on her torso. His mouth was no longer flat and hard but sensual and hot, his tongue sweeping the inside of her mouth as though he must taste every bit of her.

Dizzy, huddled against him, Marian closed her eyes, smelled his smoky, clean smell, felt the impossible breadth of his shoulders beneath her fingers, the pounding of his heart under her palms. She tasted wine and spice in his mouth, the soft sensual swipe of his lips as they slipped and slid and formed to hers, over and over.

Oh, aye. Oh, aye.

Except in her dreams, only once before had he kissed her . . . that first night in the hall, when he placed his claim on her. But this was nothing like that unemotional *taking.* This was hot and lovely, bringing her body alive and awake, making her breathless and weak.

Just as she was about to slip from the upper step into him, to lean fully against his strong body, he pulled back and fairly shoved her away. His eyes wild and dark in the sketchy light, his lips parted, breathing as if he'd just run a league, he stepped back, down, away.

"Get you away from me, Marian. Go." Will's voice was terrible. Low, but filled with loathing that matched the expression in his eyes. *"Now."*

"Will," she began, trying to collect her thoughts, wanting to drag him back down to her—but then he startled her, striding up the steps, brushing past her and ascending into the darkness above.

"Leave me be." The command filtered down to her, and the sound of his boots scraping against the gritty stone faded.

Knees weak, breathing rushed and harsh, she leaned against the wall for a moment, trying to catch her breath, to assimilate the sudden change in him: from a moment of sleek passion to one of . . . disgust.

Aye, but not merely disgust.

Fear.

It had been both that sent him away, fear and loathing. There'd been real terror in his eyes, mingling with revulsion.

She held her skirts out of the way and stepped down to reach for the foundering torch. When she lifted it, the flames tipped upright and caught more strongly. Marian hurried up the steps, her knees trembling, her fingers bracing against the gritty, damp stone, but her breathing better controlled. She wasn't certain why he'd thrust her away and run. . . . It couldn't be that *she* disgusted him, could it? No, she remembered all too well his words: *I do not deny 'twould please me greatly.*

Nay, she did not think he found her abhorrent. He might

prefer sweet, delicate Alys, or sensual, catlike Pauletta, but he was not disgusted by her. That she knew for certain.

She hurried up the stairs, and at the top of them, she came out into the darkened great hall. A few low rumbling snores met her ears, and she recognized several shapes of men slumped over the tables, well asleep. But no tall, broad-shouldered sheriff.

Disappointed, she began to walk into the hall when a shadow detached itself from the wall at the head of the stairs. "Lady Marian."

She didn't recognize the voice and reared back a bit, her heart pounding unpleasantly. Lifting her torch toward him, she demanded, "Who is it?"

The man stepped into her torchlight and she recognized one of Will's men-at-arms.

"Nottingham directed me to escort you safely to your chamber," he said with a little bow.

Marian's mouth tightened. So he had truly run away, and left one of his own men to see to her.

What she did not know was whether 'twas cowardice or disgust that had the Sheriff of Nottinghamshire shirking his duty.

Will watched from deep in the shadows as Merle escorted Marian from the hall.

To his overwhelming relief, she did not appear to be overset. There were no tear streaks on her cheeks, and although she'd started when Merle appeared in front of her, there was no terror on her face. He'd not torn at her clothing, nor pulled her hair down.

Not that he could recall anything but her taste and softness, and his own great need, once he pulled Marian against him. A whirl of pleasure and comfort, and, damn him, hope. A moment of hope.

By the saints, his fingers still shook. His lips still throbbed from their assault on her lush pink ones. His cock felt as though it were ready to explode, as if it were as hot as the smith's iron.

Yet a great emptiness left him cold and brittle. A familiar feeling, but more acute this night.

If he'd not come to his senses, he'd have rutted her against the wall right there. Like a whore—the whore he'd watched her— nay, forced her—to become. But this time it would have been without the bloody, lickspittle prince watching over them.

Will brought a shaking hand over his face. Was he going mad?

He'd protected her as well as he could, and damn him if he was actually considering ways to keep John from her. Forceful ways.

Treasonous ways.

Where was Richard? He'd heard naught from the king for three moons, after having regular missives and directives. *Watch you over my brother. Do what you must to gain his trust. Become his closest ally. What you do, you do in loyalty to Us, and We will know this.*

But for so long there'd been naught from the king. Had he forgotten his loyal man? Left him to live a life where all thought the worst of him, where he'd destroyed any chance of having the woman he loved?

Will swallowed hard, refusing to taste the bile that still churned in his belly. There was naught left to erupt but the worst of it, the acidic bitters that stung throat and mouth.

He'd believed there'd never be anything as glorious as having her, at last. And then, in all her lush, gold-brushed beauty, arched over the barrel, he could no longer find a way to avoid it.

Or so he told himself.

If he had not done so, John would have. And Ralf.

Or so he told himself.

'Twas better that he violated her than John. Or the others. Was it not?

Or had he merely lied to himself about that too?

I don't wish any *of this—you or the prince or even to be here at Ludlow. Are you mad? I wish for* none *of this!*

Those words burned into his brain, haunted his dreams even as he took and coaxed from her in the murkiness of sleep, in the deepest part of the night, in the depths of his mind. Those words wakened him in the blackness, leaving him dank with sweat and ripe with shame.

Will. Please.

He swallowed, hearing the low scratch of his throat convulsing, and scrubbed a hand over his face. When he removed it, he noticed quite by accident a lithe shadow moving across the nearly empty hall.

The slender shadow was a woman, and she appeared to be following a taller, more solid figure. A furtive one. If Will had not recognized the cloak she wore, or found the figure familiar in its shape and movement, he may not have investigated. But he knew who it was, and he eased from the shadows.

This caused her to stop in her tracks, rearing back at first in fear. But then she must have identified him, for she eased her stance. "Nottingham," said Lady Alys. "Is there something I can do for you?"

He glanced into the darkness where Alys's presumed guide

had melted into the shadows. He suspected he knew who it was. "Back out to the village again, to visit the sick?" he asked.

Her eyelids flickered. "Aye."

He noticed she carried a sack that bulged awkwardly. Presumably, she carried either her medicines or her personal belongings. "Did I not offer you escort—nay, did I not insist that I provide you with a man to ensure your safety if you were thus called again?"

"Aye, my lord, but I have my own escort. I'll come to no harm this night." Again, her eyes flickered toward the shadows.

He recognized this gesture as her nervous sense of urgency, but he was not quite ready to allow her to pass. Not until he had his own concerns allayed. In an effort to keep his next words indistinguishable to anyone but Alys, he moved closer, but took care not to block the light from an overhead sconce. He wanted a clear view of her face.

"You are a healer," he said, looking at her with unrelenting eyes. "Will the tainted meat cause harm to anyone?"

At once he saw that she understood what he knew, and what worried him. "Nay, my lord," she said, reaching to close her fingers briefly onto his wrist. "I give you my word. No real ill will come of the tainted meat. Aye, some discomfort, but that is the most of it. I swear it." She lifted a silver filigree crucifix from under her neckline, clasping her fingers about it in oath.

He searched her eyes, and saw them completely bereft of guile . . . and filled with something like understanding. Will stepped back, hooding his gaze from her knowing one, and nodded. "Aye, then, Lady Alys. You have put my fears to rest. Now, may I escort you through the bailey, at the least."

His words were not a request but a command. And when she acquiesced, he had a clearer glimpse of her guide, who'd thus far remained in the shadows. But as they walked through the hall and out into the bailey, the other man passed beneath a torch such that Will was able to see his face.

He recognized him at once: Allan-a-Dale.

A companion of Locksley.

CHAPTER 15

"*I*s he badly hurt?" Alys asked as the man led her through the darkness.

She didn't know his name. She'd awakened to her maid's gentle shaking, and gone out to see the man, who'd said only, "We need your assistance, lady healer. Will you come?"

She'd risen hastily. She knew him to be Robin Hood's companion, for she'd seen him during her short captivity in the tree hideaway. Some of her salves and herbs were already in the bag, but she shoved more in, along with a sharp knife and some clean linen cloth. Without knowing the nature of the problem they had called her to help with, she knew she must be as prepared as she could.

Outside the keep, her guide, who at last told her his name was Allan, walked quickly. Besides offering his name, he spoke not at all, and expected her to keep pace with him. She wasn't certain whether it was because he did not care that her legs were shorter or because he was in a great hurry to return, but she had trouble doing so.

"Did you fetch me for Robin?" she asked finally.

"Aye," he said, responding to her question. "We can do naught more, and he has lost much blood. The arrow slid betwixt two ribs beneath his breast and he has not been able to breathe since. 'Tis broken off inside."

Alys increased her pace, deeply worried. "Does he sound wet when he breathes?" she asked.

"Aye, as though he is breathing through water."

Nay. Oh, nay, that was not good. Alys's heart sank. "Does he speak?"

"Nay. He makes no response."

A pang struck her deep in the belly. Robin could die. He likely would. There was naught she or any leech or healer could do if the chest was pierced and the breathing was wet. And with a piece of arrow lodged within . . .

Alys drew in a deep breath, walking as quickly as her short legs would allow, her hems dragging along ground still damp from recent rain. She'd not even paused to braid her hair, merely tied it with a loose thong.

Nay. Not Robin. Not bold, foolish, grinning Robin. Robin of the kind heart and overgreat thoughts of himself. Nay.

She began to pray.

Allan led her quickly across the bridge from the bailey, down into the street of the village. Had he not brought a horse? Must they walk far into the wood? It would be hours before they arrived, and his life could be slipping away. . . . They must go faster.

A shadow pulled away from the darkness in front of them, and transformed into a man leading a horse.

"Alys," he said as they came nearer.

"Robin?" She could not contain the leap of relief, and . . . joy. "You are not hurt?"

"Nay. Not I. I told Allan to fetch you for me, for one of my men. You came." Gone tonight was the playful smile, the eyes gleaming with humor. Robin was sober and serious, cloaked in a dark wrap that added to his austerity.

She understood now the mistake she had made when Allan had spoken. "Aye, of course," she said, moving toward him. She felt nothing but an odd relief beneath her continuing apprehension.

"We will go faster on the horse," he said, as if asking permission to lift her into the saddle. His behavior was so subdued, so respectful . . . yet she sensed his underlying urgency.

"Aye, let us go quickly," she agreed.

He lifted her into the saddle and vaulted in behind her, settling his thighs about hers and his arms around her as he reached for the reins.

"Why did you send Allan for me?" she asked. "Why did you not come yourself?"

Why did you allow me to think 'twas you who lay dying?

"When last we met, you warned me never to come to you again. I did not wish to chance that you would call the sheriff or the prince's men down upon me. This night, I had no time to waste. Fergus is dying." His voice remained stiff and cool, and his arms impersonal. There was no gentle brushing against her, or surreptitious fingers over her breasts or thighs.

Not even the thought of a kiss in his glance.

Alys's mind was a whirlwind of thoughts. He had taken her

at her word. He'd stayed away because she ordered him to, and came to her only when his friend was in dire need.

Why did she suddenly feel empty and bereft? She wanted naught to do with the outlaw.

Didn't she?

But she was very aware of his presence behind and about her. And her relief when she saw him standing there, uncertain yet hale and well, had shocked her. Pure joy that, for a moment, had knocked away the urgency to get to the injured man.

"Hold tight," Robin murmured into her ear, one arm closing around her belly. The horse bolted forward, leaving the village behind and tearing into the dark forest.

Alys closed her eyes and tried not to whimper. She could see very little of the half-moon once they entered the wood, for the trees were thick and they were going so very fast. Robin's torso felt solid and steady behind her, and his legs in their tight braies kept her from tipping or sliding.

The stallion leapt and bounded and Alys clutched its mane, turning her face away so that her cheek brushed Robin's cloak and her hood protected her face. A stick scratched her arm, and another caught at her hood and in her hair, but they kept on, Robin shifting forward or to the side to avoid as much of the brush as possible.

At last she felt him draw back on the reins and even before they were fully stopped, he slipped from the saddle. Strong hands pulled her down, and she found herself faced with the same rope ladder up which she'd been taken as a prisoner by the massive John Little.

This time, she hauled up her skirts, tucking them into her girdle, and climbed up quickly. The ladder swayed as Robin followed. Alys closed her eyes—for she could see little, as it was dark—and felt her way to the top. The soft rhythmic creaking of the rope against bark and wood guided her closer to the opening in the floor above.

Inside, she found it to be even worse than she'd feared. John Little and Will Scarlet, two of Robin's other comrades, sat on small stools. The friar, whose tonsure gleamed in the candlelight as he bent his head, held prayer beads and seemed to be blessing the young man with some sort of aromatic salve. He made a cross on his forehead, and the scent of myrrh wafted through the room.

"The healer is come," Robin said. "Make you space for her."

Alys went to Fergus's side and even in the dim light from the five candles, she saw death in the color of his face. Placing a gentle hand on his chest, she felt for his breathing, and could discern the heaviness of its movement. It was slow, rough, and damp.

Peeling away the shirt that had been cut through in an attempt to remove the arrow, she looked at the wound. Someone had cleaned it as well as possible, and had even placed an herbal poultice on it. She recognized the smells of woad and hyssop.

"Good," she said, gesturing to the injury and the drying poultice. "I would have done so as well." She looked at Robin. Her breath caught for a moment as she realized how beautiful his eyes were. Something she'd never noticed before. "But I do not think 'twill be enough."

His face tight, he knelt next to her. "I feared you would say that. There is naught to be done?"

She shook her head. "Only to pray for him to go peacefully."

Their eyes met and she felt her breath hitch again as she was caught by his deep blue gaze.

Then he looked away and stood abruptly. "Allan, take her back. There is naught she can do."

"Nay." Alys reached for him, fingers around his wrist. It was narrower and more elegant than Nottingham's. And she felt a slender thong of leather encircling it.

He looked at her again, sorrow and apprehension in his eyes. But naught else. Nothing for her.

"I wish to stay," she said. And as those words left her lips, she realized that she meant them.

In more ways than one.

The sun was bringing glorious pink and orange light to the world when Fergus FitzHugh breathed his last.

Alys had remained silent, kneeling in a corner of the tree house, dozing a bit during the vigil. She'd divided her time between that, praying for the soul of the young man, and watching Robin. Trying to understand why she felt such relief when she'd learned he wasn't the injured party, while she felt remorse but no real grief for the one who was. She despised him for his lawless ways, did she not? She thought him a fool and a scoundrel.

Yet . . . her conversation with Marian rang in her head.

He does what Nottingham cannot.

Was it true? Was Robin working with the sheriff?

One thing was certain: she now saw a different side of the outlaw. One whose empathy and concern for his friend shone through, and where he did not sully it with silly flirtation or boastful claims.

He did not acknowledge her presence, and after she announced her intention of staying, he spared her not another look.

When the boy's body was empty of its life and soul, the friar and John Little wrapped him in a cloth and carried him down from the tree. Robin and the others followed, leaving Alys without a backward glance.

She watched them go, sending prayers with them, and contemplated her choice. She could stay here, or slip back to the keep. She could find her way through the forest, for the keep's tallest tower peeped over the tops of the trees and would give her direction.

Clearly, Robin cared not whether she stayed or left.

But something compelled her to remain. Mayhap it was the memory of the kiss she'd shared with him . . . the kisses. Or mayhap she merely wished to ask him about Nottingham.

Alys cleared away the remnants of the sickbed, taking the bloodied, soiled linens and adding them to the fire. They would not come clean, and no one would wish to sleep on death's blankets. She found more blankets and a few furs in a small trunk and arranged them on the pallet. She could send for more of her own linens back at the keep if necessary.

This thought halted her for a moment. She didn't mean to stay here. What would the queen say?

Nay, but she could share her comforts. She had enough in her trunks at Ludlow to furnish half the village.

The idea settled over her and Alys felt her skin prickle. Robin could distribute them if she gave them to him. He would do it, and he would not have to steal.

To take away the scent of loss, she added a handful of lavender leaves to the kettle of water simmering over the fire and tidied up the room and the four other pallets strewn about. She found a broom and swept the floor, having a moment's pause about the events of supper the night before. This broom's bristles were made of stiff straw and fine sticks, very different from the one she used in the herbary.

That one had been made with bristles of the herb called broom, which was commonly used for such an implement. It was also, conveniently, a medicinal plant used to help flush bad humors from the body, and it was that plant that she'd used to make the decoction for Marian last evening. By now, the prince and his companions should have flushed all the bad humors from their bodies and be sleeping quietly.

She hoped Marian had appreciated the reprieve.

No sooner had Alys replaced the broom and thought to look for a bite of cheese or piece of bread to break her fast than she heard sounds below.

The men had returned.

Her heart picked up speed and her stomach swished like a serf woman washing clothes, but she resisted the urge to rush to the window and look down. If Robin was there, he was there. If he was not, she would decide what to do then.

The now-familiar sound of the rope ladder creaking against the wood announced the arrival of someone, and Alys busied herself by stirring the fire. Then stirring the lavender water, releasing its clean, soothing scent into the air.

And not looking toward the hole in the floor from where a head would soon appear.

The sound of boots on clean-swept wood made soft, padding thumps instead of quiet grinding noises. The hair at the base of her neck prickled.

"I will take you back now."

She was at once grateful that 'twas the voice of Robin and not one of his men sent to do the task, and yet wounded that his first thought was to take her away.

But why would it not be? Had she not made it clear to him, more than once, that she despised him? That she would do whatever she must to bring the sheriff down upon him?

She turned and noted immediately that they were alone. The forest was silent around them. Below, and here among the trees, the only noise was the rustle of leaves brushing the walls of the hideaway and the regular conversation among the grackles and sparrows.

"I'm sorry for your loss."

His eyes flickered over her, then fell away. "I did not expect you to be here when I returned."

"Robin." Her fingers were shaking and her stomach fluttered, and she didn't know why.

"Shall we go? I must confess, I do not wish to take you farther than the edge of the village, Alys. I'm certain you'll understand why. But—"

"Robin," she said again, more urgently. "I see no need to call Nottingham down upon you if you and he have an agreement. He'll do naught but look the other way regardless."

Now she saw emotion in his face for the first time. Understanding and a sharpened stance. "What are you speaking of?"

"Robin . . . is that your true name?"

"Aye."

"You and the sheriff have been working together, have you not?"

He moved away from the hole in the floor, and began to pull up the rope ladder rapidly. Without speaking, he bundled it into a corner and closed the trapdoor. At last he looked up from his crouch, capturing her with blue eyes. The sparkle was not there, the gleam of humor . . . but there was admiration. And wariness. "And you have come to determine this how?"

"Marian and I have exchanged thoughts on the matter. 'Tis the only explanation that makes sense."

"And so now that you believe I am . . . legitimate? Is that the word? Now that you believe I am legitimate, you suddenly no longer despise me? You are willing to be here without crying down the whole of the prince's army upon me?" His words lashed out, bitter and rapid. "Simply because Nottingham blesses me?"

Wounded by his attack, Alys stood firm, refusing to allow tears of anger to gather in her eyes. "You brought me here."

"You could have left. But now you are naught more than the other ladies, aren't you, Alys? The danger, the intrigue . . . all of that has attracted you against your will, but now that you see I am no danger to you, that I am sanctioned by Nottingham, now 'tis all right for you to come to me." Disgust lined his face, yet hurt limned his eyes. She recognized it for what it was, and it gave her the courage to speak honestly. For the first time.

"Robin, the truth is . . . I could not forget you. Even when I believed the worst of you. Why do you think I had such a . . . violent reaction?"

His eyes measured her and he rose to his feet, somehow much closer to her than he was moments ago. "I've lost a dear friend this day, Alys. I have not thanked you for coming and for being honest. But you must go back to Ludlow now."

"Why?"

"Because if you do not, I cannot guarantee that my actions toward you will be honorable."

That confession, laced with a sort of despair, caused a huge warm bubble to burst inside her. Before she knew what she was doing, she stepped toward him, her fingers curling into his warm tunic, pulling him to her.

With a soft groan, Robin released himself from the frozen stance he'd assumed. His mouth crashed into hers as she lifted her face to meet it.

Ah, glorious. If she'd had any lingering doubt, it was banished by the wash of warmth and desire, of rightness, that flooded through her—from the tips of her fingers to the center of her being.

But Robin stepped back, thrusting her away. "Alys, you must go."

"Nay," she said, aware that her breathing had grown faster, and how his sudden absence left her utterly cold and bereft.

"Then I will leave, and John Little will escort you back." He turned and crouched to lift the trapdoor by its heavy leather strap.

Alys moved quickly and stepped onto the wooden plank. "Robin." She stood there until he was forced to look up at her, and when he did, the burning in his eyes sent another flash of desire through her.

"If you do not move, I cannot guarantee you will stay a maid," he said. "Please. Alys, do not—" He swallowed and turned away.

She ignored his impassioned plea and moved closer so that the hem of her gown, edged with dirt and mud, brushed over his fingers and covered the toe of his boot. His bent knee pressed into the fall of her skirt, pushing it against her calf.

Alys felt a rush of power when she saw the desperation in his eyes, when she recognized how conflicted he was. Yet her knees trembled as she stood there; her palms grew damp.

Slowly, she moved, pulling free the string that tied her hair back and tossing it aside. Shaking her head, she combed her fingers through the long curling tresses, teasing them forward over her shoulders. "Then I shall wear my hair as a maid one last time."

"Alys." His voice was choked, yet he did not move except to look down. "I cannot. . . ."

But his voice trailed off when she took a deep breath and reached forward to touch the top of his head, weaving her fingers into the warmth of his thick hair, sliding them around to cup the bottom of his chin, feeling the prickle of growth there and the wild pulse thumping in his neck.

Then she released him and began to gather up the bulk of her gown, lifting it, raising it quickly before she changed her mind . . . before she realized the madness . . . and pulled it up and over her head.

Robin gasped audibly and kept his face turned away, his gaze trained on the floor. But she suspected that he must now see her slippered feet in their cotton hose in the stead of a muddied hem cascading over it. And if he looked up, he would see her simple sleeping kirtle that ended just above her ankles, and which she now removed in another flurry of cloth.

"Alys." He said her name with reverence, and at last looked up. "Have you lost your senses?"

"Mayhap," she replied, cradling his chin with her hands again, only a breath away from her bare belly. "But I swear I will become fully crazed if you do not smile at the woman who loves you."

And that, it seemed, was the proper thing to say. For like the sun's sudden rise over the horizon, spilling light as if a pair of shutters had been thrown wide, Robin's face transformed. He smiled at her. The gleam she was used to seeing in his gaze had returned, and the roguish grin, the crinkles at the corners of his eyes. "I should be even more a fool than I already am to ignore such a threat."

Then he looked away from her face and moved out of her grip, back onto his haunches, catching her hands in his. She felt the weight of his gaze over her naked torso, saw the flash of hunger in his expression and then the wicked glint of humor back in his eyes. He surged to his feet and scooped her up in his arms as if she were no more than a goose-feather pillow.

As he strode across the room to one of the pallets, he kissed her. Nay, 'twas not a kiss so much as a nibbling . . . a gentle taste of her upper lip, playing it tenderly between his teeth, slipping a sleek tongue up and under it and then fully into her mouth. "You have the most beautiful mouth," he said against her. "'Tis like a juicy plum and I have dreamt on it for too many nights."

She was lowered onto something soft, but she hardly noticed, for he stood before her and pulled his tunic off, then his shirt, and at last she saw the fine form of his lean, muscled legs . . . and the bulge between them . . . fully outlined by his braies.

Robin's chest was fine, with wide shoulders that narrowed to a long, lean torso the color of sun-warmed honey. She'd seen bare male bodies many times as a healer, even some as well formed and muscular as this one . . . but none had made her catch her breath or wish to taste them until now. He recognized her expression, and for a moment, the cocky outlaw was back. He stilled and fisted his hands, flexing his arms in front of her so that his upper arms tightened into sleek ropes of muscle and his chest bulged.

Catching her eye, he smiled wickedly. "Aye, you like that, do you?" Then the brashness faded, replaced by something hot and liquid. "Not nearly as much as I do, Alys. I've not been able to stop thinking about you, my love."

"I thought you were the one who was dying," she said, reaching up to touch those sleek muscles. "Allan did not say who had been injured. He just told me 'he' needed me."

"And so you worried that it was my deathbed you were to visit?" He moved his elegant hands to cover her uplifted breasts. "So beautiful."

No man had touched her breasts before, and Alys was unprepared for the rush of pleasure and the instant tightening of her nipples. He sat before her, brushing the lightest of fingertips over their hard points, watching her, smiling at her shudders and the surprised gasps as her skin heated. Sharp little twinges zipped down into her belly and beyond, her body gathering up and her insides squirming in an unfamiliar way.

"Alys," he breathed, then bent forward to cover her mouth again. She felt him smiling against her, his lips curved in pure delight and laughter. He pulled up a bit to whisper, "I cannot believe you are here. I have been miserable, thinking never to see you again. Or taste you." Then he moved closer again, his tongue thrusting deeply into her mouth, tangling with hers for a long time.

She closed her eyes as the room began to tilt and shift, and flowed into him, into this slick world of tremors and heat and skin against skin. He lifted away after a long time. "I could kiss you all day," he murmured, once again sliding his tongue over and around her upper lip. "But there are other things to do. And I find that I am hungry."

Robin smiled down at her. His eyes were warm and delighted, and he moved away from her, down, down along her torso, his fingers at last settling over her bare thighs. She still wore her hose, but the cotton stockings ended near the tops of her legs . . . and left bare that full and hot place between her legs. " 'Tis long past time for me to break my fast."

Alys didn't know what he meant until he gently guided her knees apart. She gasped in surprise and at first resisted, but when he lifted his face and gave her that smile, she allowed him to part her legs.

"Ah," he said . . . but it was more of a groan. A low, deep, back-of-the-throat groan. And then he lowered his face down to her quim, which had never been so . . . opened and exposed and . . . *Oh.*

Alys nearly came off the pallet when he kissed the inside of her thigh. Just a little brush of lips, but she was so sensitive that the prickles shot all up and down, and then there were more, from every direction, as he kissed his way along her thigh, along that sensitive, soft, virginal skin, toward the cluster of golden curls. . . . She held her breath when he reached them, but he skimmed over her full nether lips, merely brushing the edges of the hair, and then settled on the other thigh.

She relaxed, closed her eyes, opened them, and vaguely saw the timber-roofed ceiling. Then she closed them again as his tongue sleeked out and his lips bussed gently against her leg, along its innermost part. . . . She sighed, no longer needing to twitch and shift with every touch. . . . She felt herself grow and swell. . . .

He lifted his head and she saw the laughter in his eyes, and the heat, the determination . . . the pleasure. 'Twas the overt delight, the lust in his own expression, that undid her and when he touched her ever so lightly, with the tip of his tongue . . .

right *there* on her tight little pearl, Alys gave a soft little cry and arched back onto the pallet.

"Aye," he murmured in deep satisfaction, but his mouth moved against her and she felt the vibration against her pip, and she writhed more because it was so . . . hot, taut, *needy*. "Ah, Alys," he sighed.

And then it began in earnest . . . first a little tickle with the point of his tongue, and then a long, slow swipe on either side of her swollen quim, down into the depths of its folds, then over and back and forth and around and inside and she could no longer follow the path, and she fell into the rhythm of it, let it suck her in . . . the pull and tug and rise and rise of warmth. . . . She felt it shiver up her legs where his fingers lightly moved, and from her belly, it coiled and spun down and around and before she knew it, she was crying out . . . for *something*. . . . She cried and begged and gasped and he slipped and slid faster and faster and finally she felt something *give*.

Just *give* . . . and then she cried out and her body was an uncontrollable mass of shiver and shudders and tears and long, great, rolling warmth.

Alys did not know how long it was before she opened her eyes, but when she did, there he was. Looking down at her with the most satisfied grin, the happiest eyes—as if he'd just brought down a boar single-handedly. Or fought off a band of raiders on his own. Or found heaven.

"Would it be fair to say you enjoyed helping me break my fast?" he murmured, trailing a sleek finger up from her still-pulsing core along the soft rise of her belly.

She could only nod, still trying to focus. "Robin. Is it always like that?" she whispered, reaching up to touch his face.

"Nay. Only if one is very fortunate." His grin grew wider. "I consider us the most fortunate of all."

"But you . . ." Her voice trailed off. There was no "us" about it. She might be a maid, but she knew enough to know that he'd not found the same pleasure as she.

He shook his head gently. "I'll not take your maidenhead, Alys. It belongs to your husband, whenever you might take one."

"What is this?" she asked, keeping her tone light. "Has the outlaw grown a conscience?"

"The outlaw . . ." His voice trailed off, then picked up more strongly. "The outlaw Robin of the Hood shall be no more."

"What?"

He pulled away, ruffling his thick hair with an energetic hand, looking across the room. "It has weighed upon me as of late, this charade I play. And I've lost a great friend this day, and I do not wish to put any more of my comrades in danger. There are other ways to help the people of Nottinghamshire. And . . . I have fallen in love with a lady that I shall not endanger. 'Tis that, most of all, that has opened my eyes."

"Endanger?"

"I'm wanted by the law—by the prince. Any liaison we have would implicate you as well." He cupped her face in his hands, seriousness in his expression. "I cannot take you as my leman, much as I want to. If a miracle happens, when the king returns and if God wills it, you'll be the wife of Robin of Locksley. But I will not despoil you before then. Much as I want to."

"But, Robin," she said, but he covered her lips with his, drowning her protests. The throb between her legs began anew along with the sleek swipe of his tongue, curling inside her. She felt his cock lift and shift against her thigh and without any further thought, Alys reached for it, slipping beneath his braies.

Soft as velvet, yet hard as iron, it grew and swelled in her hand. She almost forgot to kiss him, to taste him, as she was so enthralled by the sensation, and the burning between her legs began anew.

But he reached there, his clever fingers, and found that rising need, and he helped her slip her fingers around his cock, showed her how tightly to hold it . . . and with no further instruction, she knew. She found the rhythm, and he matched it with his fingers between her legs, and it was not long before they both cried out, their bodies sticky and slick and tangling together.

"Robin," she gasped, her fingers still curled around the softening head of his cock. A thumb stroked gently over the soft, wet rounding, and she felt him twitch gently with every little movement. She could not keep a bit of a smile from her lips. "I am a ward of the queen," she said. "Not the king."

"There is that," he said, his voice laced with satisfaction. "But she will not take my side over that of John. Until the king returns, and Nottingham tells him all, I am naught but an outlaw. My lands are gone, and I have naught to bring to you, Alys."

"But, Robin," she said, smiling against his chest, "I have plenty of lands. I am the heiress to Clervillieres."

"In Aquitaine?" He stilled against her. "You are the Lady of Clervillieres?" His voice was filled with wonder and disbelief, and rightly so. Clervillieres was a large and powerful fief on the northern border of Aquitaine.

"Aye. And," she said, her cheeks rounding further with delight, "I have already obtained permission from the queen—nay, 'twas my father who did—to allow me to wed where I will. I merely need to pay a fine—a large one, I am certain—when I do so, marrying a man that has not been selected for me. The queen will not say me nay."

At that great news, his head popped up from the pallet and he looked down at her. "You are mad, Alys. The queen would never allow that."

"But she has. My father provided her a special service—do not ask, Robin, for I cannot and will not tell you, for 'twas a most private matter for the queen—and he obtained that permission from her. Why do you think I have not yet wed?"

"Why indeed?" he murmured. "The Lady of Clervillieres. And you are quite certain Eleanor will honor it?"

"Oh, she will honor it, for the money will go into the coffers for her son's holy war."

"But I am an outlaw. She will not—"

Alys was shaking her head, looking at him affectionately. "Who knows you are an outlaw? Nottingham and Marian of Morlaix . . . and your companions. None of them will carry tales, I trow."

"John knows," he reminded her.

"But Robin Hood was captured at the archery contest. He is in the dungeon. Who is to say you are Robin Hood when he is already found?" She shrugged, spreading her hands wide.

A light came into his eyes. "Could it be that simple?"

"Your men shall travel with us—we'll leave England, and get far away from John and the others. I'll send word to Eleanor after we wed, and she'll impose the fine . . . but she will not complain. She'll take the money and grouse about it, but she'll say naught, for she is too busy trying to keep her two cubs from tearing each other's throats out."

"Or, at the least, one of them from tearing at the neck of the other," Robin said grimly.

"Aye."

He looked at her, his dimples showing fully for the first time that morning. "I do believe it might happen the way you claim, Alys. How could I be so fortunate as to find a woman who not only loves me but can free me?"

"You are very fortunate. Now you must make one more promise to me."

"Anything, my love."

"You must rid yourself of every green riband you have, for I'll not suffer you spreading them around to the ladies anymore."

He laughed, long and hard and with great delight. "Alys, my love, you are the only woman for whom I'll give a green riband. In fact"—his eyes narrowed in wicked thought—"I should very much like to see you dressed *only* in my green ribands. From head to toe."

"You have that many of them?" she asked in mock annoyance.

"Nay!" He laughed. "And that is precisely the point."

CHAPTER 16

"Nay, Marian . . . do you not see the trap into which I've led you?" Will pointed to the bishop that, if she moved her rook, would be free to slide into checkmate.

She pulled her arm back, resting its wrist in her lap, and stared at the game. Her fire-bright hair had been amassed into a loose knot at the back of her neck, but informal, curling tendrils graced her hairline. The wisps fluttered every time she moved, or whenever the breeze touched them. Marian's slender white wrist was covered by a tight-fitting sleeve of gold embroidered with red hearts and diamonds. He noticed the heavy scattering of golden freckles on the back of her hand, recalling that such coloring could be found elsewhere over her body.

On her breasts, chest, shoulders, arms, the peach-colored tones washed over her fair skin, making it appear warm and rich.

His cock shifted, reminding him how lush she'd been, sprawled on a pile of dark furs next to him in John's massive bed, her fiery hair spread all about her. And how sleek and sensual she'd been, arched over the barrel. Will tightened his lips and forced the thoughts onto the game.

She'd approached him early this morn, after the breaking of the fast, and asked if he could spare some time to teach her to play better. That she even dared to come near him after his assault on her in the stairwell was shocking enough . . . but to ask for his assistance? Will could not understand it.

Madwoman.

She should fear him. Had they been anywhere last night but that dank wet place . . .

"I do not see it," she replied, looking up at him.

He yanked his gaze away, turning his attention back to the game and away from her serious green eyes. "There. See you the bishop?"

"Ah, aye."

He glanced up to see her full lips purse in understanding, and he was overcome by a wave of annoyance and frustration. What was he doing here, sitting with Marian of Morlaix, teaching her to play chess?

And 'twas not even prudent that they meet in the great hall, for fear John would hear that they were no longer adversaries. Nor in her chamber, where he might peer through the peephole—and where there were other distractions.

Nay, they must sit out in the pear orchard, beneath a tree, behind a low, grassy hill far beyond the watchful eyes of John's court. Where they could not see . . . or be seen.

At the least, it was in the daylight.

Yet Will could not argue that teaching her to play better

chess was a fine idea, particularly in light of John's intent to entertain her privately. His "illness" had delayed this plan, mayhap even for tonight as well, but it would be only a matter of time before he recovered.

"And so, if I do such . . . ," she murmured, lifting her own bishop and moving it, "I shall prevent your little trap."

"Indeed. But do not think that I've missed your plan," Will said, lifting his queen to take her bishop. "I would not allow you to place me in check so easily."

She glanced up at him and he saw a bit of a smile twitch the corner of her mouth. He tightened his lips to keep from responding in kind.

"But you have now fallen into my trap," she said, and moved her knight. "Check . . . mate."

Marian was looking at him, arching one of those fine coppery brows in the same manner she'd done when they were younger and she'd come upon him and Locksley spying on a bathing maidservant. As if she realized that she'd won because his mind was elsewhere.

Chagrined that he'd been distracted, he looked down and saw that she had indeed won the game. He wasn't annoyed that she'd won, only that he'd allowed his thoughts to wander. Mayhap with the suggestions he'd given her, John would be distracted as well, and would allow Marian to play well enough to win.

She smoothed her overgown, which drew his attention to the curve of her breasts. Her slender hands were quick and sure, and then she looked up at him again. This time, there was a decidedly different expression on her face. One that made his mouth go dry and his palms dampen. He could merely lean forward. . . .

Nay. Lord, no.

He stood abruptly, causing her to crane her neck to look up at him. "You seem to have learned quite enough this day," he said. Glancing toward the keep, he felt a heavy weight in the pit of his belly. John had been seen up and about in his chamber early this day, slow but mobile. Marian's reprieve was soon to be over. If not anight, then the next.

Unless he could think of another way to help her evade the inevitable.

He looked back down at her, then had to drag his gaze away. She could not know how inviting her expression appeared. God help her if she looked on John with those soft eyes and parted lips.

She tried to stand, but her feet tangled in her hem and he grabbed her arm to keep her from falling. She lost her balance and fell into him, soft and sweet, and he thrust her away.

"I've been too long away from my duties," he said, giving a little bow.

And he fled.

Marian watched him go, frustration causing her to stamp her foot. However, the grass muffled any sound she might have made, taking some of the satisfaction from the movement. She could not have been more obvious if she'd torn off her clothes and leapt upon him.

She'd arranged the whole thing—the excuse for privacy, a quiet place far from the prying eyes of the keep and of Robin's men—and she could not have been more overt.

His desire was there. She could see it, hot and bright, burning in his eyes when he thought she wasn't looking. But she had been, and it had caused a slow, churning burn deep in her belly.

There was only one other explanation. It had to be that he did not think she wanted him to touch her.

So she would have to make herself perfectly, unambiguously clear.

Marian blew the horn to call Bruse, who'd been posted a discreet distance away, and gathered up the chess set. She would ensure that poor John would be sleeping like an infant this night, and William de Wendeval would find himself utterly and otherwise occupied.

Filled with apprehension, Will pounded on the door to Marian's chamber. It was late in the day, well after the midday meal from which she—as well as John—had been absent.

Upon his knock, the door opened to reveal the oft-missing maid, who looked up at him with fearful, large eyes. That was naught new, and it didn't disturb him in the least. But what disturbed him was having no idea why Marian could have sent for him.

"Your lady has called for me," he said shortly. "Is she ill?"

The maid seemed unable to find her tongue, and by way of response stepped back from the door and allowed him to enter. The antechamber was empty but for the maid's pallet and a small trunk, as well as a few neatly folded items of clothing.

Will hesitated, unsure whether Marian would come to him or whether he was to go to her, through the door and into her private chamber. But the maid gestured for him to go beyond, and with damp palms and an unsettled stomach, he moved toward the door.

Marian was within, standing as though she'd been waiting for him. Standing, not ill in bed as he'd imagined. He took in the details of the chamber and her appearance with one quick scan, his apprehension growing.

Dear God, why do you tempt me?

She was alone, and dressed simply in a white undergown so thin and delicate that he saw the shadowy curves under her breasts and the darkness at the juncture of her thighs. The tie that gathered it about her neck hung loose, leaving a good bit of skin, brushed with golden freckles, exposed. Candles lit the chamber, a variety of them on a table giving off nearly as much light as a noonday sun, and the fire burned sedately in its alcove. The scent of violets clung to the air, which was warm and humid, as though she'd bathed recently.

All her magnificent hair was unbound but for two slender braids that came from her temples and were drawn to the back of her crown. Her feet were bare. Tension emanated from her, flowing across the room as if the air vibrated. But he saw the purpose in her eyes, the determination.

His heart was pounding now, and he realized what he'd walked into. His first reaction was one of disgust and fury, but it was closely followed by the wave of desire flushing over him, sending hot blood trammeling through his body.

Nay, fool.

Curling his fingers into the sides of his simple linen shirt, he drew in a calm breath and gritted his teeth.

"What do you require, my lady?" he asked, keeping his face and voice expressionless. "My performance, I presume?"

She looked confused, but recovered. "If you wish to consider it that, then so be it."

The hope that he'd been wrong faded and Will glanced toward the tapestry, resignation washing over him, along with anger, and if he was brutally honest, he must admit there burned deep inside him that great need . . . that incessant desire that could no longer be denied. He should walk out, but he could not. He hadn't the strength.

She stepped toward him, shaking her hair out so that it fell in lustrous waves over her shoulders, glinting copper and ruby and garnet in the candlelight. But when she noticed that he was looking at the tapestry, she paused.

Comprehension flooded her face and she looked up at him, eyes wide and face serious. "Will. There is no one behind the tapestry."

As he watched her, stunned, feeling as if the breath had been knocked from him, Marian walked over to the woven picture of the knight and his horse. As he watched, she pulled up a corner of the large hanging cloth and stuffed a piece of cloth into the peephole, blocking both sight and sound. She turned back to him, raising both brows in silent question.

Flushed with shame, he stepped back, feeling his face go blank and hard. "I am sorry, Marian," he began.

"Will." She said his name desperately. He couldn't read her face any longer; he couldn't trust what he thought he saw there. "Don't."

"What do you want from me?" he snapped, angry with himself for the moment of hope, the flash of light in a dark world.

"I want you."

At first he didn't comprehend, for her response was so foreign, so impossible.

But then she said it again. "I want to be with you, Will. . . . I *choose* to be with you."

As her words penetrated, he felt as though he'd been submerged into a rush of hot water, then cold . . . and then hot again. Everything slowed and grayed and became murky and warm. He couldn't react, but she was already coming toward him and he could barely grasp the concept that she wanted him to touch her until she brushed against his body.

Some sort of trick. It must be. John must—

But she flowed into his arms . . . soft and warm, smelling of violets, smooth and rounded and woman . . . *Marian* . . . and in spite of the warning bells, he gathered her up against him, feeling the delicious press of her against his chest and the brush of her leg against the raging erection now filling out his braies. She pulled his face down and he devoured her lips, fingers sliding into the deep warmth of her hair to cup the back of her skull.

Ah, Marian. Marian.

She sighed into his mouth, stepping onto his boots with her bare feet so that she could better reach his lips. Sweet, soft, full lips . . . he felt his whiskers scrape against them and the delicate skin of her cheek as he tried to consume her . . . this woman. This woman who'd haunted him for more than a decade.

Tremors shook his fingers and weakened his knees, and he forgot to breathe.

At last. At last.

And then she tugged away, and he reluctantly let her go. Marian looked up at him with eyes that didn't sparkle, but smoldered dark emerald, and held his gaze as she smoothed her hands down over the front of his chest, then grasped his shirt as if it were a mail hauberk and lifted it over his head, the swell of her breasts brushing against him. His squire, the whores, his mistresses . . . all had done such a simple act many times . . . but never before had he appreciated it more.

He reached for her, needing to feel her skin against his, but she darted out of his range, smiling a hot, seductive smile.

Where had she learned such a thing? It was an expression of knowing, of teasing.

From John?

From Locksley?

I'll not go to Locksley.

But she had come to *him*.

Why? *Why?*

His mouth turned dry, the blood pounding deep inside him, and he stood, wondering what new torture she . . . or John . . . had devised.

Aye, he could not discount the possibility that the prince would barge into the chamber at any time and join them.

"Nay, Will," she said, positioning herself so that the bed was between them. She still wore that smile, that gentle smirking curve of her lips, now swollen from the long, deep kissing. Looking at him from beneath her lashes, she said, "I am weary of being the plaything. Of being pawed and licked and kissed until I cry for mercy. I have decided . . . aye, indeed . . . that it is your turn to be the one who is pleasured."

"Marian." His lips could barely form her name, let alone ask her if she were mad.

"Aye, Will," she said, gliding toward him from around the bed. "I wish for you to allow me to pleasure you."

The expression in his eyes—heated, blazing with desire—made her so weak it nearly sent her to her knees. Marian felt her lungs clog and tighten and her belly twist with anticipation. She wanted him, wanted to touch him, to bury her face in his chest, to stroke those long, strong arms, and to feel those powerful legs slide against hers, to be filled and caressed and loved. . . .

But then he reached out, pulling her roughly up to him. His expression had gone dark and blank again, with only a hint of the heat that had been there a moment ago. His fingers curved tightly into her arms as he looked down.

"Marian," he said, dark eyes boring into her. "Tell me that John has naught to do with this. *Please.*"

Now she saw it: the desperation, the *need* buried there beneath the cold exterior. With a rush, she understood. "Nay, Will, nay." She gripped his solid, warm shoulders. "I swear to you, on my soul, 'tis only me. And you. 'Tis my *choice*, Will. *You* are my choice. Now." She bit her lip, but the words tumbled out because she needed to erase that fear in his eyes. "Always. I love you."

She caught her breath. How could it be, after her deep loathing for him? But it was true. She felt the certainty of it, warm and full. Right . . . and almost holy.

The blackhearted Sheriff of Nottinghamshire had captured her heart.

"Marian." He said her name in a low sighing groan, then dragged her against him again. The planes of his chest moved against her flat palms as he pulled her so close she could hardly draw in a breath. "How can you . . . ?" His voice trailed off as he covered her mouth, his lips still moving.

Her eyes closed and she sank into him, against him, for a long, sleek kiss . . . and then she pulled away. "Do you not think to distract me from my purpose, Will," she said, careful to inject a clear note of teasing in her voice.

The range of emotions that had played over his face since he'd come into her chamber indicated how vulnerable and wary he was, despite the cold, brutal exterior he'd shown. She wanted nothing to bring shadows back into his eyes again on this night.

She wanted only to see the rise of pleasure and the flush of release. She wanted him to see her, only her. To say her name and know it was she who brought him there. To be one with her.

Thus, when he stepped back, releasing her, she feared he might have misunderstood. But then she realized he was no longer so wary and that a bit of a smile lurked behind his lips.

"Your purpose?" he repeated.

"Aye." She knelt at his feet and gave his hard belly a little push. Understanding, he settled back on the bed so she could pull off his boots. Then he stood while she unlaced his braies and dragged them down over his hips and the very insistent erection that jutted forth. A little drop gleamed enticingly at its tip.

Marian pulled herself upright on her knees and curled her fingers around the red purple cock. Will started, jolting against her, and then sighed as if catching himself. She glanced up and saw that he was looking down at her with hot, dark eyes, and she smiled up at him as she moved her hand. Once, quickly, suddenly, from head to base and back, she used her thumb to swipe over the glistening drip and ease her way.

He gave a little shudder and his eyes widened in response. "Marian, take care or you will overset me too soon." His voice was so deep and filled with emotion—warmth, desire, affection— that it set shivers down her spine. He'd always sounded so flat or angry, so demanding or cold. Now he sounded like the rich sable furs in which she wrapped herself during the winter.

Simply in order to be contrary, and to let him know she was in control, she gave another quick stroke that made him suck in his breath again. Then she released him and stood.

When he reached for her, she danced out of his range again. "Nay, Will, you must not touch me. Not until I give you leave."

"Marian," he protested in that low, rough voice that sent delicious shivers curling in her belly.

"Now, lay yourself down," she said. "I want to kiss you. And remember, Will . . . you may not touch me. In fact, you cannot move."

"Marian, are you *mad*?" he said. Yet he followed her direction and stretched out on the bed, lying on his back. His long legs left his feet dangling a bit off the edge, and he was so large he nearly filled the narrow pallet. There would hardly be room for her to lie next to him.

She looked at him and felt dizzy for a moment. So beautiful, so hard and dark and lean and powerful . . . from those broad, angular shoulders to the curve of the muscles in his arms, which he'd tucked behind his head. Dark hair, thick and wavy, fell from his head and half covered his wrists, exposing a face taut with desire . . . but no longer with harshness or frigidity. A shadow of whiskers brushed his square jaw and beneath his chin onto the lines of his throat. His lips, parted slightly, were full and sensual . . . so unlike the flat, disgusted grimace she'd become used to. His face like this was beautiful.

The slabs of chest muscle were covered with the same dark hair that trailed down over his belly and down to rise, thick and dark, between his muscular, corded legs. His cock stood nearly straight up, proclaiming agreement to his previous protestations . . . and she eyed it appreciatively.

This night, she would enjoy the slide of that cock deep inside her, when she could touch it . . . and him . . . and when there would be no other eyes watching and taking. When it meant aught more than a simple physical release. Oh, there would be that too . . . but more.

"Could you not at the least remove your shift so that I may look if I cannot touch?" Will asked.

"But you already know what I look like," she reminded him teasingly.

He responded with a heartfelt groan. "Please."

Licking her lips, for the deep sound made her stomach curl again, Marian glanced up at his face, and was delighted to see that he could not seem to pull his eyes away from her. So she pulled her simple gown up and over her head, tossing it into a corner. Her hair lifted as the linen rose, then fell down in a soft, sensual swirl about her shoulders, breasts, and torso. The gentle brush over her taut nipples reminded her how sensitive they were, and how she would like to have his mouth on them. *Oh, aye.*

A glance at Will, who hadn't so much as flickered an eyelash, told her that he would be more than willing to oblige. Smiling, her belly fluttering deep inside and her core already tingling in anticipation, Marian climbed onto the bed. She settled herself over his warm, ridged belly, sliding her bent legs alongside his hips, lifting her hair up and then letting it fall into place.

When she sat, her quim wide and wet over him, he drew in a long, deep breath and closed his eyes. But he did not move, though she saw the muscles in his arms twitch.

Then he opened his eyes, and they fastened on hers, avid and hot. His lips moved soundlessly. . . . *Marian . . . I love you.* The words were inaudible, as if they were too sacred to say aloud. But she read them on his mouth, and felt the truth of it in his breath and the way it radiated from him . . . now that the specter of John was gone.

She nudged herself forward, feeling the rough texture of his chest hair beneath her sensitive, swollen quim, and, placing her hands around the smooth expanse of his biceps, bent forward.

Her nipple just brushed his lips and he opened them to capture it, but she did not pause and allow him to. She tipped to one side, then the other, and back, and his tongue slipped out and flickered over one taut point . . . then the other . . . and even that brief sensation sent tingles down into her belly and beyond.

Then she settled with one breast over his mouth, her hair falling down to pool on either side of his torso. He lifted his head to close his lips around her. Marian sighed at the warm, slick sensation, the pressure, the tugging and pulling and the sliding of his tongue.

She closed her eyes and felt the familiar pooling of dampness at her quim, the sharp, tingling spiraling down from her belly to center there. Her fingers wrapped around his biceps, and she felt the smooth sensitive skin inside his arms and she bent to kiss him, tracing her tongue gently and delicately over the light-colored flesh. She took a lock of her hair and swept it lightly over his other arm, noticing how the skin leapt and trembled.

He tensed beneath her, his belly, his mouth, his arms . . . then relaxed, sucking harder on her sensitive nipple. Marian felt a twinge between her legs and a wave of delicate tremors from her little pearl . . . and she sighed as the pleasure flowed easily over her, surprising her with its intensity.

Will need have no concern that she would overset him too soon.

When she pulled away, her breast stretching a bit, he lifted his head to go with her, his muscular shoulders rising from the bed . . . but she reminded him with a sharp, "Nay, Will . . . surely you have more willpower than that."

He gave a soft, tortured laugh and collapsed back onto the bed. "Not so much, when you are wriggling and writhing over me. Have pity, Marian."

She smiled back, delighted to see his mouth curve in real humor, and bent to cover those full lips with hers again, briefly, sweetly. She pulled away when he began to shift beneath her, his breathing growing deeper and faster. Easing down his body, she found that his skin was now warmer and shiny with a faint sheen of damp . . . and musky from her own scent. She kissed a trail through the springy hair on his chest, and paused to flicker her tongue over his nipple for a moment.

But she really wanted to move lower, and though she took her time kissing and nibbling over his hard stomach, she kept moving. At the tender crease between thigh and torso, she slid her tongue down and around and finally arrived at her destination.

With a quick glance up at him, she settled between his splayed legs and cupped his erection with both hands, sliding them slowly up and down, using more of the glistening drops from its head to slick her way. Then she had an idea and, with a mischievous glance at him, slipped one of her hands into her own warm, wet folds and pulled slick fingers back out with a soft, wet sound.

Will watched avidly, heavily, as she wiped her own juices over his cock, his face raised, eyes fastened on her movements, breathing audible. She felt the surge in the hot flesh she held, felt the little rising and shooting sensations inside the warm shaft, and began to stroke . . . long and slow . . . easy . . . so easy.

She watched him, felt his body tremble and gather, focused on his face as her own body tightened, swelling and pulsing, while his face grew darker, more taut and arrested. He flushed, his nostrils flared, his lips parted, and she moved faster and faster, watching, building up and up. . . . Her heart beat harder, her breathing rose, her hand flew up and down, up and down. . . .

"Marian," he breathed, his gaze flashing to hers, eyes bright with desire, holding her as if he were touching her with his large, tanned hands.

Her chest tight, she gave in to his unspoken plea, releasing him but moving just as quickly to lift herself over his hips. Hands positioned on his trembling belly, she spread her legs wide and lowered herself onto him . . . slowly. . . .

"Lord," he hissed, "I cannot. . . ."

"Don't . . . move," she managed to say as the sweetness filled her. Nothing like the long, sleek slide of Will, filling her, up into her center. . . .

His chest glistened, his face shone, his eyes burned, yet he remained still, his hands caught behind his head, his pulse visible in the lean cords of his neck, his belly shuddering beneath her palms.

Marian settled on him, down, low, and paused to catch her own breath and steady herself. Naught that she'd experienced in the chambers with John had prepared her for this delicious warmth . . . the beauty, the connection, the sense of completion . . . of purity.

So clean and pure after the tawdriness of the Court of Pleasure.

He moved inside her, a little twitch, catching her by surprise, and she couldn't help a soft gasp of laughter. "Did I give you leave to move?" she asked, hearing in her own ears how low and dusky her voice was.

"Nay," was his rumbling reply. "But I trow the game is over." With a flash of white teeth, a humorless, fierce smile, he surged up . . . and the next thing she knew, Marian was on her back, hair tangling in and around them, and Will was poised over her.

But he paused, holding himself up on two strong arms without touching her but for the hair-covered thigh settling gently between hers. "Marian . . ." He waited, searching her face with sharp, serious eyes.

She smiled up at him, understanding his hesitation. "And so you have lost to me twice on this day. At chess . . . and in bed."

He returned the smile with one of his own . . . one she'd never seen before: warm, tender, loving. Real.

"I do not consider this"—he slipped inside her with a quick, sure movement—"losing." They both groaned with deep pleasure.

Marian closed her eyes and lifted her hips, rising to meet him and the delicious long, sleek strokes, turning her head as he buried his face in her throat, gently kissing her as he moved so slowly . . . in . . . out . . . as long, slow, sweet pleasure rose lightly inside her . . . curling, unfurling, warm, and delicious. Skin to skin, warm and damp, rough with hair, smooth with muscle, soft and lush and hard, they tangled and sighed, stroked and kissed with reverence. Without hurry. With promises.

And then with a quiet groan of acquiescence, Will lifted his face from her skin and settled back on his haunches, guiding her along with him, his hands at her hips. He moved faster now, with greater urgency, and she planted her feet on the bed on either side of him, matching the rhythm, meeting his dark eyes, feeling her tight, sensitive breasts bounce and sway and her core deepen and lengthen and swell. . . .

She made it first, just tipped over the edge on a long, downward spiral, dizzy and undulating helplessly beneath him, around him, her eyes rolling back in her head. Her toes curled.

Her heart stopped dead . . . then picked up again a moment later, pounding harder and faster.

He swore softly under his breath, more a prayer than an oath, and her eyes flew open in time to see what she needed to see: to meet his gaze and watch the flash of rapture over his upturned face, the long, sleek lines of his neck, the gentle parting of his lips.

Not the hard, triumphant expression she'd seen on John, or the shameful, desperate one from Robin . . . but an ecstatic joy, contained . . . but true. Beautiful in its vulnerability.

He said her name again, a caress of syllables that settled her pounding pulse into easy rhythm. Then, skin to skin, arms and legs tangled, they collapsed onto the bed, damp, warm, and well sated.

CHAPTER 17

*W*ill awakened abruptly. His eyes quickly adjusted to the darkness, thanks in part to the glowing coals of the fire, and his years of instant readiness in battle. Marian still slept curled against him, her soft, warm body comforting and welcome. He was covered more by her hair than the furs of the bed.

He saw the figure standing in the chamber and recognized it immediately.

"This will be the last time you invade my lady's chamber," he said, reaching for a candle. He would not conduct this conversation in the darkness.

"Nottingham." Locksley didn't sound surprised or even annoyed at discovering a man in his lover's bed. "How convenient to find you here."

The candle flared to life thanks to a sharp piece of flint and a tendril of cotton, and Will looked up at Locksley. The man seemed unconcerned by his presence, and barely cast a glance at Marian's ivory skin, more exposed than Will would have liked.

"What do you want?" Will asked.

"I came with news, and to bid Marian farewell. And since you are here as well, that makes my task even simpler."

Will sat straighter, and Marian shifted against him, waking at the sound of their low voices. "What news?" he pressed.

"Farewell?" she asked, pushing her hair out of her face.

Will glanced down at her, unable to keep himself from tensing, awaiting her reaction. But her first look was up at him with sleep-drugged eyes, and her fingers curled around his beneath the covers as she pulled herself upright. She tugged the furs to cover her breasts, and looked at Locksley . . . with naught but curiosity in her face. Will relaxed.

"I'm leaving Sherwood. Robin Hood will be no more."

"Except for the man in the dungeon below," Marian said drily, her hip and leg lined up with Will's, rubbing with little, gentle caresses.

"He's an outlaw at any rate, and will hang regardless of his name," Will told her. "He was part of the group that attacked you."

"But why are you leaving?" Marian asked, turning back to their visitor.

"My work is finished here. The queen will soon arrive and she will set all to rights."

"The queen? How do you know this?" Marian asked, echoing Will's thoughts.

Locksley flushed lightly. "Alys . . . er, Lady Alys," he corrected himself. "She has received word that Eleanor makes haste to see her youngest son. She could arrive as soon as two days from now."

Marian nodded. "Aye, the queen is a rapid traveler and waits for no one. Even the stoutest men-at-arms have difficulty keeping pace with her."

"Or so the tales claim," Will said. He looked at his former friend. "And so you leave before she arrives?"

He gave the cheeky smile that women always seemed to love, but that Will found exceedingly annoying. "Alys believes it would be helpful if I were never identified as Robin Hood, so 'tis best that we do so. We're to wed," he added, looking at Marian. "And she claims the queen will allow our union."

"I would not argue that. Alys appears to know Eleanor even better than I," Marian said, nodding.

Will looked at her in surprise, but chose not to follow that trail at the moment. "And you are leaving now? What other news?"

" 'Tis all. Just that we leave and I came to ask Marian if she wishes to go with us." Locksley looked at him, and for the first time, the rivalry between them eased. "She would be safer," he said, meeting his eyes with a sober gaze.

Will suppressed his first inclination—*nay!*—and tried to think on the suggestion clearly. Which was difficult in light of the sweet-smelling woman next to him, and the fresh memories of these last hours together.

It would be safer if she left. Locksley was right. If the queen did indeed arrive shortly, mayhap she would have word from Richard. And once things were set to right, Marian could return to him, and be protected.

"Nay," Marian said. "I'll not leave." She tightened her fingers around his hand. "And aside of that, I must speak with the queen myself. What harm can the prince do in two or three days that he has not already done?" She looked at Will, her face haughty and firm. "I do not want to leave you."

His insides warred, but in the end, he was undone by the determination that he could keep her from John for the few days remaining. The prince would not play his games when his mother was present, and if he must do so in order to guarantee her safety, Will would send Marian with the queen when she left.

"So be it," Will said. "But we must take care to keep you from the prince's sight until then."

"Aye." Marian smiled. "I shall claim illness or my flux."

"Or I shall pay five women from the village to visit the prince as a gift for recovering from his illness," Will added, feeling foolishly happy. "That will keep him busy enough for a night." When was the last time he'd felt this way?

"Very well, then," Locksley said. "Farewell, sweetling." He came closer to the bed and, before Will could react, swept down and gathered Marian up for a last kiss boldly on the mouth, with a sidewise glance at Will.

He allowed it to pass. Locksley was leaving, and Marian was staying. With him.

"Alys and I will wed, and if you cannot attend that, at the least you must visit us in Clervillieres . . . far, far from the reach of John," Locksley explained, stepping back.

"Indeed we shall," Marian replied, but Will remained silent.

He was still the Sheriff of Nottinghamshire, and he could not leave the county for any extended time. He would be attached to John through the king, and because of John's own hold over Ludlow, Will could never expect to be free of the younger Angevin.

He must serve John until he died, or unless the king released him from his position as sheriff. But then what? What would he have to offer Marian?

Unlike Robin, who'd been Lord of Locksley until the prince claimed his lands, Will had naught but his honor—which had been severely tried as of late—and many years of service to Richard.

That amounted to little when it came to settling a bride-price.

A crust of discontent settled in his belly. He was not wealthy, nor did he own anything larger than a small manor house, seated in the county. She was Lady of Morlaix and far above him in station. He'd known this all along, and even from his days at Mead's Vale he'd known she was a baron's daughter . . . and he'd reminded himself of this when she arrived here at Ludlow. But then the battle of wills with the prince had arisen, and Will had taken the opportunity to have what he believed he'd never touch.

Bitterness soured his happiness, and he felt a wave of self-revulsion. Clearly he'd not spent enough time on his knees in the chapel.

"Will?" Marian was looking at him, and he gave himself a bit of a shake.

"You must go with him," he said, easing away from her. Chill settled over his skin when they broke apart. "John will have recovered from his sickness, and he will be more determined than ever to entertain you. There is little I can do to stop him, save violence."

She was shaking her head. "I'll not leave you, Will," she said again. "He will not dare to truly harm me. He dares not leave lasting hurts on a noblewoman; he merely wishes to play. And it is not as if I've not had to suffer his hands on me before. 'Tis no pleasure, but there could be worse things—such as being called out for treason."

He realized dimly that Locksley had left the chamber, but it was not too late to send her after him. "Marian, you needn't take that chance. I'll not have him put his hands on you again. Do not ask it of me. I could hardly bear it before, but now . . ."

She was watching him so closely, he swore she could read his inner thoughts. "Will, I cannot leave you. I won't. Do not try and force me."

"But I have forced you into all of this, have I not?" he asked, suddenly blackly furious with himself and John, and with Locksley, the king's rapacious war . . . with it all.

"You've forced me into nothing. The queen sent me here, knowing that John would want me," Marian told him. Whether by accident or design, the furs had slipped from her hand and now she sat bare to the waist, her lovely hair tangling about her.

As tantalizing as the sight was, he could not allow it to distract him. "The queen sent you to be John's leman?"

Marian reached for him, her fingers on his arm. "Not to be his leman, although 'tis certain she suspected it would happen. She set me to spy upon John, for she suspects his plotting against Richard."

Will looked at her, unsure whether to believe her words. They were shocking, but certainly rang true from what he knew of Eleanor. And he had seen Marian looking through John's papers. "She will protect you, you are certain?"

Marian nodded. "I am certain of it. I have long been one of her favorites, and I've done what she wished. And I suspect that when she learns how you've acted to protect the people of

Nottinghamshire in the face of John's greed, she'll have much to say to the king. He loves her above all people, you know. And she loves England too. More so than the king himself."

"I know that." Then he looked at her. "You believe I've protected the people? Only two days ago you accused me of senseless cruelty and dark deeds."

"But is that not what you wanted me—and all—to think? How was I to know that you and Robin worked together? Once I realized that, I understood most of it. But why did you burn the houses? That I cannot comprehend. I do not believe you did it out of cruelty. But why?"

He could not help it. Her faith in him, her understanding, and her bravery brought his hand forth to touch her hair, sliding his fingers down over a thick lock to caress her smooth arm. Even though he knew it was folly to prolong this. He should be setting her away, leaving, then sending her off to safety.

"The houses were old and falling apart. They were dangerous and needed to be replaced, but I thought if they were rebuilt on the far side of the village, where John does not go, he would not see them. New buildings would be too much a sign of prosperity for him to resist, and he would ask for more than they could give—they are already so overtaxed for this bloody war."

"And so you made a show of burning them in order to further blacken your reputation." Marian was nodding. "And then Robin was tasked with helping to rebuild the houses. With your help in the way of resources. Lumber and other, aye, Will? Is that how it was? And you would meet with him or leave messages to tell him where and how to get the materials?"

He nodded. How had she figured it all out? No one else had seen through it. Then he noticed she was looking down, as if ashamed. "What is it, Marian?"

"I felt so badly for Robin all of this time—believing he was a hero while being painted an outlaw, a lawless man. How difficult it must be, I believed, for him to be thought so evil while he did so much good. But now I realize it was you all along. How you were hated and feared because of what we saw—or were meant to see—while all along you were the hero. You were the one who made sure the villagers were cared for, and the woods kept safe." She lifted his battle-scarred hand to her lips, looking at him.

"I had already begun to love you before I knew that, and I confess, I fought the feelings. I didn't want to love such a loathsome man . . . but you were so kind to me, I could not—"

He snorted in disbelief. "Kind to you?"

The look she gave him was melting and sent a new wave of affection and desire coursing through his body. "You were most kind to me in John's chambers. Did you think I did not know what you were doing? Protecting me, giving me pleasure, all the while pretending to be as evil as he? Refusing to allow me to touch you when it was clear you wanted me to?"

He looked away. When she spoke it like that, he almost believed he'd done the right thing.

"If you'd not been there, I cannot imagine what it would have been like."

He didn't know what to do with these feelings she roused in him, so he pulled her close and buried himself in the warmth and comfort of Marian.

It was many hours later that they disengaged themselves as a knock came at the door. The maid poked her head around, eyes wide and looking everywhere but at Will. The sun had risen long ago, and it must be near the midday meal.

"Begging pardon," said the maid. "But word has come that the prince is looking for you, my lord."

"Better me than you," Will said to Marian as he slipped from her bed. Duty beckoned. His knees were a bit weak, but he felt more alive and awake than he had for years. "Does he know that I am here?" he asked the maid sharply.

"I have not told anyone of your presence," she said. "As you ordered, my lady. 'Tis just that the news has come from below that he is looking for you."

"Aye," Will said, relieved at that bit of information. He looked at the maid, whose name he would someday have to learn. "I task you to bring this day the meals to my lady, for she is ill and is not to be disturbed."

He dressed quickly and left, reluctant, but knowing that Marian would be safe as long as he spread the word she was ill and she remained in the chamber.

John received him in his private chambers, which in the light of day appeared tawdry and base. The stink of illness, plus old wine and coupling, permeated the well-lit space, reminding Will yet again of how fortunate he was to have found more than the mere act of coupling with Marian.

The prince wasted no time. Having fully recovered from his illness, he was possessed of great energy and plans. "Robin Hood shall be hung," he began. "On what day?"

"A sennight hence," Will told him, presuming that the queen would have arrived by then and all would be sorted out. But now that Locksley had gone away, it didn't really matter whether the outlaw was identified as Robin Hood.

"Good. Aye, 'tis a good thing that he has been captured at last. And now you must find the rest of his men. Go you into the forest and round them up. Without their leader, I trow it shall be as simple as coddling a babe."

"Aye, my lord," Will said. He'd go into the forest, but Robin and his men would be long gone. He'd return with the tale and evidence of the dispersal of the outlaws, and all would be settled.

While he was in the forest, he would set a watch for the approach of the queen's traveling wagons. The sooner he learned of her approach, the better he'd feel.

"At once, Nottingham. I have waited much too long."

"Aye, my lord," Will said, keeping his voice easy and mellow as always. "I will attend to it at once."

Just as he was about to dismiss him, John lifted his hand and beckoned. A large man-at-arms appeared from the door of the chamber. "I shall send Jem with you. He is quite handy with the sword, and I do not wish for any of those outlaws to escape."

Will felt a prickle of unease down his spine. John had never bestirred himself to send any of his men with him before. But he merely nodded and smiled as if privileged that a royal servant would assist him in his task.

Yet as he left John's chambers, the muscular Jem behind him, the back of Will's neck felt exposed. He gripped his sword's hilt unobtrusively, knowing he must remain on his guard. When they reached the bridge from the inner yard to the village, Will paused and spoke with the watchman so that he could measure Jem for a moment.

"Any sign of approaching travelers? Large trains with great amounts of baggage?" Will asked, eyeing the prince's man. He carried a long sword and a leather-bound shield, the latter of which was not only unnecessary but unwieldy when tracking outlaws in the wood. Either he did not know any better, or he had been ordered to do so.

Will's sense of unease lifted a notch and he did a quick scan of the bailey as he continued his conversation with the watchman.

"Nay, my lord sheriff. Naught but a small group of a dozen men coming from the east. They are traveling quickly, but do not appear to be a threat."

Will nodded absently, for he'd just seen Bruse, Marian's master-at-arms, crossing the yard. He hailed him and pulled quickly away from Jem before the other man could think to follow him and listen in.

"Your lady. Keep close with her. She is very ill and cannot be disturbed," was all Will had a chance to say before Jem approached.

Bruse's sharp eyes met his, and Will saw understanding and determination. *Aye. Good.*

Then he swung away, Jem and four of the sheriff's other men following as they went off into the forest.

The back of Will's neck still itched. He might be in danger, but Marian would be safe.

Marian dared not leave her chamber, but she found the space confining after Will left. She worked on a piece of embroidery that had long suffered neglect, and then found herself pacing the room.

The sun was high in the sky, warming the chamber as much as it ever could, when the door opened. There stood Prince John, with a goggle-eyed Ethelberga cowering behind him.

"Ah, Lady Marian," he said in his smooth voice. "I see that, contrary to rumor, you've recovered from your illness quite well. I'm delighted that you're feeling better, for I no longer have to delay my congratulations to you for winning the golden arrow."

He extended his arm in an offer that she could not refuse.

She did not even have the chance to retrieve the sleeping draught that Alys had made for her, for John took her arm and escorted her quickly from the chamber.

CHAPTER 18

"Why, Lady Marian, you seem a bit reluctant," John said. He had seated her on the edge of the massive bed and now stood in front of her.

It was the middle of the day, an hour past the midday meal. That fact alone made her feel out of sorts, for she'd never been summoned to John's apartments other than at night. A single guard had been posted outside the door, and other than she and the prince, there was no other person present in the chambers. It felt odd to be in this place of hedonism in the full sunlight, with all its accoutrements showing in full, garish detail. The empty restraints, the massive bed with the curtains pulled away, the table of half-eaten food and drink and its array of crumbs and crusts and spills. The heavy smells of profligacy seemed particularly foul in the full light of day.

Marian swallowed and tried to appear as if the very thought

of John's hands on her didn't make her skin crawl with revulsion. She looked up at him, at his greedy dark eyes and full red lips, and kept her face blank.

"I *am* reluctant, my lord," she said. Had a woman ever told him nay? Mayhap he thought she was willing, or, at the least, not averse to sharing his bed. After all, he was the prince and likely heir to the throne. Most women would not complain at the chance for the wealth, privilege, or power that came with being a royal mistress.

"Is that so?" he asked, reaching to touch her hair. She hadn't bound or otherwise confined it, and now it streamed over her shoulders and pooled on the bed. "I am sorry for that, for 'tis much more enjoyable with a willing partner."

"My lord, please. I am flattered by your kindness and your attentions, but I pray, please release me. I have no desire to share your bed." There. She'd spoken plainly. If he had any conscience, he would release her.

" 'Tis a disappointment that you feel thus, Lady Marian," he said, stepping closer to her. His leg brushed her gown and the wayward edge of his tunic's hem curled atop her lap. "For I shall not release you."

His hands cupped the top of her skull and smoothed down over the long strands of hair along her shoulders and arms.

"Please, my lord."

"Stand," he ordered, his tone brisk and his eyes bright, as he pulled her to her feet. "I would see you clothed in naught but your hair."

Marian stood reluctantly, and glanced toward the chamber door. Will could not know she was here. He was busy with his duties and thought her safely in her chamber.

But what could he do about it, in any event, if he knew?

In fact, it would be best if he did not know.

The realization struck her then. If Will found out she was here with the prince, he would react angrily, possibly violently. He'd already said it: *There is naught I can do but violence.*

Violence against the prince? That would be treason and would destroy his honor. Either he'd die or he might as well be dead, for he'd abhor himself for turning against his liege.

Marian felt nauseated, and it had little to do with the fact that John had not waited for her to remove her kirtle. He had begun to untie the string at the neckline and was tugging it off her shoulders.

"Oh, and did I forget to mention"—John lifted the kirtle up and over her head; she raised her arms reluctantly and it slipped off, leaving her naked— "that Nottingham will be unable to join us? I've sent him off on a task that should take a good while." He smiled knowingly at her, brushing away the hair that had fallen into her face. "So you need not watch the door."

She braced herself when he leaned forward to kiss her, suffering the full, wet lips over hers and the hands that never seemed to stop touching her hair: brushing, combing, wrapping, lifting it.

Marian closed her eyes, realizing that it was best this way. If she did not fight him, if she pretended to participate or at least allowed him to do what he wished, it would be over sooner. It would be no worse than submitting to Harold's fumblings. And once she escaped from his chamber, she would hide and he'd never find her.

And, most important, Will would never find out. She shivered.

Did he not realize whatever the prince did to her meant

nothing? Naught more than her husband pumping and groaning over her?

"Ah, so you do like that," John murmured, lifting his face from her neck, where he'd been gently biting along her shoulder. "I am not surprised. You are a passionate woman. I've seen evidence of it."

He pulled her onto the bed and fell with her, taking her hand and bringing it to the great bulge between his legs. She fumbled with it through his braies, trying to think on anything but what she was doing.

But then he was fondling her breasts, kissing and licking her nipples, and she felt his breathing rise and the insistence in his movements as he pushed her back flat onto the bed. He straddled her now, and she closed her eyes, unwilling to look at his face as he prepared to push himself inside her.

A sharp tweak at her left nipple had her crying out in pain and her eyes flying open. "Do you not think to pretend disinterest," he said, his face very near hers. Warm wine breath puffed over her and he smiled. "I expect that you will be a willing participant, Marian, or I might become annoyed. I do not believe you'd want me to be annoyed with you."

Remembering the restraints, and the whips on the other side of the chamber, and the chessboard he'd made on the back of a woman who'd angered him, Marian kept her eyes open after that. Even when his fingers delved deep inside her, stroking and pinching and squeezing, she did nothing but bite her lip and try to think of something else. She dared not close her eyes again, but she wished to be somewhere else.

She'd tried the tactic of playing with his cock, trying to make him excited enough to get the act over with, to finish and be done with it . . . but he'd only enjoyed that more, and made her stop and start over and over again, as if it made his pleasure grow to come so close and then to have the finish delayed.

He bade her wrap her hair around his cock and use the bright red locks to stroke him, but that made for awkward movements and he became frustrated with the game. Tearing off his braies, he took himself in hand, poising in front of her on the bed, and Marian thought at last it would all soon be over.

Just then the door opened and closed, silently. She didn't hear but saw the movement behind John, or she might not have been aware that Will had just entered the room.

He had a sword in his hand, and he looked as if he'd just come from a battle. The expression on his grimy, sweaty face was the same blank, cold one she'd seen many times. Will didn't look at Marian other than a brief glance, but he moved forward and pressed the tip of his sword into John's back just as the prince seemed to sense his presence.

"Move away from her, my lord," Will said in a tense voice.

"Will," Marian said desperately. It had almost been over. And now . . . he'd drawn a sword on the prince!

"Nottingham." John turned warily, seemingly unaffected by the fact that he was naked from the waist down and that he had an impressive erection poking out from beneath his tunic. "I had expected Jem to keep you occupied for much longer."

Then he seemed to notice the blade and his face turned darker. "You dare come into my chambers armed? And draw it on me?"

"Marian," Will said without taking his eyes off the prince, "leave now."

"Will, *nay,*" she began, seeing that he had no intention of dropping the blade from its threatening stance until she obeyed.

"Do not be a fool, Nottingham," John said, reaching forward

to jostle one of Marian's breasts, giving his adversary a mocking smile. "You cannot keep me from what I desire. You've partaken and you will no longer hold me off."

The sword tip moved closer, pressing into John's tunic, and Marian gasped. She looked at Will, her eyes pleading with him not to continue with the madness, but it was already too late.

John's face had gone dark and wild. "You'll hang for this, Nottingham. I would have permitted a bit of insolence, but you go too far."

"Marian, you must *leave*."

"The woman is not worth your neck," John said angrily.

"Aye, she is. Remove your hands from her, or I will drive this straight through."

Marian felt tears welling up in her eyes. Fool! Fool! Did he not know what he was doing? He'd hang and she would be left alone.

"The queen is due to arrive any day," Marian said.

John looked at her, his eyes narrow. "You lie."

"Nay, I do not. She comes to see what you have plotted against the king."

"Marian!" Will cried.

"I would know if a message from my mother had made its way here. She is not coming, and if she were, I—"

"You would . . . ?"

The strong, calm voice from the doorway stopped all of them.

Despite her nakedness, Marian dropped to her knees at the miraculous sight of Queen Eleanor. Her clothing was dusty from travel, her snow-white hair wisping from behind her traditional veil. But her blue eyes were sharp and clear as a bird's.

Will dropped his sword and fell to his knees as well. Marian caught a glimpse of his face; it was back to dark and emotionless once again.

"John? You were saying?"

The prince adjusted his tunic so that it covered his sagging cock, gave a little bow to his mother, but remained silent.

"Lady Marian. From the sight before me, it appears that you have at the least accomplished the task I set you?"

Marian nodded, feeling John's and Will's eyes on her. "Did you receive my second missive, Your Highness?"

"Aye, I did indeed, and that is the reason I made such haste getting here. As you can see, I have just arrived. It was suggested by my half niece, Alys, whom I met in the bailey, that you might be in need of my . . . presence." She turned and looked at John, her eyes cold. " 'The wild dog'?"

"Your Highness, I can—," he began.

"Put your breeches on," Eleanor told him. "And you'll need to clear all of your . . . eh . . . belongings . . . from these chambers. And have the space thoroughly cleaned. For they will be mine whilst I am here. Which, my dear John, shall be for the foreseeable future."

Then, for the first time she appeared to notice Will, who'd remained on his knees, head bowed. "And who is this who dares threaten my son?"

He lifted his face and Marian saw the grave seriousness there, reflecting his acceptance that his dishonor had been not only witnessed, but witnessed by the queen. "I am William de Wendeval," he said in a strong voice that made no attempt of concealment.

Eleanor's face lost some of its sharpness. "William de Wendeval, the Sheriff of Nottinghamshire?"

"Aye."

She nodded. "Indeed. Well, then, I have much to say to you. You will attend me in two . . . nay, three hours. Now, go. And take this lady of great distraction and her impossible hair with you."

With that, they were dismissed.

CHAPTER 19

"*Y*ou could have been hung," Marian said, splaying her fingers through the dark hair on Will's chest. "You *should* have been hung."

"So you have reminded me. For nigh on three moons now, Marian," he replied with an aggrieved tone. His broad hand smoothed up and down the lowest part of her back and she arched automatically against him. "But methinks I am already fairly . . . hung."

She laughed as he gently prodded her belly with his very interested cock. A surprising sense of humor had lurked beneath his dark personality, only recently beginning to shine through. Marian found it utterly delightful, even if most of his jokes were of the bawdy type.

" 'Twas fortunate that the queen was so angry with John that she chose to overlook your . . . uh . . . misstep. Will, you were so foolish!"

"Marian, 'tis finished. We're far from John's reach here in Normandy, and here is where we shall stay."

"But when he is king?" Her humor faded into the black worry that seemed to always hover about, even on the sunniest of days, such as the one on which they'd been wed.

It was her greatest fear. Richard appeared to be uninterested in siring an heir, and it seemed clear that someday John would take the throne. Mayhap sooner than later, if one took into account Richard's penchant for war.

Will pulled her close, kissing the top of her head with a soft buss. His arms were so warm and strong. . . . She felt safe and loved there. But John would never forgive Will for what he'd done, and when he came to power, he would have his revenge.

"Marian, you know that when I attended Eleanor as she requested, she spoke plainly. Aye, John will never forgive me. And that is why we had to leave England."

"That I know," she interrupted. "But when he is king, and Lord of Normandy—"

"There are times," he said, sighing heavily, "that I wish you were the quiet, submissive woman you pretended to be at Ludlow."

"I did not pretend to be quiet and submissive," she retorted. "Did I not poison the prince? And attempt to negotiate with him over chess? And did I not accost the gruff Sheriff of Nottinghamshire and argue about his legal decisions?"

"Aye . . . that is so. I must have a faulty memory. Or mayhap it was only that I *wished* for it."

She yanked playfully at a lock of long, dark hair and then brought his face down for a luscious, thorough kiss to let him know she did not mean it. "And did I not," she murmured against his mouth, "win the archery match against Robin Hood?"

He nodded against her. " 'Twas a very proud moment for me, my dearling. To see his very large head deflated so. My only other wish was that I had been the one to do it."

"Now that we have veered far away from the matter at hand," she said, "may we return to your private conversation with the queen?" It had never occurred to her in the three moons since they'd left England that he had not told her the entirety of the conversation with Eleanor. "There is something you did not tell me?"

All she'd learned was that they were to leave and return to Morlaix, her lands. This sanctioned escape was recompense for her work for Eleanor, and in thanks for Will's loyalty to Richard.

"Ah . . . aye. The queen and I agreed that John has a long memory for even the smallest slight, and so we are safe here until he takes the crown. Of course, you know all of that. But because of my service to Richard, she and he have also gifted me with the fief of Leurville, in southern Aquitaine, and that is where you and I will go when John becomes king. 'Tis small, and a vassalage to the queen, but we will never be required to go to court, to pledge allegiance to John. He will not know we are even there. If he even manages to retain his hold on the French lands when he is king."

He looked down at her, his eyes sober. "I did not tell you for fear you would not agree to leave Morlaix and go into hiding, for that is what it will be as long as John is in power. I will go to Leurville when it becomes necessary, but you do not have to go with me."

"Morlaix or you? Will, I truly begin to believe you are the veriest of fools. I would never leave your side. For any reason."

She pulled herself up on her palms to look into his hand-some, serious face. "I love you. I do not care if we live as chatelaine and steward in a small manor house for some great lord, or if we have our own lands. As long as we are together, I care not."

His eyes crinkled at the corners when he smiled. "I confess, I prayed you would say thus, but then I was not certain how much like Eleanor you are. She would forsake her own sons or husband for land rather than give it up."

"She is the queen. I am merely Lady of Morlaix. And now . . . Baroness Leurville." She smiled up at him. "I am quite fulfilled."

His eyes grew smoky and heavy-lidded. "Did you say that you were ful . . . filled?" he asked . . . and slid himself inside her. Filling her. Fully.